Ken Ward's *SIX FEET* instantly conjures up the pleasure I have always found in walking English footpaths: the history, the magical vistas, the glory of English mud, the pubs where they look at you sideways when you admit you travelled from the Bahamas to walk into their village, the comfortable feeling that surely part of me belongs here....

Chester Thompson
Nassau, Bahamas
Commander D-Day landing craft LST 527

This book is a page turner which arouses fond memories of walking adventures in England.

Doug McKeen
Ottawa, Canada
GM, Glebe Apothecary

SIX FEET to LAND'S END skilfully recalls the magic to be found walking along England's footpaths. Ken Ward's tale of a 300-mile adventure is stuffed with history, spectacle, drama – and even romance. His humour is as gentle and sly as the pub lunch delicacy of Spotted Dick.

Michael Marzolini
Toronto, Canada
Çhairman, POLLARA Insights

Ken Ward delightfully reminds us that England's history comes alive every time we cross the Atlantic to walk her glorious footpaths, and it's on these paths that we discover the English.

Clem and Carolyn Patton
North Carolina, USA

2010 first published in the UK by
Footpath Touring
Beer, Devon
EX12 3AE
www.footpathtouring.co.uk

This second *revised* edition published 2011

The novel is a work of fiction. Although some names and characters do
belong to actual persons.

Cover artwork by Bob Bradshaw/www.JurassicCoast.ws

Printed in Great Britain by
SRP Ltd
Sowton Industrial Estate. Exeter, Devon

Thomas Jefferson once wrote to his nephew, 'The object of walking is to relax the mind. You should not therefore permit yourself even to think while you walk'.

Ken Ward has mastered the art of walking as a form of relaxation, but in *SIX FEET* he not only *allows* thinking, but positively encourages it, especially regarding the walkers' surroundings, history, culture, economy – and more.

He has given us a fictional walking trip filled with vivacity and adventuresomeness. All who have trod the footpaths of *This Sceptered Isle* can relate to the characters and to the story. Many of the paths and places – even some of the puddles – will be familiar.

The reader is cordially invited to join Budge, Twirly and the Major as they take their places with such Dickens characters as Mr. Micawber, Miss Havisham and Little Nell. The journey will amply reward all who choose to take it.

Willis P. Whichard
Associate Justice (ret)
Supreme Court of North Carolina

My mind is filled with memories of the hills and valleys of Cranborne Chase while training for D-Day as a young parachutist with the 1st Canadian Parachute Battalion.

Now today, more relaxed, I greatly enjoy returning to England to walk the magical footpaths which history has left behind – and Ken Ward's *SIX FEET* reminds me it is time to do it again.

Jan de Vries
Toronto, Canada
Member of the Order of Canada
French Légion d'Honneur

Also by Ken Ward

South West Peninsula Coast Path
(with John Mason)
Letts Guides – Charles Letts & Co.Ltd

Book 1 Minehead to St. Ives
Book 2 St.Ives to Plymouth
Book 3 Plymouth to Poole

Footpath Touring with Ken Ward
Jarrold and Sons, Norwich

An Introduction
The Best of Lakeland
The Cotswolds
Exmoor and Lorna Doone
Land's End and The Lizard
North York Moors

RAC Going Places – North West England
RAC Publications, London

Discovering Backpacking
Shire Publications, Aylesbury

SIX
FEET
to
Land's End

For Brian

Ken Ward (signature)

Ken Ward

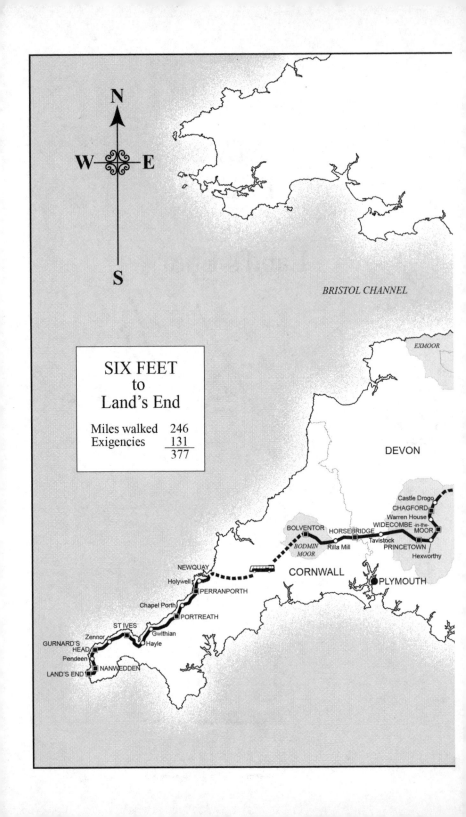

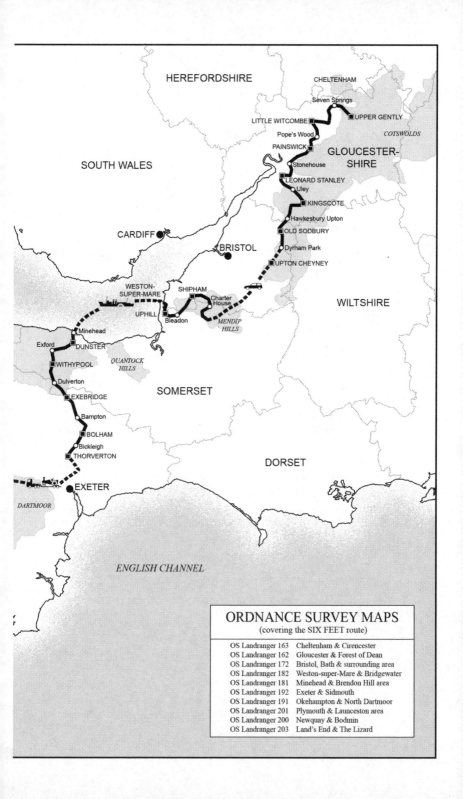

HEREFORDSHIRE

CHELTENHAM

Seven Springs

SOUTH WALES

LITTLE WITCOMBE

UPPER GENTLY

COTSWOLDS

Pope's Wood

PAINSWICK

Stonehouse

GLOUCESTER-
SHIRE

LEONARD STANLEY

Uley

KINGSCOTE

CARDIFF

BRISTOL

Hawkesbury Upton

OLD SODBURY

Dyrham Park

UPTON CHEYNEY

WESTON-
SUPER-MARE

SHIPHAM

WILTSHIRE

Charter
House

UPHILL

Bleadon

MENDIP
HILLS

Minehead

Exford

DUNSTER

QUANTOCK
HILLS

WITHYPOOL

Dulverton

SOMERSET

EXEBRIDGE

Bampton

BOLHAM

Bickleigh

THORVERTON

DORSET

EXETER

DARTMOOR

ENGLISH CHANNEL

ORDNANCE SURVEY MAPS
(covering the SIX FEET route)

OS Landranger 163   Cheltenham & Cirencester
OS Landranger 162   Gloucester & Forest of Dean
OS Landranger 172   Bristol, Bath & surrounding area
OS Landranger 182   Weston-super-Mare & Bridgewater
OS Landranger 181   Minehead & Brendon Hill area
OS Landranger 192   Exeter & Sidmouth
OS Landranger 191   Okehampton & North Dartmoor
OS Landranger 201   Plymouth & Launceston area
OS Landranger 200   Newquay & Bodmin
OS Landranger 203   Land's End & The Lizard

Chapter One

Monday 6th July 1998 *Day one*

'Stop right there or I'll blow your heads off!'

The coarse bellow slashed across the valley like tearing linoleum.

Budge Ballflower – forty-five-year old stonemason of the Cotswolds village of Upper Gently – snapped from his summer's day reverie and slammed a boot into the dry turf.

The snarling voice again:

'Get orf my land!'

Budge squinted down the field. The bright afternoon sun made it difficult to see.

Hell's going on?

Suddenly about thirty yards ahead a wide figure stepped from the shade of a lightning-scorched ash tree.

Perhaps it was the heat haze but he appeared to be swaying. However, there was no doubt about the object at his waist. A double-barrelled shotgun.

Budge's nape hair stiffened. A cold punch thudded into his gut. His already dry mouth clacked like a chisel striking granite.

He slid a quick glance at the old soldier a few yards to his right standing frozen mid-stride like the statue of Smuts in Parliament Square, with the sun gleaming on ridiculously luxuriant silver locks cascading from a pork-pie hat.

The voice bawled, 'I seen you coming. Ratbag ramblers.'

Budge held up his map and took a pace forward.

'I think there must be some mistake . . . '

Stubby red fingers slid along the gun barrel and two loud clicks marked the release of both safety-catches. A black and white dog crouching by the man's boots edged forward through the long grass like a mamba snake.

1

The old soldier – Major Legge-Wellesley – hissed without turning his head, 'For God's sake, Mr Ballflower, can't you see he's stoned out of his mind?

'Stand still.

'Don't look at him.

'Don't look at the dog.

'And stop waving that bloody map!'

Budge growled with fury.

First day of leading a couple of geriatrics on a 300-mile walk, and we're threatened by a lunatic with a gun.

He heard the Major continue his clipped diatribe.

'Do nothing. Just wait. Let *him* make the next move.'

Then as a wistful aside, 'Let's hope that Corporal Whippet back up at the gate will create a diversion.'

'Whippet?' snorted Budge.

Good grief. Upper Gently's favourite poacher, scrounger, and village idiot.

He scowled at the tall, white-haired Major, still in his Smuts pose.

Pompous twit.

By a gate at the top of the field, Twirly Whippet paused in his labours at the bone-dry water trough. With a thin brown arm he brushed sweat from his eyes and continued scraping rust from the jammed ballcock with his ex-army clasp knife.

Snorting cattle, mad with thirst, pushed and jostled around.

He lifted his head.

Someone shouting?

He tilted his head to one side. There it was again.

He snapped shut his knife, and clambered on top of the trough to look down the field to where Budge and the Major should be.

There they were, standing like two forgotten gateposts in the middle of the field. Beyond them was a stranger.

Behind the stranger, at the bottom of the field, was a dark Bedouin encampment of a farm surrounded by rusty tractors and discarded Land Rovers. Alongside was a green pond.

The stranger appeared to be waving a stick.

2

Twirly peered – and gasped.
Not a stick! A gun.
'Stab!' he swore.

His mind raced at flashback speed.

Two weeks ago he'd been in Upper Gently's Five Bells opposite St Amand's church, celebrating the arrival of a large cheque from the idiot Water Board, with landlady Doll drooling, 'What you going to do with it, m'duck?'

Go to Land's End. That's what. Three times saw it from troopships. For fifty years have wanted to get there.

Then these City lads doing the Cotswolds Way came in wearing expensive bright jackets, boasting they had walked from Bath.

'Seventy miles in six days,' they said.

Brigadier Hill would have fell over laughing. In 1942 he marched us one hundred miles in two and a half days, with everyone carrying sixty pounds of kit. Automatic RTU for those who didn't make it.

Incensed, Twirly had clambered on to one of Doll's chairs and made a blurred statement to Gently and the world.

HE WOULD WALK TO LAND'S END!

Then in the days that followed – Lord knows how – the Major and Budge Ballflower took over HIS walk.

The Major, who only speaks to him on Armistice Days.

Budge Ballflower, owner of Ballflower Stone Restorations, who once threatened to report him for nicking a lousy lump of limestone for a doorstop.

Now here they both were, standing as helpless as day-old calves.

'STAB!' he said again; and one of the heaving young bullocks pushed him off balance. Dislodged from the rim of the trough he crashed down into it's dry bottom to lie with his wellingtons in the air like a cast ewe.

In that instant he knew what he had to do.
Saw Tom Mix do it.

3

Stampede in Coffin Gulch, Palace Cinema, Saturday morning Children's Club, 1938.

He scrambled from the trough, pushed and punched his way through the wild-eyed panicking herd with saliva-slimed mouths, and sweet warm breath, and hurled himself at the decrepit gate.

The rotten orange binder-cord fell apart and the gate lurched open.

For a frozen moment the cattle stood stunned and stupid – then surged through the gateway. The ground shook as they stormed down the field sounding like a creeping barrage of 25-pounders.

Twirly chased after them.

'Major!' he yelled.

'MAJOR! The gate to the left! Run like hell, Sir!'

He grabbed the tail of one of the beasts, and with legs revolving like the blades of a beet-cutter, joined the charge.

Budge turned around to look back at the commotion, saw the avalanche of dust, and heard the roar of head-down beef thundering towards him.

Above the hammering hoofs he heard Twirly's shrieking voice.

'Run! RUN! To the gate!'

Budge shot a glance at the crazed farmer and the bright green pond behind him, weed covered and stagnant, but nevertheless containing *water.* Twirly's thirst-crazed cattle were hell-bent for it.

Down in a hedgerow to the left was a gate on to a lane: the very gate they'd had been heading for . . .

Budge glimpsed the evil dog retreating towards the barns with its tail tucked under its belly. The drunken farmer stood aghast with mouth agape.

Budge scooped up his map from the grass and yelled, 'C'mon, Major!'

But the Major was already leaping like a long-legged colt in the direction of the gate.

Budge overtook him.

Over his shoulder he saw the herd trample the terrified farmer and splash spectacularly into the iridescent pond.

4

He yanked open the gate wide enough to let the Major and Twirly through, and sagged over the green-encrusted top rail.

For several minutes no one spoke.

In the silence of the valley, the Major briskly recovered and efficiently produced a half-bottle of brandy from his green canvas satchel.

'NAAFI break, I think, gentlemen.'

Budge, still draped over the gate, murmured, 'Wonder if he would have fired . . . '

'Be thankful we didn't find out,' snapped the Major – and for some strange reason found himself putting his hand to his forehead, expecting to find it sticky with blood.

The narrow, serpentine lane was oven-hot, but tall hedges provided patches of merciful shade.

The Major flicked at dusty and drab sprays of cow-parsley with his cane and watched Budge striding ahead with his faded blue Karrimor backpack.

He breathed deeply. Pale pink and creamy dog-roses filled the lane with soft perfume.

He turned to look at Twirly strolling behind who was switching from side to side and peering over gates, and poking at clumps of bright yellow St John's wort with a stick he had cut from a hazel bush.

The Major was surprised how well the walk had begun.

Ballflower, the local builder, appeared to have appointed himself navigator, logistics expert, and billeting officer –- like a newly arrived reinforcement from Sandhurst eager for promotion. Pleasant field footpaths had led easily up from Upper Gently to Needle Hole with its jamboree of power pylons.

Lunch at Seven Springs Inn on the A436 made a welcome and shady stop. The Hook Norton had been most acceptable, and his three-cheese Ploughman's – adequate.

He thought perhaps the builder had been unwise with his choice of meat and potato pie on such a sweltering day, and marvelled at the speed and vigour with which Whippet demolished the pile of sausage and mash with extra onions.

The sun blazed down as they contoured the magnificent Hartley Hill.

Below them stretched Cheltenham, once so full of retired people back from serving the Empire in the British Raj that it was known locally as Colonels-and-Curry.

Hidden in the heat haze to the north was the famous racecourse and, rising to the east, was the superb escarpment of Cleeve Hill topped by its skeletal aerial towers.

The scene was blighted by the Lego-like lump of the Eagle Star building that had been dumped on the town by aliens whilst people from Planning were taking a late lunch.

It was only when Whippet located the sabotaged footpath signpost buried in brambles and they were mobbed by dehydrated bullocks, that Ballflower's navigation seemed to go awry.

The Major checked the time. Half-past four.

Ballflower had said accommodation was booked in the village of Little Witcombe, with an ETA of five o'clock.

A bend in the scented lane revealed a line of red-brick council houses, followed by a cluster of flower-decked cottages in Cotswold stone.

A bent gentleman with a sweat-stained trilby hat and a wavering stick stood with leisurely interest. He watched the Major approach and nodded.

The Major returned the nod – then realised that the man nodded all the time.

Around the next bend stood Ballflower studying his map and looking perplexed.

Here we go again.

The Major called cheerfully, 'Everything all right, Mr Ballflower?'

The eyes of the Navigation Officer remained glued to his map.

'This is Little Witcombe. Ordnance Survey says there's a pub. Can't see one.'

Now the straggling Whippet had caught up, and called, 'It's just up there on the left. The Crickley Hill. It's open and the barman's name is Ned.'

The Major glared.

'The nodding man told me, Sir.'

The bar was pleasantly dark and cool, and smelt soothingly of spilt ale, varnished timbers, and Mansion polish.

Budge got the beers in – Morland's Old Speckled Hen.

Halfway through his second pint, Budge called across to the barman who was out of sight behind the bar, clinking bottles.

'Do you know Glebe Cottage?'

Voice from behind the bar:

'Mrs Bowman? Yes, just up the road on the right. Opposite the church. Pink with a stone-tiled roof and hanging baskets which need watering. She's expecting you.'

Budge began assembling himself into his large pack, while Twirly hauled on his antique rucksack.

The Major slipped his modest canvas satchel over his shoulder and creaked open the heavy oak door. The sun flooded across the stone slab floor.

Budge called to the barman, who was studying a carton of Walker's crisps. 'You know Shurdy Farm, about a mile from here?'

Ned grunted.

'The farmer – is he a bit odd?'

'He's barred from here.'

Budge continued, 'We were coming down the footpath past his farm and he threatened to shoot us.'

Ned continued to be fascinated by the crisp box.

'Yeah. He does that.'

Budge frowned.

'Does he ever hit anyone?'

Ned stabbed the carton with a lethal-looking knife.

'He's a rotten shot, sir.'

In seventy-three years the Major has learnt *exactly* how tall he is – when to duck and when not to duck. He ducked now through the doorway of Glebe Cottage and bowed and smiled at the wide floral apron that was Mrs Bowman.

'I've put a jug of water in all three of your rooms. You must be parched.'

She looked to each in turn for approval.

'Dinner seven o'clock?'

With a yellow duster she flicked at an imaginary speck of dust.

'I'm doing something light tonight,' she beamed. 'Poached local salmon with broad beans and new potatoes.'

She nodded fondly at a framed portrait above a polished black marble clock standing on a lace-covered sideboard.

'My late husband's favourite.'

At dinner the Major was careful to sit with his back to the late husband who might resent strangers partaking of his favourite meal. Ballflower and Whippet sat at opposite ends of a hand-embroidered tablecloth with precisely positioned green and gold table-mats.

While they were taking coffee, Mrs Bowman said, 'Breakfast at nine?'

'Half-past eight?' asked Budge.

Mrs Bowman looked round for any other offers.

The Major said, 'Eight o'clock?'

Mrs Bowman smiled. 'Eight o'clock it is. You walking far?'

Twirly sniffed. 'Land's End.'

Mrs Bowman raised her friendly grey eyebrows in admiration. 'But . . . not tomorrow?'

The Navigation and Logistics Officer replaced his coffee cup in the rose-design saucer.

'No. We're walking to Stroud.'

'My goodness! How far is that?'

'About sixteen miles.'

'I say!' said wide-eyed Mrs Bowman.

The Major carefully smoothed his folded napkin, stroked his magnificent snow-white moustache and cleared his throat.

'If you don't mind me saying so, Mr Ballflower, that's quite beyond the men's capabilities. Sixteen miles is *ridiculous*.'

The black marble clock beneath the photograph of the late-departed ticked disapprovingly loud.

Chapter Two

Tuesday 7th July *Day two*

The Major sat on the edge of the bed massaging his lumpy knees.

It was six-thirty and already the sun, eager to start the day, was bestowing its favours on the floral-papered room.

On the window-sill a single crimson peony in a slender vase stood tall like a red-turbaned Rajasthani camel-boy. There was a hint of lavender somewhere, but he hadn't located the source.

He wondered about the wisdom of volunteering for this particular operation, and concluded that his normal rational thinking had been thrown off-guard by a worrying letter recently received from the Honourable Cynthia Withers.

'Sorry to hear about Mary. Will be in Cheltenham shortly to stay with dear Humphrey Berkeley. Would love to meet you. Talk about the past – and the future . . .'

Cynthia first appeared after he had left the Fusiliers and moved to the family tea plantation in Darjeeling. During a spell of UK leave in 1951 he gave a lecture on tea-growing at a symposium organised by the British Tea Council at Brighton's Metropole Hotel. Her father, a colonel in the Army Catering Corps, had been chairman. She attended the final social evening.

He sighed.

In those days she was acceptably attractive. And there were drinks . . .

He should have stuck to tea.

Now he urgently needed a temporary posting away from Gently.

Then the day after her letter arrived, Doll in The Five Bells announced that Whippet was embarking on this eccentric venture – and was expecting to be away for three weeks.

Three weeks!

A private soldier attempting such a campaign obviously requires the leadership of an officer who once held His Majesty's Commission. It was his duty *to take command.*

He plunged his arm into the bed to recover his *dhobi* work: two long green socks and blue Marks and Spencer Y-fronts which he had rinsed in the handbasin last night before dinner and dried in a towel. Two hours ago he had slipped them into the night-warm bed to air.

From the bedside chair he took a light-as-a-whisper purple silk housecoat, a birthday present from Mary, and a souvenir of happy days when shopping was done at Gieves, Bond Street, before it became Gieves and Hawkes of Savile Row.

There was only one bathroom.

It was locked.

Blast!

But as he turned in peeved retreat, the agreeable sound of a sliding bolt signalled salvation. The door opened and out stepped Budge Ballflower; broad, glowing, tanned, modestly covered by a hand-towel, and swinging a leopard-skin toiletries bag.

He spoke curtly.

'Morning, Major.'

'Yes, of course. Good morning.'

Steaming slightly, and smelling strongly of manly scent, the builder disappeared down the corridor. Muscular arms. Massive shoulders. And legs the size of Napoleonic cannon, easily capable of carrying a man to Land's End and beyond.

Back in his room the Major heaved up the mattress to recover his immaculately pressed cotton and polyester olive-green breeches – made-to-measure with deep thigh pockets, two Velcro fastening rear-pockets, and a cunning security pouch in the waist-band; all cut and

11

stitched in less than two hours for the cost of a double gin-and-tonic in an alcove behind the United Services Club of Calcutta.

In his Tilley's *Lord Winston* khaki shirt, all pockets and epaulettes, he checked himself in a full-length mirror.

Ready for inspection, Sir.

The Major found Twirly in the sun-filled dining-room, enthusiastically attacking a full English and wearing a striped yellow and green rugby shirt.

'Morning, Whippet.'

Mrs Bowman must have been on 'sentry-go' because she instantly swept into the room as bright as a buttercup and with a beaming smile.

'Hope you slept well.'

She nodded in the direction of Twirly's plate and raised her eyebrows to their full arched and fluffy height:

'The same, Mr Legge-Wellesley?'

The Major hesitated.

Mrs Bowman understood.

'I've got a lovely ham in the kitchen. Perhaps a slice of that with a poached egg and a home-grown tomato?'

'Capital.'

Twirly bayoneted a thick pork sausage.

'Have you seen Budge?'

'Yes.'

'He all right?'

'Well, he looked all right.'

Budge had been up since five-thirty, not pleased.

These nincompoops, questioning my schedule.

He crossly remembered how he got involved in this nonsense.

With his banker shop crammed with £12,000 worth of carved Guiting stone, everything had been ready for installation to begin at Lambley Hall on Wednesday, 1st of July.

Then one evening, Doll, uncharacteristically glum, said she was worried stiff because Twirly had announced he was intending to walk to Land's End. The situation was not helped by the Major insisting he accompany him.

Harry Lemming who drives lorries for Heygate's flour mill told her it was two hundred and fifty miles, along busy, dangerous roads.

'They won't last a week,' he forecast.

Budge had tried to reassure her.

'Doll. Twirly is a country lad. He won't walk along roads. He'll go by footpaths.'

England's network of legal footpaths is unique. A hundred thousand miles of them. Ten times the distance from London to Sydney. Some were ancient before the Romans arrived. Most of them pre-date William the Conqueror. There is not a hamlet, village, town, nor city that cannot be approached by a footpath.

Doll had glared.

'How can poor Twirly know where the paths are?'

Budge had laughed. 'Well, Doll, in *theory* he can use established long-distance walking routes. They're mostly waymarked, and have guidebooks.'

Budge knew immediately the route Twirly could take.

Cotswolds Way down to Bath.

Somerset Way from Bath to Minehead.

South West Coast Path to Lynmouth.

Two Moors Way south across Exmoor and Dartmoor to Plymouth.

South West Coast Path to Falmouth, Lizard, Michael's Mount and on to Land's End.

Then the disaster.

Brussels Health and Safety issued a four-week Order of Closure on Lambley. No visitors. No workmen. The whole of Upper Gently was stunned.

All except Doll, who appeared to be cheerfully buoyant.

13

'What will you and your men do, Budge?'

Budge shrugged.

Doll smiled.

'Have this one on me, m'duck.'

Budge frowned. Doll was as crafty as a carpet-seller in a Moroccan *souk*. He looked around for the free mint tea.

As she pulled his pint, Doll nonchalantly suggested that if he filled this waiting period by escorting Twirly and the Major on their walking adventure, she would pay all his expenses.

Budge was aghast.

'Doll,' he exploded. 'Spend three weeks with those two! I would rather have earache.'

Doll purred, and with an expression as inscrutable as the plastic Guiness toucan perched on a shelf behind the bar, softly made him an offer he could not refuse.

'If you could get them both to Land's End and safely back, m'duck . . .'

Budge waited.

' . . . I would be happy for you to have the lintel.'

THE LINTEL?

Budge stood stunned.

He had been needling Doll to let him remove it from her club-room ever since he discovered its secret. But she had always refused.

Until now!

Budge swept into the dining room wearing a fresh open-necked shirt.

He nodded at Twirly, and graciously accepted Mrs Bowman's offer of the statutory breakfast.

'You are fortunate, Mr Ballflower,' oozed Mrs Bowman. 'Your friend was out early this morning and brought back some lovely field mushrooms.' And she flashed Twirly the affectionate smile usually reserved for the portrait of 'the late'.

Twirly sniffed.

'Saw a likely field as we came into the village,' he confided to a forkful of baked beans. 'And I checked with the nodding man.'

Mrs Bowman turned to the Major.

'Would you like some mushrooms with your ham? There's plenty. Your friend's handkerchief was *full.'*

The Major shuddered, and declined.

'We still walking sixteen miles?' asked Twirly.

The Major discreetly checked that his cutlery was properly aligned in readiness for the arrival of his ham, while Budge glared at Twirly's energetic mopping-up operation.

'Told you last night I would look at the route.'

Twirly's mopping up became vigorous plate-polishing and the Major was reminded of a batman he had in Ceylon called Sabdar. Cleaned everything in sight. He either cleaned it or stole it.

Twirly sniffed.

'And?'

'While you were gathering toadstools, I devised a shorter day. Probably eight to nine miles. So I've cancelled the accommodation in Stroud and I've booked us into The Falcon in Painswick. All right, Twirly?'

'Satisfied, Major?'

At that moment the ham arrived.

At nine o'clock the Major leaned over the churchyard wall and inspected a colourful display of lupins and empty lager bottles.

In a big blue sky the sun was preparing to be hot again, but great clumps of snowy white cumulus were lurking with the promise of merciful periods of shade.

Traffic could be heard pouring along the A417 close by the village.

He noticed Budge further along the churchyard wall studying the handwritten notice:

PLEASE DO NOT CUT GRASS ON OTHER GRAVES – ONLY YOUR OWN.

At the door appeared a grey canvas shape with numerous dangling straps of webbing, followed by Twirly.

Mrs Bowman exclaimed with pleasure at the flower-baskets now cascading with water. She smiled at Twirly.

15

'Very kind.' Then, 'What exactly *is* your name?'
'Albert.'
Her smile grew wider and softer.
'That was my husband's name.'
The smile was suddenly switched off.
'But they call you 'Twirly'.'
Twirly sniffed.
Mrs Bowman leaned forward to hear the confidential explanation.
But Twirly merely wriggled into his webbing straps.
'It's a long story . . .'
'Let's go,' said Budge.

Budge's map promised a footpath that rejoined the Cotswolds Way near Woodlands Farm, not far from where they had detoured so dramatically down into Witcombe yesterday.

Although it was clearly marked on the map, Budge was well aware that the path might be impassable. Normally the chance of completing six miles on footpaths in Gloucestershire without encountering an obstruction is less than one in ten.

But this morning Gloucestershire County Council redeemed itself. In Great Witcombe was a gleaming new sign: Link path to Cotswolds Way.

Hallelujah!

For the first time since waking, he relaxed and noticed that it was a beautiful morning. With pleasure, he realised that the new schedule would allow time to visit Painswick churchyard, the most glorious in all England.

He even smiled guardedly at the Major when they entered a high-hedged lane.

'The Roman Ermin Way,' he called.

The Ermin Way had once been an important highway between the Roman city of Cirencester and the depot for retired soldiers at Gloucester.

It was built by the extraordinary soldier-engineers of the Second Augusta Legion under Flavius Vespasian, an ambitious commander who eventually became Emperor of Rome.

Budge was vaguely aware of Whippet poking his stick into mud near Willow Farm.

The field footpath rose steeply up to the green duvet of Witcombe Wood and levelled off into a typical English woodland path, winding and gently undulating, and a delight to walk. On the right, descending steep banks were covered in a maze of saplings, allowing brief glimpses of green meadows.

On the left, beech trees and firs crowded up to the Birdlip road, and thin tree roots stretched across the path like veins on the back of an old woman's hand.

The heavy smell of damp moss and rotten fallen logs was relieved by the fragrance of white lily-of-the-valley, and the sickly odour of Bird's Nest Orchid. Clumps of tiny yellow cow-wheat tucked coyly beneath statuesque green and rust-speckled ferns.

At a clearing, tall stems of yellow-flowered nipplewort grouped protectively around a signpost marking a path going up to Brimpsfield.

'Mr Ballflower,' called the Major.

Budge stopped and looked back.

The Major was advancing, breathing heavily. Twirly was dawdling along in the rear.

The Major gasped, 'Is it absolutely essential, Mr Ballflower, that we march at Light Infantry speed – one-forty paces a minute and all that. Mustn't push the men too hard, you know. I fear the rear-guard – Whippet – is falling way behind.'

At an opening through the saplings down on the right a string of fairy lights twinkled: the sun reflecting off windscreens of cars travelling south on the M5 two miles away.

The beech trees on the left were more sparsely spaced now, standing like worshippers outside a church on a fine Sunday morning.

'The thing is, Major,' sighed Budge, 'I have to remind you of our schedule.

17

'On Monday third of August I am contracted to begin the delayed work at Lambley Hall. Scaffolders booked. Plasterers booked. Carpenters booked. Labourers booked. Everybody booked. So it's essential I'm back in Upper Gently by Saturday, first of August. That's in twenty-four days.

'I have spent a great deal of time devising a route along historic footpaths which will show Twirly, and yourself, some of the best of the English landscape.'

He flourished an explanatory hand.

'Along this Cotswolds escarpment down to the city of Bath, the Mendip Hills, the Quantocks, Exmoor, Exe Valley, city of Exeter, Dartmoor, Bodmin Moor, and the magnificent coastline of the south-west ending at Land's End.

'I estimate this distance could be about three hundred and fifty miles. To do this in twenty-four days means an average of fifteen miles a day.

'We have already discovered this is probably too much for yourself and Mr Whippet, and it may be necessary to revise this route. However, I think it's important that we cover as much ground as possible NOW, before we get tired, or have bad weather; or . . .'

He shrugged dismissively.

Above them in the trees a couple of wood pigeons indulged in a noisy wing-slapping tiff.

Twirly arrived and handed out mint toffees, which Budge recalled seeing in a bowl on the bar at Seven Springs.

'Anyway, Major. This splendid Mark Richards guidebook says there is a café on the path about ten minutes away. Let's go and have a coffee.'

Sure enough, at a cottage almost submerged beneath a crowded garden, stood a sign propped against a wall:

THE HAVEN TEA GARDEN
Teas
Coffee
Snacks
Drinks
A supplementary sign said: CLOSED

The path curved round to the left and led up through trees on a steep hillock scrubbed bare by a million slipping, stamping boots.

'Cooper's Hill,' gasped Budge.

At the top, beneath a flagpole topped by a cockerel with a red coxcomb, Budge threw off his pack.

'Suggest we take five minutes. Could have done with that coffee.'

The Major slumped down, and instantly stretched himself out with his head on his satchel.

'Could also do with a *wahad wad*.'

Twirly sniffed, plunged his hand into an outside pocket of his commando rucksack, and withdrew a foil-wrapped package.

'From Mrs Bowman. Home-made bread pudding.'

Budge contemplated the forty-five degree slope dropping down below them.

'They hold an annual cheese-rolling event here. Double Gloucester cheeses are hurled down the slope and monstrously fit imbeciles chase after them, attempting to catch them.'

Budge looked around for some response from the horizontal Major and Twirly.

There was none.

He continued.

'A special cheese prize is presented to the winner – or his next-of-kin.'

Eventually Twirly sat up and gazed across the feet of his muddy black wellington boots at the wonderful sunlit valley stretching below.

Multicoloured fields. Isolated farms. Barns. Woods in every shade of green. Quiet enough to hear approaching gamekeepers two hundred yards away.

He noticed that Budge was now also flat on his back, gazing up at the enormous sky.

He looked at the Major, who appeared to be deeply asleep. Feet crossed. Hands clasped on his chest. Looking exactly like the stone effigy of Giles Berkeley lying in Cobberley church, four miles from Upper Gently.

Sir Giles had been to the Crusades, and his heart is buried in the church wall – the rest of him is buried in Little Malvern Priory.

As a young lad Twirly and his mates used to walk to Cobberley to put wild flowers on the grave of Lombard – Sir Giles's horse – buried in the churchyard.

Suddenly Twirly leapt to his feet.
VROOM!
VROOM!
Two fighter aircraft roared down the valley, so low that he could have waved at the pilots had he been quick enough.

The noise blasted his ears and shook the trees. Seconds later the roar rushed back again in a deafening echo from the hillside opposite and dispersed in a sky full of protesting birds fluttering like scraps of charred paper above a bonfire.

Budge and the Major shot up like skittles on the devil-among-the-tailors in The Bells.

Just as suddenly the valley returned to its vow of silence.

Ant-sized horses in an L-shaped meadow slowed their stampede of alarm.

Birds slowly settled and unruffled their feathers.

The valley made itself comfortable and prepared to doze off again.

'Budge,' Twirly called. 'Does your map show heights?'
'It does.
'Does it say it's about eight hundred feet up here?'
Budge unfolded his map and did some reckoning.
'Yes,' he said. 'Two hundred and sixty-eight metres. Which I make about eight hundred and seventy feet.'
The Major grunted and struggled up to join Twirly gazing out over the glorious landscape.
'Well done, Corporal,' he said softly.
Twirly nodded.
He knows how I know . . .

Chapter Three

The path from Cooper's Hill dropped into Brockworth Wood and became a wide switchback of ups and downs.

Soon the trees on the left were replaced by a low stone wall enclosing a field of waving green oats. On the right the beech and sycamore of Upton Wood plunged steeply down the hillside.

'Hell we got here?' growled Budge.

The Major joined Budge in one of the dips of the roller-coaster.

'Up there,' nodded Budge.

Three hundred yards ahead on the summit of one of the rises and backlit by the sun, was a slow-moving tangle with a puzzling configuration.

The apparition disappeared into one of the dips and after a few moments rose back up into view; an odd mass supported on a jumble of legs and sticks.

'Have you seen *The Lion King*, Major? Think this must be their travelling show.'

The group again sank from view, but in a few moments the leader appeared: a man in red, with wild ginger hair and an untrimmed ginger beard, looking like a face peering through a hedge of copper-beech. He was walking with a stick in each hand.

The rest of the group were similarly supported on two sticks, so there appeared to be more sticks than legs.

The Major said, 'It's a new fad dreamed up by the walking-stick industry. Supposed to relieve pressure on the knees. All nonsense, of course. My uncle, Rear-Admiral John Hanky Wellesley would have been very sceptical. Used to insist, "Always keep one hand for the ship, lad."'

Budge said, 'It's a marketing wheeze: buy one, get one free.'

Twirly came up.

'All need elbow replacements in a few years' time.'

The group processed slowly by, waving and smiling and prodding and clicking and clacking.

The Major shook his head.

'Looks like an insectarium of praying mantis.'

'Had a praying mantis as a pet once,' said Twirly. 'Used to live on the locker above my bed-space. When I came into the billet and whistled, it used to leap on my shoulder.'

Budge said, 'Did you know that the female praying mantis bites the head off the male immediately after mating?'

The Major said, 'I hope, Private Whippet, you made it clear that your relationship was purely platonic.'

By the path a low patch of dark green leaves sprinkled with frothy white flowers engulfed them in the pungent aroma of garlic, and Budge was suddenly reminded of a plate of *spaghetti aglio*.

'If we can keep moving, Major, we can be troughing in five minutes – and, what's more, with one of England's maritime monarchs.'

The instant increase in pace was impressive.

The reward was The King William, nestling amongst the birch and wild cherry of Pope's Wood on the A46 Cheltenham to Stroud road.

King William IV served for ten years with the Royal Navy in the West Indies.

He later cavorted with a buxom actress called Dolly Jordan and produced enough bastard children to man a frigate.

The Major had always had a soft spot for Silly Billy.

In 1944, in disgust at being posted to a tent-repair depot in Bridgwater, he applied for a transfer to the extraordinary and secret Phantom organisation, whose headquarters was located in Petersham Lodge in Richmond Park, the very house where Silly Billy and Mrs Jordan were wont to frolic.

The Major was devastated to be rejected. His interviewer was the film actor, David Niven.

He remembered Niven taking him to the bar to console him.

'Give this man a stiff whisky.'
Barman: 'A double, Sir?'
Niven: ' Good Lord, no. A single. But make it a *stiff* single.'

The King William was crowded, but Twirly discovered a small private room just inside the entrance.

It was dark, empty and cool, with a stone-paved floor, high-backed settle seats and comfortable blue cushions.

As he supped his Newcastle Brown, the Major studied their private room.

'Do you know the ancient Haunch of Venison in Salisbury, Mr Ballflower? This hideaway is similar to the compartment to the right of the entrance.'

Budge didn't.

But Twirly had been stationed on and off at Carter Barracks, Bulford, and Salisbury was only a twelve-hour pass away.

The timber-framed pub has been serving ale since 1320, nearly two hundred years before Columbus stumbled upon America. The vestibule on the right of the entrance was for ladies, who were not permitted in the men-only public bar. A small hatch gave access to the bar and, when husbands remembered, they would instruct the barman to pass through to the 'little lady' a glass of small beer or, if he was feeling frisky, a cheap port.

The Major was fascinated by the short-skirted young lady who floated around their table like a Flymo mower. With the grace of a smiling ballerina, she served them with cheese and apple ploughman's.

'Have you only got one pair of trousers, Private Whippet?'

Twirly looked down at his grey flannels as if he had never seen them before.

'I've got two.'

'With you?'

'No. Arthur Gilkes has borrowed one pair. He's due in court on Thursday.'

The Major crunched on a slice of apple.

'Can't wear trousers to dinner if they are soaking and covered in mud. Mess Presidents don't allow it.'

The young lady returned to perform an exquisite *pas seul* and collected the empty plates.

'You need another pair for evenings, Corporal. Better see the Quartermaster. Or buy yourself a pair in Painswick.'

'Sah!' said Twirly. The Major ignored the hint of insubordination.

Back on the path, the Major was relieved to see that fluffy clouds had assembled in the heavens and the temperature was pleasantly amenable. He found himself smiling.

Not done a lot of smiling since Mary went eighteen months ago. In fact, not done much of anything. Perhaps that was what Doll was implying. 'It'll get you back to your old self, Major.'

They sped past the secretive Castle Court Hotel and the smartly disciplined Painswick Hill golf course, and contentedly scrambled along the exhilarating ridge of Beacon hill-fort with its deep ditches and small craters.

In September 1643, after lifting their four-week siege of Gloucester, an unhappy Royalist army spent a wretched and damp night up here amongst the long grass and muddy puddles.

King Charles sensibly exercised his divine right and spent the night in a warm, plump bed in the Court House in Painswick.

The views across the valley were stunning.

As Budge led the way across the golf course he eyed the handful of golfers with suspicion.

He waved - dutifully.

They waved back - dutifully.

Golfers are convinced that walkers are idiots, despite walking every bit as far themselves.

Likewise, walkers are convinced that golfers are idiots with their mania for striking at a ludicrously small white ball with a metal-tipped stick.

For a moment Budge lost the line of the path across the immaculate greens, but soon located the mystic symbols of the Cotswold Way on a gatepost: a white spot with a yellow arrow.

Further on, he stopped in amazement.

A track beyond a gate was lined on both sides by carved masonry stacked on a row of pallets. He scratched the white stone and rubbed the dust between his fingers.

'Bath,' he said.

Beyond a straggling hedge of fuschia stood a six-foot statue of Aphrodite in pink stone, steadying a pitcher balanced on the head of an unhappy-looking lion. Behind her was scattered a Portmeirion of architectural miscellanea:

A dismantled footbridge in black and gold.

Stone pillars.

Slabs of marble.

Bricks in all colours and sizes.

A collection of red and gold lacquered wooden panels which Budge thought may have been the set of a touring *Madame Butterfly*.

He consulted his Mark Richards:

Catsbrain Quarry Architectural Reclamations.

A scraping noise came from behind a white gazebo with a green copper roof. A man in flapping shirt sleeves with a knotted red headcover was chipping paint from a wrought iron gate.

Budge stepped forward.

'May we?' he called, with a wave in the direction of the treasure-trove.

The man shrugged without ceasing his chipping, which probably meant 'carry on'.

On the far side of the collection, beyond a black stone sphinx, stood a row of doors in all sizes and colours. In the centre was one in bright blue with a black metal sanctuary ring and a splendidly engraved brass plate bearing the legend: TOILET.

Twirly sidled up to Budge.

'The outside-closet at my Fish House wants a new door.'

Budge strode towards the door, carefully skirting the sphinx which was probably Belgian Tournai marble. He watched as Twirly turned the sanctuary ring and began to open the door.

A loud scream filled the quarry, and Twirly fell backwards over the sphinx.

The door was slammed shut.

The man with the red handkerchief did not look up from his chipping.

'That's the wife in there,' he said.

Over to the left stretched a wonderful Cotswolds valley backed by the tree-topped slopes of Saltridge Hill, and the sun picked out the cottages of the village of Slad where Laurie Lee took cider with Rosie.

'Budge', said Twirly, 'do you think this town will have a shop where I can buy jeans?'

'It'll have a shop where you can buy trousers, Twirly. But you don't want jeans. Jeans are for poseurs. Useless for serious walking. Rain makes them cold and soggy. Take weeks to dry.'

A green and gold sign at the head of a long curving drive announced: PAINSWICK HOUSE AND ROCOCO GARDENS.

Budge looked at his watch. Three o'clock.

'Do we want to visit the gardens? Fabulous. Meet afterwards in the tea-room? Say half-an-hour?'

The Major was enchanted. The colours. The scent-filled valley. The cunning mix of formal order and flamboyant asymmetry. And the shrubbery with many of the species he and Mary had planted in their Residency garden overlooking Upper Gently.

He sat in the sunshine outside the Red House looking down the length of the valley garden.

She would have loved it.

He remembered the idyllic few days they spent in Ravello on the Amalfi coast two years before she was diagnosed.

They had sat like this in the magical gardens of the Villa Rufolo. The smell of flowers. The sharp scent of lemons. The busy

26

cicadas. The domed towers. The unbelievably blue sea. The smudge on the horizon which was Capri.

Afterwards they had taken lunch as guests of the genial Vincenzo Palumbo in his breathlessly-sited Villa Maria restaurant...

He jumped up and checked his Army issue G1098 watch. Time to be at the tea-house.

Budge had visited the gardens a few years ago when working on Painswick church and he was eager to see again the famous follies, full of cunning optical tricks suggesting height and depth.

After making his tour of the estate's delights, he sat on the balcony of the Eagle House overlooking the flower-filled valley, and unfolded his 1:25 000 Explorer map.

Maps have fascinated him since he was a bare-kneed Boy Scout, and he considers those produced by Ordnance Survey to be the finest in the world for those who walk footpaths.

English maps began with Major-General William Roy, FRS.

During the Jacobite rebellion of 1745 the English army found itself at a disadvantage, continually getting lost in glens, along by lochs, through burns and over ben, and taking the high road when they should have taken the low.

Eventually, in exasperation, the military surveyor William Roy was commissioned urgently to produce a map of Scotland.

When, fifty years later, the French made pathetic attempts to invade England via Bantry Bay in Ireland and Pembrokeshire in Wales, the Board of Ordnance, housed in the Tower of London, decided it required a map indicating which roads in the south were capable of taking heavy guns to discourage these foolish French incursions.

After a period of perplexity, someone remembered the techniques developed by Roy, and the first map – one-inch-to-one-mile covering part of Kent – was completed.

It is still the Ordnance people who produce England's maps, unmatched for their accuracy and imaginative detail.

They indicate if a minor road is more than twelve feet wide, and if it's fenced. They show if a place of worship has a steeple or tower, or neither. They differentiate between sandpits, gravel pits, slag heaps and refuse dumps. They inform whether an area of trees is a forest of firs, a wood of oak and ash, or just someone's orchard. And the patch ahead shimmering in the sun is identified as water, or wet sand, or shingle, or plain English mud – or merely a gigantic greenhouse.

And the symbol like a blue rising sun warns German tourists when they are standing at an Aussichtspunkt.

Budge's thoughts were arrested by a loud shout that shattered the peace of the flower-filled valley.

'Hi YOU!'

From his left came the shout again.

'Hi! What are you doing?'

It came from a shirt-sleeved man running along the valley from the Snowdrop Grove, waving a hoe.

Budge saw that he was heading for the fish pond, where a figure was kneeling with both hands in the water.

What's he doing? Stealing the exotic fish?

The running man shouted again, waving his hoe with more urgency.

The figure by the pond straightened – and Budge groaned.

He was wearing a familiar yellow and green rugby shirt.

Chapter Four

In the *Coach House Café* they had buttered date-and-walnut cake, with tea served in tiny finger-lifting cups of translucent china.

The Major perfected the positioning of his cravat.

'Wonderful part of the country, this.'

Budge agreed. 'The *real* heart of England.'

Millions of years ago, enormous pressures pushed up a band of limestone curving across England from Dorset in the south, to the North Yorkshire Moors. Near the Severn estuary this limestone weal tilted so it lay like a slice of birthday cake on its side. The high ridge on the west formed a steep escarpment which gradually sloped down to the east and the Thames Valley.

This piece of cake, with its lush grass valleys, rolling hills, rivers and woods, was once inhabited by more sheep than people, and came to be known as The Cotswolds: 'cots' meaning sheep pens, 'wolds' meaning hills.

Budge watched Twirly crumble the remains of cake into his mouth.

'Piece more, Twirly?'

But Twirly revealed that he was holding a reserve slice in his other hand.

The Major topped up the teacups.

'Twirly,' said Budge, 'down by the pond there appeared to be some shouting.'

Twirly shrugged:

'Some people love shouting.'

He stood up from the table with its lacy cloth and bowed to the Major.

'I'll deal with the bill, Sir.'

He performed a smart about-turn, marched over to the cashier's table, and grandly produced from his rugby shirt a red card.

Budge raised his eyebrows at the Major.

The Major raised his eyebrows at Budge.

'Hell's he up to now?' murmured Budge.

The Major slowly stirred sugar into his tea.

On the way down into Painswick a little lad wearing a birthday-present-bright Manchester United shirt peered at them from behind a low garden wall.

'Dad! There's some walkers.'

The unseen Dad growled, 'Heave half a brick at 'em.'

In front of them lay the stone-built and once prosperous wool town looking like two dozen oysters in a basket.

Budge loved this place.

He loved the soft grey stone which was able to capture the sun's heat during the day, to release it as a warm glow in the evening.

He loved the beautiful ashlar stonework

- the load spreading arches
- the hood-mouldings protecting beautifully proportioned windows
- the shapely mullions
- and the graceful draping of stone roof tiles.

They turned right into New Street – it was 'new' in 1250.

Along the narrow stone slab pavements they walked crab-like to avoid being dragged into the non-stop chaos of cars which hate Painswick and all who tread in her and crouched fearfully away from thundering, belching mobile warehouses carrying Guernsey flowers to Glasgow and Arbroath kippers to Kent.

England's oldest post office – timber-framed Tudor and dated 1482 – skulked in terror up against a small grey neighbour.

They passed grand seventeenth-century Palladian facades built with wool money; peered in pretty little shops selling trinkets to delight visitors; resisted welcoming tea-shops; and lingered below hanging flower-baskets dazzling in their multitudinous colours and spilling fragrance.

The slender spire of the church of St Mary's soared up from a grey and green churchyard.

'Did some work in this church once, Major.'

Opposite the church stood the three-storey Falcon Inn and Budge led them through the smart white doorway with its overhead brass lantern.

'You're in a nice double room on the first floor, Mr Ballflower,' smiled a fair-haired girl who looked too young to be in a pub. She carefully selected keys from a rack beneath an archway bearing two eight-foot duck-shooting guns. 'The other two gentlemen are on the second floor.'

In a corner bar a pimply young barman with a smile stretching from earstud to earstud poured three pints of Abbot's Ale.

'You going to get some walking trousers, Twirly?'

Twirly, with froth on his top lip, nodded.

'I'll dump my pack and come with you,' said Budge.

The pimply barman suggested a shop in Bisley Street.

It was next to a National Trust bookshop which had once been the *Little Fleece* pub with an arched doorway and an oak studded door through which lines of packhorses once passed daily bearing panniers stuffed with raw wool.

'Walking trousers?' said a long young man with a remarkable lurching gait.

'Sure. Walk this way,' he challenged.

They did their best.

Budge selected a pair of navy quick-drying, rip-proof Regatta trousers with more pockets than a dozen kangaroos.

Twirly proudly clutched his Cotswolds Outdoor bag as Budge led them along Friday Street which in 1941 had been blasted by a rogue German bomber; then along St Mary's Street and past the iron 'specs' stocks looking so much more unfriendly than the standard wooden models; and so into the rear gate of the churchyard.

31

By a low, decaying table tomb Budge said, 'The Falcon is just across the road, Twirly. Think I'll stay here and poke about amongst these tombstones.'

Twirly shook aloft his purchase bag.

'Thanks, Budge.'

Budge raised his hands in dismissal.

Twirly plunged his hand into a pocket.

'You know all about stone and things. Thought you might like this.'

Budge took the fragment of red pottery and studied it.

'Where'd you get this?'

'On that Roman road we crossed. Saw it in the mud by the stile.'

'You know what this is?'

Twirly nodded.

'It's Samian ware.'

Budge studied Twirly with his white wispy halo and nut-brown head and eyes as innocent as a koala bear.

It was indeed Samian.

The fine red, glazed tableware originally from the island of Samos off Turkey, and later produced in Gaul, was shipped in large quantities across Oceanus Britannicus for use by the elite of Claudius's occupying army

.

Twirly continued, 'When we were young a Mr Tom used to come to the village with a box strapped on the back of his bike. He gave us money for any bits like this we found in the Roman site down past the lake on the Woodbridge road. *He* told us it was Samian ware.

'He used to give us a penny for every piece we found. He used to give us tuppence for bits of metal; and sixpence for any old coin.

'We got good at finding things.'

Budge ran a finger over the glazed surface and the embossed pattern.

Twirly shrugged.

'Thought it must be Samian, so I washed it in the pond in those gardens.'

Budge understood.

'Is that where the gardener spoke to you?'

Twirly laughed.

'Yeah! He knows Upper Gently, *and* Doll, *and* The Five Bells. Used to work for the National Trust at the Roman villa at Chedworth a couple of miles away. He said he's heard English Heritage are looking for a herb-gardener to work in Gently – and did I know about it .'

He turned to go.

'Twirly! That red card you had in the tea-room . . . ?'

Twirly grinned:

'*He* gave it me - said to get our teas with it. Staff meal voucher.'

The evening sun hung over Scottsquar Hill in the west, and turned the weather-vane on the church spire into blazing Aztec gold.

A 9th-century Pope decreed that all churches should display a cockerel on steeples and towers as a reminder of Peter's denial; but they suffered from high winds. Then some genius mounted them on a swivel and they survived. With the addition of north-south co-ordinates they became wind direction indicators.

Budge strolled amongst the neatly trimmed yew trees standing like busby-topped guardsmen, said to total a hundred.

But it was the collection of seventeenth and eighteenth century stone memorials which fascinated him. Slabs, table tombs, and glorious 'tea-caddies'. Outrageously decorated with crumbling scrolls, hearts, skulls, sprays, ribbon, sea shells and other rococo devices. Most of them the work of a local family of masons. One of them, John Byron, described as a 'carver', made sure that his final resting-place would be memorably distinctive. It's a six-foot high pyramid, a replica of the hundred-foot high tomb of the Roman colonial magistrate Caius Cestius, erected in 20 BC near St Peter's gate in Rome.

At the church Budge smiled up at the many-faceted stone on the roof of the surprisingly modern porch, a twenty-sided icosohedron.

He had helped students mark out the stone for this fiendishly complicated test-piece.

Inside he discovered the Major, already dressed for dinner: immaculate knife-edged creased trousers, indigo shirt and a yellow paisley cravat.

'Ah, Mr Ballflower. Finished my *dhobi* tasks and slipped out for a breather – and a look at your church.'

Budge said, 'D'you know the work of the poet Spencer?'

'Well . . . yes. Some of it.'

'I think as a military man, Major, you might be interested in this . . .' And he led the way into the north aisle.

'During the Civil War the Royalists attacked Painswick, and the Parliamentarians established defensive positions inside the churchyard walls. But the Royalists pushed them back into the church and set up a siege to starve them out.'

Budge stopped by an octagonal pillar near the pulpit and bent down, and traced with his finger.

'See here, Major. A soldier trapped in here, keeping his head below musket balls fired through the windows, found time to scratch these words:

Be bolde. Be bolde.

But whereas Spencer in his *Fairie Queen* continues:

And everywhere be bolde, the soldier had sensibly cautioned:

But not TOO bolde.

Near the entrance to St Peter's chapel, Budge pointed out a mason's registered identification mark.

In the church there were other craftsman's trademarks: tiny friars in the corners of stained-glass windows by Whitefriars Glass; and engraved spiders' webs in windows designed by Geoffrey Webb.

'That ship,' said Budge, pointing to a six-foot model ship on the wall high above the font.

'*HMS Bonaventure,* took part in seeing off the 1588 Armada. And above the door, the coat of arms of our host at lunch – King William IV.'

34

As they left the church the Major paused by a window bearing the badge of the Argyle and Sutherland Highlanders, a memorial to 2nd Lieut Michael John Douglas Cawthorne, aged twenty-one years, killed in action in Korea, 4th April 1951.

The Major shook his head.

'Year of the battle of Imjin River.'

'You there, Major?'

The Major strode through the door, and through the porch, and stood to attention in the sunlight. He nodded.

'Attached to the *Fighting Fifth* – the Royal Northumberland Fusiliers.'

'Hey, Budge!' called Twirly, ensconced with the landlord at the corner bar of the Falcon Inn. 'Something else for you.'

The landlord was holding a curved chunk of orange stone.

'Think this comes from your village.'

Budge examined it, laughed, and shook his head.

'Not from Gently, sir. It's from Guiting Power. About seven miles from us. Coarse limestone. Where did you get it?'

'We were up there on a shoot. Found it sticking out of a wall. Unusual shape. Thought it might have some value.'

Budge replaced the stone on the bar-top.

'Do you know what it is?'

The landlord shook his head.

Budge smiled.

'No value at all, I'm afraid. It's the great stone-pipe scandal.'

In the 1800s an extraordinary steam-operated machine arrived at the quarries in Guiting Power, capable of cutting cylinders from stone.

The Stone Pipe Company was formed to supply the city of Manchester with sixty miles of pipes in all sizes for the sum of £36,000 pounds. The company neglected to point out a flaw: the pipes disintegrated under pressure.

Manchester was obliged to replace every one with cast-iron pipes, which, ironically, cost considerably less than £36,000.

The inhabitants of Guiting Power still deny any responsibility and are careful to point out that the directors of The Stone Pipe

Company also happened to be on the board of Manchester Water Works.

Twirly proudly showed his new trousers to the Major.

The Major approved.

Twirly sniffed.

'I'm keeping these for walking,' he said and he looked down at the mud-splattered trousers he was wearing.

'Clean these up for evenings.'

The Major muttered something about keeping up the standards of the Corps.

In his second-floor bedroom Twirly stood bare-legged at the window, vigorously brushing mud from his flannels onto the ceaseless traffic in New Street below. The church clock struck six.

Budge had said his double room contained a trouser-press. If Twirly wished, he would press the cleaned-up grey flannels in time for dinner.

'You can't miss my room, Twirly. It's opposite the top of the stairs.'

Twirly was loathe to put on his new purchase which smelled wonderfully of Aunt Maggie's linen cupboard, so in his long yellow and green rugby shirt and black socks, he tripped along the carpeted landing and tapped at the door at the top of the stairs.

The door opened.

It wasn't Budge!

She was slender and curved and loosely wrapped in something thin and pink.

'Budge-in-here?' stammered Twirly.

The apparition tilted her head and smiled.

'Mr Budgineer? No. I think you must have the wrong room.'

She had the greenest and most beautiful eyes that Twirly had ever seen.

He turned and fled.

Chapter Five

Twirly raced to his room and slammed the door. He pressed his back hard against the far side of the stout mahogany wardrobe.

On poaching forays his father had drummed into him, "When there's trouble, don't move, Twirly lad. Flatten yourself against a tree and become ivy. People only see things which move.'

He listened for pounding footsteps.

An angry husband?

The squeaking shoes of Management?

A gamekeeper?

A heavy thump shook the door.

Aargh!

Another thump and,

'Twirly. It's Budge.'

Twirly leapt to the door.

It *WAS* Budge – and he was alone.

'You said you'd let me have your trousers to press.'

Twirly eagerly thrust the brushed trousers into these friendly hands, nodding furiously with relief and appreciation.

'Right!' said Budge. 'Come and collect them in about an hour. They'll have creases you can shave a pig with.'

As he departed he called, 'I'm in the room opposite the stairs *...on the floor below.'*

'Stab!'

The Major clutched his scotch and *billayati pani,* with no ice.

Never ice. Can't trust the beesti-wallahs. *Never know where the hell they get the water from.*

He studied a framed watercolour of a crowded stagecoach waiting outside the pub, looking much as it did now.

There has been an inn here since 1554, and in 1760 it became a bustling posthouse for always-in-a-hurry stagecoaches.

Intrepid travellers assembled here to join the midday stage to Cheltenham, where they changed to the Royal Mail coach which left every evening of the year, whatever the weather, for the hundred-mile, eleven-hour journey in various levels of discomfort to arrive at the Belle Sauvage, Ludgate Hill at 5:00 am.

'Evening, Major.'

Budge's two-day tan glowed against a crisp white open-necked shirt.

The Major motioned with his glass at another frame on the wall.

'You seen this, Mr Ballflower? Extraordinary.'

It was a framed certificate dated 1678 attesting that Henry Bridges had been buried in a shroud of wool as required by Parliament.

They sat on a high-backed pew by a stone fireplace filled with pink and blue lupins.

Budge said, 'In the fourteenth century we exported tons of wool. The north of Europe should have been ideal for sheep farming but they still had wolves – and they also had wars – because whenever we fought the French we were careful to do it on *their* territory.

The Major checked his watch.

Private Whippet is late on parade.

Budge continued, 'In the 1700s linen began to take over and wool went into decline. This corpse thing was an attempt to boost the home market. Strictly enforced. A non-wool shroud meant a five-pound fine: half went to the informer, other half to the poor of the parish.'

Twirly walked stiffly in, wearing his pressed and mud-free flannels – and his yellow and green shirt.

The Major made a mental note: have a word with the Quarter-Master; this man needs a different shirt.

The softly-lit dining-room smelled of warm gravy. Subdued conversation mingled with the clink of cutlery on china plates.

A highly-polished waiter bowed them to the only empty table, and the Major scanned the room. Businessmen; farmers; tourists; and a lady of mature age with hair as white as his own but glistening like moonlight on a lake. She looked up at him and smiled.

'Nice place,' he said, and turned to the menu.

Budge said, 'I assume the *leak soup* is a misspelling.'

Halfway through his roasted prime rib of beef *au jus*, the Major managed to twist his head as if easing his neck inside his cravat. The silver-haired lady was wearing a blue silk dress with a pearl necklace. Opposite her sat a much younger woman with remarkably attractive green eyes.

Twirly had his head down into his steak and kidney pudding and Budge was briskly dealing with his golden roast potatoes.

The Major leant forward.

'The lady to your right is obviously English, but I rather suspect the younger girl is American. She is performing that knife and fork juggling thing they do.'

The Major and Budge ordered the *coupe poire belle Helene;* Twirly - jam roly-poly and custard.

Budge said, 'Think you're wrong about the girl, Major. She's wearing a small red and white brooch. Bet a corbel to a crocket it's a maple leaf flag. She's Canadian.'

Twirly resolutely kept his eyes on the menu and mumbled that he preferred tea to coffee.

The Major suddenly straightened himself and flicked his moustache; the ladies were preparing to leave.

As they approached, he clutched his napkin and rose sharply to his feet.

Twirly bent to retrieve the Major's cutlery from the carpet.

The Major bowed and smiled.

The silver hair nodded and said, 'Good evening.'

The green-eyed girl stopped by Twirly, who was still groping on the floor for a fork.

'Hello again,' she murmured kindly.

Twirly grunted a noise.

A silence enveloped the table until the ladies disappeared from the room.

'Hell is that?' demanded Budge.

'You know them, Private Whippet?'

Twirly stirred his tea with the retrieved fork.

'Seen the girl,' he mumbled.

Wednesday 8th July *Day three*

The sun had risen over the valley and was already delighting the golden cockerel on its all-seeing perch.

Twirly sat on the wall around the war memorial opposite the pub, polishing his black wellington boots with lavender floor polish loaned him by the lady called Housekeeping.

Painswick was awake and bustling. Shops to open. Children to get to school. A living to earn. Cars rushing because they were late, and lorries snorting because Aberdeen is a long way.

The Major, cane under his arm, strode across the road ignoring the traffic and glared approvingly at Twirly's wellingtons and new trousers.

He turned to Budge.

'Great improvement in the turnout of the men, Sergeant Major.'

Budge rolled his eyes.

They left Painswick up Edge Road, opposite the lychgate built from eighteen-inch oak beams salvaged when the tall spire hurtled down during an 1883 thunderstorm.

The Cotswold Way turned left down through Hambutts Field owned by the Open Spaces Society, where a wooden bench remembers that Helene Brotherton found beauty and peace here.

Budge looked up from his map. Before them stretched a shimmering backcloth of green fields, grey cottages, and woods in an assortment of geometrical shapes:

'Let's make this fast,' he said.

An hour later they crossed the Gloucester-Stroud road near the Edgemoor Inn and, beneath an already scorching sun, climbed a thin path zig-zagging through saplings of silver birch, tall grasses, dandelions, wild oats and the mauve flax flowers which seventeenth century apothecaries were wont to infuse in white wine to provide a potent purgative.

In Maitland Wood the path was lovingly tended as only the National Trust seems able – or prepared – to do. In a cool cavern of shade they descended between tall, smooth grey beech trees like elephants' legs.

Budge recalled that Queen Victoria had once royally commanded that only the sweet-burning beech was to be fed into royal fireplaces. Non-obeyance would cause her to be unamused.

Through saplings at the bottom of the slope were glimpses of a promised land of sun-bathed fields.

Yellow and white honeysuckle smothered a low hedgerow.

Breaks in the canopy overhead gave dappled reminders that the sun was still up there searching for them.

The Major was striding ahead, and he stopped and pointed with his cane.

'You ever build houses like that, Mr Ballflower?'

Budge peered through the trees at a single storey hexagonal cottage with a red pyramid roof.

Ah. The cottage orné.

'No, Major, I don't build houses.'

The Major protested, 'Yes, but you have men: bricklayers, labourers . . .'

'They don't build houses either.'

Twirly took over the lead.

As they rounded a bend he put a finger to his lips and pointed to a squirrel in the centre of the path counting beech nuts. As they approached, it leapt up into a sycamore tree for a display of aerial acrobatics. Branch to branch. Twig to twig.

On reaching a high fork it sat to peer down at them with eyes like wet grapes, awaiting the applause it deserved.

41

Twirly tossed a mint to the base of the tree.

If the squirrel had been streetwise he would have left a cap there.

A high-hedged lane marked the end of the wood. A bungalow on the right was called 'No Turning'.

A steeply-gabled stone shelter dated 1870 stood over a well, but the well was blocked by concrete and covered with dead beech leaves – and a discarded white button. Someone had scratched, 'Edith Baron, 1891'. Perhaps it was *her* button.

It was eleven-thirty when they arrived at Haresfield Beacon hill-fort on the end of a spectacular isthmus,with the Severn Valley gloriously spread beneath them.

Budge said, 'Suggest we take five.'

Twirly and the Major sank to the ground as if they had been pole-axed. Budge slid down with his back to a trig-pillar.

Before them stretched sunlit fields of every colour like a vast artist's palette: pale yellow cornfields, startling gold fields of rape, rectangles of blue flax, a striped patch of pale green and yellow where a mown hayfield awaited harvesting and green grazing fields dotted with toy animals.

Below on the right, a mile away, ran the railway, the M5 motorway, the A38 old Roman road, and a glistening strip of hand-torn kitchen foil: the Severn estuary.

Budge checked his watch and closed his eyes.

He awoke when he heard the Major struggling to stand.

'I approve of the new trousers, Whippet. They make you look taller.' He adjusted his satchel. 'Always think baggy trousers make a man look impotent.'

Budge looked up into the bright dome of sky.

'Did you see the weather forecast this morning?'

The Major scowled.

'Thunderstorms this evening. Been pouring all over the country. Lucky so far.'

Budge said, 'You got raingear, Twirly?'

42

Twirly blinked up at the sky and grunted a sort of 'yes'.

Budge persevered.

'*Proper* raingear?'

Twirly sat up, dragged his great rucksack on to his lap and extracted a fawn mackintosh with frayed hems and cuffs.

'Hell's bells,' said Budge.

Twirly sniffed.

'A gift from the king when he decided he didn't need my services any more.'

The Major snorted, 'Good God, Whippet. That must be fifty years old.'

Twirly stroked the fawn bundle with affection and gazed at the Major.

'Its twenty years younger than you or me, Sir.'

Budge stood up and harnessed himself.

'I suggest we leave the Cotswold Way here and drop down into Stonehouse – there's a good pub there. After lunch we'll get you a proper rain jacket.'

Several days of sun had burnished the steep grass slope as smooth as a child's slide, and Budge went down sideways, digging in the edges of his Vibram soles as carefully as if he was descending the *Eigergletscher* above Kleine Scheidegg.

He declined to look up and embarrass the others in their shuffling, slipping, snorting descent, but a lone skylark – the *alauda arvensis* – was not so considerate, and in the heaven high above, it hovered in trilling hysterics.

A grey and green metal footbridge took them over the railway at Stonehouse station and they walked down Burdett Road towards a stone church with a stubby steeple.

Next to a Bethal chapel the Frying Machine had a notice:

Due to demand we now produce a cheese and onion pattie.

We assure regular customers that this in no way affects the quality of our famous meat and potato patties.

In a few yards, large gold letters on a long, low building proclaimed they had arrived at the watering hole of the Woolpack.

West Country Ale. 1760. Best in the West.

'Better get this man a waterproof jacket first,' said Budge.

In Queen's Road they passed a green and cream tea-room, starkly empty except for an optimistic notice:

More seats upstairs.

Next door was a shop called Equestrian Requisites. A bell clicked as they pushed into the fug of leather, warm stables, disinfectant and dubbin.

From behind racks of riding jackets and a stack of plastic bags stuffed with straw, emerged a chubby-faced girl who hadn't had time to rake her hair.

Budge explained what they wanted.

'Rain jacket. Breathable. Long – no point in keeping the bum dry if rain cascades down on to the legs. Big pockets – with big flaps to stop them becoming panniers of water.'

Twirly chose one in fluorescent orange.

It fitted fine.

Budge yanked up the zip to the top so that Twirly looked like a neck-ringed Kayan woman from Chiang Mai.

'Right,' said Budge. 'Lunch.'

But the zip had jammed.

Twirly, with the startled look of a rabbit in a trap, attempted to free himself.

Budge violently shook the zip, and Twirly.

The Major tried kindness, but the stubborn zip was unimpressed.

Twirly said to the girl, 'It's faulty. Is there a discount?'

He stood motionless as a highway cone, while the young girl scurried behind the bags of straw 'to ask'.

Budge studied the stock.

Tins of Propert's saddle soap; Hobbs's velvet riding-hats; Buxton and Liverpool bits; kicking straps; felt numnahs; snaffle bridles; Boswell's loin covers; plated trouser-lifts; gentlemen's open-

44

bottom stirrups; tins of Parkin's saddle-sore ointment; and whips to meet every equestrian fancy.

'Twenty-five per cent off,' said the breathless young lady.

'I'll take it,' said Twirly.

The Major exploded.

'Whippet. You can't walk all the way to Land's End looking like a fire-beacon. Put the rest of the men at risk.'

Twirly gave a monstrously unsubtle wink, and Budge paid.

Chapter Six

A few years ago Budge spent three weeks working on the church of St Swithun in Leonard Stanley, and often walked to the Woolpack pub in Stonehouse.

In the seventeenth century it was a private house, which converted to a pub about the time of Waterloo when commerce relied upon the existence of thousands of sturdy packhorses travelling the country in slow-moving trains. An old photograph in a corridor shows the pub forecourt crowded with packhorses laden with bales of wool.

The ceiling was low, with dark posts and wooden partitions. Stone floor slabs were polished and cool. A collection of eighty mugs dangled from overhead beams. Above the fireplace hung a rare cylindrical brass document-carrier.

A blackboard said the dish of the day was calves' liver and smoked bacon with caramelised onion, and apple-and-garlic mash.

Budge and the Major were still cogitating when Twirly strode in with his new orange jacket slung over his arm like a Spanish bullfighter.

'How'd you do that?'

'A lad in the garage opposite sprayed it with WD 40.'

'You give him anything?' demanded Budge.

'A slab of Mrs Bowman's bread-pudding,' said Twirly. 'Is this pint mine?'

They decided upon the liver and mash, and the waitress, whose name was Valerie, promised she would ask the chef to make the portions small.

She obviously didn't.

They left Stonehouse down Regent Street. The shop on the corner, Flower Creations, was once part of the pub's stabling block.

They crossed the busy A419, noting the turgid waters of the old Stroudwater canal, once a throbbing link between London and Bristol, but now an unlovely smear of waterweeds and shipwrecked supermarket trolleys.

From the tiny green of Stanley Downtown, Budge led them along an ancient field footpath, and stopped by a pile of red earth and a hole in a bank beneath tall foxgloves.

He waited for Twirly.

'Rabbits? Fox?'

Twirly thrust his hand into the pile of earth and dry grass and presented Budge with a black bristle.

'Badger.'

Budge remembered. Female badgers are houseproud, sending the males off while they change the bedding and drag in flowers to make their underground home smell like Sundays.

At Grange Farm they eased through a squeeze-stile which Health and Safety had missed, and emerged opposite a bungalow with a dismal garden of uneven and cracked concrete slabs and featuring an attractive red watering-can marked 'weed-killer'.

In the village of Leonard Stanley, Budge stopped at a red brick house which was probably once a vicarage.

'You fond of ballet, Major?'

The Major began, 'Mary . . .'

'You'll love this place.'

He pushed open the purple gate marked 'La Fonteyn'.

A figure swathed in a black jump-suit with a bright red sash leapt from the purple and gold door and stood *à la quatrieme derrière*.

'My *dear* Mr Ballflower. How *wonderful* to see you again. *Dabro pazhalavat!*'

Her heavily mascared eyes dazzled like stage spots. An arm grandly extended to present Budge with a pale limp hand.

'So pleased.'

She turned to stare at the Major. The arm unfurled again, but the smile was now modified. Pencilled eyebrows were raised in imperious query.

'Legge-Wellesley,' bowed the Major.

She beamed.

Now a quick revolve in the direction of Twirly, but the arm remained taut with a suggestion of diminished enthusiasm.

'Whippet,' said Budge.

'I'm sure,' smiled Camilla Sutovic, retired ballet star of Moscow, New York and Paris, aka Mavis Plumple of Bolton.

Her bright red shoes pirouetted indoors and she indicated they should follow.

She was exactly as Budge remembered, and the green-room had not changed. The dark walls were a festival of photographs, framed programmes and faded handbills. Huge glossy plants in exotic brass and porcelain urns might have come from a theatre prop-store.

'I do think you are so brave to walk all the way here,' she gushed, and she waved *a-potage* towards a row of gilt and red velvet chairs.

'*Sivodnya prikrasny dyen. No ochin zharka* – you poor darlings. I have some marvellous elderflower-sparkle to cool you,' and she disappeared behind a blue velvet curtain with golden ties.

Budge nudged the Major and nodded at an assemblage of photographs cunningly positioned to draw attention to one larger than the rest.

Madame Sutovic wooshed back through the curtain bearing a tray with three tall glasses clinking with ice.

'Ah,' she chuckled, 'admiring my foolish photographs, I see.'

And she rushed over to point to the largest.

'That's me with Nureyev and Margot – New York, spring 1963.'

'Good Lord,' said the Major.

'So kind.'

And with a superb *êrte derrière*, she announced, 'And that's me with dear Fred Ashton when I was invited to join the Ballet Opera Corps. Did you know he was Peruvian?'

'Amazing,' said the Major.

Madame's eyes softened into pools of star-struck adoration, and she turned to Budge.

'I *love* your pa-pa.'

'Now Mr Ballflower – is dinner at five-thirty appropriate?'

Budge looked at his watch. It was four o'clock, and he muttered something about it being a bit early.

Camilla raised herself to *sur la pointe* and cried, 'But my darlings, the concert begins at seven, and you *must* be there by six-thirty.'

Budge looked blank.

Camilla sank to earth with a look of horror.

'You didn't know!' She clasped her hands in despair.

'My dear Mr Ballflower, it's our music festival week. Thought that's why you are here. I have already got you tickets,' and she performed a dramatic exit-left through the curtains.

Budge watched Twirly swoosh his elderberry-sparkle into a brass-potted rubber plant.

Two bars later she was back brandishing a buff leaflet.

'*Voila. C'est le programme!'*

Budge scanned it.

Music at the Priory of St Swithun's, Leonard Stanley, Wednesday 8th July, 1998. Cheltenham Symphony Orchestra.

He raised his eyebrows in query at the Major.

'An overture by Mendelssohn. A Quiet Stroll – Charles Williams. Concerto for Trombone and Orchestra by Lars Eric Larsson, soloist Emily White. Lark Ascending by Vaughan Williams, soloist Nigel Smith.'

The Major fiddled with his moustache for a tantalising moment.

'Perfect.'

Budge handed back the leaflet.

'In that case, Camilla . . . Dinner at five-thirty sounds *magnifique.'*

She beamed.

'*Otleechna!'*

St Swithun's stands at the side of a group of farm buildings which once formed an Augustinian priory.

In 1979, to commemorate the 850th anniversary of its consecration, a week-long programme of concerts was arranged, and they have continued every July since.

The church was almost full with hub-bubbing concert-goers, and from the rear came the sound of more shuffling arrivals. A floral lady clinked coins into a Sharp's Toffee tin.

On a blue carpeted platform beneath the crossings tower, the dinner-jacketed orchestra sat below looped bell-ropes making their tuning-up noises.

Budge said, 'In the interval, Major, I'll take you up into the chancel. There's a remarkable primitive carving of Adam and Eve stamping on a serpent. And there's two wonderfully carved Norman capitals – one has Mary giving birth to Jesus and an angel drawing back the curtain of a four-poster bed with a wide-eyed ox looking on.

Twirly sniffed his unenthusing sniff.

Budge continued, 'And Twirly will kindly nip out to the White Hart opposite and get three beers in.'

Twirly brightened and straightened, and took a greater interest in the proceedings.

But not for long . . .

He suddenly slumped in his chair.

'You all right, Twirly?'

Twirly nodded towards the stage.

'Sitting near the front. Them two women.'

Budge and the Major peered.

At that moment a silver-haired lady turned and smiled directly at them.

'Good Lord,' said the Major.

The Mendelssohn overture ended in a blaze of glory and enthusiastic applause, and Twirly stood to leave.

The Major snapped, 'As you were, Corporal. *I'll* tell you when.'

The Charles Williams piece followed.

An interval was announced and the silver-haired lady was swept along the aisle towards them by a flood of concert-goers heading for the refreshment table beneath the stained glass West window.

The Major said, 'Suggest we get coffees for the ladies.'

Twirly sniffed.

'Thought we were going to the pub for beers.'

The Major glared.

'Corporal. It is mess etiquette to look after lady guests.'

Twirly sniffed again.

'We were never allowed lady guests in the NAAFI.'

'That, Corporal, is because you were an Other Rank. Other Ranks were not to be trusted with ladies.'

The silver-haired lady beamed.

'We thought it was you. We saw you come in.'

The Major bowed and said, 'May we get you coffees?'

The Major led them out into the still bright sunlight and they sipped coffees grouped around a table tomb, and helped themselves to biscuits from a large plate which Twirly had considered it his duty to confiscate from off the font.

'Did you walk all the way here? We think that's marvellous. We were making an early visit to the church in Painswick and saw you leave.'

The green-eyed girl said, 'You on a walking holiday?'

Twirly sniffed.

'We're walking to Land's End.'

The Major saw the two ladies turn to each other and noted the significantly raised eyebrows.

Budge bent to read aloud the tomb's inscription in memory of a yeoman who died at the age of ninety-three.

> *Stop traveller; turn your eye*
> *A solemn thought – you're sure to die.*
> *Remember that you shortly must*
> *Lie here as I do; merely dust*

'I'm Annabelle Clayton, and this is my niece, Sophia Forrest.'

Budge nodded.

'Charmed,' smiled the Major. 'Robert Legge-Wellesley at your service. And this is Budge Ballflower.'

The green-eyed Sophia appeared to have a moment of revelation.

'Budge? Ah. Of course – Budge-in-here,' she said and smiled at Annabelle and Twirly with their private joke.

The Major waved his free hand towards Twirly.

'And this is . . .'

Twirly whipped his nose from his cup and said, 'Albert Valentino Whippet.'

Lightning flashed, and the Major noticed for the first time that over beyond the farm buildings the sky was threateningly dark. A heavenly timpani rumbled in the distance.

All conversation stopped and the musicians stubbed out their cigarettes and turned to hurry back into the church.

Sophia curled round to gaze at Twirly.

'What a delightful name – Valentino.'

A second blast of thunder exploded, rocked around the churchyard, rattled the pantiles on the lych-gate roof, and the concert-goers began to dawdle back to the concert.

The Major smiled at Sophia.

'You are American?'

'Canadian. From Toronto.'

Budge flashed a look of triumph at the Major.

The Major curled his top lip to activate his moustache.

'Budge is a builder.'

Budge collected the cups.

'Stonemason,' he corrected.

The Major chuckled.

'Quite. He builds in stone: we don't have many bricks in the Cotswolds.'

The green eyes smiled at Budge.

'So do you create mullions, and hood mouldings, and capitals and corbels? And do you carve statues to place in niches on the west face of cathedrals?'

Budge stared for what seemed a long time.

Her eyes were certainly magnificently green.

He quickly recovered and turned to point at the church wall beyond the open door.

'Have you noticed the carved calf's head protruding from the stonework? Most unusual.'

The Major sighed.

'Budge is our expert on churches.'

The ladies beamed at each other, and Annabelle said, 'My niece is over here on a six-month sabbatical and is obsessed by English churches. We have been chasing all over the country.'

The niece said, 'I think they are England's treasure-houses. We've been to the Victoria and Albert in London, of course, but I think England's real treasures are in the thousands of churches.'

'Seventeen thousand churches,' prompted Budge. 'And may I suggest that after the concert you go round to see the amazing Norman archway over the west door.'

The Major interrupted.

'Time to get inside, I believe.'

Just inside the door stood a slim girl in a maroon backless dress clutching a trombone. The conductor was already on the stage.

'Mrs Clayton,' called Budge as they hurried down the aisle, 'Ozleworth church. Ten miles south of here. Your niece would love it.'

Another rumble of thunder; and as the music began, an unscored percussion solo of heavy rain battered the wagon-roof and spat at the tall round-arched windows.

Thursday 9th July   *Day four*

The morning was soggy with all-night rain. Heavy, soaking rain, and Budge was not happy. He hates rain. All masons hate rain.

When mighty cathedrals were built the site was first marked out using magic set-squares and knotted string. The flatness of the site was checked using milk-settling pans filled to the brim with water. The orientation was checked to confirm that the alignment conformed to the position of sunrise on the feast day of the cathedral's patron saint -

then a shelter was built to keep the masons dry.

Budge recalled that five weeks ago he had a meal in the Thai Orchid restaurant in a cosy building on Exeter cathedral green, originally built to house the masons. And he was recently in the tiny Old Watling pub tucked away near the Mansion House, originally built by Wren to keep his hydrophobic masons dry and happy when building St Paul's.

It was nine-thirty and Twirly was stomping about in the downpour eager to start walking and to test his new waterproof.

'This way,' growled Budge, splashing along Gypsy Lane where yellow puddles were combining to form yellow lakes.

At the end of the long wet lane a brick-built bungalow huddled close to the ground, and the rain beat a tattoo on a sign reading:

MANURE £2 a bag

The bread-winner, a small dappled pony covered by a soggy flour-sack, stood with its head over a fence, apparently asleep and not yet ready to begin producing. Twirly strode up and made a clicking noise.

The pony opened its sad eyes and stared morosely. Then it slowly turned and plodded muddily away to stand amongst thistles and nettles in a less crowded part of the field.

The lane became a footpath squeezed between hedgerows where tall wet grass smacked at their waterproofs. Now dense branches crowded in to form a gloomy tunnel filled with rain-mist seeping through sodden branches.

The path began to rise steeply, and the banks on either side rose higher still, and Budge recognised this as an old packhorse route where over the years a thousand sharp hooves had chopped the clay into a yellow slurry to be swept down into Leonard Stanley. The path climbed relentlessly upwards, and became a narrow trench down which gushed a custard-coloured torrent over a slimy mulch of last year's beech leaves.

On either side, the thirty-foot high banks were topped by weeping trees leaning inwards at a threatening angle.

Budge climbed at a crouch, his fingers clutching at the clay, and he twisted round to look at the Major who was slipping and sliding immediately behind – a wretched ammunition carrier on the Somme.

Twirly in his orange jacket was far away in the rear.

Budge continued to slip and slide slowly upwards, struggling to remain on his feet, only pausing when an overhead branch suddenly decided it was overloaded with rain and released a pounding deluge on to his hood.

He swore.

At that instant from behind came a shout – and Budge heard a loud, sickening crack.

He spun around.

The Major was crouched forward on his knees, very still, with his face buried in the wet mattress of coffee-coloured beech leaves.

Chapter Seven

Budge splashed and slewed down to the figure slumped in the yellow gulley.

'Major?'

The Major raised his head, his ashen face plastered with beech leaves, reminding Budge of the green man he had carved last year for Wittingham church.

Budge knelt by the trench, peeled away the leaves, scooped mud from the eyes, and squeezed mire from the drowned moustache.

The Major gasped.

'It's broken.'

Budge looked wildly around for misshapen limbs.

The Major plunged an arm into the porridge of dead leaves and extracted his brass-topped cane – or at least half of it – and examined it with dismay.

'Applewood – unreliable rubbish.'

Twirly arrived in a welter of ooze and orange nylon and flung himself down by the Major.

'Sir?'

The Major's face cracked into a glutinous grin.

'Bloody stupid, Corporal. Get me to the RAP and I'll survive.'

'RAP?' Budge queried

Twirly waved his hand dismissively.

There is a belief amongst English military that it is written in King's Regulations that wounded soldiers making it to the Regimental Aid Post are forbidden to die. This despite the fact that the RAP may be equipped with little more than sulphanilamide powder, a pile of shell dressings, tins of mixed tea, sugar and powdered milk, and weary medics with a laconic optimism.

The Major struggled to raise himself up on to his knees and thrust a slime-entombed hand into the side pocket of his satchel, from where he extracted his half-bottle of brandy to take a shaky draught.

'Anyone?'

Twirly and Budge shook their heads, and put a hand under each arm and lugged him upright.

He stood gently swaying like something from a murky underworld until Twirly thrust the stick he had cut from an ash in Gypsy Lane into his hand.

The Major braced himself and, with a sucking sound, lifted a sludge-enhanced brogue and shakily resumed his sliding, slurping ascent.

Budge took the lead.

Soon the slope became less acute and the banks on either side became less daunting; until at a crossroad of grass-filled gullies stood a solitary post bearing a yellow arrow and a white spot.

They were back on the Cotswold Way.

The gasp of relief would have filled a balloon.

Ahead stretched a wide grassy path decorated with soft leaves and crunchy pine cones as far as he could see. Friendly ash and hazel trees lined banks gorgeously smothered in purple lady's-slipper.

Twirly forayed forward to make a celebratory issue of cream biscuits – souvenirs of last night's concert.

Soon the mature trees were replaced by young saplings which dropped steeply down into the valley on the right, and the sky magically reappeared. It was no longer raining, although the old trees on the left were still fussily shaking themselves dry.

Budge and the Major stripped off their wet-gear. Twirly was loath to dispense with his, and walked with it flapping like a badly erected E.P.I.P. tent.

Budge checked his watch. Despite the painful slog up into Stanley Wood, they had made good time.

'Should be in the pub in a couple of hours,' he murmured to an immaculate line of nodding foxgloves.

The steepness of the descending bank on their right meant they could now see over the tops of the saplings. The Severn valley was steaming itself dry, and in the far distance mauve hills floated above the mist like fairytale islands.

At a sudden clearing a glistening silver pylon stood perched on the edge of the path with its far legs braced well down the slope. Noisily spitting cables looped down to damp fields six hundred feet below. He half expected to see a red cable car come creeping up on its way to Waldspitz, but the snarling sound of a motorcycle in the trees on the left destroyed the illusion. He retrieved his map from its comfortingly dry pocket:

'Can hear traffic on the B4066 Dursley to Stroud road,' he called.

He looked back for a response, but the Major and Twirly were fussing over a bedraggled black and white collie dog which might have been dragged from a canal.

Twirly grinned.

'Joined us back there,' he shouted. 'Keep telling it to go home, but it just sits on its haunches with its head on one side wondering if we really mean it. Next thing it's trotting beside us again.'

'Get rid of it,' called Budge.

The Major ruffled a wet canine ear and peered over the valley at the distant mauve islands.

Poor wretch. Probably escaped from a wet Welsh farm.

He said softly, 'Go home, boy-o.'

The path abruptly emerged onto a park-like area of mown grass, with a decrepit stone building bearing information boards made indecipherable by green mould.

Coaley Peak picnic park.

Dark, dripping picnic tables were scattered like abandoned cars, their wooden tops scarred by black rectangles where campers on happy dry days had lit their disposable barbecues.

'You want to rest here, Major?'

But the Major didn't hear, or chose to ignore.

Beyond the edge of the seven-hundred foot escarpment, Budge could vaguely see buildings.

Berkeley power station, eight miles away on the banks of the River Severn.

A stone pillar topograph suggested they could see the Malvern Hills, the Brecons, and the flat-topped Cam Long Down, but it was lying. The sad-eyed dog peed on it and they left.

The gun-metal sky was slowly breaking up, and cracks revealed a marbling of bright blue. Suddenly the sun leapt into a fissure larger than the rest; it beamed down, punch-drunk but triumphant.

Budge looked back at the PDSA carers.

'Hell you doing?' he shouted.

Twirly looked startled.

'Giving the dog a sweet.'

'Hell's bells. You'll never get rid of it. Send it off. Can't follow us all day.'

They watched as the dog carefully dropped the sweet into the wet grass and proceeded to crunch it with hungry relish and darting suspicious eyes.

'Got a bad feeling about this dog, Budge'

'So have I. Get rid of it!' He turned on his heel and marched towards one of the most unsatisfactory sections of the Cotswold Way.

For several yards at this point the route entails a walk along a narrow grass verge alongside a road where glazed-eyed drivers hurtle past in speeding cars and monster lorries, too big for these roads, thrust aside hedgerows, traffic signs and unwary walkers.

Budge climbed up steps from Frocester Hill quarry on to the verge and was immediately engulfed by a great plume of spray thrown up by a vehicle planing at high speed through the standing water.

He swore.

And he swore again at the next. His shirt, which had remained more or less dry beneath his rain jacket, was now soaked.

The dog moved to the front and was now happily trotting ahead, turning and grinning in patient encouragement, with a great lolling tongue.

Budge gave it a scowl.

The dog stopped with ears alert.

Suddenly it streaked across the glistening road as if shot from a gun. Incredibly a hell-bent car missed it, the horn blaring and rear wheels skewing.

'Stupid bloody dog!' shrieked Twirly.

The dog turned to look at them across the spray-cloaked road, obviously planning a return dash.

They all shouted.

They waved their arms.

The dog had never known such attention.

It lowered its nose and eagerly headed back across the killing field.

A speeding plume hit him with a metallic *WHUMP!* and tossed him into the air. He landed in front of a second plume which pounded the body into the road. A third car roared along like a coastal corvette and the dog became a fur-covered mess.

Budge saw Twirly throw off his rucksack. He leapt at him, and smashed a hand onto his shoulder – a hand which could prevent a two-ton block of granite from sliding down a ramp:

'NO, TWIRLY! DON'T EVEN THINK ABOUT IT,' he shouted.

Then more quietly, much more quietly, he said, 'Nothing you could do, Twirly.' He shook his head. 'That's no longer a dog lying out there. C'mon. Let's get away from this place and these lunatics.'

The fiercely scowling Twirly wrenched himself free from beneath Budge's grasp and stomped off along the verge towards a Cotswold Way sign.

His eyes were stinging.

Stupid. It was only a dog. He remembered the blokes in the wadi below Djebel Mansour. And the bobbing heads in the waters around HMS Abdiel after it hit the mine in Taranto harbour. And the mess

60

the mortars made outside Minden. And his mate who asked him to tell his wife . . .

  With shoulders thrust forward, he pushed past the sign announcing: *Coaley Wood - Woodland Trust.*

Through the gap in the hedge he charged down a straight clear path which dropped steeply to the valley floor.

At the bottom he slammed to a halt.

Standing by an open-fronted shed stood Aunt Maggie.

Except it wasn't her, of course.

It was an ivy-covered tree stump standing in the damp mist near a dilapidated hovel.

But he had seen her wink, and heard what she said.

'Wahad shai, Twirly.'

Quite right.

He whipped off his rucksack and pulled out his bulky tinker's kettle, and motioned to Budge and the Major to take a seat amongst the assorted agricultural machinery assembled in the shed.

The kettle was filled from a gurgling jet of water still pouring from the lowest corner of a rusty corrugated roof.

A dry tinder of dead leaves and spongy rotted wood was taken from the interior of the stump. Extra burning material came from splinters of timber from inside the shed and a handful of yellow paper serviettes borrowed from Stonehouse's Woolpack.

With the aid of his screwtop tin of stormproof matches, the fire was lit. Tea bags and sugar sachets had been donated by Painswick's Falcon Inn. And a tube of Nestle's condensed milk came from Mrs Audrey's in Upper Gently.

Within three minutes he called, 'Let's have your mugs.'

The Major, his ruddy face washed clean by perspiration, shakily applied a tincture of brandy to each mug.

They sat in silence, and sipped.

Glorious hot sweet tea. The British Army's great secret weapon.

The path rose steeply, and the long wet grass whipped their legs, but now the sun was confidently beaming, and coaxing wisps of steam to rise from every soaked surface, and for the first time that day they heard birds singing. Below them the Severn valley sparkled as if it had survived a session in a dishwasher.

Budge was reminded of the view from Inspiration Point overlooking the Borrega desert to the east of San Diego, on the outskirts of the small ex-mining town of Julian, famous for its apple pies.

He had walked the old Butterfield coach route, staying in gleaming white-washed adobe lodges, and had been lucky enough to be there during the annual Blooming, when wild flowers sprang up to smother the prairie in a startling carpet of colour –- and a week later as quickly disappeared.

He remembered the gorgeous suntanned Belinda-Ann, a student from LA, who walked fast with handsome legs, chewed a lot, and occasionally said, 'Yah!'.

At a viewpoint picnic table where the path briefly nudged the B4066 Budge studied his map while the Major and Twirly sat nibbling biscuits.

'I think we should leave the Cotswold Way here. Would like us to see the wonderful hill-fort at Uley, but, more important, there's a splendid pub just below.'

The Major sat with his head lolling on folded arms. 'Perfect,' he murmured.

'Great,' said Twirly.

Budge added, 'After, we could go onto Owlpen which Prince Charles recently described as the "epitome of the English village".'

The response was disappointing, and you could hear youthful breezes playing amongst the trees.

Then, 'What does that mean? *Epitome*?' asked Twirly.

Budge thought for a moment.

'It means he's educated.'

The rectangular hill-fort of Uley is located at the southern end of a steep-sided spur and provides one of the most scenic high-level traverses in the west of England. The plateau of thirty-two acres is surrounded by two enormous defensive ditches, and in forty-something AD was wrenched from the Dobunni in a desperate attack by soldiers of the 2nd Augusta Legion. A gold coin believed to have been dropped in the melee is now in the lost property office of Gloucester museum.

Walking on the wide grass circuit was easy and fast, and an ecstatic skylark urged them on like a fife player with a marching column.

Budge halted and searched heaven for the songster, and found it, and pointed.

'Listen to that. Wonderful.'

He turned to the Major.

'Last night. That Vaughan Williams thing. Perfect.'

The bird above sang its agreement.

To the south-west the tree-capped Downham Hill rose spectacularly three hundred and fifty feet above the floor of the valley, but Budge saw only a pair of green eyes.

The rapidly recovering Major was walking briskly in tandem with Twirly, both with eyes fixed firmly on the seductive level path ahead.

Budge attempted to draw their attention to the rich landscape spread all around.

For instance, the wooded spur of West Hill to the North.

West Hill was a holy place with a series of shrines and temples long before the Romans arrived to take over the site. The head of a six-foot statue of Mercury found here is now on display in London.

The Major stopped, turned to Budge, and pointed with the borrowed ash stick. At the bottom of an excessively steep field dotted with especially hill-trained cows, a church tower poked above trees like a guiding beacon.

Budge called, 'St Giles's in the village of Uley.'

'Is Uley a good Christian village?'

'Indeed it is, Major. Pub is just across the road.'

The Major slipped into fifth gear and Twirly rode pillion.

On a bench outside the long white Old Crown Inn, Budge watched the Major remove his mud-oozing shoes, peel off his long green socks and take a plastic sack from his satchel.

He extracted a neat bundle of clothes carefully wrapped in rolled Lovat-green trousers with knife-edge creases, and from this he pulled a pair of clean green socks and sighed with satisfaction.

He stood in his bare feet and walked into the pub.

Beneath the wooden beams, amongst the horse brasses and old photographs, and by an enormous hundred-gallon sherry drum on stone slabs just inside the door, the Major smiled at the bright-eyed brunette behind the bar and held up his hand in supplication.

'A dark rum with a dash of blackcurrant and a modicum of hot water, if you please.'

Budge called, 'Make that three.'

And added, 'Better make that doubles.'

He winced.

NOW I have to tell them.
We have no accommodation booked for tonight.

Chapter Eight

Uley was once a prosperous cloth-producing village.

During the Penninsula War it became famous for a blue serge supplied in vast quantities to the military, with eighteen mills working full-time along the River Ewelme.

However, when Napoleon was safely tucked away, the orders disappeared and the mills closed. In 1873, the biggest employer, who built Gatcombe Park, now home of the Princess Royal, went bankrupt.

The villagers emigrated in droves. Only two mills were left, making a soft cloth which America bought in bales for babies' blankets.

'You here for the bowls?' asked a craggy man wearing a cap and sitting by the brandy barrel with knees projecting like a crouching grasshopper.

His left hand rested on a knobbly stick and shook like a leaf on a twig. However, his right hand was steady as a block of Duston sandstone and held a pint mug full to the gunnels.

'No, sir,' grinned Budge. 'We're here for the beer.'

The craggy man shook his head.

'Won't be no bowls today. Green'll be one damn gurt puddle.'

And he chuckled wheezily and came dangerously close to spilling a drop of his beer.

Twirly entered the pub carrying the Major's shoes, now cleared of mud inside and out, but attractively speckled with grass cuttings from the recently mown green outside.

The brunette barmaid looked at the shoes, and then at the bare-footed Major.

'Give them to me, love,' she said.

To the Major, she said, 'And give me those wet socks, grandad,' and she disappeared with them through an archway.

Budge asked, 'You never wear boots, Major?'

The Major carefully sipped his rum.

'Stomped about in military boots for eight years, Mr Ballflower, and came to the conclusion they are overrated. Those shoes are Church's handstitched Wayfarer brogues – considerably more civilised.'

Budge and Twirly ordered the day's special: homemade faggots with onion gravy. The Major hesitated, and finally agreed upon a slice of cold lamb with assorted pickles.

When Budge considered they were sufficiently relaxed, he said, 'About accommodation tonight . . . We have nothing booked.'

Days ago Budge had made a provisional booking with the Hunter's Inn near Kingscroft, but when he phoned from Painswick to confirm, they were sorry but a wedding which had taken everyone by surprise – including the bridegroom – had unsportingly booked all the rooms.

The faggots arrived in a thick swirling sauce and smelled delicious.

'Last night I spoke to a four-star hotel outside Kingscroft, and they can have us, but they want an arm and a leg.'

'So where do we sleep?'

'This morning I spoke to the hotel manager asking if he could give us a special price.'

Budge didn't think it necessary to mention to the Major that he had explained to the manager that he was escorting two elderly gentlemen engaged on a walking pilgrimage.

'He suggested I ring back this afternoon.'

The Major's lamb arrived, lightly pink, and adorned with caramelised red onions, two new potatoes and a little pot of Sainsbury's mint jelly.

As they were assembling themselves to leave, the brunette produced the Major's shoes looking dull but dry and devoid of mown grass.

'The dried socks are in this Tesco bag. Enjoy the rest of the walk. I'm Sandra,' she said as they all shook hands.

The craggy man's tankard was empty and both hands were now shaking as if he was playing a piano. He called, 'You want to watch them lady bowls players. Tricky as gypsies selling pegs.'

Budge led the way from the pub. They walked fast down between the high hedges of Fiery Lane; past concrete mounting steps; past cottages with chocolate-box gardens; past Marling End, and finally up left to the tiny church of Holy Cross in the secret hamlet of Owlpen.

The heavy wooden door creaked in disapproval as Budge pushed it open.

The interior was black and cold.

Twirly pointed to a glowing orange neon button.

Budge pressed it.

WOW!

The church interior burst into a festival of light and colour.

Twirly staggered.

It was like St Amand's Feast.

Every February at St Amand's Feast time, portly Mr Billings used to arrive on Upper Gently's playing-field with his convoy of belching steam engines, overloaded lorries, gaudy caravans and tanned children who never went to school and said awful words.

Then every night for three nights Twirly and the children of the village assembled in a cold-breath group by a large roof-topped steam engine as it hummed and hissed and snorted and rocked and smelled of hot chip fat, and dropped white hot ash from its belly to scorch the playing field turf, and envelop them in nose-twitching smoke.

Mr Billings, wearing a bowler hat, would carefully remove a chained watch from a plump shiny waistcoat and at six o'clock precisely would throw a switch on the dynamo nestling at the base of the tall spark-shooting chimney.

AND IN A FLASH, FAIRYLAND ARRIVED IN UPPER GENTLY.

Twirly remembered the coloured lights, and the tented stalls, and the tall shiny frame of the swing-boats, and the loud music, and the smell of feast-rock and hot salted peanuts, and the six pennies clutched inside his woollen glove.

Budge stood open-mouthed.

The church had instantly expanded like the Tardis, and seemed warmer and welcoming.

A bright blue ceiling was ablaze with golden stars and sunbursts. Dazzling tiled walls were covered with angels, and rose trees and lilies, and clumps of crocuses, and snowdrops in mother-of-pearl, and crowns of gold.

In the far corner stood an organ with grey and white pipes topped with outrageous orange coronets with leaping tongues of fire.

'Mosaics done by Italians working for Whitefriars Glass Works,' murmured Budge.

'Magnificent,' breathed the Major.

Outside, in a cavity in a pillar by the south wall, was a large bronze bee.

'Memorial to a Michael Lewis, bee keeper and director of a local weaving company,' said Budge. 'Shall we visit the Manor house? It's open to the public. Fifteenth century. Famous for its collection of seventeenth century painted wall cloths, an economical substitute for expensive tapestries.'

The Major tapped a grey tombstone with Twirly's stick and considered.

'If we may have to search for a hay barn in which to sleep, Mr Ballflower, I rather suspect it would be wise to get moving.'

Budge agreed.

'I'll phone as soon as we get up out of this valley. My stupid telephone has no signal here.'

The path from the Manor House ran along by the Ewelme stream, passed an old grist mill, now a holiday cottage, and climbed steeply up a field into Ruin Wood and on to the Dursley to Nailsworth road.

Budge unloaded his telephone and called Kingscroft Court Hotel.

The Manager in soft superior vowels revealed that the Agincourt Suite was in need of refurbishment. It had twin beds in one room, with a single in an alcove.

As a personal favour for him and his pilgrims he was prepared to let them have it at a special price.

Budge beamed as he tucked away his machine.

'Relax, Major. We have beds.'

Kingscroft is a small Cotswold village of snuggling cottages and tidily groomed gardens, with a Post Office shop and a granite horse trough full of silver-white salvias.

Two modern workshops are located in an old stable yard, one a grass-cutting-machine repair place, the other a wood turner.

A little way outside the village a large blue board with gleaming gold letters proclaimed:

Kingscroft Court Hotel. AA RAC 4-stars.

At the magnificent entrance, two golden lions supporting black shields and perched on tall stone pillars glared down defying anyone to pass. Particularly anyone not in a company car.

The Major was astounded – and suspicious.

'Here?'

Budge nodded.

As they crunched along a wide drive, curving between manicured lawns, the Major studied Twirly's yellow and green striped shirt and wondered what effect it was having on Security sitting in front of their monitors.

Perhaps reaching for rifles.

Grey gables and buttresses and oriel windows appeared strangely familiar; probably a favourite of producers of television costume dramas.

An arched front doorway was wide enough to accept a small bus if it could be persuaded up the steps.

Inside, a high timber-vaulted ceiling dominated Reception. Dark linen-fold panelling bore illuminated heavy gilt frames with portraits of bewigged persons. Immediately to the right of the doorway stood a fearsome suit of foot-tournament armour. A card announced it had been tailor-made at Almain armoury in Greenwich Palace and worn by a Sir Thomas Erpingham at Harfleur.

In the centre of the hall a tall floral island of purple Vanda orchids arose from a surf line of ermine white Madonna lilies and the Major remembered orchids were Mary's favourite.

'Suggest you sit there,' ordered Budge, pointing to a dark settle within arm's reach of the armoured figure, and he strode over the sound-absorbing carpet to a polished oak reception desk where sat a smiling young lady looking like a portrait on a fifteenth century illuminated manuscript.

The Agincourt Suite was remarkable.

Pale wainscoting.

Royal blue walls with hanging banners bearing gold embroidered *fleur-de-lis.*

Two single beds covered in the same blue and gold.

Snow-white sheepskin rugs on a tiled floor.

A wide archway leading to a grey alcove with a single bed covered by a cream spread with blue stars.

Afternoon sunlight streaming through mullioned windows illuminating wall sculptures of white Portland stone.

'Beats a hay-barn, Major,' said Budge.

Bathed and rested, and smelling of honey, the Major idly leafed through a velum portfolio listing the in-house services.

Budge said, 'Considering afternoon tea, Major?'

The Major grunted, 'Have you seen the menu – and the prices?'

Twirly, spread-eagled on the blue stars in his alcove hideaway, sniffed.

He sat up and extracted from a deep trouser pocket the waxed envelope – Army Form W3118A Casualty Ship Label – and fondled the folded ten-pound notes which Doll, licensee of The Five Bells, village counsellor, and money launderer, had given him in exchange for the Water Board cheque.

The cheque.

He sighed.

The cheque which had dumped him on this poncy bed, sharing a room with an ex-officer and a stonemason who owns a Porsche

He lay back and gazed at the star-decorated ceiling, and imagined he was lying by the forced rhubarb in the garden of his Fish House looking up at the Plough…

The fourteenth century Fish House on the bank of Booky Tweet was built by the monks of Lambley monastery, four miles from Upper Gently.

When Twirly returned from the army in 1948 after deferring his demob for three years during a period of black depression, Fish House belonged to the Ministry of Works – later English Heritage – and he was allowed to take possession for a peppercorn rent.

It was a stone-built one-up and one-down cottage which still smelled of fish and unwashed monks.

Unfortunately, every February the Booky Tweet rises above its crumbling banks. Sometimes it creeps into his Fish House, and Twirly is obliged to scrape frog-spawn off his door-mat and rescue minnows slapping about on the stone slab floor.

He has written several letters pointing this out to the Water Board, but they have usually been returned marked 'Undecipherable'.

Last year Upper Gently's retired Head Teacher, Maurice Kensing, agreed to write for him. Since his stroke poor Maurice can hardly speak – but he writes a lovely letter.

The Water Board wrote back claiming it was not their *water which flowed into his cottage.*

Then last August, during the annual hosepipe ban just before the Gently Flower and Produce show, when Twirly was filling a bucket from the brook for his delphiniums, Fred Gurney from Northleach turned up in his Water Board yellow van shouting he was not allowed to take water from the stream.

Twirly knows him well. Only things he has are this yellow van, a Company waistcoat, and a nagging wife.

71

Twirly growled, 'If it's not Company water when it's in my cottage, Fred Gurney, it's not Company water when it's in my bucket.'

The Company man grabbed the bucket and there was a tussle.

Portly Fred Gurney was winning when Twirly remembered 'negative resistance' taught him by Sgt Instructor Slater – and he let go.

Fred Gurney flew backwards, bucket on his chest, muddy water soaking his Company-issue waistcoat.

The Water Board man was not happy. He whacked the bucket away and it smashed into a pile of glass from a collapsed cucumber-frame which Twirly had stacked by his gate in the hope that the binmen might take it away.

Maurice Kensing wrote an imaginative letter.

Ten days ago a cheque for £250 had arrived from the Water Board: Without prejudice – towards replacing your greenhouse.

Budge slid off his bed and called, 'Come on you two. Tea is on me.'

Afternoon tea at the Kingscroft Hotel was served in the Garden Terrace Room.

A spiky-haired young man wearing black velvet breeches, a frothy white shirt and a black waistcoat ushered them to a group of lusciously comfortable chairs by a series of french windows overlooking formal gardens and briskly produced a silver tray with cups and saucers and small plates decorated with tiny violets.

With a shoulder-of-mutton sleeve held artistically behind his back, he skilfully poured tea from a Queen Anne teapot and deposited a three-tiered stand of dinky sandwiches shorn of their crusts and no larger than first-class stamps.

The room was empty but for a middle-aged couple with a spoilt-looking daughter of about sixteen with long fair hair also taking tea, and Budge took pleasure in watching the girl secretly stroking the serving boy's sleeve, and even naughtily sliding her arm down his velvet breeches.

Twirly scooped up a handful of miniscule sandwiches and rose to his feet.

'We having dinner here?'

Budge shook his head.

'Suggest we retire to the Hunters' Inn just up the road.'

'See you later then,' said Twirly, striding from the room.

The Major said, 'Conscientious man. Probably preparing his kit for dinner.' But they later saw him scurrying across the garden carrying a white plastic bag.

Budge snorted.

'Hell's he up to? Into the village to flog the hotel's toiletries?'

It was music night at the Hunters' Inn.

'The Kilkenny Drovers' included a slip of a bright-eyed, black-haired girl feverishly playing a fiddle, a long thin boy wearing large boots playing Irish elbow pipes, and a chubby man rolling a piano accordion across his paunch and singing.

The piano accordion man later did the slightly rude 'one-armed flautist' and everyone cheered, pretending they hadn't seen it before.

The chicken and chips were fine, although the Major was obliged to request that the ever-faithful Twirly relieve him of most of his chips.

It was a beautiful evening with a massive moon.

Earlier, on the way to the pub, Budge had noticed a wicket gate leading into the hotel grounds. They now took this to avoid the walk down the road to the main entrance.

The moon threw sharp origami shadows from the bushes as they headed for the line of illuminated french windows of the Garden Terrace Room.

Twirly led the way, followed by the Major.

A silver owl sounding a warning hoot, shot from a Cedar of Lebanon, and streaked above their heads.

An eerie gleaming statue stood in the centre of a sunken rectangular lawn . . .

Except it wasn't a lawn.

Twirly went in first – *splash*.

The Major followed – *SPLASH*.

Budge checked himself and watched black patches developing around their knees in the duck-weed covered pond.

Chapter Nine

Dorothy Burnlystock, licensee of The Five Bells in Upper Gently had called 'Time' twenty-minutes ago and was now noisily collecting glasses and moving chairs.

She was irritated and worried.

It had been four days now. She'd had no news of Twirly, and Budge Ballflower was not keeping his side of the bargain by telephoning regularly.

'Goodnight, m'duck,' she said to the last customer, and she locked and bolted the door and straightened the tatty mat she tries to remember to throw away.

She thought about this morning's visitors . . .

It had just gone eleven. She was having her morning port, and Shaun was stacking Babycham and Britvics.

'Customers!' called Shaun.

She slipped the port beneath the counter and peered out to the cobbled car park in front of the pub.

By a large black car stood a man in an open-necked pink shirt and two men in lightweight suits wearing dark glasses – one carrying a briefcase.

'Looks like the Mafia,' said Shaun.

'Mafia don't dress like that.'

'Perhaps they are plain-clothed Mafia.'

The pink-shirted man stepped warily into the bar and his quick brown fox eyes flicked around the room.

'We were hoping to find Mr Albert Whippet here.'

She studied the suits. Expensive: certainly not Fifty Shilling Tailors.

He continued, '....Mr Whippet of Fish House, by the clapper-bridge.'

Doll put her bracelet-jangling hand on to one of the pumps and smiled her gin and tonic smile.

'What can I get you, m'duck?'

'The road sweeper said we might find *Mr Whippet here.'*

She tossed her head and chuckled.

'Poor old Arthur has been sweeping in Upper Gently for twenty-five years. He gets confused.'

She called to Shaun.

'We need another crate of Old Speckled Hen.'

Doll served them three pints of best bitter.

Halfway through his pint the pink-shirt said, 'We're from English Heritage,' and he nodded towards his two restricted-vision accomplices. 'These gentlemen have come up from London.'

'Chose a lovely day,' she smiled.

'I wrote to Mr Whippet three days ago to say we were coming.'

She shrugged and shook her head.

'Regular postman is away on a week's holiday in Playa Blanca. Been no post.'

The pink-shirt took a sip of his beer, and peered at the dark glasses.

'Mustn't forget we have an appointment at Hailes Abbey at twelve.'

The pink-shirt headed for the door and the two suits both blundered into the same table.

She poured the three half-empty glasses into the ullage barrel which the malt-vinegar company empties every two weeks.

In the moonlit gardens of Kingscourt the Major staggered and spluttered, marooned in a black and green puddle.

'Give me a hand if you please, Mr Ballflower.'

Soon the Major and Twirly stood on the ornamental pavement, cascading water like down-pipes after a storm.

'I'll nip back to the room and collect towels and dry trousers,' said Budge.

'And meanwhile?' asked the Major.

Budge looked around.

Twirly pointed.

'There!' he said. Along a gravel spur, in the moonlight, glowed an octagonal summerhouse wedged between two giant rhododendrons.

'Capital, Corporal.'

Budge nodded, and sped towards the french windows of the hotel.

The Major and Twirly sloshed along the gravel.

Fortunately, the summerhouse was unlocked and they squelched into the dark interior, pushing between wicker chairs, folding tables, and canvas-covered bundles smelling of creosote and damp.

The Major growled.

This is not how a respectable ex-member of His Majesty's Forces should be conducting himself.

He longed for the comfort and familiarity of his timber-built bungalow high up on Beacon Hill overlooking Upper Gently.

The Residency had been inspired by a pavilion five thousand feet up at Shillong in the breathtakingly beautiful Khasi mountains in the Indian state of Meghalaya where he and Mary . . .

'Someone coming,' whispered Twirly.

Light steps along the gravel, and hushed giggles.

The Major pressed Twirly back against a croquet mallet frame and they became garden statues.

In the moonlit doorway appeared two figures: a shapely young girl with long fair hair, and a boy whose spiky hair glistened like a silver-paper crown.

More whispering as they entered into the darkness.

The Major tried not to imagine what was happening:
whispering, hissing, rustling, and breathless gasping – it sounded like a busy laundry room in a vow-of-silence nunnery.

Twirly poked a finger into the Major's ribs. And then the Major heard what Twirly had heard.

Heavy footsteps advancing along the gravel.

The rustling stopped.

Deep breath-held silence – and the relentless crunching grew closer.

From outside a soft urgent voice ordered, 'Come out of there you two, and get those wet knickers off!'

It was Budge.

The girl shrieked and rushed out of the hut.   The boy, clutching his nether garments about him, legged after her.

In the Catherine bar the Major and Twirly stood reassuringly clad in dry trousers, with Budge attempting to hide a bulging plastic bag which was leaking.

'Three double brandies,' he ordered.

The Major purred, 'There's a hair-dryer and an iron in the room.'

Budge grinned.

They all three grinned.

Budge dug his nose deep into his brandy glass.

'Must telephone Doll tomorrow.'

Friday 10th July   *Day five*

It was a beautiful morning.

'Hell's Twirly?'

The Major shrugged.

'Left the room early. Bulling his wellingtons perhaps.'

'Or flogging more shampoos,' said Budge. 'He's missing a good breakfast.'

The fresh grapefruit and poached halibut had been wonderful, and the Melba toast was fragile perfection.

He watched the Major poking a finger through a basket of small jars of preserves.

The Major explained, 'Mobile canteens in Burma sometimes turned up with small tins of apricot jam. Unbelievable treat. Welcome change from corned beef and hard biscuits. Still adore the stuff. Gorgeous canteen girls.'

At that moment the flush-faced AWOL Twirly strode rapidly into the Field-of-the-Cloth-of-Gold breakfast room.

'Major!' he said, and he thrust forward a pale polished cane fitted with the Major's old brass top.

A sharp sniff.

'Got the wood-turner in the village to do it last night. It's ash. Won't break. Used for hockey-sticks.'

They marched briskly in step along the lane and Budge noticed the wedding-party cars were still sleeping behind the ivy-covered Hunters' Hall Hotel.

Distant fields were lightly cloaked in late rising mists, and the sun was carefully filling in all the colours.

In a field on the right, just past Bumper's Isle Farm, a group of lumpily-shorn sheep were ignoring the grass at their feet, preferring to stretch over a low wire-topped wall to nibble at the long dew-damp grass of the verge.

A large ewe with its head trapped in the wire turned insane watery eyes on Budge with fearful apprehension, and broke into furious and unscientific attempts at disentanglement.

Budge called to Twirly in the rear of the column.

'Should we try to free it?'

Twirly gave the prisoner a brief glance and carried on.

'Forget it, Budge. Be stuck again in five minutes if you do – all sheep are born with a death wish.'

Budge checked his map. Ahead was the telecommunications tower of Goose Green.

By a letterbox on a post at a crossroads in the hamlet of Bagpath, Budge located a bridleway sign, and at a gap in a hedgerow a narrow stony track dropped steeply down into the valley.

He slung off his pack.

'You two go on. I'll follow. Must telephone Doll. There'll be no reception down there.'

'How are they, m'duck?'
'Fine, Doll.'
'Both of them?'

'Bit tired, but fine.'

'Been worried, not hearing.'

'It's only been four days, Doll. They are doing well.'

'Like to hear, you know, Budge; not necessary *every* day of course . . .'

Budge noted the censure.

'I've been worried too, Doll. A gardener at some large house told Twirly that English Heritage are getting involved in something in Upper Gently. Do you suppose they know about the Roman stone?'

Silence.

'Doll?'

The licensee of the Five Bells usually spoke first and thought afterwards. Now she was carefully high-heeling across a muddy car-park.

'English Heritage *were* in the village yesterday, Budge. But not about the lintel.'

She speeded up.

'Budge. You get them safely to Land's End, m'duck, and our arrangement is firm. That stone will be yours.'

Last year, when Doll persuaded the brewery to remove the plaster in her club room, no one commented on the oddly-shaped stone lintel revealed above the small window by the fireplace.

At one end it was triangular, with a line of rosettes at the other, and a pattern of incised lines in between. Budge noticed that it was not in the local marmalade-coloured Guiting stone, nor the warm grey of Painswick. It was pure white, like stone taken from the underground quarries in the Devon fishing village of Beer at the southern end of the Roman Fosse Way.

Then, during an unexciting dart's match against Shipton Oliffe, Budge realised what it was.

The stone had originally stood VERTICALLY with the triangular gable at the top.

Dodging the darts, he examined the markings more closely and found the letters D and M. In the remainder of the pattern he found LEG II AVG, and H S E.

D M for Dis Manibus *(To the spirits of the departed)*

LEG II AVG for Legionis II Augustae *(Second Legion Augusta)*

H S E for hic situs est *(Here lies)*

INCREDIBLE!

A memorial stone for a Roman soldier, probably looted by the pub builders from the nearby Chedworth site.

Priceless!

At the end of the stony track a wicket gate led into a green lush valley, fresh and beautiful, lit by a sun eagerly peering over woods high up on the left, and highlighting green fields up on the right, with a large white building which Budge's map suggested was probably Ashcroft House.

A faint track wandering through long grass and leading easily down was marked by waymarks on wooden posts. It eventually joined a stream. At first the stream ran in a deep gulley, but as the valley flattened the stream became wide and shallow.

The Major, gently teasing a clump of shoulder-high thistles with his new cane, called, 'Quite charming, Mr Ballflower. Rarely seen such a serene and silent valley.'

Budge nodded.

Up in the woods a few birds were holding an early morning Songs of Praise, but the loudest noise came from crickets by the path, and the chuckling, babbling, sparkling stream weaving past their feet and playfully nudging bright yellow spearwort paddling at the edge.

It's like the Yorkshire Dales with the added advantage of balmy southern sunshine, and to confirm this, up on a hillock on the left perched a Yorkshire forage barn.

The Major asked, 'Do you suppose that anyone else knows about this perfect place? Should be called *Shangri-La.*'

Again Budge checked his map. He grinned.

'It's called Ozleworth's Bottom.'

Half a mile further on, Budge stopped to examine a narrow battered stone bridge from where ornamental cap-stones had fallen into the stream, which had now become a deep gulley called Marlees Brook.

Here they turned to the right on a farm track heading up the steep valleyside towards Walker's Wood. A single small crab-apple tree had fruit the size of green marbles.

'Where's lunch?' asked the Major, scrambling onto a flat farm trailer by the side of the track.

Budge pointed across the valley.

'Five miles to the south of here. Should be there about one. First doing a short diversion to see a remarkable little church which I know you'll love, Major.'

The Major glanced unconvinced at Twirly, who had clambered up beside him.

Twirly dived into a deep trouser pocket and extracted three plastic spoons. From his rucksack he produced three small cartons of fruit yoghurt.

Budge said, 'From the breakfast buffet?'

Twirly peeled off the foil cover and plunged in his spoon.

'From a silver tray outside the Harfleur Suite.'

Stepping out of Walker's Wood was like Dorothy leaving Kansas and arriving at the start of the yellow-brick road. A sandy track ran along the centre of a forty-foot wide mown gallop with an avenue of recently planted saplings. Either side were pristine paddocks. Handsome, nervously prancing horses followed the walkers with wide-eyed, well-bred curiosity.

Budge reflected that had the many fences been gleaming white he could be back in Lexington, Kentucky.

Ahead lay an ornate archway with pristine buildings and a conservatory and a grey slated roof topped by a cupola where a clock pronounced the time to be five minutes past ten o'clock precisely.

Immediately before the archway a Gloucestershire notice announced a statutory order diversion, and they were led round to the right by a beautifully carved wooden signpost indicating: To the church.

The neat path crossed a pretty little stone bridge with a miniature lake with lilies, and superior-looking ducks with wings gleaming like Quality Street wrappings, and a House-and-Gardens waterfall running down to manicured flowerbeds and an immaculate tennis court.

A stubby church tower appeared over a high stone wall.

Budge said, 'Unique in England, Major. A circular churchyard.'

In AD 509 Pope Gregory commanded that pagan sites should be taken over by Christian churches. This was probably the reason a wooden Saxon church was built on this ancient circular spot. Later, Normans replaced it with an unusual hexagonal stone tower, and then added extensions to the east and the west.

Budge saw the Major pause by the metal gate to the churchyard to fussily check the alignment of his green jungle hat and give a couple of flicks to his snow-white moustache.

Then, twirling his new cane like Beau Brummell entering Vauxhall Gardens, he passed through the gateway.

The hexagonal church squatted to the left, but ahead, on a large slab of red granite, was living proof of the Major's unerring sixth-sense.

Chapter Ten

Silver-haired Annabelle Clayton rose smiling from the red slab and advanced towards the Major with her hand extended.

'Lovely to see you again, Robert.'

The Major beamed.

'Extraordinary!' he said.

And he called to the young niece, 'Good morning,' and watched her rise and sway towards him in a sunflower-yellow linen suit.

'Major Legge-Wellesley,' she smiled. 'Aunt is *so* clever. She guessed you would come here, and calculated it would probably be this morning. She wants Mr Ballflower to tell me all about the church.'

He saw Annabelle smiling proudly as she watched her niece saunter happily towards Budge by the church porch.

'She can't believe she has met a real stonemason who knows all about English churches.'

The Major said, 'First class. But where have you come from this morning?'

The aunt laughed.

'We're still at Painswick!'

Painswick? That was two campaigns ago.

The aunt continued, 'It's only half-an-hour by car.'

Budge watched as Sophia approached along the straight-as-a-cloister mown path.

'Good morning, Mr Ballflower,' she called with her perfect teeth and green eyes. 'We love your church. It's *darling*.'

Budge winced.

She waved a slender arm and tossed her pale auburn hair.

'And so beautifully located.'

Budge turned to the church.

84

'Probably originally built by Roger de Berkeley at the beginning of the twelfth century as a single-storey chapel. Two other levels added later – you can see the string-courses.'

'String-courses?' From an olive-suede shoulder-bag she extracted a blue paperback. 'I have this book . . .'

Budge took it, looked at it, and handed it back.

Discovering Church Architecture. Mark Child. Yes, I know it. Excellent.'

'I've been using it everywhere. Don't think it mentions string-courses.'

Budge looked over her shoulder at Twirly swerving purposefully around tombstones and heading for the east wall where a man was mowing grass.

The Major and the aunt were still by the red slab, deep in discussion, with the Major occasionally throwing back his head and laughing aloud and with the aunt smiling, and admiring.

Budge took a deep breath and turned towards the church and said in his schools lecture voice, 'Church walls were built on a stone foundation – the tablement. The master-mason carried a pole, called a latt, trimmed to the height the walls were expected to reach in the first stage of building, probably ten or twelve feet.

'He would stand this pole upright on the tablement to measure the progress of the stone courses, and check that the height was constant all round the building. When the full pole height was reached, that often marked the end of the building for that year.'

Budge turned to look at her. She was standing rapt.

'Work invariably stopped during winter months to allow the wall to stabilize, and because of frosts. The top of the wall was protected by thatch or projecting slabs.

'When work recommenced in the spring, this line of slabs – the string course – became the new tablement from which progress was measured by the latt pole.

'On high towers you can usually see several string-courses, all marking the building periods.'

He ended his lecture and spoke more softly.

'Understand?'

The green eyes smiled. Her soft fingers touched his arm.

'That's fascinating. Thank you.'

Inside the porch he showed her the remarkable carved leaf-sprays around the doorway; and in the white walled church with its splendid floor of red encaustic tiles he pointed out a damaged corbel where a carving had been attacked by a well-intentioned iconoclast; and on a windowsill the naval hatband of HMS Grayling, an armed trawler built in 1942 with money contributed by surrounding villages.

He showed her the incredible example of thirteenth century stone-carving where a tangle of chevrons appears to stand clear of the tower archway and which stoneworkers from all over Europe come to see.

Budge said, 'Imagine, Sophia, the vision of the mason who conceived this design, and carried it out. And imagine, too, in a church lit by candles, the multiple dancing shadows it must have thrown. More watchable than some television.'

Sophia purred.

Time to get moving.

Outside Budge looked around the churchyard.

'Hell is Twirly?'

The Major called, 'Mr Whippet!' and Twirly came cheerfully leaping over the graves.

'Been talking to the gardener.'

'Know him?'

Twirly shook his head:

'Showed me the grave of the last man hanged in England for highway-robbery.'

They all walked round by the great house of Ozleworth Park with its six-pillared portico and closely mown lawns and elegant bushes and spectacular flowerbeds. Here the aunt and niece were to turn right for the car-park.

The aunt placed her hand on the Major's arm.

'I hope you will come to Tunbridge Wells to find me, Robert.'

The Major nodded.

'And next time you are in Cheltenham, come to Upper Gently. Anyone will point out The Residency, high up on the hill.'

The Major's eyes were shining brighter than they had for several days. Budge watched him remove his hat, and step forward, and gently take the aunt by the shoulders. He kissed her softly on both cheeks as if she tasted of apricots.

Budge checked the time. Ten-thirty. Blast!

Need a fast pace now until lunch.

Down into the valley to cross Marlees Brook, and steeply up across a field towards Holwell Farm – a red-ochre-washed building reminding Budge of Abisko and Kebnekaise on the Swedish long distance path of *Kungsleden,* the King's Way.

Immediately past the farm, the track became rougher and curved to the left. It ran along the bottom of a deep V-cleft beneath banks twenty feet high, probably the result of a landslip from the steep Hen's Cliff above.

It quickly became a damp narrow trench hidden from drying sun and winds, and Budge watched Twirly stomp over the rough and boggy turves.

The bright blue sky became obscured as trees and great holly bushes came together overhead to make a damp and oppressive tunnel.

Twirly stopped, confronted by an impassable barrier of green leaves, tangled branches, and boughs thick as a man's leg.

'Fallen sycamore tree,' called Twirly. 'Ripped from the top of the bank. Probably the high winds we had in June.'

Budge joined Twirly and peered up at the side-banks, too steep and muddy to climb, and probably too dangerous to slide down beyond the tree.

He took out his map.

Running late. Must avoid returning to the valley.

Twirly pushed himself into the foliage and returned with fire in his eyes and twigs in his hair.

'We can do this. It's only a tree. We've all climbed trees. Just up-and-over.'

Budge was not convinced, but the Major swung his satchel to the rear, rammed his jungle-hat down over his ears, handed his cane to Twirly and commanded, 'Right! Off you go, Corporal. If Wolfe could scale Quebec's Abraham Heights, so can we.'

Budge called after them, 'General Wolfe *died* at the top, Major.'

He watched them disappear and followed their progress marked by thrashing branches, and tumbling twigs and scattering leaves, and the confused sound of snapping, splintering, scuffling and swearing.

Soon the struggle passed out of sight; they were over the summit.

Budge sighed and prepared to follow.

But then . . .

A CRACK! Like a rifle shot.

A snapping bough.

Followed by a series of cries descending to the floor of the cleft.

Then stillness.

The old fool's fallen.

But then the Major's voice calling, 'TWIRLY!'

Then renewed cracking and crunching, and Budge knew the Major was fighting his way down to where Twirly must be.

Budge leapt to the steep bank where the branches were jammed into the turf and with the aid of desperation he climbed, and kicked and clawed and cursed until he could see down into the bottom of the trench.

Hell!

The Major was on his knees by the side of Twirly, who was spreadeagled on a pile of tree debris. From his lofty viewpoint Budge could clearly see blood oozing through the Major's fingers where he was gripping the blood-soaked sleeve of Twirly's striped rugby shirt.

But worse . . .

Twirly's left leg was lying at a sickening right-angle to where it should be.

'Steady, Corporal,' whispered the Major, and he increased his pressure on the bloody arm.

He heard Budge scrambling down the high bank and demanding, 'How is he?'

The Major did not look up.

'He's alive.'

Budge ripped off his pack.

'I'll ring for an ambulance.'

'Good grief, Ballflower!' shouted the Major. 'Talk bloody sense. Never get a signal down here. And take an ambulance two days to get to this filthy begotten no-man's land.'

There was a moan from Twirly.

The Major quickly released one gory hand and gently prised open Twirly's left eye.

He said softly, 'Twirly?'

Then louder and more sharply, 'Corporal!'

The head moved, and Twirly licked dry lips and murmured, 'Whippet. Five-eight-four.'

Good boy.

The Major released his grip on Twirly's forearm and struggled to his feet.

'Here, Mr Ballflower. Take over pressure to the wound while I check the damage,' and he snatched off his Paisley cravat and threw it down at Budge. 'Make a pad with that, and hold it hard.'

The Major noted that Twirly's pallor was becoming less ghastly and the limp body beginning to look more like Twirly.

He looked up at the splintered branches.

Not fallen any great height. Mostly bounced from branch to branch. Will have adopted regulation landing-in-trees position. Knees up. Feet tight together. Arms across face. Probably a bit of concussion – and this nasty wound.

The Major knelt down and did a quick check of neck and limbs, prompted by grunts from Twirly.

Finally he stood.

'Corporal Whippet. Once that arm is dressed you'll be fit for guard duties, fatigues, and cookhouse.'

'Stab!' feebly complained Twirly.

Budge, still applying pressure, exploded.

'But his leg, Major.'

'His leg?'

'His leg, Major. BLOODY LOOK AT IT!'

89

'Ballflower,' snapped the Major, '*you* concentrate on controlling that blood flow. His legs appear to be fine. Both of them. A wellington boot has come adrift, that's all!'

And to prove his point he tossed the offending boot a couple of yards up the trench.

Twenty minutes later Twirly staggered to his feet, his lips no longer blue, parted in a weak grin.

His sleeve had been slit open from cuff to elbow.

A folded clean handkerchief, smothered with the contents of a tube of Boots antiseptic cream, had been placed over the wound and held in place by a tightly-bound two-inch bandage.

The Major was content.

A long tear. Should knit together more quickly than a cut.

The ripped and bloody sleeve was safety-pinned up near the collarbone to make an effective sling.

'Well done, Corporal. Get you to the MDS as soon as possible.'

He produced his brandy bottle, took a quick swig himself, and passed it to Budge.

'Well done, Budge,' he murmured.

He then poured water over his hands and wiped them on the grassy bank. He handed Budge the water bottle.

'Suggest you do the same, otherwise they'll get sticky as strawberry jam.'

He gave Twirly two pain-killing tablets and said gravely, 'You know the wound will begin to stiffen shortly.'

Twirly nodded, but protested, 'Don't usually bother with pain killers, Sir.'

'Don't usually fall out of trees, Corporal.'

Twirly was given the Major's satchel to carry, while the Major eased himself into the Commando rucksack.

'Good Lord! Whippet. Hell you got here? Far too heavy. Hold a kit inspection when we get to the billet. Lot of this stuff must be surplus to requirements and should be returned to the QM's stores immediately.'

90

And then, 'Right! Mr Ballflower. When you are ready. *Slowly, slowly* – walking wounded speed, if you please.'

Budge nodded and set off *slowly,* as instructed.

The path ran steeply up until it was level with the tops of fir trees in the combe below Hen's Cliff, and Budge paused in the burning sunshine and pondered.

The pub is four miles away. Can't let Twirly walk that far. However, the hamlet of Tresham is only about a mile. Will ask at a cottage about local taxis. We'll ALL ride to the pub, never mind the World War II warriors protesting with their nonsensical heroics.

Then we'll reappraise the situation.

While he waited for Twirly with his attendant commanding officer, he watched ecstatic bees fumbling the purple finger-stalls of foxgloves as they lay back and thought of England. A waymark on a gatepost indicated they were now joining the six hundred and ten mile Monarch's Way that follows the supposed escape route of Charles II after the Battle of Worcester.

In a field on the left a whitewashed trig point marked the height of 675 feet, and this grass-topped, sunbathed summit provided magnificent, unrestricted views in all directions.

In the hazy distance he could see two pillars with two-storey windows, brilliant white in the sunlight, one of the River Severn bridges.

Normally this viewpoint would be a place for celebration, where he might even suggest to the Major that he produce his brandy bottle.

But there is nothing to celebrate now.

It was always a ridiculous adventure, of course. Only the fifth day and already the pace is killing them. First the Major's fall. Now this disaster . . .

There is no way that Twirly will stand on the cliffs of Land's End searching for the ghosts of troopships.

And the Major will retreat from his glorious campaign and become a lonely, reclusive widower again.

And the Roman stone will remain in Doll's club-room – or pass to English Heritage.

The Monarch's Way left the wide grass track and crossed a field to a stone stile where a path led over a neat lawn surrounded by laurels and dotted with croquet hoops.

A grey-haired lady in Burden Court Cottage, dressed as if she was expecting visitors, was understanding and instantly helpful.

'Taxi will be here in fifteen minutes. Perhaps your friends would like some tea when they arrive.'

At that moment Twirly and the Major appeared amongst the croquet hoops.

'Good heavens!' she cried. 'Walking wounded.'

She rushed over to Twirly and examined his gory make-shift sling.

'Think we can improve upon that.'

She disappeared through a canary yellow doorway and re-emerged later with a tray bearing large scissors, little boxes, and a wicker basket of bandages.

'Maisie is making tea,' she said.

In no time at all the taxi appeared, and Budge watched the Major replace his cup on the tea-and-biscuits tray, and nod towards Twirly who was now posing heroically with the rugby-shirt sleeve replaced by a gleaming white sling.

'Most grateful, ma'am,' said the Major. 'A great improvement on the RAP job. Should suffice till we get to the MDS.'

She laughed.

'I was an ex-army nurse.'

The Major smiled.

'My late wife was a QAIMNS with SEAC.'

'I was an SN with a CCS for 16 BMH, BLA.'

Budge sighed.

Who are these guys?

Chapter Eleven

The maroon Mercedes was driven fast and confidently along a roller-coaster route of narrow lanes through the villages of Alderley and Hillersley, with a perfunctory pause at the Wickwar junction.

As they sped past the hundred and thirty foot high pillar in memory of General Lord Edward Somerset who gloriously commanded a brigade of cavalry wiped out at Waterloo, Budge turned to squint at the rear seat passengers. Twirly, with head lolled back and eyes closed, was nursing his wounded arm as if it was a baby. The Major rolled from side to side as if watching tennis, but serenely asleep.

Budge made up his mind.

I'll tell them during lunch.

Opposite a group of expensively renovated barns a sign began to read: *Hawkesbury Upton welcomes careful . . .*

But the Mercedes didn't read English.

Outside a cream washed building shimmering with a Hanging Babylon display of flower-filled baskets, the Mercedes applied a powerful reverse thrust, propelling Twirly and the Major forward into wakefulness.

'Beaufort Arms,' announced the driver. 'Four pounds fifty.'

Half-hidden by the baskets was a large round yellow enamel sign.

'Remember those, Major?'

In the early days of motoring the Automobile Association erected 40,000 such signs all over England with the name of the village and indicating the distances to the next village and London. In 1940, when England hourly expected to be infested by stubble-chinned nuns asking, 'Wo wa ist mich?', the signs were removed.

The Beaufort Arms bears one of the few signs reinstated. The distance from London is shown as 103 miles, with the distance to the next village one mile – ironically a village called Dunkirk.

'What happened to *you?'* asked the landlord, glaring at Twirly.

'He fell out of a tree,' said Budge ordering three pints of Wickwar Brewing Company's Old Bob ale.

The landlord paused from his pulling.

'A tree?' He shook his head and slid a full pint towards Twirly.

'How *old* are you?'

'He's seventy-three,' said the Major.

The landlord reached for another glass.

'Does he talk?'

With a shaking hand, Twirly carefully lifted the brimming pint towards his dry lips.

The landlord suddenly stopped pulling and commanded, 'Put that ale down, young tree-climbing fellar. Got the very thing for you,' and he disappeared through a doorway.

In a couple of minutes he was back.

'Duke of Beaufort's famous kill-or-cure. Egg yolk. Brandy. Worcester sauce. Scrap of chilli. It's on the house.'

It was the last ingredient which went a long way to curing Twirly's arm.

He struggled to focus on a glass panel lit from below, set into the wooden floor by his bar stool.

'It's a well,' explained the landlord. 'Sixty feet deep. Water as pure as me, but Brussels have condemned it. Bastards.'

The Major handed Twirly a menu, but his eyes found it fuzzy.

'Have the home-made oxtail soup,' advised the Major.

'Me, too,' sighed Budge.

While the Major and Budge dealt with their 'afters' – custard sponge puddings – Twirly looked around the bar for somewhere to curl up with his throbbing arm, but Budge loudly cleared his throat and dabbled his spoon in the remains of the thick custard.

'Been thinking . . .

'This is our fifth day of walking and we've covered something like forty-six miles.'

He pushed away the plate and the spoon.

'I reckon we've got another three hundred miles to do to Land's End.'

Twirly watched as he groped for words.

'As you know,' continued Budge. 'I *have* to be back in Gently by the beginning of August to start work at Lambley.'

He straightened a Wickwar Brewery beer-mat, and looked up to check the ceiling beams were also correctly aligned.

'There is not a cat-in-hell's chance of getting to Land's End in time.'

Twirly peered at Budge, examining his words, and then turned his attention to a fly buzzing dangerously near a crimson-shaded wall-lamp above their heads.

He turned to watch the Major, who was staring down into the condemned well.

Budge coughed liked a politician.

'Big disappointment, of course. All done so well. But I'm sure it's sensible that we abort now, before we go any further.'

Twirly's lacerated arm was beginning to burn and on the low table his glass of Old Bob ale was advancing and retreating like a swaying cow's tail.

He heard the Major say, 'FINISH? Right *here* at this pub?'

A noisy tractor towing a trailer loaded high with hay slowly passed by the window, blocking out the sun.

Budge nodded.

'Got the taxi-driver's card. He could get us to Yate railway station in ten minutes. Be in Gently in time for tea.'

The concerned landlord called from the bar, 'Everything all right, gentlemen?'

Twirly tugged at his sling and said to the Major, 'You got another of those tablets, Major?'

The Major checked his watch.

'Better wait for a bit if you can, Twirly.'

Budge peered into their faces.

The Major spoke softly.

'Mr Ballflower, this morning you were *determined* to get us all to Land's End. It is true that we have been advancing more slowly than your programme demands, and the unit suffered a slight set-back this morning . . .'

Twirly watched Budge stride across to the window.

The Major called after him, 'If I might say so, Mr Ballflower – Budge – it is uncharacteristic of you to change your mind so rapidly.'

Budge returned and placed both hands on the bar and knew he was right.

Budge does NOT *change his mind rapidly.*

In fact he rarely does anything *rapidly, and this has always been the case.*

He was born on 4th June, 1953 two weeks overdue and his mother used to joke he was waiting for a better offer.

He was never a toddler *and never bothered to walk until he was three. He always sat with a contented smile in the busiest part of the rectory while the family stepped over and around him.*

He heard, 'Come on, BUDGE!' so often he thought it was his name.

And he has answered to it ever since.

When he was eight years old the family decided he was too large to step over. So he was packed off to a boarding school in Weymouth.

There his contented quiescence served him well, and he became the star goalkeeper of the school football team. He achieved this by never *leaping about the goal-mouth but firmly standing his ground and developing strong, far-reaching arms like windmill-sails and being more or less in the right place for at least half of the goal attempts.*

The school called him Rock of Aegis.
His real name is John Christopher Ballflower.
Church commissioners and architects know him as JCB.

The Major spoke like a judge.

'May I suggest, Budge, that we continue the campaign until this evening's *laager*. Things always appear clearer after a night's kip. Make a decision in the morning.'

Budge considered, then suddenly slapped the bar.

'O.K. Let's go to Old Sodbury.'

He peered at Twirly.

'You all right to walk? Two hours? Map says it's all flat.'

Twirly sniffed.

'Let's just get going.'

Outside the pub Twirly blinked in the blinding sunshine; his face was afire, he was perspiring like a cow in labour, and his wellington boots staggered about like newly-born lambs. He could hear S.I. Slater bawling, *'Stop wobbling, that man!'*

His lips were sloe dry.

'You all right, Corporal?'

He swayed as he considered.

'I'll do,' he said eventually.

The path was a wide sandy track with grass verges, and smooth as Compton Abdale bowling green. He could hear skylarks but didn't bother to check. Budge would do that. Meadow Brown butterflies skitted gaily along in front of him like insensitive teenagers.

Down to the right was the deep valley of the Severn and the sunlit patchwork of fields swayed like hammocks on a troopship.

By the crumbling ruins of a barn they paused while Budge made decisions about turning right to follow the Cotswold Way, or continuing ahead on the Monarch's Way.

Twirly stepped into the shade of the bare walls and remembered a smouldering barn by stunted olive trees from which vicious rounds were ricocheting, and where he had thrown himself down alongside three still and silent parachutists of the 551st

Parachute Infantry Battalion, US 7th Army, who had jumped earlier that morning over Le Muy in the invasion of southern France.

Poor lads – they would never see the States again.

In a beech wood near Horton Court they crunched over a carpet of dead leaves and old nut husks.

'All right, Twirly?' Budge asked. 'Map shows a post office in Horton, the next village. It might also be a shop where we can buy cold drinks. Or ice-cream.'

It wasn't a shop.

Wasn't even a post office.

But a dark-haired lady in the garden of Post Office Cottage put down a small red trowel, peeled off green rubber gloves, and disappeared to quickly return with a jug of water clinking with ice and three glasses.

Twirly saw her stare at his arm, then give him a kind smile, and he remembered the old lady who had smiled sadly at him as she silently handed him an orange in the ruins of the mortar-battered *villagio* of San Basilio-Mottola as he lay waiting for the stretcher bearers.

Budge stopped at the top of a steep grassy bank beneath overhead cables, by a small lake with a dam. The Major took hold of Twirly's good arm and steadied him down the slope.

It was like the painting *Comrades* with a weary lieutenant helping a wounded squaddie into a shell-hole in Ypres, which hangs by the fag machine in the British Legion Club at Shipton.

Twirly reluctantly sniffed his thanks and swept away sweat which hung from his eyebrows like drops of rain along the top bar of a gate.

Through Little Sodbury they stopped at a bend in a lane where a clump of Giant Hogweed stood ten feet tall.

There was some discussion.

Apparently the Cotswold Way follows the lane to the left then up and over a hill-fort used by Romans, Vikings and finally an English army on its way to fight a battle at Tewkesbury.

On the other hand, a footpath leads directly ahead across fields flat as last night's beer.

'Sod Sodbury hill-fort,' growled the Major.

Twirly heard Budge tell the Major that grassy banks on the right of the path were pillow mounds.

Twirly knew differently, but it didn't seem important. They were old warrens built to provide rabbits for the manor or the church – and woe betide any poor bastard caught poaching them.

The path went through a farmyard where Budge tried to interest them in three heads carved in stone sticking from the gable of a barn.

'Yes, yes,' said the Major. 'Is it far?'

Budge smiled like Mrs Tarry when she looked at the clock and it was two minutes to four.

'Major! Beyond the farm gateway lies the B4040 road . . . This *is* Old Sodbury.'

Twirly sank down on to a low wall by a garage which slowly drifted backwards and forwards like a Tunisian desert mirage.

Budge pointed to a thatched cottage with a low white fence.

'That's Tunnel Cottage where we're booked in for the night. We can check in with Mrs Wallington now, or we can first nip next door into the Dog Inn for a quick one.'

Twirly sighed. He desperately needed to kick off his hot boots, fall on to a soft cool bed and lay his arm somewhere comfortable.

The Major elaborately licked his dry lips and nodded towards Twirly.

'Attend to the men first.'

Twirly's room was small and white, with neatly trimmed thatch overhanging a tiny window. It was as cool as Doll's beer-cellar where orange stains run out of white-painted stonework behind the barrels.

He lay on the high patchwork quilt and nursed his arm. It was throbbing as if his thumping heart had slipped down inside it beyond his elbow. He wondered if the Major, in an unexplained act of betrayal, had bandaged his arm with barbed wire and live electric-fencing. The ends of his fingers felt as if they were growing long fragile shoots like seed-potatoes in the box under his stairs.

He closed his eyes and they filled with stinging sweat.

He thought of Fish House. And Doll. And Ratcher, his black-as-a-moonless-night cat whose full name is Rat-Catcher because that is what he is for, but 'Ratcher' slips more easily off the tongue – although the cat declines to recognise either. He was acquired a few years ago when rats began swimming over Booky Tweet from Bob Dunkley's rickyard.

The cat has a purr like a rusty drill and is ugly. It has only one eye; a rat took the other. The scrawny tail has a ninety-degree kink in it, result of an encounter with a slamming barn door.

He wondered if Alf Smith was feeding him properly and . . .

When he awoke he could hear Budge talking downstairs. Mrs Wallington didn't do evening meals but she recommended The Dog next door.

Twirly splashed water on his face and tottered down the narrow staircase in his sticky socks and said he would skip dinner.

After Budge and the Major left, Mrs Wallington pointed to an armchair and he found it easier to sink down than protest.

On a spindly coffee table by the chair she placed a bowl of steaming soup.

It was French onion.

'C'est délicieux,' murmured Twirly, not quite certain where he was.

'C'est Baxter's,' chuckled Mrs Wallington.

The windows were open, and the evening air was still and sweet. In the depths of this buzzing silence he detected a faint tinkling noise, which slowly got louder.

He strained to listen, and realised it came from the spoon in his empty dish. It was gently rocking to and fro.

Then he heard the cause.

Outside in the far distance came a deep approaching double beat.

THUMP-THUMP.
THUMP-THUMP.
THUMP-THUMP.

He clenched his eyes and strained to think. He knew the sound, but couldn't place it.

Mrs Wallington appeared with some cold apple tart.

She smiled.

'The noise? It's a train. Just behind the house is the entrance to Sodbury tunnel, on the London-Bristol line.'

Of course. A slow goods train. He used to hear them on clear frosty nights doing guard at Bulford Depot a million years ago.

Mrs Wallington went to stand by the open door.

'Germans tried to bomb the tunnel during the war,' she said.

The thumping continued.

'Well, that's what they said, although my father, who was the village Air Raid Warden, he used to say it was nothing to do with the tunnel. A plane from a bombing raid on Cardiff docks, probably lost, just dumped his bombs and went home.'

The thumping suddenly ceased as the train was swallowed by the tunnel.

Mrs Wallington turned from the doorway.

'The bombs just dropped in fields up on the hill behind us. Except for one which landed on the Land Army Hostel by Plough Farm.'

Twirly stiffened as the air was ripped apart by a great roaring squeal of an express train which burst free from the tunnel, to rattle rapidly away in the direction of Bristol.

Mrs Wallington continued.

'If you're interested, my father kept a scrapbook about the war. It's got a cutting from the *Chipping Echo*. It mentions him helping some of the poor girls who were wounded.'

Twirly's delicately bursting head was still pounding from the blast of the express train.

I should go up to my room – NOW.

Mrs Wallington produced an open red and grey album.

'It don't say it was Sodbury, never did, always somewhere in the south-west . . . but the photo *is* of my dad.'

The book was thrust on to Twirly's lap.

He couldn't focus properly.

With a shaking forefinger he followed the words under the dappled photograph . . . *the bravery of the local warden . . . the destruction of the hostel . . . seven girls seriously injured . . .*

'Could I have a glass of water, please?'

Mrs Wallington bent forward with concern.

'You all right, Mr Whippet? Is it the arm? Got some pain killers which my doctor says . . .'

Twirly shook his head.

His finger followed the words: *one girl was killed . . .*

His sigh was deep and painful, for he knew what was to come.

'R. Burnlystock of Cheltenham.'

He closed the book, and the room swayed as if he was clinging to a piece of green debris on a Mediterranean sea.

He turned to reassure Mrs Wallington, but couldn't see clearly through the screen of wet eyelashes.

He shook his head and tried to make his quivering lips speak.

He looked down at his black socks and murmured softer than a dropped rose petal, 'I knew her.'

Chapter Twelve

William Tyndale was a chaplain and tutor in Old Sodbury.

Henry VIII was not well pleased when Tyndale produced his translation of the Bible into English, and in 1536 the king had him strangled.   Two years later he had second thoughts about the translation, and issued a decree that every church in the land must own a copy. Tyndale stayed strangled.

In the 1830s Isambard Kingdom Brunel pioneered his Great Western Railway through here with a two-mile tunnel just behind Mrs Wallington's Tunnel Cottage.

In the 500 year old Dog Inn at a table by a beam-topped open fireplace, the size of Upper Gently's bus shelter, the Major fingered his menu.

Perhaps the fish?

He watched Budge struggling to make a decision and heard him mumble, 'Pity about Twirly. D'you think he could have carried on walking?'

The Major put down the menu and said firmly, 'Not could . . . He *can* carry on walking, Budge.   Men of Corporal Whippet's generation learnt to accept and *deal* with difficulties. Discomfort and hardship were part of normal life. They are wary of comfort. Notice how they invariably sit on the edge of a chair which looks too inviting. Anything easy is suspect.'

Budge turned to the menu as a young lady in a red blouse materialised with an expectant smile and notebook at the ready.

'Local trout with bacon,' said the Major.

Budge played for time.

'The steak and kidney pudding. Is it a slice of a large pudding or an individual pudding?'

The young lady looked hurt.

'It's a small pudding made by Arthur.'

'Arthur the chef?'

'Arthur comes in just to make the puddings, sir. Nobody makes steak-and-kidney puddings like Arthur.'

'You get gravy?'

The girl sighed. 'You get a small jug of hot gravy, sir.'

Budge nodded.

'One of Arthur's puddings – with hot gravy.'

The Major carefully aligned the cutlery and wondered if he would get a fish knife.

'You understand my problem, Major, about Land's End? It's essential I'm back in Gently by the end of July. Don't think we can do it.'

The Major stared at Budge. He hadn't previously noticed his intensely blue eyes.

'We've been averaging less than ten miles a day, Major, and to get to Land's End in time, I reckon we've got to do fifteen miles a day. *Every day.* Can't be done.'

The Major leaned back in his chair.

'Budge,' he said, 'the walk to Land's End belongs to *Twirly.* Not us. We are merely acting in a supporting role. It's not for *us* to declare the operation cancelled.'

'You think he could get there without us?'

The Major laughed aloud.

'Mr Ballflower, Private Whippet once made his way alone across twenty miles of enemy-occupied Provence. He is quite capable of reaching the south-west corner of friendly England. He is a survivor.'

The young waitress appeared, looking flustered.

'Sorry, gentlemen. Forgot to ask. Is it chips or new?'

Mrs Wallington was worried about her guest. She asked if he had been inoculated against tetanus. He had.

She asked when.

Twirly said he thought it must have been 1942.

Without consulting him, she arranged for him to be seen at the surgery in the rear of the Post Office at eight-thirty in the morning.

Saturday 11th July *Day six*

The Major heroically demolished a plate of kidneys, black pudding and scrambled egg, and was about to rise when Twirly strode through the front door.

A gleaming white NHS sling was strapped across his chest, stark against a blue Peter England shirt – a gift from Mrs Wallington.

'It belonged to my late husband.'

Mrs Wallington beamed at the casualty.

'More porridge?'

Twirly grinned wickedly, but shook his head.

The Major said, 'Well, Corporal?'

'MO says I'm fine, Sir. If he'd seen me yesterday he would have stitched it and given me excused duties, but it's knitting together nicely. He said there'd always be a long shiny scar, but he laughed and said it's cheaper than a tattoo. He goes walking in the Dales.'

'Come and sit down, Corporal. Have some of my tea.'

However, a smiling Mrs Wallington got there first and pressed a steaming mug into Twirly's hands.

'Corporal. Mr Ballflower insists it is only possible for him to remain on the nominal roll if we can be certain of reaching Land's End by the end of the month.'

Twirly sniffed into the mug.

'That's no problem, Sir.'

The Major heard Budge coming down the stairs. He emerged into the dining-room - not wearing boots.

He nodded curt greetings all around.

'Mr Ballflower, Corporal Whippet is convinced we can be at Land's End by the end of the month. I am also of that opinion.'

Budge glared.

'Full English?' asked Mrs Wallington from the kitchen doorway.

Twirly's keen eyes crouched behind his mug.

At the table Budge reached for a clean cup and saucer, and said to the teapot, 'Twirly, do you realise that in five days we have covered only forty-six miles? That's an average of nine miles a day, and I estimate we still have three hundred miles to do. That means we must average about fifteen miles a day if we are to complete by the end of the month.'

Twirly sniffed.

'What was that?' snapped Budge.

Twirly's eyebrows rose high above his mug and he said quietly, 'We can get there in time. We'll play it by ear.'

'Hell does that mean?'

The Major smiled.

'I think the Corporal means we'll temporize to meet the exigencies of the service.'

'And what does *that* mean?'

The Major's eyes blazed and he spoke with grim severity.

'It means, Mr Ballflower, that when opportunities occur, we'll cheat.'

'Right, Corporal Whippet. I'll be carrying your rucksack again today, but I'm damned if I'm going to be burdened with half the quartermaster's stores. It's kit check time.'

The tinker's kettle was left with Mrs Wallington.

Also tossed aside were:

A yellow block of Sunlight Soap as hard as Baltic amber with deep black fissures.

A copy of the 1972 *Thomas Cook Railway Timetable* marked property of Cheltenham Public Library.

A framed yellowing photograph of The Bells decorated for Mayday celebrations in 1935, with a surprised looking ten-year old Twirly in the foreground wearing an enormous cap, large boots, and tubular trousers reaching below his knees, and coyly holding the hand of a fair-haired girl with a large ribbon.

Twirly let the frame go, but insisted on keeping the photograph.

A foil-wrapped slab of WD Emergency Ration – only to be consumed with the permission of an officer – dated 1940.

'And what on earth is this, Private Whippet?'

Twirly peered in surprise.

'Where was that?'

'At the bottom of the Bren-magazine pocket.'

It was a Mills Mk 34 hand grenade.

Twirly took it outside and dropped it down a drain between the Dog Inn and the bus shelter.

It was nine-thirty by the time Budge had changed, ready to move.

Mrs Wallington at her front door asked, 'Where today, Mr Whippet?'

Twirly pointed to Budge.

'Following the Cotswold Way to The Bull at Hinton for lunch. Then past Dyrham House . . .'

'Dyrham?'

She was ecstatic.

'It's their Annual Féte today.'

Twirly watched Budge scowl.

She continued, 'You *must* call in. Produce tent and flower show. Chipping Sodbury Brass Band. Refreshment and bar marquees. Horse carriages and classical vehicles. And a Spanish man comes every year and does rope tricks and throws knives at his wife.'

Budge looked unmoved.

The Major's eyes were aglow.

'Flower show?'

Twirly asked, 'Is it always the same wife?'

Budge charged down Chapel Lane and climbed a stile into fields opposite the 1835 Tyndale Chapel, now a private house.

Up on the left was a castellated tower.

He heard the Major call, 'The tower, Mr Ballflower?'

Budge kept moving.

'One of six ventilation shafts of Brunel's tunnel.'

A hostile sign by a stone stile warned that walkers MUST keep to a footpath through a field of waist-high wheat.

The generous landowner permitted a path barely six inches wide.

Budge was indignant.

Doddington Park. Built with dubious wealth from West Indies sugar plantations, and today insisting we shuffle along as if shackled in leg-irons, although the law clearly states footpaths through crops must be three feet wide – 'to allow burdened wayfarers to pass'.
Bastards.

Doddington House, complacently gleaming in the sun, with its six-pillared portico and green clock tower, is owned today by a man who invents vacuum cleaners and wheelbarrows.

Doddington's extensive parkland was landscaped by Lancelot 'Capability' Brown and included groups of trees he liked to call 'clumps'.
Hammersdown Clump. Vineyard Clump. Bailey Clump.
He named a larger wood 'Frenchpiece', although it is said he indulged in a little frivolity here and identified it on his original map as 'The Frenchpiece Would'.
A few gnarled trees, grandly called Cuckoo Pen, reminded Budge of men with drooping fags, standing around waiting for a betting shop to open.

The park ended in a large bright green field patterned with stripes of yellow hay. A tractor towed an orange device which every few yards disgorged a gleaming black roll as high as a man.

Budge watched as the Major beckoned Twirly and they walked over to one of the rolls and pushed with their shoulders in an attempt to move it. First it merely rocked back and forth, then reluctantly edged forward an inch.

'Very satisfactory,' said the Major when he returned.
'Hell is?'
'Proves that two determined men could move one of those rolls of cocooned hay.'
'Hell anybody want to do that?'
The Major shrugged.
'Je n'en sais rien.'

On the outskirts of the village of Tormarton the Compass Inn is built of Virginia creeper, topped by a red tiled roof with dormer windows, and surrounded by flower-boxes overflowing with a massive display of colour.

Budge checked the time.

Eleven o'clock.

Perhaps too early to stop, especially as the air was not actually perfumed with roses, but with the twentieth-century stench of exhausts, burning oil and scorched rubber.

Minutes later they stood on a roundabout bridge peering down at the M4 motorway and a dizzying, speeding, *foreign* world.

The Major sighed.

'All power corrupts,' he said. 'Especially horse-power.'

As they passed a high-fenced concentration camp called Tormarton Maintenance Compound, Twirly held up his hand to call a halt.

'The smell. *That's* not traffic any more.'

He sniffed deeply.

'That's frying onions.'

He skipped down stone steps and pushed through a hedge.

Wow!

Picnic tables. A scattering of empty containers. An opulence of glistening foil wrappers. A brick built toilet-block. But best of all, a cream and green refreshment van issuing odours impossible to resist.

Budge threw off his pack.

'With mustard, everyone?'

The path through Beacon Lane Plantation opened on to a wide track between trees and endless blue-green wheat. In the blue canopy above, a network of aircraft trails had been stretched by stratospheric winds into a sunlit veil of white Honiton lace.

In the distance the M4 rose out of its cutting to climb up into the landscape like a blue ski-slope, and they headed south along an exhilarating footpath running between cropped fields, some with shimmering oats the colour of asparagus, and some full of Shredded Wheat ready to be boxed. On the right the fields dipped down into the familiar magnificence of the Severn valley.

Budge watched Twirly striding along in front, whacking at nettles with his good arm and a newly-found stick.

The Major behind him turned to call, 'Wonderful country, Mr Ballflower.'

Budge grinned.

There were skylarks – and he sun-dreamed of Ozleworth.

The path emerged onto a tarmac crossroad and Budge saw Twirly halt to await instructions.

Budge checked with his guidebook.

'Ah,' he said, 'half a mile down the road on the right there's a hill-fort.'

He read, *'In the 6th-century three local British kings banded together at this hill-fort in an attempt to stem the advance of invading West Saxons under their king, Ceawlin. But a bloody defeat drove a permanent wedge between the Celts of the south-west and those of Wales, making this one of the most decisive battles fought on English soil.*

Budge closed his guidebook.

'Also down the hill is Hinton, where the The Bull pub is famous for its good ales and fine food.

'BUT . . . along the lane ahead lies Dyrham Park where we are advised by Mrs Wallington there will be food, drink and jollity.'

'How far is the pub?' sniffed Twirly.

'A mile.'

'How far to the fete?'

'Twenty minutes straight ahead and downhill all the way.'

Budge hurriedly stuffed the guidebook into a trouser pocket and chased after the two who were scurrying down the lane like chickens running behind a hen.

Twirly was painkiller happy.

A garden fete.

After darts-team annual dinners, garden fetes are his favourite things.

He skipped along the lane, clutching his sling across his chest like a reserve parachute.

The verges were smothered in clumps of red ragged-robin and blue tufted vetch and the air was heavily perfumed by yellow and orange honeysuckle so that it smelt like Doll's bedroom when he did her windows on Saturday mornings.

Ahead lay a group of poplars standing guard above barns with corrugated-tin roofs graded from silver grey to gingerbread rust.

He heard Budge behind shout, 'To the right! And follow the wall.'

But Twirly waited, and stood fiddling with his sling.

'Major, Sir,' he said. 'Can you get rid of this? Feel like somebody in *All Quiet on the Western Front*.'

The Major hesitated.

'Not sure I should, Corporal. The MO . . .'

'Sir! He's bound it tighter than a spinster's elastic stocking. I'll tuck my hand into my shirt like Napoleon. Be fine.'

The Major reluctantly obliged, and folded the sling and stuffed it into one of the pockets in Twirly's emaciated rucksack.

Down in the hamlet of Dyrham, a dilapidated blue gate led to a drive and a church. A few yards further on was another gate with a large sign: GARDEN FETE. At a small table covered by a clean flag of St George of England sat three smiling people looking like a visiting bowling team waiting for the sandwiches.

Another sign, thoughtfully providing shade for a full crate of milk, said:

National Trust members free. Non-members £5.

Budge fumbled in a pocket.

'You a member, Major?'

The Major nodded.

'Me, too,' said Budge. 'You, Twirly?'

Twirly sniffed and shook his head.

Whippets don't pay to go into garden fetes. Specially not into garden fetes in deer parks with two miles of crumbling walls

'You go ahead. I'll see you in the beer tent in five minutes.'

He called after them, 'It's a matter of family principle.'

'I worry about Twirly, ' said Budge.

'Try not to,' said the Major.

Budge recalled coming here two years ago to replace three ornamental urns along the rooftop balustrade. He remembered silent and serene green lawns with discrete and orderly flower beds, with the squat tower of St Johns peering authoritatively over a shrubbery wall, and the only noise coming from a group of unruly crows and a squeaking wheelbarrow.

Today a line of colourful stalls stood along the left. Along the right was a marquee identified as Flower and Produce. A conclave of flags surrounded a sign - Food Village - and from an encampment of tents and caravans rose a pot-pourri of edible vapours.

Ahead, on the high terrace running the length of the fifteen-bay mansion, the high-noon sun glinted off the perspiring heads and gleaming brass instruments of a band playing *When the saints come marching in* with fete-day abandon. In front of the terrace a marquee was labelled BAR, and for this they headed.

They gasped.

Inside, the biblical five thousand were congregated, demanding sustenance.

Budge growled; the Major snorted.

'One would have thought the National Trust could organise a queue system with posts and ribbons like the Post Office. Here the day belongs to those with the thickest skins and sharpest elbows.'

But clear above the thirsty, mumbling, grunting clamour rang a voice.

A familiar voice.

'Major!'

They spun round.

There in the marquee entrance, framed in sunlight with a fluffy halo of glistening white hair, stood a beaming Twirly.

More important, he held a tray of beers.

They stood by a sun-bathed stone urn draped in purple wisteria and luxuriated with the remarkably cool beer.

Budge licked froth from his lips.

'How the hell, Twirly?'

Twirly chuckled.

'That crate of milk by the table where you had to pay. Picked it up and carried it to the refreshment tent. A lady in a green smock waved and said, "Over behind the table, please". Then she said, "Go behind the bar, find Maurice, and ask him for a beer. Say Sylvia said so."

'I found Maurice, and said "Sylvia said so", and asked for three pints.'

The immaculate lawns were littered with people. Some meandering aimlessly. Some studying programmes to discover why they are here. Some parents looking for lost children. Some children not looking for lost parents. Some striding tight-lipped with desperate purpose towards a line of blue and grey Portaloos standing like Daleks by laurels near the gate.

Budge could not believe what happened next.

A broad squat man striding by in ginger trousers with a moustache of the same colour suddenly stopped, turned, and glared at the Major.

His mouth fell open and he whispered, 'Chota?'

The Major pulled himself erect and peered at him with fiercely blazing eyes.

The man said again, 'Chota? Colonel?'

But then he shook his head.

'No. Can't be you. You're dead.'

Chapter Thirteen

The Major stared at the ginger man.

Never seen him before.

The man shrugged and grinned and prepared to continue on his way. He raised a forefinger to his forehead and gave a flicked salute.

The Major cried, 'Good Lord! Quintin. Quintin Bathhurst.'

How could he forget?

India. January 1944. Just been made captain. Posted to the 28th Field Regiment RE, at a ghastly camp in the low-lying delta area of Bengal. Kicking his heels on detachment with the Royal Northumberland Fusiliers.

That's when he first saw Quintin, sweaty and apprehensive in the rear of a 15-cwt truck.

They had both responded to a call from Div HQ for volunteers 'to undertake tasks of particular danger'.

That afternoon they were flown from Jessore by Dakotas of the RAF 357 Special Duty Squadron to 103 Special Training School in Kandy, Ceylon, along with five other Joes.

'QUINTIN!' called the Major.

The man stopped mid-stride and threw up his arms in joyful surrender.

'It *is* you! Colonel Robert Legge-Wellesley, Royal Engineers, late of His Majesty's Special Forces. They said you were dead.'

The Major laughed aloud and thrust his cane into the hands of Budge who stood open-mouthed, while the two ex-warriors advanced upon each other and collided, and hugged, and rocked and laughed, ignoring alarmed fete-goers who adroitly altered course and averted eyes from the embarrassing coupling.

They eventually pushed apart and examined each other.

114

Quintin is wider than he was when the Major last saw him in Pakasut camp near Gurun Batu Puteh, fifteen miles south of Cameron Highlands.

He still has his moustache, but now it's neatly trimmed, not the ginger hedgehog he sported then.

His face is better fed and pinker – and devoid of scratches and open jungle-sores.

But his eyes are the same. Twinkling like lights on a fairground roundabout, but without the haunting dark caverns of fatigue.

He also has the same growling laugh.

'Kandy said the Japs got you.'

'Cut away the same night,' laughed the Major.

Quintin nodded.

'Like they taught us, "Flit while you're fit".'

'And Vanrenan and Stanley?'

The Major remembered them.

An incredibly brave Dutch rubber-planter, and a sergeant-signaller from Durham.

The Major shook his head.

'No. Not them.'

In the silence which followed the Major became aware of the presence of Budge and Twirly.

'Ah. Quintin. This is Mr Ballflower, my line-of-march and billeting officer, and this is . . . Whippet, *Twirly* Whippet, the pride of the regiment.'

He turned to Budge and Twirly.

'And this is Quintin Bathurst. Ex-Royal Wiltshire Yeomanry. Ex-Force 136 and SOE. Explosives expert and dangerous maniac.'

Grunts and nods and handshakes.

'So what are you doing here, Chota?'

'Mr Whippet is walking to Land's End. Mr Ballflower and I are his support platoon.'

Quintin stretched his top lip to exercise his ginger moustache and laughed aloud.

'Think I need a brandy. We *all* need a brandy. Have you time, Sir?'

'Quintin. As our Chinese friends used to say, "A wise man can always find time to enrich his soul."'

Quintin nodded.

'In that case, follow me, gentlemen.'

On an area of gravel to the south of Dyrham House, a dazzling display of two dozen classic cars was precisely positioned in three perfect rows. In the bright sunlight they looked polished and burnished and too hot to touch.

Quintin marched directly towards them in surprisingly long strides for one so portly, stepping illegally over immaculate beds of bright lavender.

Without slowing he called in a loud voice, 'TUCKER!'

From beneath the raised bonnet of a dark green and black saloon, smaller than some of the magnificent monsters on parade but nevertheless grandly impressive, a head arose.

'Tucker! Break-out the emergency supplies.'

By the time they reached the car, the bonnet had been lowered and Tucker, in faded blue overalls, stood stiffly at the alert with a painted tray bearing several gleaming glasses and a squat bottle of XO Imperial Courvoisier.

At a nod from Quintin he also produced a tin of Crawford's Cream Delights.

The Major realised his glass was trembling as he struggled with a confusion of memories.

Quintin was babbling non-stop like an auctioneer.

'So many questions, Colonel. So much to tell.'

The Major saw Budge check his watch.

Quintin noticed, too.

'Ah yes,' he said, slowing down. 'Actually we are awaiting the scrutineers. You know what they're like. Eager to grope the Duchess's bodywork. Fondle her upholstery. Peer up her exhaust pipe. And all that. Afterwards we are obliged to take part in a six-mile procession outside the grounds. Should be back about three. You still be here then? Spot more brandy? How far you walking from here?'

The Major indicated Budge, his routemaster.

Budge sighed and said, 'Really should be going. We've got accommodation booked near Lansdown, about three hours walk from here.'

'*Lansdown!*' exclaimed Quintin. 'Good Lord. That's less than two miles from my place. You staying in a hotel? I could come and find you. We could talk over a drink after dinner.'

'It's a farm bed-and-breakfast.'

'*Farm?*'

'Lower Langridge Farm.'

Quinton shuddered and scratched his ginger lip, then spun round to confront the Major.

'Tell you what, Sir. Why don't you come and spend the night at my place. Love to have you. You and your chaps.'

Budge shook his head and frowned.

'Already booked the farm.'

Quintin waved his arm in wild dismissal.

'Pah! Tucker has one of these portable telephones. He'll cancel it. Tomorrow you can carry on with your little outing.'

The band at the front of the house burst into a spirited rendering of *Congratulations.*

The Major's eyes met those of Budge and Twirly in a silent discussion which ended in resigned acceptance.

Quintin slapped his podgy palms together.

'That's fixed then, Colonel, Sir. Off you go and get some lunch. Me and Tucker will go and tour Gloucestershire. Meet you back here at four. The Duchess will have us at Upton Cheyney in time for tea.'

It was obvious to the Major that lunch was not going to be easy.

From the door of the Orangery restaurant wound a column of fully paid-up members of the National Trust demonstrating their willingness to suffer for the good of the nation.

The bar refreshment tent was stuffed to overflowing.

Even more depressing was the crowded chaos of the Food Village.

The Major snorted, 'I have always regarded queuing for food, gentlemen, as only one step up from cannibalism.'

Budge said firmly, 'It'll be three hours till tea at your friend's. Need something.'

The Major agreed.

'Corporal Whippet. What do you suggest?'

Twirly did not hesitate.

'Picnic, Sir.'

'Picnic?'

'Y'Sir. Up on the grass hill behind the fancy cars. Up by the statue. Away from the civvies.'

The Major considered.

Twirly continued, 'In the Produce Tent there's a sale of entries at half-past-one – proceeds to Sodbury Gardening Club. In the Trade Tent they'll be giving away free samples and flogging special offers. And I bet . . ..'

The Major cut him short.

'Corporal Whippet . . .'

'Sir?'

'You are i/c foraging party. Mr Ballflower and I await your instructions.'

Half-an-hour later they sat high up on the slope with their backs to a statue of Neptune, examining their spoils:

A ready-cooked chicken from Wiltshire Farms.

A wedge of Somerset Blue from Hinton House Supplies.

Generous free sample of Chipping Sodbury Peach Chutney in a plastic cup.

Baked-this-morning bread rolls from Avon Bakeries.

Six large tomatoes from a man in a straw hat who complained they should have come First.

An abandoned and slightly distressed lettuce.

A jar of Victoria plums unplaced in the Home Bottling class.

A carton of double-cream from Compton Dando Dairies.

A bottle of pink Elderberry and Nettle wine entered by Flora Millder, Honey Cottage, Puckleworth and marked down to 50p.

Three yellow plastic feeding bowls from the Playgroup bric-a-brac stall – buy-one-get-two-free.

Accompanied by an assortment of plastic cutlery, paper plates, acrylic glasses, foil-wrapped butter, sachets of salad cream, and a pile of *Have-a-Big-Mac* paper serviettes, all scooped up by Twirly, who smiled at everyone as if he knows their parents.

Budge lay back on his elbows and pushed out his legs in the long grass. He watched Twirly making up three plates of food.

Very pleasant but they should be walking. And he has not warned them that he has a problem with the route.

From here to Bath is easy – follow the Cotswold Way into the city centre. From there we can strike west across to the Mendips and Cheddar Gorge from where the well-marked West Mendip Way leads directly to the coast. But between Bath and Cheddar is terra icognita. Laurence Main's Bristol Countryway long-distance route covers the twenty-mile gap, but has no waymarking.

This means two days of pioneering with guidebook, map, compass, and fragile tempers, with his two companions falling asleep whenever he stops to check.

Of course he could ask at Bath Information Centre, but they tend to be knowledgeable about bus routes and car parking. Know absolutely nothing about footpaths.

But here, prostrate in the shade of Neptune, he accepted that this was not the time to make decisions – except how much to eat.

The sun and Neptune smiled down at him, and a grasshopper sang in his ear.

The Neptune statue was once the base of a twenty-foot high fountain from which water cascaded down over two hundred steps to a canal bordered by orange and bay trees. Recognised in the 1700s as one of Europe's finest water gardens. All allowed to decay and crumble.

Budge waved a chicken leg.

'Major,' he called. 'Your friend – Quintin. He sometimes calls you Chota, and sometimes Colonel.

The Major chuckled.

'British army humour, Budge. I was once six-foot-five tall. *Chota* is Anglo-Indian for 'small'.'

'And Colonel?'

The Major twirled his chicken leg between his fingers like a cobb of maize.

'In April'44 SOE inserted Quintin and myself into Malaya to locate a group of incredibly brave soldiers and civilians who had melted into the jungle when the Japs invaded two years before. These extraordinary people more or less survived operating an allied resistance movement. Now they had been ordered to put us in touch with the Chinese MPAJA, the Malayan People's Anti-Japanese Army, who were also fighting as guerrillas.

'The MPAJA didn't trust the British, of course, but were prepared to accept help in their long-running war with the Japs – and Kandy thought they might be more impressed if I was made a temporary lieut-colonel.

'The Chinese called me 'Colonel Tuan'.

'Over a year later, in August, '45, the atomic bomb was dropped with the approval of a newly-elected Labour government. On that *very* day, a *box-wallah* – safely housed in London – returned early from lunch in order to demote me back to Major: with-effect-from.

'Bastard.'

Budge watched Twirly busily collecting up the debris.

The Major dusted himself down.

'First class, Corporal.'

He flicked away a shred of lettuce from his shirt.

'Pity about Mrs Millder's wine.'

'Almost two hours to wait before we see your friend,' said Budge.

The Major suggested, 'Perhaps a little snooze?'

But Budge had higher plans.

'Major, you talked about finding time to enrich the soul.'

'Ah yes. Attributed to the soldier-statesman Chu Teh, and often quoted by the commander Lim Bo Seng at our Larek Tin Mine camp.'

'You fancy visiting the house?'

Silence.

'Wonderfully furnished.'

Still silence – except for heavy breathing in the long grass enveloping Twirly.

'Marvellous paintings. Three were once in Fonthill Abbey before it fell down because it had no foundations. Moved to the ceiling of the Theatre Royal in Bath, covered in tar from tobacco smoke – almost ruined. Now restored – and here.'

Budge, still talking, scrambled to his feet.

'There's a famous *trompe-l'oeil* mural which makes a corridor appear to go on for ever. Wonderful perspective. Artists come from all over the world.

'There is also a secret licensed bar in the Orangery.'

The Major prised himself from the grass.

Budge said, 'Twirly?'

But buttercups and daises were gently stroking Twirly's ears, and bright chamomile flowers were threatening to drug him into insensibility.

He opened one eye a fraction, and shook his head.

'I'm excused duties and doing billet-orderly. I'll keep stag for our transport.'

Seated inside the car they were speechless with admiration, and Quintin beamed like a new father in a maternity home.

The car was a 1936, twenty-five horse-power Austin Mayflower, with a fragrant interior smelling of polished leather and warm sewing-machine oil.

Quintin drove, while Tucker sat beside him as co-pilot and flight engineer.

Budge recalled the Humber which his father worshipped back at the Rectory, and of which his mother was properly jealous, and he sighed with pleasure as the car, heavy on its springs, crunched grandly over the gravel, and rose royally up Dyrham House drive past the hungry-looking statue of Neptune.

The car purred as it moved onto the highway, taking bends as sedately as an ocean liner pulling away from 55th Street Passenger Terminal, Manhattan. It protested genteelly whenever Quintin mistimed the double-declutching, and it rocked as demurely as a lady in a crinoline.

Quintin squirmed round in his seat and slid back the glass screen.

'What do you think of her, Chota?'

'Wonderful.'

Quintin turned back to concentrate on avoiding a milk-tanker.

'Like all women, all she needs is a few kind words and an occasional pat on the backside.'

He laughed.

'She can be temperamental. And coy.'

To demonstrate this, he tugged an ivory button dangling by his ear, and a pink damask curtain slid across the rear window.

'And canny. A button down by the passenger seat gives access to a spare petrol tank.

'And flighty. Loves to feel the breeze up her skirts,' and he pulled a lever above the dashboard and the windscreen tilted up to fill the car with a thrilling draught of Gloucestershire air.

They crossed the A420 Bristol-Chippenham road.

'Of course, she's a star and she knows it. Twelve times on television. Four times in films. Hundreds of indecent proposals.'

The car free-wheeled gleefully and illegally down Hanging Hill.

'Only one fault. She has a drink problem. Eleven miles to the gallon.'

The Duchess coughed discreetly, and majestically heeled over to navigate between towering stone gateposts.

'Here we are, gentlemen – Upton Cheyney House.'

The Duchess sighed happily like a horse scenting its stabling and lolled easily up the winding drive to the magnificent three-storey mansion, with a slated roof sprinkled with numerous dormer windows and topped by a glorious dome of green copper.

Budge watched the Major flick a hand through his white locks and straighten his jacket.

As they disembarked, the Duchess eased herself up on her springs, while her six-cylinder engine turned over as smoothly as a bacon slicer.

'Welcome to the *kampong,* Chota.'

The afternoon sun illuminated the green dome and Budge recalled the day when, at eight years old, his father delivered him to Winterborne St Martin boarding school near Weymouth.

Budge looked across at the Major – looking remarkably like the grey-haired housemaster, Mr 'Bootsy' Brown.

The Major sensed the gaze and he turned to nod his silver hair and smile knowingly.

And Budge felt acutely that his education was about to be continued here at Upton Cheyney – and that great things would shortly come to pass.

Chapter Fourteen

Upton Cheyney House was built by the celebrated architect, Sir Roger Pratt – the first English gentleman-architect to be knighted – and from the 17th to the late 19th-century was the family seat of the de Chednet family, who once owned 8,000-acres of the surrounding countryside.

When brick became unfashionable in the 19th-century, it was clad in stone and tall corner chimneys were added. A formidable entrance was constructed, including a grand Palladian staircase adorned with whimsical statues.

Pitt the Younger, the Duke of Wellington, and Kaiser Wilhelm II were all entertained here. To celebrate the end of the South African war in 1902, King Edward VII planted a cedar in the twenty-acre grounds. It was felled by the ferocious gales of January 1990.

In the entrance hall, staircases swept up to the right and left to meet at a central landing. High peach walls were covered by gold-framed paintings. From the moulded cream ceiling hung a gilt chandelier reminding the Major of the nave of Milan's cathedral of St Augustine.

'Fiona will be sorry to have missed you, Chota. Staying the weekend with a daughter in Andover.'

He led them to a mahogany side-table bearing a large silver model of a submarine.

'Recognise this, Sir?'

'Good Lord. The *Statesman*. How on earth?'

Quintin turned to Budge and Twirly.

'Your Colonel and I travelled in this Free-Dutch Navy submarine from Trincomalee to the island of Pangkor on the western coast. Took six days.'

Quintin grimaced.

'You remember that sweaty wardroom, Chota? Six-feet cube. Sleeping beneath the table. Like trying to kip in a garage inspection pit. Everything tasting of diesel.

'After the war I was able to trace the captain. This model is a gift from the Dutch,' and he pointed to an engraved tablet on the polished wooden base:

To all those brave unknowns who travelled with us beneath the waves.

In a green room with massive armchairs, any one of which could overpower the unwary, tea was laid for four.

The Major extracted an egg-and-cress sandwich.

Quintin gestured at the wall between two sash windows draped with olive velvet curtains, where a red pennant with three yellow stars was surrounded by two small plaques.

'Recognise them?'

The Major put down his pink and gold teacup, heaved himself out of his *howdah*, and crossed to the wall.

Quintin called, 'Lim Bo Seng gave me the MPAJA flag when we finally left in August '45.'

The Major shook awake his memory.

These days he finds it difficult to remember where he is – or who he is. However events of fifty years ago usually present a perfectly clear picture, with the paint still wet.

He joyfully turned to Quintin and tunelessly sang, *'Pyow yang di hong-chi,'* and they both laughed.

The Major said to Budge, 'First line of *The Peoples' Flag* in Chinese.'

Budge scowled.

'Those guerillas – they Communists?'

Quintin roared with laughter and slapped his chubby thigh.

The Major chuckled, and instantly sobered.

'Budge. For these fearless and fanatical young people, Russia was the Promised Land. *But they were fighting the Japs.* That was good enough for us. We trained them and armed them.'

He turned to a small red shield bearing a sword and XIV.

Fourteenth Army.

He peered at a second shield with a white disc and a blue phoenix rising from red flames.

'S.E.A.C.?'

'South East Asia Command,' said Quintin, and he turned to Budge.

'Or as our gallant American allies used to insist, "Save England's Asiatic Colonies."'

Quintin strode over to a window and slipped his hand behind a curtain.

'May I suggest we meet down here for dinner at seven? Eddie will show you to your rooms.'

Summoned by some secret signal, a slight man appeared in a green waistcoat, thin grey hair, a face scored by deep laughter lines, and eyes which blazed like hot coals.

'Eddie and his wife Jemma have been with me since the fifties. He's an old Ox and Bucks man.'

Since arriving at the house, Twirly had been subdued. Now he sat up and stared at the man.

'What battalion?' he demanded.

'Second, Sir.'

'Rhine?'

The man peered hard and nodded.

'You?'

'Three Brigade.'

The man grinned.

Dressed for dinner, Budge found the Major and Quintin deeply engaged in re-winning the war.

' . . . wasn't he the bounder who mistook a box of mustard for egg-powder and almost wiped out the Household Brigade?'.

However all reminiscence was abruptly halted when Twirly appeared.

He looked resplendent.

His usual halo of wispy hair was plastered to his nut-brown skull. His cheeks glowed from unaccustomed scrubbing. A starched khaki shirt – yet another gift from Mrs Wallington of Tunnel Cottage – obliged him to walk unusually erect so that he looked imperious. Even in his plimsolls.

But what stopped the conversation was his exuberantly knotted tie, a glorious device of golden damask lined with crimson silk.

The Major and Quintin quickly recovered and their war continued.

Budge clutched his Campari and soda and leaned forward and whispered, 'Love the tie, Twirly.'

Twirly grinned.

'Round a curtain in my bedroom.'

Budge was aghast.

'Hell's bells,' he hissed, 'he'll recognise it.'

Eddie appeared with an unsolicited pint of bitter and thrust it into Twirly's hand with a powerful wink.

Twirly took a long slurp.

'Don't worry, Budge. No man ever knows the colour of his curtains.'

Eddie approached Quintin and nodded meaningfully.

Quintin instantly held up an arm just as the Major was saying, '. . .always spit when I see a Suzuki . . .'

'Gentlemen! I think they are ready for us in the dining-room.'

He turned to the Major. 'I've asked them to do better than a cigarette tin of rice with curried pig-tailed monkey.'

The Major ginned politely.

'I was rather hoping it might be well-hung rat with tapioca, baked inside a piece of bamboo.'

The two Force 136 men chuckled all the way to the dining-room.

Budge approved of the pork loin, with honey and mustard sauce, and vegetables from the estate, followed by whortleberry and apple pie.

He leaned across the polished walnut table.

'By the way, Twirly, how's the arm?'

Twirly sniffed.

The Major explained Twirly's indisposition to Quintin.

'Good Lord! Eddie shall take you to Jemma. She'll look at it. Was a matron at Keynsham Boys' School.'

Clutching his brandy, Twirly was escorted away for treatment.

Back in the green lounge with brandy refills, Budge and the Major sank again into the armchairs, while Quintin perched upon a Louis XIV cabinet.

Budge studied the view through the tall windows. A great chestnut dominated the parkland which dropped down to the Avon valley. In the hazy distance dozed the green-grey whaleback of the Mendip Hills.

Should be there in three day's time.

Budge passed a dish of pretty little *petit fours* to the Major.

'So were you both in the jungle for about a year?'

The Major munched pink and yellow marzipan and squinted back into the past, and remembered.

'Think it was about a year . . .'

'One year and four months,' interrupted Quintin. 'Living rough. Eating local food. No leave. No R-and-R. Constantly looking *for* Japs, or hiding *from* Japs. The jungle biting us, burning us, drowning us, and scaring us stupid. We both weighed less than nine stone when we finally got back to Kandy.'

The Major said, 'You would never believe, Mr Ballflower, how effective those guerrillas had been. Incredible. In one particular fortnight in 1942, eight trains were derailed, fifteen bridges damaged, the railway cut in sixty places, and more than forty vehicles destroyed or damaged.

'But Quintin taught them *new* tricks.'

Quintin chuckled.

The Major accepted another morsel of marzipan.

'Although the Chinese cut field-telephone cables almost on a daily basis, the Japs easily located the breaks and repaired them. Quintin showed them how to loop the cable, slit the insulation, and completely remove about an inch of wire. After the cable was fondled back to look as good as new, the break was impossible to find. Japs had to replace the whole length.

'He also taught them how to stuff eighteen-inch lengths of bamboo with five pounds of gelignite.

'He introduced the awful ruse of placing a Mills grenade – as if dropped by mistake – in the path of an advancing Jap patrol.

128

Quintin showed them how to first remove the ten-second fuse and carefully replace the spring-clip, so that it exploded as the grenade left the hand.'

The Major looked around at the sound of raucous laughter coming from somewhere in the house.

He watched Quintin stand and stride swiftly over to the window and again stroke the magic curtain.

Eddie instantly appeared, buttoning up his green waistcoat.

'Eddie! What the devil is going is on down there? If it's that new gardener's lad, send him to bed with a flea in his ear.'

'Sir,' bowed Eddie. He wheeled around and, to the Major's surprise, gave him a smile – and a secret wink.

Quintin continued, 'You remember the first supply-drop, Chota?'

He explained to Budge, 'Kandy signalled that two Liberators of 357 Squadron would take off from Jessore with four Euro personnel, one Chinese, and two tons of supplies.

'Incredible

'Three thousand miles.

'Fifteen hours at two-twenty-five miles per hour.

'Flying at fifty feet over the Bay of Bengal to avoid radar.'

He sighed deeply.

'I was blubbing like a baby when those bloody great birds roared over – chutes tumbling out like tufted seeds from a thistle.'

The Major nodded and remembered: 'Sapper Newberry. Major 'Wicked' Watts, RAMC. Henk Dekker, the Dutch planter who spoke Malay. And Ling Peng. And the signaller with the new R201 set.'

Quintin added, '*And* the tins of edible food and two bottles of scotch. And what about Kandy's delightful lady doctor?'

He jubilantly turned to Budge.

'She inoculated us, dosed us, checked us; and in return we would take her to dinner at the Queen's Hotel on the edge of the lake near the Temple of the Tooth.

'And that splendid girl had bullied 'Wicked' Watts to conceal in his leg-valise a tin of ridiculously sweet blocks of *jaggery* – dried palm syrup – which she knew we both loved.'

129

The Major rolled his glass fondly between caressing hands.

Quintin continued.

'I can see her now. Suntanned. Tousled fair hair. Full red lips.' He frowned. 'Can't remember her name.'

'Her name was Mary.'

Quintin smiled. 'So it was.'

The Major nodded, and spoke carefully. 'Major Miss Mary Brownlie, RAMC.'

Budge saw the Major gazing well beyond the brandy glass.

'I married her.'

Sunday 12th July   *Day seven*

Budge stood silently watching the cascade of rain sluicing down the dining-room windows.

The whole world was engulfed in a grey damp gauze, backed by a sky as black as a coal-hole. The splendid chestnut tree looked as dismal as a war memorial.

'Hell is Twirly?' he growled.

'Not like him to be late for breakfast,' said the Major. 'Can't think why he didn't come back from the MI room last night.'

'You suppose he is all right?'

'Of course he is *all right,* Mr Ballflower. Whippet is *always* all right. Its just worrying what he may be up to.'

The door wooshed open and in plunged Quintin passing a two-finger squeegee across his moustache, and flicking rain off his ginger hair.

'Been exercising the dogs. Like walking through a car-wash.' He looked around. 'No breakfast yet?'

He threw back his head and bellowed, 'EDDIE!'

Instantly Eddie appeared, negotiating before him a long squeaking trolley bearing a row of gleaming covers.

'Morning, gentlemen. Bacon. Sausage. Scrambled eggs. Beans. Saute potatoes. Black pudding. Please help yourselves.'

Quintin declined to sit at the dining-table and stood by the trolley:

'Well, Chota, I see the Frogs thrashed Brazil to win the World Cup,' and he crunched into a noisy slice of toast. 'What's your operational plan for today?'

Budge glanced at the Major, and said, 'We hope to walk a mile to North Stoke to rejoin the Cotswold Way. Then five miles into Bath. Lunch and a look at the Abbey.'

Quintin stopped crunching.

'What? In this filth?'

He lifted a dome and extracted a sausage with his fingers.

'Then what? Where you aiming for?'

'I've booked accommodation in Dunkerton to the west of Bath.'

Quintin was biting on his sausage and eyeing Budge intently, demanding more.

'Tomorrow to Compton Martin. Next day to Cheddar Gorge and Shipham.'

Quintin snatched the sausage from his lips.

'Cheddar Gorge? You're going to take three days to get to Cheddar? Dammit, it's only half-an-hour away. Tucker goes there for cheese.'

Budge looked at the Major for support.

The Major looked around and said, 'Can't think what Whippet is up to.'

Quintin licked his fingers and turned to Eddie standing by the trolley.

'Go and tap on his door. Tell him he's late on parade.'

Eddie hesitated, and Budge thought he was about to speak, but he disappeared in a puff of obedience.

Quintin growled, 'Chota, I think you've been at the filtered Brasso.' And he nodded in disgust towards the window.

'How can you even *consider* setting off in this monsoon? Best let Tucker run you into Cheddar in the Daimler and take the day off. Go to church.'

The Major smiled.

'It's Whippet's wish to *walk* to Land's End. It's an Approach March exercise, Quintin.'

Quintin lifted the cover protecting the black pudding, frowned, and closed it.

The door opened and in stepped Twirly and Eddie. Twirly looked remarkably well. It looked as if his arm had been re-bandaged, this time with considerable padding.

The Major said, 'No breakfast, Whippet?'

Twirly looked sheepish, and the man Eddie stepped forward and addressed Quintin.

'Last night, Sir, Mr Whippet and I discovered that we had once been running around in the same woods not far from each other. East of the Rhine, Sir. And then all the way to the Baltic together to thwart the Russians who were hell-bent on invading Denmark.

'Had a bit of party last night. This morning Jemma insisted on doing him breakfast in our kitchen, Sir.'

Quintin threw back his head and laughed.

'Bloody wonderful. Knee-deep in reunions here, Chota. Must do this on a regular basis. Put the flags out next time.'

The Major nodded sagely, and smiled, and adopted his CO's Orders voice.

'Corporal. In view of the weather our host is generously offering to transport us to Cheddar.'

Silence.

'Mr Ballflower thinks it would take us three days to walk there.'

Twirly sniffed, then grinned, and turned to the Major.

'Permission to extemporize, Sir?'

They were in Cheddar by eleven o'clock.

Chapter Fifteen

In the twelfth century the village of Cheddar was famous for its mild farmhouse cheese which Daniel Defoe, author of Robinson Crusoe, *declared to be the best in the land.*

Today it is better known for the deep gorge gouged out of the Mendip Hills by Ice Age meltwaters a million years ago.

High limestone cliffs soar almost vertically above the conclave of car-parks, cafés, and cleverly lit caves where prehistoric man once lived.

Budge pushed through the straggle of brightly waterproofed visitors coming down from the coach parks. The rain was losing interest, and up on the towering cliffs little ledges of glistening greenery caught the light of an unseen sun.

The Gough Cave Café offered TEA, COFFEE, FRESHLY BAKED SCONES, and an eight-thousand-year old skeleton.

Cheddar Cheese Shop displayed a gold embossed letter from Brigadier Maurice Hunt Davies:

'The Duke of Edinburgh has asked me to write and thank you for the wedge of Cheddar you kindly sent him – 26 July, 1993.'

Opposite the Edelweiss Restaurant with its flower-filled tubs and fete of coloured umbrellas, Budge located the twist of concrete steps marking the beginning of a footpath leading up on to the eastern cliff.

After a climb of two hundred feet through bushes, briars, pink rosebay willowherb and discarded plastic bottles, he suggested they pause for breath.

He leaned against the green metal tower which tops the Jacob's Ladder running up from the gorge, built by an eccentric Rowland Pavey who thought he could fly, but fatally proved he couldn't.

Half-a-dozen horned goats tripped up the last of Mr Pavey's two hundred and seventy-four steps looking around in ragged astonishment - or perhaps guilt because they hadn't paid.

The rain had stopped, and clouds drifted idly apart, coyly revealing hopeful patches of blue 'enough to make trousers for a sailor.'

In the west, the sun dappled the surface of the circular mile-wide Cheddar reservoir.

Ten miles to the south lay Glastonbury, where a lighthouse-topped island floated in a hazy expanse of green.

Alongside the path of red earth and white limestone ran a hedgerow, smothered by a fanfare of brilliant white trumpets of hedge-bindweed.

On the left, a pulpit of boulders perched on the very edge of the gorge. It was stained pink by the boots of a trillion neck-craning walkers seeking a vertiginous fix with a dizzy view of the meandering road five hundred feet below.

On the right, in a clearing of young ash trees, lurked a handful of late bluebells. Budge remembered discovering a similar clearing when he was a fluffy-chinned student. He remembered the magical afternoon he spent studying fauna and Flora.

He wondered what happened to her.

'Careful, Major,' he called as they slithered and slipped down the wet track descending steeply from the gorge's eastern cliff between squat yews and slender silver birch.

As they crossed the B3135 at the bottom he heard Twirly call, 'When is it trough-time?'

Budge was aware that Twirly was subdued, and lagging far behind. He shook his head.

How does he do it? That arm.

'You coping, Twirly?' he called.

'I'm fine. It's just that I'm carrying three heavy slices of cherry and almond cake from Jemma.'

In the secret valley of Black Rock, Ayrshire cows were conscientiously working as lawnmowers for the Somerset Trust for Nature Conservation, and the trimmed grass was soft as tufted Wilton.

Budge noticed that although the cows ignored the Major and himself, they studied Twirly's every move, instinctively recognising three generations of cowmen.

Multicoloured lichens daubed two hundred-year old walls. Yellow wall-peppers and delicate spleenwort-ferns clung with tenuous fingerholds. Behind the walls rose high banks of ash and blackthorn gently shaking off the recent rain.

The air was fresh and disinfectant clean, and Budge filled his lungs with deep, satisfying breaths.

'Coming to an old Roman road, Major,' he called. 'Built by Roman soldier engineers in a hurry.'

When Claudius ordered his legions to cross Oceanus Britannicus *in AD 43 it was partly to placate the Senate.*

But there were other reasons.

One was the need for silver to meet the enormous demand for coinage in the empire's single currency.

For several years Rome had been purchasing great quantities of Mendip lead for its cupellation system of producing silver. Now the lead became victors' spoils.

Over a stone stile into the grassy dry riverbed of Velvet Bottom, the walking was again easy, although a succession of five stone dams – part of the lead settling process – called for serious knee-bending. The valley floor had no trees, except for a few elders clinging to the dam walls. And the high lead content made the valley unsuitable for cattle, so the grass trimming was left to a million rabbits, who had more on their naughty little minds than the dangers of unprotected lead poisoning.

Grassy hollows marked the remains of circular *buddles* where, in the Middle Ages, water was added to crushed rock to produce a slurry, from which heavy ore settled out for smelting.

Patches of black slag fragments glistened in the sun like Victorian jet jewellery.

The Information Office in Cheddar had kindly arranged for the enthusiastic and knowledgeable wardens in the Outdoor Activity

Centre at Charterhouse to provide a modest lunch. They sat beneath a photograph of an ingot of Mendip silver preserved in St Valery-sur-Somme, marked *2nd Augusta* and dated AD 74, and feasted on ham and cheese sandwiches, tea, and custard tarts.

'Interesting name this place has, Major. Carthusian monks were granted the right to mine here and they named the area Chartreuse after their mother church of Grande Chartreuse, near Grenoble.

'But the English don't care for fanciful French names: they preferred to call it Charterhouse.

'It's like the stream running through Upper Gently. When the Normans built Lambley monastery the stream was full of trout. So they built Twirly's Fish House and called the stream *Beaucoup de Truite'*.

'We find it easier to call it Booky Tweet.'

Budge continued, 'Four years ago I was walking on the North York Moors, along Ryedale, and passed a farm which the French builders of nearby Rievaulx Abbey called *Arriére Terre Ferme*.

'The locals demurred from twisting their tongues around all that French stuff. Today it's shown on OS maps as Harriet Air Farm.'

After profusely thanking the wardens for their ministrations, Budge led up the steep little Rains Batch lane to the telecommunications tower.

A steady climb followed to the hump-like summit of Beacon Batch, at 1066 feet the highest point of the Mendips. A wide grass path climbed through pink and purple heather and acres of bracken: a dark green blanket patterned with patches the colour of rusty bed-springs with young timid shoots curled like green snake heads.

The spoilsport clouds had now departed in search of distant Sunday open-air events to disrupt, leaving a vast unblemished blue sky stretching from horizon to horizon.

The Major was struggling someway behind, with Twirly proceeding slowly even further back.

Budge slung off his pack by a trig pillar which gleamed white at the centre of a bright green sheep-trimmed lawn surrounded by a halo of golden gorse.

The views in every direction were breathtaking.

To the northeast lay glistening Blagdon Lake. To the south stretched the green Somerset Levels where a dejected king was once scolded by a peasant housewife for allowing her cakes to burn; and where two thousand of the Duke of Monmouth's protestant pitchfork army were slaughtered. And where now baskets are weaved from willow.

Beyond, Budge could see the blur of the Quantocks, and the haze of the hogs-back hills of Exmoor.

But twelve miles away in the west was the sight to excite all islanders: the sea. Blue and beckoning.

This precious stone set in a silver sea . . .
This blessed plot . . . This England . . .

The Major arrived puffing and gasping and Budge watched him stand and gaze wide-eyed at the sea-edged England laid out below.

'Magnificent, Mr Ballflower.'

'Take this,' said Budge, handing him one of three cans of Boddington's.

He called to Twirly, 'A dozen more paces and this beer is yours.'

Twirly grasped the can of the hair-of-the dog and wheezed, 'Thank God for the NAAFI', and he put his back to the trig pillar and slowly subsided.

'Corporal,' said the Major.

'Sir?'

The Major thrust a water bottle at him.

'Jemma's instructions. Tablet time.'

Twirly luxuriously supped the Boddington's, and watched Budge flick through a newly-purchased guidebook.

Budge finally looked up. 'That's interesting. These lines of grass-covered cairns stretching down the slope below us: thought they must be prehistoric. This book says: *The rows of stubby pillars were erected during the Second World War to prevent enemy gliders landing.*

Twirly sniffed.

'You all right, Twirly? Arm giving you trouble?'

Twirly said, 'You get that book in Cheddar?'

Budge grunted.

'How much?'

'Three pounds fifty.'

Twirly sniffed again.

'They saw you coming.'

A couple of sheep that had been quietly nibbling near the pillar moved nervously away.

'Budge. That book – it's twaddle.'

Twirly, miraculously resuscitated by the Boddington and two tablets, waved towards the green plain between Cheddar reservoir and the coast.

'Look at that flat space, Budge. They could build another Heathrow there. Then look at the side of this hill. Steeper than a hayrick thatch. Even the looniest Kraut wouldn't dream of trying to land his troop-carrying DFS on a slope like this.'

Twirly continued.

'And anyway, stone pimples like those would mean nothing. Gliders were made of plywood. Undercarriage designed to rip off on landing. Those stubs might slow them down and make it a bit bumpy for the ten armed men squeezed inside with their boots lifted off the deck and arms linked. But that's all.'

A deep Mendip silence.

The two sheep, reassured, returned to renew their nibbling.

The Major pulled his jungle hat down to shield his eyes from the sun.

Budge snapped shut his guidebook.

'Know about gliders, do you, Twirly?'

Twirly sniffed and stooped to stuff the empty beer-can into the Major's satchel.

'The corporal does, Budge. And he is right. This site has nothing at all to do with 'anti-airborne defences'.

The Major continued firmly, 'I know about this place. It was intended to act as a decoy to confuse German bombers.'

In the Second World War it was recognised that during night raids German bombers tended to drop their bombs on to fires already burning, so in a crafty top-security operation, several sites were rapidly built to deceive the attackers about the location of their intended targets.

When switches were thrown, this particular Secret Fire site magically became Bristol's Temple Mead railway station, five miles to the north.

Ealing Film Studios provided many of the special effects.

The rows of stone 'tumps', many built by hundreds of volunteers in the evenings and weekends, were topped by light boxes to resemble a sidings complex. Spasmodic red and green lights simulated signals. Other lights were intended to resemble partly blacked-out warehouses.

Tall frames covered in roofing-felt, with white interiors, were fitted with lamps which lit intermittently to give the impression of doors opening and closing.

When bombers were overhead, fifty-gallon tar-barrels and sandbags of cordite could be electrically detonated to suggest bursting high explosive bombs. Metal troughs filled with combustible materials could be fired, and randomly sprayed with liquids from three tanks. Paraffin for sudden bursts of flame. Diesel oil for swirling black smoke. Water for clouds of steam.

A massive undertaking which sometimes worked.

'Budge,' said the Major: 'Your guidebook is merely repeating the lie put about at the time to reassure the local populace. And lies tend to last longer than truths.'

Twirly scrambled to his feet. He was annoyed with himself.

Stupid to feel so groggy. Perhaps it's this throbbing arm. Perhaps the late drinking session last night. Perhaps seven days of walking every day – ALL day.

Or perhaps he was missing Upper Gently . . .

A sudden chirruping sound shattered the silence of Beacon Batch.

All three stood puzzled.

Then Twirly watched Budge gasp, rip off his backpack, plunge in his hand and pull out his mobile phone, as big as a box of liquorice all-sorts.

With the phone to his ear, he shot a glance at the Major.

'Doll!' he whispered, and proceeded to nod and grunt and smile and frown.

Then, with his hand over the phone, he said, 'Twirly! Some English Heritage men are in the pub asking if they can have the key to Fish House. They want to look around. Doll wants to know what she should do.'

Twirly looked startled.

Fish House? His landlords? Stab!

'Tell her . . .'

And his brain revved like a tractor in a muddy gateway.

He held up his hand.

'Tell her not to give them the keys, but get Arthur Wilkins to go and unlock for them. Goes in every morning to feed Ratcher.'

Budge relayed the message and continued to nod and grunt, then, 'I'll phone you tonight, Doll, to see what develops.'

He stabbed a finger at the device and stuffed it back into his pack.

Twirly scowled.

The hell they up to? Have never missed paying the rent. Never heard from them before, not for thirty-eight years.

They better not upset Ratcher.

Where the field path opened out on to a narrow lane by a broken backed barn, an East Mendip Way signpost promised. 'SHIPHAM 2 miles'.

Walking past Tynings Trekking Centre – *indoor stalls and livery vacancies* – Twirly breathed the familiar farm smells. Warm horses. Full wheelbarrows of muck. Sharp whiffs of brass polish and burnished leather. And a nose-twitching hint of a farmhouse's all-day frying sausages . . .

From the farm a muddy track led into the shady tunnel of the Forestry Commission's Rowberry Warren.

Twirly watched the Major and Budge slither and slip along a deep mire of spongy leaf mulch beneath the trees. He sloshed along in his wellingtons and smiled.

Up on the right rose Scots and Corsican firs completely blotting out the sky. Those on the left dropped down more thinly, revealing patches of pale green sunlight. The air was heavy with the smell of damp pine.

A family of wood pigeons fluttered amongst the pine tops like hymn sheets tossed from a high church gallery by mischievous choirboys.

After about five minutes the left-hand trees disappeared and there was sky was again. Here the track was sun-dried with firm red earth and gleaming white stones and lush grass verges.

'How far now, Budge?'

Budge stopped.

'You got that heavy cake handy?'

On the left of the track a fallen log was covered in bright green moss and adorned with a scattering of blood-red elf-cup fungi.

Budge and Twirly sank down onto this convenient bench.

The Major moved to a patch of sun-blest grass which sloped down to a sparkling stream. Twirly watched him disintegrate and with a loud sigh stretch out full-length, crumbling Jemma's cake all over his chest.

Pale blue harebells were caught by a gnat's breath of a breeze which set them trembling like teacups in a nursing home.

Twirly pondered over Doll's phone-call. English Heritage? Fish House?

He thought of his snug bedroom, wallpapered by his brother who, thirty years ago, was suddenly packed off to Australia. He remembered the pattern of young roses climbing urgently up yellow bamboo; now the roses had lost all ambition and the bamboos were brown with damp. He thought of his bed, as high as a farm trailer, with its tarnished brass bedstead as impressive as the gates of Lambley Hall, and with a patchwork quilt which arrived during the war in a bundle-for-Britain from a kindly lady in Kentucky who signed herself Mary-Ruth.

He thought of Ratcher.

He thought of his armchair with the red velvet cushions, which came from the church vestry after a visit by the bishop.

He thought of sitting with his arm resting on pillows soft as whipped-cream – and not hurting.

He thought of being gently fed with Marmite soldiers dipped into soft-boiled egg by a crisp brown-eyed BMH nurse smelling of Dettol.

Beyond his fancies he heard Budge say quietly, 'You asleep, Major?'

No response.

Twirly looked down to the bottom of the grassy bank, where a gleaming stream babbled like women at a bus stop.

The opposite bank rose up steeply to a low hedge, beyond which stood a smart cream bungalow with a green back door.

In the front garden a slim housewife in a pink blouse appeared to be raking up grass-cuttings.

Across the lane in front of the house stood three Lombardy poplars, with a patchwork of fields reaching up to the horizon . . .

Twirly stiffened.

Something moved. By one of the trees.

Again it moved and Twirly scrambled to his feet.

'Budge. You got your binoculars a minute?'

Twirly focussed the little wheel, and wobbled his head until he found what he was looking for.

'Budge. What do you make of that bit of black behind the middle tree?'

Budge took the glasses.

'Don't know . . . Could be the elbow of a leather jacket.'

'I think it's a man,' said Twirly.

Instantly the Major sat up, his nostrils flaring, his old-warrior instincts sensing action.

'What is it, Corporal?'

'Not sure, Sir.'

The Major leapt to his feet, staggered giddily, and brushed crumbs from his shirt.

'Get the men to stand-to, Corporal,' he snapped.

Chapter Sixteen

Apart from the gentle chuckling of the stream, the valley hung silent and still.

Budge scowled.

He looked at his watch.

'Pub is only a mile away, and we sit here getting excited about an elbow.'

The Major murmured, 'Quiet, if you please, Mr Ballflower.'

Over to their right in the west, the sun, thinking of calling it a day, was hovering before commencing its descent behind the trees.

Twirly slid the Major's satchel from his shoulder and placed it by a clump of yellow horseshoe vetch where three chalkhill blue butterflies were performing an unconcerned balletic *ménage à trois*.

'That's definitely a man,' grunted Twirly.

Budge snorted.

'Probably an illicit lover checking the coast is clear.'

The Major turned to Twirly and asked quietly, 'You have string, Corporal?'

Twirly plunged a hand into one of the seven pockets in his new walking trousers and held up his Boy Scout length of string.

'Sir!'

The Major nodded in approval.

An innocent breath of wind frolicked up the valley in carefree anticipation of the sun's downfall.

Twirly noted Budge scratching his cheek in doubt, peering at the scrap of black.

The silence was oppressive.

Twirly sniffed.

Like the silence below Gué Hill near Beja.

He remembered crouching at its base and Sergeant Hutton saying quietly, 'Wait for it, lads. Wait until I say.'

The tension was slightly relieved by a song-thrush unhurriedly tapping a terrified snail on an anvil stone, idly contemplating a light repast of *escargot au naturel*.

Suddenly a squadron of rooks in the tops of elm trees burst into a noisy protest.

A sunset-coloured pheasant exploded up from the field across the lane and chortled blue murder. It hurtled over the stream and whirred over Twirly's head like an incoming mortar.

The black elbow became a leather jacket.

Budge rammed his binoculars to his forehead.

'There!' hissed Twirly.

A thickset figure leapt from the tree, and glanced quickly left and right.

He lurched across the lane and thrust the garden gate open.

Budge dropped the binoculars on to the bench.

Twirly winced when the woman screamed, shrill as a Stuka.

The sky filled with a melee of panicking birds.

The woman threw down her rake and, with arms raised, rushed into the cottage.

'NOW, MEN!' cried the Major. 'Mr Ballflower, get across the stream, if you please – up through the privet and to the back door. Go in and hit him. No politically correct reasoning. No playful poke – go in and knock his head off.'

He himself set off bouncing down the slope, calling over his shoulder, 'I will be at your elbow as reserve, Mr Ballflower.'

As he splashed across the stream he shouted, 'Whippet! Through the hedge into the *front* garden. Block his escape when we flush him out.'

He paused at the base of the opposite steep bank and called loudly in the voice which born leaders find when required, 'Let's get this right first time, gentlemen.

'AND GOOD LUCK.'

Twirly slid down to the stream and swept across, and grabbed at the turf of the opposite bank, aware that Budge had not yet moved.

Then he came.

Twirly heard him pounding down the bank like a charging bull, splashing wildly, shouting, scrambling up the bank and crashing through the hedge like a thirty-two ton Sherman.

As Twirly breathlessly pushed through the privet he heard the sound of splintering timber and tinkling glass and knew that the massive strength of the mason had breached the back door.

Twirly chased round to the front of the cottage in accordance with the Major's battle-plan and saw a yard-brush leaning against a trellis porch.

On the lawn lay the abandoned rake.

He scooped this up at the gallop like a Lancer in a peg-sticking competition, and rammed it through the trelliswork about a foot from the ground.

He grabbed the broom and, standing to the side of the path about three feet from the porch, he raised it high above his head.

Amongst the shouting echoing through the open doorway was another scream.

Footsteps pounded towards the door.

Twirly tensed and raised the brush higher.

Would it be the woman? Budge? The Major? Or the man.

It was the man.

The ruffian flew out of the doorway like a rabbit with a ferret on its tail, tripped on the rake and threw both arms forward, wildly clutching at handfuls of air.

NOW!

Twirly brought the yard-brush down firmly on the man's head.

THUMP!

The howl of pain came from Twirly himself; he tossed away the broom, and gripped his re-wounded arm.

The man sank as silent as a sack of soot.

Twirly leapt on to the back of the concussed heap and grabbed his arms and lugged them to the middle of the man's back. He saw the Major shoot out of the doorway, fling away his cane, and hurl himself down on his knees at the man's feet.

While the Major wrenched off dirty white trainers as big as disposable nappies, Twirly produced his string and speedily formed two small loops to make a clove-hitch which he slipped over the man's right thumb and jerked it tight.

With a look of urgent disgust, the Major ripped off a greasy grey sock, slammed the man's foot back, and called, 'STRING!'

Within twelve seconds the man was trussed like an Aylesbury duck with both big toes tied tightly to both thumbs, centred in the small of his back.

The Major struggled to his feet gasping – and nodded.

Budge rushed from the doorway with fists clenched.

He gazed down at the bound intruder with eyes as big as badger burrows.

'Is he . . .?'

But the Major cut him short.

'Water, Mr Ballflower. At the double! AT THE DOUBLE!'

For a few seconds Budge stared at the criss-crossed man, and fled back into the house.

'Well done, Corporal,' said the Major, brushing down his shirt and wiping his hands on a spotless white handkerchief.

Twirly shrugged.

Budge appeared at the double and thrust a trembling glass of water towards the Major, who studied it with disgust for several seconds, finally taking it and drinking it in one gulp.

But Twirly knew what was wanted.

Into the kitchen, and out again, with a large blue plastic bowl.

The Major nodded towards the man and Twirly deluged the supine figure with a Niagara of soapy water – and two spoons and a pretty pink-and-white saucer.

The effect was instant.

The man jerked violently as if he had been kicked by a horse, spluttered like a dog thrown into a pond, and began lugging at his bonds.

'Suggest you stop tugging, laddie,' reasoned the Major. 'You'll pull off a thumb.'

In the tidy pine and porcelain kitchen Budge stood gently comforting the sobbing woman, while Twirly assembled tea-brewing equipment.

147

The Major removed four mugs from a china cabinet:
'Make them sweet and strong, Corporal.'

'The police should be informed,' said the Major, putting down his empty mug. 'And, if you can, my dear, it would be better if *you* made the call. We have to get on our way.'

They stood in the kitchen and listened while she talked on a telephone in the hall.

'I'm calling from Longbottom Cottage, just past Longbottom Farm, south-east of Shipham . . .'

The Major said softly, 'As soon as we hear the police, we should scarper. They will almost certainly provide this charlie with money for a new pair of socks and his bus fare home. We, however, will be detained overnight for questioning.'

The lady returned and smiled with her red-rimmed eyes.

'They say they are coming.'

'Then we will leave you.'

Budge nodded. 'We have to get to . . .'

'Cheddar,' snapped Twirly. 'Cheddar Gorge.'

Budge stared and looked across at the Major, who stood impassive as a barn owl.

Then Budge understood.

'Yes . . . Cheddar,' he said.

The young lady dabbed her wet face.

'You walking?'

'That's right,' and he glared at the Major and Twirly and said, 'We left William up on the path beyond the stream looking after our packs.'

Twirly turned to the Major with raised eyebrows. The Major's expression was of angelic approval.

'So there are *four* of you?'

Budge looked as pleased as Ratcher delivering a messily mauled mouse. Twirly could almost hear him purring.

'Good man,' murmured the Major.

The lady sniffed.

'I can't think what would have happened if you . . .'

148

But they had gone.

They did not stop until they reached the village of Shipham and pushed into the sanity of the crowded bar of the Miners' Arms.

Landlady Georgina in blue and red striped trousers beamed at them as she pulled three pints of Theakston's.

'Had a good day?'

They drank with obliterating enthusiasm.

The Major examined this friendly redoubt across the foam of his second pint. Red carpet. Blue-cushioned high-backed settles. Collections of brasses, double-handed mugs, and forks and spoons and ladles. But most pleasing, a reassuring display of noble malts.

Suddenly the hubbub around them was hushed. The local radio was announcing a news item.

'A man on early release from a six-year prison sentence for rape was detained this afternoon near Shipham.

'To assist them with their enquiries the police are urgently seeking four male hikers in the Cheddar area.'

Georgina smiled and advised them that dinner was roast local beef with Yorkshire pudding, potatoes roasted in dripping, and cauliflower and carrots; followed by rice-pudding with strawberry jam.

The Major remembered it was Sunday.

He spruced himself up and paraded himself to evensong at St Leonard's church a few yards up the road.

Monday 13th July *Day eight*

'Your friend had his breakfast ages ago,' called Georgina. 'He's gone out.'

The Major poked his head outside the pub door to see who his friend was.

It was Twirly.

He sat by the iron railings around the war memorial on the green, opposite the garage, polishing his wellingtons with unusual ferocity.

The Major remembered the significance for Twirly of this particular date in July, fifty-five years ago.

He shook his head and murmured, 'Incredible.'

He sniffed the air. It was a beautiful morning. From a sky of blue infinity hung snow-white balls of cotton-wool clouds. Outside a shop across the green, beneath optimistic yellow sun-blinds, was arranged a harvest festival of fruit and vegetables balanced on empty orange boxes.

He turned to re-enter the pub, and bent forward and rubbed the backs of his legs.

Budge had said last night that he hoped they could do twelve miles today.

Twelve miles!

He winced at the thought, and pushed into the dining-room through french doors at the end of the bar.

'Will you be having the full English?' asked Georgina.

Budge blundered into the dining room with his rucksack already packed.

'Twirly about yet?'

'Doing a bit of bull by the war memorial.'

He helped himself to a slice of the Major's toast.

'He all right?'

'Think so. Although his wound opened and bled when he did his head-tapping act yesterday.'

Budge scowled and crunched into the toast.

'Bit worried how we left that wretch.'

The Major reached for the marmalade.

'I strongly recommend the local pork sausage.'

Breakfast finished, the Major excused himself.

Budge called after him, 'We begin our second week today, Major.'

The Major turned and smiled.

He watched Budge wrench tight a strap on his pack

'Still two hundred miles to go. Only eighteen days. Need to do some serious miles today.'

As the Major eased himself up the narrow staircase he felt his knees creaking and he groaned and leant against the wall.

I'm seventy-three, for goodness sake. Sod Cynthia.

As they passed St Leonard's, the Major called to Budge who was striding along like a point-man in search of promotion.

'Fascinating little church, Mr Ballflower.'

But Budge was not doing churches this morning.

On the outskirts of the village, by an electricity transformer on poles, a signpost indicated a footpath to Shute Shelve Farm. Up concrete steps, over a stile, and on to a narrow path between high hedges. This soon opened out to become bracken and fir trees and tall foxgloves followed by soft pastures full of daises and buttercups and rare cowslips.

Beyond the red-roofed barns of Winterhill Farm they turned onto a wide, rutted, and quiet grass lane, obviously an old drove road.

The Major knew about drove roads.

Before refrigeration was commonplace, the only methods of preserving meat were by smoking or salting, and it was necessary to consume meat as soon as possible after slaughter. It meant moving animals close to the point of consumption while they were still capable of walking.

This involved driving great herds over enormous distances by tough and wily men as colourful as cowboys of America's Wild West. In the sixteenth century it became necessary to pass an act restricting droving to licence holders, 'to discourage those seeking to leave their honest labour, and only to live easily.' A requirement was that all applicants should be married and at least thirty years of age.

It has been estimated that the two main drovers' routes from Wales and Scotland probably annually delivered 100,000 head of cattle and 750,000 sheep to Smithfield market in London.

This morning the lane was empty and tranquil, except for sudden protests from startled birds, and urgent scurryings down at the path-side amongst cow-parsley, red campion, and low drifts of snow-white stitch-wort.

The Major peered ahead.

Budge was standing with his portable telephone to his ear.

He packed it away as the Major approached.

'That was Doll,' he called. 'Last night she had a Cynthia Withers in the bar who insisted that she must contact you urgently.

' She wants to talk to you about getting married.'

Chapter Seventeen

Beyond a honeysuckle-draped hedge the land rolled away and in the distance shimmered a village of red-roofed houses with yellow walls.

'Sidcot,' called Budge flourishing his map. 'Tree-topped knoll behind is probably Banwell hill-fort. Glistening strip – the Severn estuary. Dark smudge behind could be the Brecon Beacons.'

Geography lesson over, Budge turned and sped off again into the distance like an unsympathetic Army Physical Training Instructor on temporary detachment.

The Major heard Twirly call from behind, 'Sir!'

He scurried up, waving his hand like an Egyptian gully-gully-man producing a live chicken from an egg and held out a banana.

'Instant energy, sir. Got it from the man in the shop while you were having breakfast. He's got a brother who used to live in Shipton Oliffe.'

Ahead, the Major could see green slopes looking like Cheltenham's Cleeve Hill where he and Mary used to walk on Sunday mornings, with lunch at the Rising Sun.

He tilted his head and listened.

A distant tractor?

Traffic noises?

The Sergeant Instructor reappeared to investigate this tardiness and shouted, 'The A38!' and impatiently waved them on.

The hedges became higher, the path narrower and increasingly claustrophobic, until it suddenly opened into a gravel drive for a handful of secret houses with small, closely shaved lawns, and red geraniums looking too hot to touch.

They rushed across the A38 Bristol/Exeter road, near a blue-roofed FINA garage, dodging lethal lorries and surly speeding saloon cars.

By King's Wood smelling of wild garlic, an information board advised them they had reached Wavering Down where thirty-six commoners still hold grazing rights.

The board recommended they look for yellow bird's-foot trefoil.

Twirly squinted at the illustration and sniffed.

'We call it 'bacon and eggs.'

Wide paths of sheep-trimmed grass led steeply up through high bracken. In the distance, a white trig-pillar topping the high point, looked like a Nepalese *chorten*. The sun was hot, the day silently still, and occasional user-friendly snatches of breeze from unseen *punkahs* gently caressed their sweating backs.

The views became progressively more magnificent.

The Major swished a hand across his dripping forehead and eased the straps of Twirly's huge rucksack.

Come on, knees. You can do it.

He remembered toiling up the sun-baked Horton Plains in Ceylon.

In 1955 his father had pulled strings in the tea world to get him the position of manager in a small tea plantation below Nuwara Eliya.

Mary joined him after six months and they bought the pretty villa known as Rose Cottage opposite the golf course and the Nuwara Hill Club.

During a few days off they stayed at the seven-room Farr's Inn near Ohiya on the seven thousand-foot high plateau of the island's hill country. After idly meandering over the sparsely populated grasslands, they made the four-mile trek to the World's End to stand on the edge of the breathtaking sheer drop to the coastal plain five thousand -feet below – one of the scenic wonders of the world.

'You all right, Sir?'

The Major snapped round in surprise.

'Your legs were going up and down, Sir, but you didn't seem to be advancing forward.'

At a recently whitewashed trig point they found Budge slowly revolving like a kebab-spindle, binoculars in one hand, map in the other, mumbling a commentary to himself.

'Village of Axbridge.'

'Cheddar reservoir.'

'Nyland Hill.'

He lowered his accoutrements, acknowledged their presence, and nodded in the direction of a great green dome, around the base of which wound the distant twin grey snakes of the M5.

'Brent Knoll. Once stood in the middle of flooded lowland and known as the Island of Frogs. Beyond that, gentlemen, lies Bridgwater Bay – and the sea.'

The Major fumbled in his pack to produce a tube of melting Jaffa cakes.

Budge continued his commentary.

'I think that's the Quantocks to the south-west. And the dark hump to the right could be Dunkery Beacon on Exmoor. Should be there in a few days.

'THAT'S IF WE KEEP MOVING.'

He poked the slushy Jaffa cake into his mouth, licked his fingers, put away his map, and strode off at speed across the soft grassland.

Shortly he turned to wave a hand ahead to a summit crowned by a coronet of rocks: 'Crook Peak, ' he called.

The Major smiled at Twirly. They were still by the seven hundred feet trig-point gazing at the glorious distant sea, enjoying the few moments of euphoric mutiny.

A hang-gliding buzzard soared nonchalantly high up on their left.

A handful of sheep paused in their feverish nibbling to view them suspiciously through rheumy eyes.

The Major ignored a trickle of sweat running down his cheek from beneath his jungle hat and, although he tried not to, he sighed.

Quite wonderful. Mary would . . .

Twirly sniffed and tucked his bandaged arm into his shirt.

'Let's go, Sir,' he said.

A wide farm track curved below the rocky summit and suddenly they were looking down on the M5 motorway, a noisy obstacle between them and the sea.   Pure science-fiction.   Once again the Major growled with displeasure at this display of nonsensical urgency.

'Idiots,' he grunted.

Mahatma Ghandi once said, 'There should be more to life than merely increasing speed.'

Budge was waiting impatiently for them on the motorway bridge.

He waved a hand at the red-roofed architectural jumble which they had just passed.

'Webbington Hotel,' he said. 'Designed by Lutyens.'

And he was off again.

The Major stood in disbelief.

By Lutyens?   Sir Edwin Landseer Lutyens who designed the Cenotaph in London, and the magnificent Gate of India standing over the Raj Path in Delhi?

He shook his head.

'Looks more like a job by Anglian Windows,' and he bent forward to encourage his unhappy knees with a quick fondle.

Budge stood by a stile at the end of the motorway bridge scowling at a paddock which resembled a scene on the Somme. It was littered with lumps of agricultural machinery and a few shell-shocked cows standing up to their teats in mud.

A sign erected by the people-loving National Farmworkers' Union commanded: KEEP TO THE FOOTPATH.

'*What* footpath!' cried Budge.

He crossed the stile and the Major watched him as his boots plunged through a thin sun-baked crust into an ankle-deep mire, sinking deeper with every step.

Halfway across he stopped. His monstrously smothered boots were more restricting than lead weights. And he raised his arms, and shouted to anyone who could hear,

'A POX ON LOXTON!'

But the villagers of Loxton cowered behind locked shutters.

Just before a gate at the far end of the field the churned morass appeared to become a mercifully smooth patch of slate – but Budge instantly discovered it was a stinking slurry.

He sank almost to his knees.

'BASTARDS!' he shouted.

The cows looked on with mournful agreement.

The Major noticed that Twirly was grinning, but he refrained from doing the same.

Noblesse oblige and all that.

Instead, he set off on a circuitous route, hugging the tangle of barbed wire and nettles forming the farm boundary, and arrived at the gate and lane remarkably cleanly shod.

He crossed to Budge, who sat on the verge angrily attacking the filth with handfuls of crackling grass.

The Major turned to Twirly, who was calmly making his way across the bog in his lucky black wellingtons.

'Whippet! Mr Ballflower needs something to clean his boots.'

Budge did not look up when the Major joined him, but continued frantically wiping.

The Major handed him his ever-ready flask of brandy.

Still with no eye-contact, Budge grunted, 'Thanks.'

Twirly arrived with a balding broom and a metal tub of clear water. He dumped it down beside Budge.

'Hell you get that?'

'Tap,' said Twirly vaguely as he took a swig of the Major's offered brandy.

'Well done, Corporal,' said the Major jauntily.

'Pleasure,' said Twirly.

The Major scowled.

It is contrary to King's Regulations for other ranks to wink at commissioned officers.

By an iron post commemorating sixty years of Queen Victoria's reign the Major asked, 'Mind if I take a look at your map, Mr Ballflower?'

Budge, still engaged in boot ablutions, waved towards his pack and the protruding map.

After a few moments study, the Major said, 'Looks as if we have a stiff climb ahead. Probably half-an-hour up to Loxton Hill. Perhaps an elevation of five hundred feet.'

Budge nodded without enthusiasm and scrambled to his feet.

'How can anyone drink milk from cows which have to live in pus like that? Where are the Health and Safety people?'

The Major and Twirly were ahead and hardly heard, but the Major recalled the caution of King George V and his Queen Mary when they sailed on the *Medina* for the Royal Durbar of 1911. They took three of their own cows and a milkman.

The narrow path climbed past knee-high green oats whispering encouragement, while on the opposite side the trees of Loxton Wood swept down into the carbon-monoxide filled motorway valley.

The Major quickly adopted his customary long-climb posture, holding his cane with both hands behind his back, sliding his feet along the ground like a guardsman doing a ceremonial slow march and softly singing a hymn.

The Major used this technique twenty years ago on the three-hour climb from the village of Jorsale on the banks of the Dudh Kosi up to the eleven thousand-feet village of Namche Bazaar.

He remembered the hot Nepalese sun, the clean smell of fir trees, heavily-scented magnolias, and the first disturbing effects of altitude.

He also fondly remembered how Nima, his siddar, *stopped him five hundred feet into the climb and insisted he take a drink from a grubby plastic bottle of milky-coloured chang, as he pointed out the distant smoking summit of Everest peeping coyly over the ridge between Lhotse and Nuptse.*

He heard Budge breathing heavily behind him.

'This is the top, Major . . . made good time . . . now along a high level Roman road, then mostly downhill. Be in Bleadon pub in less than an hour.'

A red-topped green woodpecker bobbed gleefully above in its up-and-down flight, entreating everyone to be happy.

At a quarter past one they stood transfixed in the cool bar of the Queen's Arms. A rank of tapped barrels was lined up ready for inspection, each topped by a white cape and bearing honourable labels: Old Thumper, Tanglefoot, PG Stream, Bishop's Tipple, Black Sheep Best Bitter, Wadworth 6X, and Eldridge Pope Hardy Country Bitter.

Their packs slid to the stone-slabbed floor.

The pub's walls of terracotta red were adorned with items of horse harness and an array of antique agricultural implements.

An overhead beam was inscribed:

A man should only drink when he is dry,
Or because he may be, by and by,
. . .or for any other reason why.

'Quite right,' said the Major, and ordered three pints of Bishop's Tipple, with three chasers of rum to help dry Budge's dampened enthusiasm.

'I still feel as if I am standing in a swamp', growled Budge. So they trooped outside and watched him remove boots, gaiters and socks, to stand barefoot on the hot stones of the paved pub-yard.

Twirly heroically and gingerly took the stinking boots as if they were recently lifted anti-personnel mines and carefully placed them on a low sun-bathed wall.

'Well done, Corporal,' said the Major. 'We can sit and watch them decompose.'

Halfway through the second round of the Bishop's Tipple they decided to eat and went inside to find a table near the door.

Red leather menus on the tables were supplemented by various chalked boards. It was the usual pub fare – except for one item: *dhal-bhat-tarkaari.*

The Major wondered how this staple Nepalese dish would be interpreted in this very English pub, and he mused aloud, *'Mi t-ho chaa?'* – Is it good?

The sound of a chair scraping on the stone floor came from across the room. At a table on the far side of the bar a broad-shouldered, sun-tanned man in a bright yellow shirt turned and smiled.

159

'*Hajur! Mitho chha.*'

The Major peered into the gloom, slowly rose to his feet, placed his hands together, and said, '*Namaste.*'

The man stood and did the same, then stepped forward with his hand extended.

'Greg Howard.'

'Legge-Wellesley.'

The man smiled and studied the Major's weathered features.

'You were with the Gurkhas?'

The Major hesitated, then said, 'Royal Northumberland Fusiliers actually, but attached to 153 Gurkha Para Battalion for the drop on Rangoon. Operation Dracula. May '45.'

Greg Howard smiled.

'I spent several years managing a hotel in Darjeeling. *Ma ali ali Nepaali bolchhu.*'

The Major's fluffy white eyebrows shot heavenwards.

'Good Lord – Darjeeling? Which hotel?'

Greg twirled a finger indicating all three half-empty glasses.

'Same again?'

He continued, 'Helvellyn Hotel, on Observatory Hill.'

The Major's eyebrows eased up a little higher.

'Know it well! Wonderful hotel. My father was at the nearby Temi tea plantation. Have stayed at the Helvellyn, and often eaten there.'

Greg Howard chuckled.

'Scones and onion tart for tea in the music room?'

'Exactly. And beef steak and claret for breakfast in front of an open wood fire.'

They both laughed, and Greg turned to look down at Twirly's mud-smeared Wellingtons and Budge's pink bare feet.

'We're having fun on a walking holiday,' explained the Major.

'*Tapai kahaa janne?*'

'Ah,' said the Major. 'Lands End – eventually.'

'*Hunch-ha!*' and he raised his eyes to the beam on which was carved the legend:

Distance is never a problem: it is taking the first step that is difficult.

160

'Where you staying tonight?'

The Major turned to Budge.

'Weston-super-Mare,' said Budge.'

'But where?'

Budge glanced quickly at the Major and said, 'Not sure yet. Thought we would have the luxury of studying the options.'

The man stroked his top lip with a forefinger.

'One moment,' he said and swiftly stepped outside.

'Does he keep speaking Hindi?' asked Budge.

'Nepali.'

'But Darjeeling is in India . . .'

'Nepali is the official language in Darjeeling.'

The yellow-shirted man swept back into the bar with a portable telephone in his hand. He looked very pleased with himself.

Chapter Eighteen

The Major pulled rank and sat on the front passenger seat of Greg Howard's four-by-four.

A sticker on the glove-box entreated:

'PLEASE USE YOUR SEAT BELT – See Genesis 45:24'

As the bulbous black vehicle trundled up onto Bleadon Hill a ragged sea-mist flirted across the windscreen.

They passed through an estate of bungalows and small houses with more burglar alarms than chimneys, and Greg turned from the wheel.

'I'm sorry, Legge-Wellesley, I didn't catch the names of your comrades,' and he nodded towards Budge and Twirly on the rear seats.

'Ah,' said the Major. 'Behind you is Mr Ballflower, a stonemason. With him is Mr Twirly Whippet,' and the Major turned and smiled at them to confirm that he was correct.

'Twirly?' said Greg, peering up at the rear-mirror to study his passengers. 'Unusual name.'

The Major explained.

'We are all from Upper Gently in the Cotswolds; five-miles south-east of Cheltenham.

'There is no road running through the village. It lies at the head of a valley, and is an isolated community with old-established families.

'Nicknames are common, and these often get passed from generation to generation. Twirly's nickname belonged to his father, and his grandfather before that.'

Grandfather Whippet had been a cowman – man and boy.

He used to rise at four to fetch in the cows for morning milking.

His working day ended about half-past five in the evening when the afternoon milking was finished, the shed swilled down, the cooler cleaned, and the cows back in the field.

Then he would walk down into the village for a pint in the Five Bells opposite the church.

However, during the First World War, workers in England's industrial towns often forgot to go back after their lunchtime drink, and so endangering the war-effort. In 1917, the teetotal Prime Minister Lloyd George introduced legislation to close pubs between two-thirty and six-o-clock.

This law also applied to remote pubs like The Five Bells – but unfortunately no one told the cows.

Consequently, Grandfather Whippet continued to arrive at The Bells well before opening time.

In all weathers he would sit on the pub's front step awaiting six o'clock.

If the landlord or his wife appeared he would grin up at them hopefully and ask, 'Am I too early?'

Eventually they began to refer to him as 'Too-early'.

In time this became 'T-wirly'.

The Major noted that a railway was crossed.

And the A370.

In the village of Uphill where the sea-mist was denser the car slowed opposite The Dolphin pub and turned left onto a driveway where two stone creatures squatted with thick forelegs, bulging eyes, and lolling tongues - daubed with splashes of red dye. Above loomed a high archway of scalloped pink and red stone. Large gold lettering proclaimed:

FAR PAVILIONS HOTEL.

'Yahar!' purred Greg. ' *Mero bhatt..* My hotel.'

The car crept through the arch and up a paved pink drive lined with blanco kerbs, and verges of luscious grass trimmed short-back-and-sides, and glossy green shrubs, and blood red poinsettias, and large pink pitchers overflowing with yellow and gold nasturtiums.

Ahead, among a group of dark timber and red-tiled pyramids, rose a high dazzling white *chorten* topped by a soaring golden, gleaming spigot.

'Think I've been overdosing on the *chang,*' murmured the Major, and Greg chuckled with pleasure.

A slim, dark-skinned youth on the verge, wearing a fresh-from-the-*dhobi* long white shirt, jumped to prop a long-handled hoe against a grey-green juniper. He clapped his hands together, and mouthed a beaming 'Namaste'.

The four-by-four stopped in the centre of a paved area at the foot of a wide stone staircase lined by more stone statues – elephants, snarling lions with curly manes and weird beasts wearing stone crowns. From white flag-poles drooped the orange, white and green flag of India, the red and blue double pennant of Nepal, and a surplice-white flag of St George.

A young man in a long cream jacket, white jodhpurs and a red and green *topi* forage-cap leapt towards the car. His beaming smile was an advertisement for tooth-paste, and he flung open the car door.

'Welcome to Far Pavilions, Sahib.'

He waved his hand to the mist-hidden horizon, widened his already stretched smile, and said softly, 'Sorry for mist.'

The Major stepped stiffly from the car.

Beyond the paved area, the hill dropped sharply down towards the sea, but in the lazy haze he caught a glimpse of a stone windmill, and a church tower beyond.

Exactly on cue, nature took over with a breath-taking wide-screen experience.

The mist rolled majestically away to reveal a distant brilliant blue sea, stretching for eternity to touch the hem of a clear, pale blue sky.

The Major thought there should be a fanfare of French horns, with jubilant violins.

Far below, to the north, gleamed the glistening yellow sands of a curving two-mile beach: Weston-super-Mare.

In the far distance the blue and mauve hills of South Wales were topped by an icing of white clouds looking like the Himalayas seen from Darjeeling.

Out at sea, two islands sat like naval ships moored off Trincomalee.

The Major stood and stared.

It's so beautiful . . . why aren't you here?

He turned to Twirly, who stood open-mouthed.

'Well? Corporal Twirly Whippet?'

Twirly turned to the Major with eyes moist with wonder, and he sniffed with approval.

Hajur!' cried the young man in jodhpurs, and loudly clapped his hands.

Down the staircase skipped three giggling girls in bright *saris* and purple *churidar* trousers, bearing aloft orange garlands of marigolds which they threw over the heads of the three travellers.

'*Dhanyabhad,'* murmured the Major. He looked across at Budge, who gave him a quick grin of embarrassment.

He heard Twirly growl, 'Marigolds are supposed to be good for haemorrhoids.'

The young man quickly collected the rucksacks and satchel and rushed to the rear of the vehicle and opened the door. He looked puzzled.

'Baggage, Sahib?'

Budge shook his head.

The young man looked even more confused, and peered more intently into the vehicle.

The Major chuckled.

'Budge. A shaken head to a Nepali means yes.'

He called to the young man and waved his hand.

'*Chaaina.* No baggage.'

'Hajur!' cried the young man, not exactly approving of the *sahibs'* irregularity, but with a wave of his hand indicated they should follow him.

The Major turned to Greg standing by the car like a headmaster proudly observing his pupils.

'*Raamro,* Mr Howard.'

The man bowed slightly.

'Everyone at Far Pavilions is pleased to welcome you.'

He signalled to the driver of the vehicle to drive off.

'I understand Pertemba has put you in one of our three-bedroomed family compounds: the *Kush Mahal* – the Palace of Happiness. I hope you and your friends enjoy your stay, Legge-Wellesley.'

The high ceiling of the reception area was of dark mahogany panels hung with enormous paper lanterns. The air was heavy with musk and the rich aroma of *masala* spices. Somewhere the Major could hear the plaintive strains of four-stringed *saringhis* and whining flutes and unhurried drum rhythms.

In his double-room leading off their private central lounge, the Major tossed his satchel onto a long-armed planter chair, levered off his shoes, and sank onto a wide bed of carved manayo wood wonderfully adorned with Varanasi brocades and silks which may have come from Bombay. A lilac counterpane was of finest *shahtoosh*, which Mary never tired of explaining was shorn from the throats of mountain ibex.

They met for dinner in the long, bright conservatory of the *Ukaalo Pavilion*, redolent with the aroma of exotic spices, newly baked bread, and a subtle suggestion of jasmine.

The Major was impressed by Whippet, who appeared in a smart purple shirt he had not seen before. His whispy halo was brushed and held into place by a perfumed gum taken from the collection of outrageously packaged toiletries stacked in their gleaming state-of-the-art *nuhaane thaau*.

Budge announced he had already studied the ten-page menu and asked the Major if he thought they should opt for the recommended Maharajah-special-of-the-day.

Minced duck with cinammon and cardomom
Chicken korma with Madagascan prawns, spinach and potato
Slow-cooked Lucknow lamb with dhal
Pineapple curry
Kulfi coconut ice-cream with roasted almonds

Tuesday 14th July *Day nine*

Breakfast at the Far Pavilions Hotel was served from seven o'clock. It was now only six-thirty.

Twirly stood outside on a crunchy gravel path and took a deep breath of the sea air.

At dinner the Major had said Raj bungalows were often surrounded by gravel paths to deter snakes and prowlers, and his guilty poacher's feet stepped instinctively on to the dew-wet grass.

The sky was a high blue canopy over a shimmering sea. It could have been the bay of Naples seen from the 103 British Military Hospital at Sorrento.

He ran his hand down his right thigh to feel the deep groove gouged out fifty years ago by an angry chunk of red-hot shrapnel. The medical officer had warned him there would always be a scar – he didn't have time to make a joke about tattoos.

The two islands off Weston are smaller versions of the two he used to look down on from the hospital balcony. One day two of the nurses took him and a foreign-speaking gunner from Glen Cannick over to Capri for convalescent therapy. They made him climb with his crutches up zig-zag steps to a tiny café in a clock tower overlooking Piazza Umberto, where they drank ice-cold beer and limoncello, and ate crusty bruschetta with tomato and mozzarella cheese.

But now, standing in the Far Pavilions gardens amongst silent bushes and green and black bamboo, he stiffened.

He was being observed. Someone – somewhere – behind him. Careful now.

Slowly he raised his arms away from his sides and turned . . .

About fifteen paces away, half-hidden by glossy-leaved japonica, stood a slim figure robed in white. In one hand was a red flag, and in the other a handgun. But most alarming was the size of the head.

Enormous.

Brightly coloured: red, blue, and gold with protruding eyes and fearsome teeth. And rocking from side to side.

Then Twirly remembered he had seen heads like this before.

It was a papier maché carnival mask!

When in 1944 Jerry scarpered from the south of France the locals held a wild party along the Promenade des Anglais of Nice, and some had pranced about in heads like this, while the Brits soberly got drunk on beer provided by the American navy.

Twirly cautiously called, '*Sai-ida!*'

The figure gave a startled jump.

The flag and gun were dropped, and arms thin as cinnamon sticks shot up to snatch off the mask, revealing a brown face wrinkled like a seed-potato, with golden wire spectacles, and a streaky flimsy beard.

Twirly looked down and saw that the 'handgun' was a football supporter's wooden rattle.

The face broke into a wide gappy grin.

'Do not be minding me, Sahib. I am very nice man. I am Passang Temba: hotel seagull man.'

Twirly stared.

Passang continued, 'Seagulls very naughty birds, Sahib. Make dirty, dirty on Sahib Howard's nice roofs. Make him very angry.'

Passang stepped forward and confided, 'Sahib Howard says I am very good seagull man. He says, "You make them pissorf, Passang."'

At that moment two gulls swooped down with defiant shrieks and crash-landed on to a nearby roof.

Passang slammed his mask back on, and with great leaps of his scrawny brown legs and much flag waving and noisy rattling, he scampered into action.

The breakfast buffet table ran the length of the room and the Major took one of the small *kan tok* baskets filled with chunks of paw-paw, papaya, melon and mangosteen.

A smiling girl in a purple and green *sari* brought him a glass of ice-cold *lassi* yoghurt.

Ten minutes later, Budge joined him carrying a plate of fruit, and a dish of prawns in ginger.

The Major smiled.

'How far today, Mr Ballflower?'

Budge explained that he had originally hoped they could go down on to Weston beach and stand on the pier, but they were seriously behind schedule. Instead, he thought they should walk down the coast to Burnham-on-Sea and find accommodation in Puriton on the River Parrett. Three days from now they could be at Minehead and stomping about on Dunkery Beacon.

Alone on the terrace by the flagpoles with their softly tapping halyards, Budge looked at his watch. It was nine o'clock, and no sign of the Major or Twirly.

Before him the peninsula hill of Brean Down poked into the blue Bristol Channel, and, about six miles out, sat the two small islands of Steep Holm and Flat Holm. In the distance a fishing boat was ploughing purposefully towards Weston beach.

He turned to the south and studied the coast where they would soon be walking. About ten miles away were the white monoliths of Hinkley power-station, backed by the purple Quantock Hills.

To the north, across the estuary, the Black Mountains of South Wales were lit by the morning sun giving a more welcoming appearance than usual, and the coastal towns of Barry and Penarth flashed friendly messages of reflected sunlight.

'No other hotel in England has such magnificent views,' said Greg Howard striding down the steps towards the terrace. 'Guests have assured me that you can sometimes see Pen-y-Fan in the Brecon Beacons fifty miles away.'

Behind him paraded the Major, bright, brisk and eager to begin the affray with his haversack and cane at the alert.

'You seen Corporal Whippet?' he called.

Greg Howard laughed.

'Apparently your friend met up with Passang Temba, our seagull man. . .'

He continued with a knowing nod, ' . . . and Passang served with a Gurkha battalion in Tunisia.'

Budge did not understand.

Greg frowned.

169

'But wasn't your friend in Tunisia?'

Budge turned to the Major with his eyebrows raised.

The Major nodded, and Budge grimaced and shrugged.

Greg continued with a chuckle, 'Passang insisted on making him a breakfast of *gurr* potato pancakes with *pakora* onion fritters – generously washed down with Passang's lethal home-made *rakshi*. You may have to carry him.'

At that moment Twirly appeared at the top of the steps looking more flushed than usual, one eyebrow oddly raised as if someone had just poked him in the back. With his good arm he was dragging behind him his rucksack like a favourite teddy bear.

He solemnly swayed down the steps and stood before the Major. He slowly raised his arm and Budge thought he was going to salute. But he was merely correcting his balance.

He breathed a soft, 'Sah!'

Budge looked out to sea again and noticed that the fishing boat appeared to be quite large, and originally must have been further away than he supposed. He could clearly see twin derricks and it was trailing a wide white wake.

He took out his binoculars for a closer look.

And gasped.

It wasn't a fishing boat.

Chapter Nineteen

'That?' called Greg Howard. 'That's the *Waverley* – world's only sea-going paddle-steamer. Comes here every July and does excursions.'

The hull was white and long and slender, with side paddle-wheels like panniers. What Budge had supposed to be derricks were funnels.

He stood wide-eyed with wonder.

History sailing just below him.

'See that, Major?'

But the Major was bobbing up and down like a Gilbert and Sullivan policeman, flexing his knees in preparation for the coming onslaught. Twirly was struggling to make sense of the straps of his upside-down rucksack that he insisted he would carry this morning.

'Is it putting into Weston?'

'Sure,' said Greg. 'Then sails to Penarth or Minehead.'

MINEHEAD?

Budge's mind raced.

'But which?' he demanded.

Greg shrugged.

Budge glared, demanding a proper answer.

'Pertemba!' called Greg. The white jodhpurs arrived at the trot and Nepali words were rapidly exchanged.

'He says it's Tuesday, so it's Minehead.'

Minehead – three days walk away.

WE COULD BE THERE IN TIME FOR TEA.

He quickly glanced at the two old soldiers.

Three days ago the Major had boasted, 'We'll temporise to meet the exigencies of the service. If opportunities occur, we'll cheat.'

'Major! If we took the boat . . .'

The Major was attempting to manoeuvre Twirly into his rucksack.

'Ship,' he corrected.

Old fool.

'Greg! What time does the *Waverley* leave for Minehead?'

Greg and Pertemba conducted another foreign debate.

Budge stood twitching, tense as a tight-rope walker, desperate for a result.

The *right* result.

Finally Greg said, 'Pertemba often arranges trips for guests. It leaves at ten o'clock.'

Wow!

Budge furiously checked his watch.

That's forty-five minutes.

'Major. Twirly. It is my opinion that we should take the ship. It'll save us three days walking. Put us back on schedule.'

The Major and Twirly stared at him blankly.

'Well?' Budge snapped.

The Major spoke. 'Mr Ballflower. You must remember that Corporal Whippet and myself are old soldiers. And soldiers do not always agree with, or understand, what they are expected to do. But something is instilled in us. *Discipline*, Mr Ballflower. Never lose it. Tell an old soldier what is required of him and, although he may grumble, he will do it. Whatever the cost.'

Yes? Well?

The Major continued, 'You want us to take the ship?'

Budge nodded with urgent vigour.

The Major shouldered his cane.

'C'mon, Corporal. It's troopship time.'

Greg pointed out that Weston harbour was at the far end of the beach and three miles away. They must leave NOW.

'The 4x4 will take you.'

'No!' Pertemba said. 'The 4x4 is at the cash-and-carry.'

'Blast,' said Greg.

'*Burra Sahib*,' said Pertemba. 'The *gharry* is harnessed up ready to do a pick-up from the railway station at ten-fifty-three.

'Brilliant,' said Greg. 'Get Jangpo down here *chitto*.'

He explained to Budge and the Major, "Bought this marvellous barouche-carriage from Woburn Estate last year. Use it to ferry guests between the town and here. They love it. Jangpo will get you to the harbour in time – if he gets a move on.'

A distant explosion of shouted commands.

Jingling harness.

A whinnying horse.

Greg spoke quickly into his portable telephone. He nodded at the Major and whispered, 'Harbour Master.'

' . . . important friends of mine, Rodney. Thanks.'

He stuffed away his telephone.

'He'll do his best to hold the *Waverley.*'

Now from beyond the magnolias came a clattering of hooves and a high-pitched voice shrieking, *'Chhitto! Chhitto!'*

'STAND BACK EVERYBODY!' shouted Greg, and from behind a tossing clump of cabbage palms leapt a chestnut mare, ears forward, nostrils flared, forelegs flaying – and the staring eyes of a horse out of its equine mind.

Behind, lurched a gleaming black open carriage on whirling, slender wheels.

Sliding from side to side on a high front bench rocked a stocky Nepali wearing a red jacket with golden epaulettes and a black and gold pillbox hat, and eyes as wild as the mare's.

'Yahaa! he cried.

The carriage slewed to a halt and the mare tossed a flaxen mane, prancing like a nervous boxer awaiting the bell.

Greg quickly gave the driver urgent instructions and bundled the bewildered Upper Gently Three aboard - Budge with his back to the driver clutching his pack and Twirly's rucksack, and the Major and Twirly on the facing seat.

The carriage rocked like a dinghy.

Shouted farewells, a slapped mare's rump, and they were away at the gallop.

The Major braced himself as the carriage dashed through the archway and keeled hard over with no lessening of speed onto the main road.

Twirly slid to the floor.

Furiously fast down a steep hill, past houses and a church. Ahead the long yellow beach and the pink promenade road stretched like the twin runways of Nice airport.

The Major watched Budge briefly turn to look over the driver's shoulder to observe their progress, and saw his white knuckles suddenly grip the sides of the carriage, abandoning the packs, which tumbled down to join Twirly in the well.

At a boatyard at the bottom of the hill the red-coated driver did some desperate heaving on reins, and the carriage lurched to port and swished on to the beach.

It was past high tide and the sea had retreated, and the wheels of the wildly rocking carriage hissed and splashed over wet, rippled sand.

The Major snatched off his jungle hat and clutched it to his person, his white hair streaming out in the sea-weed scented air.

'You all right, Major?' he heard Twirly call. He looked down and the corporal was grinning like a five-year old at a fun-fair.

Ahead a cloud of seagulls ceased picking at a disgusting breakfast and swept into the air like water birds taking off from Lake Timsah. Their non-flying mottled brown youngsters were abandoned, and they waddled crossly away like old ladies scurrying between tour coach and toilets.

The carriage swished past a banner announcing Mr Tapnell's Traditional Donkey Rides. The line of normally patient donkeys twitched nervously as they passed, and one confused creature broke ranks and galloped after them like an unseated horse at Aintree.

Children with buckets and spades waved with delight.

Twirly waved back like the Queen of Tonga.

Now, to the Major's horror, the gharry swerved from the beach to join the traffic up on the red tarmac of Promenade Road, and the narrow-tyred wheels bounced high with bone-shaking bumps.

The shouting, waving driver honked a rubber-bulbed horn at dithering pedestrians, and the mare furiously tossed her mane with every blast.

On and on.

Past a putting green.

Past the Tropicana Pleasure Beach.

Past the Aquarium – *open till late.*

Past the massive red-brick Atlantic Hotel.

Past the Grand Pier – *Bingo at 2:30.*

And into the melee of traffic at a roundabout near the Winter Pavilion.

The Major was aware that the driver was pointing over to the left where the black and white *Waverley* sat tucked against the grey wall of the tiny harbour.

The carriage swept into the forecourt of the glass-fronted Harbour Inn, and the driver stood and heaved back on the reins.

'Bistaarai haknus,' he cried.

'Bistaarai. Roknus. Roknus.'

The sweating, frothing mare slowed to a heaving halt and stood scraping restless hooves on the cobbles.

The Nepali spun round and grinned. His face was glistening, and a black fringe was plastered to his forehead below the askew pillbox hat.

He waved to the *Waverley*.

'Big ship, Sahib,' he cried.

A red sandstone Victorian clock tower by the harbour wall declared it to be four minutes past ten.

Budge shot into action, struggled to his feet and tumbled out of the carriage. He snatched up both packs.

'Come on. Come on. Can't miss her now.'

The Major leapt after him, clutching his satchel to his chest. Twirly was already speeding towards the ship.

As he ran, Budge gasped at the beauty of the *Waverley*. It was magnificent. Bright and pristine. Multicoloured flags tugging from soaring mastheads. Black smoke issuing urgently from red funnels topped with black and white collars.

Every part of the ship's white superstructure was covered by heads and waving arms like an overturned centipede, and Budge could hear a mixture of abuse and cheering from impatient passengers.

A brass band on the cobbles by the ship's side was blasting out a boisterous version of *Life on the Ocean Wave* and the conductor eyed them crossly as they sped past. Budge rushed up a red gangplank on to a platform above a black and gold paddle-box, followed by Twirly and the Major. Unsmiling seamen thrust the three aside and slammed shut a gate in the ship's rail.

The passengers cheered.

Immediately there were shouted orders.

'Away forrard!'

'Away midships!'

Three blasts from the ship's siren sounded the 'I-am-going-astern'.

On the dockside the band's bass drum sounded a loud *pom-pom* beat and the music stopped as abruptly as if the band had struck an iceberg.

The mighty paddles on either side of the ship thundered into powerful life, pounding the water into a massive head of white foam.

'Away aft!' and a hemp hawser as thick as a giant conger was hurled from a dockside bollard and dragged dripping on to the deck.

The gleaming stern of *Waverley* swung away from the quay and moved slowly astern into clear water, causing yachts moored nearby to nod a silent *bon voyage*.

A signal bell rang.

The paddles froze, pouring with sun flashing cascades of green water.

Another signal bell.

Again the paddles leapt into life and the ship surged, this time forward, with a turning circle as tight as a London taxi, clearing the end of the sea wall with several inches to spare.

The old lady *Waverley,* already at maximum speed and heading for the horizon, settled down into the swell to make herself comfortable for the ninety-minute run to Minehead.

The Major, still gasping, managed to speak.

'We need a drink,' he said.

The Jennie Dean's Lounge was cool, dark – and empty.

An oily-haired barman with gold rings of rank clipped to his lip looked up from a newspaper spread on the bar.

'You with the Legion?'

Budge shook his head.

'Not necessarily.'

The barman gathered up the newspaper.

'Supposed to be a private cruise. Summer outing of the Bristol branch of the British Legion. Told there would be no one in here. All be supping at the free bar on the after-deck.'

'Three pints of McEwan's,' said Budge.

The Major sat at a copper-topped table by a window, watching the dark green foaming ocean hurtling past just inches away from his shoulder, and toyed with his half-empty glass.

He remembered a shallow river-boat sweeping along in the current and Lim Bo Seng hissing, 'Keep your head down, Colonel. Yellow bastards everywhere . . .

'Excuse me, Sir.'

It was the barman.

'Did you want another beer?'

The Major blinked.

'I'm thinking of closing the bar, Sir. Only you here.'

The Major looked around. Budge and Twirly had disappeared.

He shook his head, said, 'Thank you,' and headed for the door. Stepping out into the bright sunlight, and the salt air, he headed in the direction of the strains of *Mademoiselle from Armentiéres* being buffeted from aft.

Near the steps to the Lower Saloon, a red-faced man was pushing and pulling a piano-accordion across his casemate stomach. One foot furiously thumped out the beat, causing numerous empty glasses grouped around his chair to tinkle and clash like a novice percussion section.

The milling, swaying crowd could have filled Gently's Memorial Hall: upright weathered men even older than the Major, sporting blazers with embroidered badges; stooping thin men who had forgotten how sergeant-majors once stretched them upright;
rotund men the shape of barrels and already half-full of free beer.

177

Ladies in bright dresses and pink cardigans with lips as red as a poppy-seller's tray fearing for their sea-cruise coiffures; fragile white haired widows with darkly veined hands desperately clutched heavy handbags of ballast as a precaution against being blown overboard.

A jolly parade-ground voice boomed, 'All fall-in for the Hokey-Cokey!'

The Major fled.

At the base of one of the funnels the Major discovered a polished brass plaque recording that this particular *Waverley* was built in 1947 by the London and North-Eastern Railway, replacing the vessel which in 1940 had steamed heroically to Dunkirk.

On Wednesday, 29th May, loaded to the gunnels with weary, wounded men, the original Waverley *valiantly struggled to keep up with the escort of bustling destroyers, but Heinkel bombers found her, sunk her and three hundred men died.*

Beneath the plaque was a wooden enclosure filled with bright yellow lifejackets. He recalled Churchill's insistence that he would only travel on ships with Italian crews. He used to growl, 'No nonsense with *them* about women and children first.'

The Major prodded the jackets. Soft. He eased himself into this luxurious bunk and adopted the recovery position.

Budge stood alone on the deserted foredeck like Nelson on *Victory* with legs apart, chin up, eyes on the horizon and swaying to meet the roll of the ship.

If I had been in their *war, it would have been the Navy.*

Bright sunshine skimmed off the waves to be tossed aboard by a brisk slipstream and he licked salt from his lips.

A tiny trawler rocked past, accompanied by a screeching fan-club of wheeling, diving seagulls. A toiling fisherman looked up and waved.

The high stays of the *Waverley* whistled a continuous shanty, punctuated from time to time by a loud slap from a blue and gold flag fluttering from the main mast. The huge paddles thrashed away at the turquoise sea with a steady, confident rhythm.

He turned to look aft from where odd snatches of singing attempted to force their way forrard, and he approved of the way the *Waverley* jettisoned these discords overboard, so they disappeared into the wide foaming wake stretching behind them as straight as a Roman road.

Twirly thrust his way through the swaying, laughing, singing crowd and helped himself from a plate of sandwiches.

'Ham with mustard,' winked a lady as large as an inflated dinghy. He smiled and scooped up a few more – haversack rations for the Major and Budge – and retreated from the heaving jollity.

Up behind the bridge, a small dark cabin displayed a handwritten 'Reserved' sign pasted on to one of the windows. He stopped and peered.

Budge made his way down to the Engine Room Viewing Gallery and stood by polished brass rails.

Three massive pistons slid effortlessly backwards and forwards, sucking and sighing in a sweet aura of warm oil, acrid steam, and perfumed furniture polish. An enormous fly-wheel turned at an unhurried fifty revolutions a minute.

On the far wall, mahogany panels bore dials encased in gleaming brass, surrounded by a maze of coils and burnished copper tubing.

'Isn't she beautiful,' said a voice at his elbow.

The speaker was shaped like a channel buoy and wearing a black Paddle Steamer Preservation Society jersey.

'You seen the Jenny Nettle rods?' he asked.

Much later Budge headed back to the lounge in search of his shipmates.

A 'Reserved' sign on a half-hidden cabin caught his attention, and as he passed he dimly saw a handful of red-coated gentlemen of the Royal Chelsea Hospital, sitting like a collection of Toby jugs.

He stopped and stepped back.

In the gloom amongst the black tricorn hats and polished silver buttons was a familiar suntanned tonsure. Two eyes glared at him through the spray-dashed window.

Chapter Twenty

Twirly burst out of the Pilot's cabin.

'Budge!'

He stood like Puck, sprung from a below-stage trap, waving a half-filled tankard.

'Come in. Meet some of my old mates.'

In the tiny cabin smelling of peppermint and mothballs, four red-coated ex-warriors sat on a narrow bench, with chests emblazoned by a military pageant of coloured ribbons and gleaming medals.

In the centre sat a wide figure with knees apart like a Zulu chief, bright penetrating eyes glinting from pistol-holster leather.

'Sergeant-Major John Cormack,' announced Twirly.

The man tipped a white-gloved forefinger to his three-cornered hat.

Above the black cuff was a large coat-of-arms device worked in golden thread. High on his right shoulder was a small golden-winged parachute badge.

Budge leaned forward and deferentially shook a proffered hand:

'You know Twirly?'

The *Waverley* lurched, but quickly regained her sedately rolling progress.

The Sgt-Major raised his eyebrows.

Twirly leapt forward.

'They know me as *Whippet*, Budge.'

The Sgt-Major relaxed with a bellow of a laugh.

'That's right. Whippet! Sometimes Private Whippet, sometimes Lance-Corporal Whippet, and sometimes Corporal-acting-unpaid Whippet – but mostly Private Whippet. Only NCO in the British army with stripes on press-studs.'

He shared this merry joke with his fellow survivors.

181

'A hero of the First Parachute Battalion, and best sanitary orderly in the whole of the Middle East.'

A barrage of heaving guffaws filled the confined cabin, and Budge studied the slight figure of Twirly staring into his tankard to check there was no treacherous King's Shilling lurking at the bottom.

'Don't remember you saying you were in the paras, Twirly,' murmured Budge.

Twirly briefly withdrew from the tankard and sniffed.

'Don't remember you asking, Budge.'

The Sgt-Major roared, 'Don't suppose he told you about his GOC's Certificate of Commendation either?'

The tightly-wedged comrades rocked in unison.

A group of passing passengers paused to shield their eyes and peer briefly into the gloom.

The Sgt-Major commanded, 'Whippet, lad. Why don't you go and get a drink for your young friend? Take this tray and bring up urgently needed supplies.'

Twirly took the tray and made his escape.

The Sgt-Major pulled forward a stool from a hidden corner and indicated with a nod that Budge should sit.

This was going to be a long war.

'You see, Sir, it was November, 1942. First Parachute Battalion – that was us – dropped and took Souk el Arba airfield four-hundred miles ahead of British and American troops advancing along the coast of Morocco and Tunisia and we were to hold it until the rest of the brigade reached us.

'My company, B Company, became responsible for constructing battalion latrines. I detailed half-a-dozen blokes, including seventeen-year old Rifleman Whippet.

'I tell you, Sir, he was amazing. No squatting over rough trenches with him.

'He knew about digging ditches from working for the Council in civvy-street, and he was a genius at scrounging.

'Stole timber from a sloppy Pioneer unit.

'Turned his red beret inside out so he looked like a tank man, and returned from the lines of the snooty 17th/21st Lancers with a load of tarpaulin.

'Built wonderful six-foot high screens with proper door flaps. Borrowed desks from an empty *froggie* school to make lovely seats. Toilet-paper holders from empty butter tins.

'Wonderful.

'And you should have seen the OFFICERS ONLY. They called it the Evacuation Club. He fixed it with running water, and scrounged a crate of Lifebuoy from a NAAFI bulk store in Algiers.

'The CO promoted him to Battalion Sanitary Corporal.

'Then one day old 'Technicolour' visited us.'

'Technicolour?'

'Colonel Malcolm MacEwan, RAMC.

'A World War One pilot who got the DFC. He got other medals in the Russian Civil War. Became a doctor. Was with an artillery unit at Dunkirk and got another medal. He became Commanding Officer of the first Parachute Field Ambulance. Everyone called him 'Technicolour' because he had more ribbons across his chest than the ruler of a banana republic. He was in wars only *he* knew about.'

A tap on the *Waverley* cabin door announced Twirly's return from a successful supply mission.

The ale was distributed, and Budge noticed that whilst he and Twirly sat on hard stools, the Chelsea gentlemen were cosseted on thick blue cushions.

The Sgt-Major continued, 'Technicolour made Whippet responsible for hygiene throughout the whole Brigade. Excused parades, PT, and guard duties. And no-one ever knew *where* he was supposed to be, or *what* he was supposed to be doing.'

Everyone chuckled.

Budge leaned forward.

'And his Certificate of Commendation?'

Twirly leapt to his feet with a hand raised, calling for silence.

The *Waverley's* tannoys were talking.

'We're coming into Minehead,' Budge said.

He turned to the warriors:

'You disembarking here?'

The Sgt-Major shook his head.

'They're picking up Minehead Legion members, then we sail on to Lynmouth.'

Budge quickly drained his glass.

'Come on, Twirly!'

Hands shaken, hats touched – and Twirly demonstrated to Budge how a parachutist does a fast exit.

'Don't forget, Whippet,' called the Sgt-Major, 'Utrinque Paratus!'

Ready for anything.

Twirly hunched his shoulders and they dodged along the busy deck towards the paddle box and he heard Budge call, 'Hell is the Major?'

He was not at the rails where the gangplank was being manoeuvred into place.

Budge cried, 'He's *your* officer, Twirly!'

Twirly scanned the craning crowd. No Major. Pushing himself ramrod stiff with his thumbnails feeling for the seams in his trousers, he threw back his head.

Cormack had taught him, 'Not from your throat, Whippet – from the gut, and shout as if a bayonet has been stuck up your arse.'

Twirly did just that.

'MAJOR!'

The *Waverley* fell silent. So did the passengers. So did the startled crew.

Twirly bellowed again.

'OFFICERS - ON PARADE!'

A commotion amidships. The confused crowd parted to allow the bustling arrival of the Major fumbling his hat and juggling his satchel and cane.

He nodded at Twirly.

'Thank you, Corporal. Get the men fell-in on the dockside.'

Still blinking himself awake, he followed Twirly and Budge down the gangplank and smilingly pushed through the waving and shouting group waiting to embark.

Beyond the yacht-filled harbour arose a high tree-covered hill. To the right stretched a coast of hump-back cliffs like a line of half-submerged water-buffalo. To the left a beach ran to the town.

A steam-whistle blasted and the prima donna *Waverley* re-took centre stage, with the whole harbour a besotted audience.

Elegant yachts and work-weary fishing boats bobbed and bowed, restrained by a cats-cradle of new nylon painters and old ropes with beards of green. Shining wire stays slapped against metal masts. Mini-tsunami waves crashed against harbour walls and swept up and down ancient seaweed-slippery steps.

Onlookers waved, and pressed small silver cameras to their foreheads, and a little boy cheered.

The Major looked around for Twirly.

He was striding along the quay away from his past.

Even when *Waverley* signalled her departure he didn't turn round for a farewell glance.

Now it was the Major's turn to bark an order.

'Whippet. AB-O-UT - TURN!'

Twirly stopped and turned.

The Major stood pointing with his cane.

Up on the roof of the Promenade Deck lounge stood the four men of Chelsea silhouetted against the Legion-blue sky like new red skittles.

The Sgt-Major particularly presented a splendid figure with his right arm raised in a magnificent salute.

The Major watched Twirly slam his wellingtons into the cobbles and snap to attention and instantly recognised his dilemma.

Article 342. Members of His Majesty's Forces will only salute when wearing regulation headdress.

He snatched off his jungle hat and skimmed it frisby fashion to Twirly, who jumped forward, caught it, and slammed it on his head.

He performed a perfect longest-way-up, three-second-wobble, shortest-way-down – *two-three*. A salute which would have won the battle of Waterloo without the help of Blücher.

Good man.

Now, with a slick guardsman's about-turn and precision stamping, Twirly marched off. *Leet-right. Leet-right.*

185

When he finally stopped to look around, the *Waverley* had disappeared behind the high sea wall, leaving only a thrashing wake.

The Major sighed, knowing that Twirly's First Parachute Brigade was not only fifty-three years away. It had departed from England for ever.

Minehead harbour existed more than a thousand years ago, and once belonged to the Saxon son of Lady Godiva. The stone quay was built in the seventeenth century with ships trading as far afield as Portugal, Africa and North America. In the 1930s it also had a fine pier, frantically dismantled when Hitler's invasion was expected, and still lies stacked in Newport awaiting a come-back-all-is-forgiven.

It was twelve-thirty.

They needed lunch.

The flower-bedecked Old Ship Aground was full to the gunwales and overflowing with visitors who had come to see the *Waverley.*

'We'll do better grabbing something as we go through the town. Got to keep moving,' declared Budge.

They walked briskly past a row of thatched cottages looking like a strip from a Dulux colour chart.

'Minehead?' said Budge. 'Did they mine here, Major?'

The Major, struggling to keep up, replied, 'No mining.

'The great hill was a landmark for fishermen and sailors. The Welsh called it *Mynydd,* Celtic for mountain. The tolerant English adopted the name, but corrected the spelling.'

'Speak Welsh, Major?'

The Major shrugged. 'Mary and I used to walk a lot in the Black Mountains. Stayed in a little hotel in the ruins of Llanthony Priory near Abergavenny. And there was a restaurant called The Walnut Tree . . ..'

Budge pointed to a small blue cottage with the pretty name *Gwely a Brewcast.*

'What's that mean?'

'Bed and Breakfast,' said the Major.

'And that: *Ar gau?*'

186

'Closed.'

On a high balcony of a red three-storey hotel with a large green dome, a fair-haired girl in a white bathrobe waved to someone, and Budge wondered if it was him and waved back just in case. He stopped at a signpost pointing up stone steps.

SOUTH WEST WAY.
Poole 630 miles.
Land's End 264 miles.
Affixed to the wall was a small bronze plaque:
'John Mason – who knew and loved every inch of this path.'

Twirly, who had been trailing behind, joined them and pushed past up the steps.

'Hold it, Twirly,' called Budge. 'Not going that way.'

Twirly turned and scowled.

Budge shook his head.

'That path dawdles around every cove and fishing-village in the southwest. Magnificent – but take us ages. Couldn't do it with our schedule. Devised a shorter route dropping south across Exmoor and down to Exeter, then south-west across Dartmoor and Bodmin. Join the coast path at Newquay and on to St Ives and Land's End.

'It's brilliant. Trust me.'

Beyond the sea wall on the other side of the road the restless waves thumped and sighed and scraped.

Twirly watched the Major grimace and awkwardly rub his back.

Then he gave a deep investigative sniff.

He sniffed again.

He nimbly skipped down the steps and held up an authoritative finger.

His expression was blissful.

'Fish and chips,' he cried. 'Not far from here.'

He set off sniffing like a hedgehog, aware of the Major and Budge eagerly following like bloodhounds at point.

The fish and chips were on Twirly. As were the various treasures extracted from his rucksack. Sachets of vinegar, coloured sauces, and paper serviettes bearing various legends.

Budge contributed soft, warm, buttered rolls.

The Major produced three oranges.

As they sat on a sea wall in the hot sun, packing away empty plastic cartons, the Major said, 'You should get a hat, Corporal.'

Twirly stroked his brown pate.

Budge waved his hand inland towards a high horizon of steep green meadows, dark bracken and blue-black fir trees.

'Other side of that ridge is Dunster. Shops there. Be there by four. Sure to be somebody selling hats.'

Now walking, Budge paused by a hissing railway station, where behind a red paling fence rested three magnificent cream and brown Pullman coaches, a blue saddle-tank engine, and a long green tender with the initials GWR. An artistic maroon and gold sign declared:

TOILETS – PASSENGERS ONLY.

They hurried past a narrow strip of beach dotted with striped windbreaks, deck-chairs, sleeping bodies, children leaping, shouting, screaming, sobbing and having a jolly seaside holiday.

At a holiday camp dominated by a multi-spiked silver tent, they turned inland to cross the new A39 and the *old* A39.

Past a rugby ground.

Up the steep Dean Lane – no longer a lane but a sparkling stream rushing down a deep trench of red earth and polished stones.

He watched Twirly joyfully stomping up in his wellingtons.

He looked at the Major's polished brogues.

'Going to get your feet wet again, Major.'

The Major shrugged.

'A SEAC medical officer once assured me that the human skin is more or less waterproof,' he said and he splashed up after Twirly.

Soon high-level gusts eased the heat of the sun, and several times they paused to gaze back at the coast. As they climbed higher and higher, the sea horizon stretched further and further, until it appeared as an endless sheet of purple silk, marbled with meandering streaks of dark blue.

At last they topped the hill and Budge studied his map.

'Twirly,' he said. 'Does your built-in altimeter tell you we are two hundred and thirty feet above sea level?'

But Twirly was busy digging into his rucksack, and without comment he handed out crumpled British Legion ham and mustard sandwiches, and some boiled sweets discovered in a Waverley locker marked 'Crew Only'.

The Major masticated his ham and mustard.

'It's a question of Twirly's parachute training, Budge.

'During practice jumps it was usual to exit at a thousand feet.

'The twenty seconds of descent just about allowed time to release your leg-valise and feed it out on its rope so that it hit the ground before you did; enabled you to shuffle your behind out of the harness seat-strap, kick like a running dog to get rid of any twists in the rigging lines, reach up for the lift webs and pull down to reduce oscillation, if possible identify the RV point on the DZ and assess your line of drift in preparation for landing.

'On the other hand, when the sky was noisily unfriendly, it was sensible to get the hell down as quickly as possible, and you preferred to exit at about eight hundred feet or below.'

Budge folded his map.

'Sure.'

Ten minutes later they were down on Priory Green admiring Dunster's High Street.

It was three-thirty.

Budge decided Dunster must have been built as a film-set for a mediaeval costume drama.

On the left the 3-star Luttrell Arms, once a fifteenth century hospitality suite for nearby Cleeve Abbey, is still filled with architectural treasures and conceals a secret perfumed garden which only the determined find.

In the centre of the surprisingly wide street, on a cobbled pavement, a grey slated octagonal roof was once the venue for Irish traders selling wool to Somerset weavers.

Low cream, green and pink cottages down one side of the street.

Tall Tudor houses with carved oak doorways on the other.

At the far end, on a mound of green, rose a Sleeping Beauty cluster of red turrets and towers: Dunster Castle.

'We made good time,' said Budge in the Colonel Wyndham pub where they drank Old Speckled Hen and collected their room keys.

'Visit the castle. Part Norman part National Trust?'

Twirly said his injured arm didn't care for castles, and anyway he had seen some people arrive which he thought he perhaps knew. . .

The Major demurred.

'How many miles tomorrow, Mr Ballflower?'

'You'll *love* the castle, Major. And tomorrow is tomorrow.'

The Major was charmed by the leather wall coverings – cheaper than tapestries. The wood carvings – cheaper than stone. The story about a seven-foot skeleton with iron shackles found bricked-up in a wall. The room in which poor William Prynne spent eight months, imprisoned by Cromwell for 'seditious libel', and which he only left twice. Once to have the letters S and L branded on to his cheek. And once to have his thumbs cut off.

'Fancy a cup of tea?' asked Budge.

As they walked down from the castle gatehouse they could hear music.

Sweet Lass of Richmond Hill.

Outside the Courtyard Gallery on an area marked COACHES ONLY a small crowd was gathered. In their centre leapt a team of Morris dancers. Yellow and red ribbons flying from black straw hats. Black breeches tucked into long white socks gartered with jingling sleigh bells. Billowing white sleeves waving Persil-white handkerchiefs. All cavorting with joyous abandon.

But the Major was attracted by the antics of a tall brown-coated figure topped by a grotesque horse's head with staring green glass eyes which leapt and skipped amongst the dancers.

Protruding from its rear was an obscene horse's tail bound with a bright red tail-bandage, and it delighted the crowd by heading for groups of ladies, turning its back on them, and jostling this protuberance into their shrieking midst.

Occasionally it pranced around with a sequined collecting bag.

The Major turned to Budge.

'Authentic Elizabethan bawdy humour.'

Suddenly the apparition stood still and bent forward with its ridiculously large head and its staring eyes.

'Good Lord,' said the Major. 'Heading for us. Got any change handy, Budge?'

But the sequined bag was not proffered. Instead the figure leapt, and bowed and to the delight of the crowd turned extravagantly to treat the Major to vigorous prodding with his impertinent tail.

The Major was aghast.

'Steady!' he blustered as he squirmed to avoid the jostling.

The crowd laughed and clapped, and the bagman retreated to the centre and mingled with the dancers, lifting up his brown skirts and performing a series of frenzied leaps.

And that was when they both saw . . .

The equine bagman was wearing polished black wellingtons.

Chapter Twenty-one

'Private Whippet will not be joining us for dinner, Mr Ballflower.'

'He all right?'

'He's fine. He's explained his affinity with the Morris dancing people. Apparently he often acts as bagman for the Chedworth team, so he's familiar with the procedures. Yesterday the Polden Hills team arrived in Dunster, complete with its ancient horses's head, but the usual man was trapped in traffic in Taunton.

'Whippet gamely agreed to take his place. All goes to charity, you know.'

Budge sipped his beer and studied the golden grapes wound around timber pillars growing from the bar.

The Major continued, 'Landlord has arranged a roast-pig barbecue in the car park for the dancers and their camp followers. Whippet has been invited to join them.'

He nursed his Campari and soda.

'Whippet is an enigma.'

The bar with its green walls and light woodwork was almost empty, but raucous noises came from behind a door marked Fitzgeralds's Cellar Bar.

'By the way, Mr Ballflower, I have noticed you appear to be paying for all Whippet's accommodation.'

'Ah,' said Budge. 'Doll at the Bells insisted on giving me a substantial sum to do just that. Concerned that Twirly doesn't realise that two hundred and fifty pounds doesn't make him a millionaire.'

The Major nodded.

Budge continued, 'Don't you think that a little *odd*, Major: Doll paying for him?'

The Major shook his head.

'Not at all, Mr Ballflower, not when you *remember* . . .'

'You ready to order, gentlemen?' asked an attractive waitress who suddenly stood at their table.

Budge was charmed. She wore a loose white blouse. A complexion soft as a peach. And she smiled with eyes of green.

Of course, not as gloriously green . . .

She recited, 'The chef would like to recommend tonight's special: roast saddle of venison marinated for three days in red wine with juniper and thyme. Served with redcurrant jelly, game chips and puree of chestnuts.'

It was an historic choice.

Wednesday 15th July *Day ten*

Twirly watched the Major blink as he stepped from the white and green pub into the bright sunshine. He blinked again when he saw the hat Twirly was carefully smoothing.

'Hope you are not thinking of wearing that on parade, Whippet. Frighten the horses.'

Twirly looked down at the black straw boater hat presented to him last night by the Morris men and sniffed.

He liked it.

Before breakfast, despite a thumping head, he stripped off the artificial flowers and with the aid of his army-issue 'housewife' fashioned the yellow ribbons into a long chinstrap. When he chose not to wear it, he would hang it around his neck like Tonto.

He placed it squarely on his head and adopted a Clint Eastwood scowl of defiance.

Budge burst on to the cobbled pavement struggling into his backpack, and glowered at the black hat.

'Hell is that? Somebody died?'

Twirly glared in disapproval.

His mother didn't allow jokes about death – always invited trouble.

'Let's go,' said Budge. 'Long day today,' and he charged off at his light-infantry pace.

Twirly saw the Major wince, stretch himself to his full height, and gamely follow round the corner by the Cage gift shop. Along by a grey tile-fronted building Budge called over his shoulder:

'Fourteenth century. They call it the Old Nunnery. Never was, of course. We'll nip into St. George's church, once a Benedictine priory *and* parish church.'

They clattered up the central aisle.

'See that oddly-shaped arch? Initially elegant and narrow, but not wide enough to allow processing monks to pass through in pairs – resulting in unholy fisticuffs deciding who should go first. The mason who was paid to hack it wider must have wept.'

Budge charged to the end of the south aisle:

'Come and see this.'

Twirly stood and waited with his hat dangling over his back.

Not a great church man. Armistice and funerals. Used to go a lot. After school every Friday. Helped his mother sweep; clean the brasses; clear dead flowers from vases; and empty the ashtrays in the vicar's vestry.

He heard Budge telling the Major, 'Roundheads were billeted here when they besieged the castle during the Civil War. Drilled these holes so they could play Nine-men marbles.

'Longest rood screen in Europe,' he called as they left by an open door in the north aisle.

'Memorial garden,' he cried.

Twirly blinked in the walled garden full of sunshine and flowers. He called, 'Morning!' to a grey-haired man in a blue pullover who was reverently deadheading roses into a bucket.

The church clock struck nine and the bells played, *Oh God our help in ages past.*

'Oh yes,' wheezed the old man, 'plays a tune every morning at this time. Tomorrow it'll be *Home, sweet home.'*

Twirly sped after the Major as fast as his throbbing head would allow and sighed.

Home, sweet home?

At this hour he would normally be sharing breakfast with Ratcher. Perhaps sitting outside looking down on to the clear waters of Booky Tweet, with its lazily writhing yellow and white water-crowfoots, and the big willow idly stroking the water with its slender leaves. And on the opposite bank, tall Indian balsam, topped by turban-like purple-pink flowers standing like skinny Lascars at Port Said waiting for a ship.

This morning – why does he have to run along with FSMO, carrying a wounded arm and a head full of lead?

'Stab!'

Beyond a school, Budge led them through a tidy cemetery where Twirly acquired a waxy white gardenia to tuck into his shirt pocket.

A gate at the rear opened on to allotments from where a wicket-gate led into a wood cloaking the hillside.

The path wound up to the right in cool shade where hostas and clumps of pink rosebay willowherb were still glistening under a sprinkling of dew from a heavenly aspergillum.

As the path got steeper, it became buried under dead oak leaves, brittle as cornflakes, and Twirly slid his wellingtons noisily through like snow-ploughs.

At last the trees thinned and the path became wider and dappled with sunlight. Finally, it turned sharp right and glorious blue sky appeared between the trees ahead.

By an inviting wooden bench and a National Trust *Grabbist Hill* sign, the trees disappeared.

It was like the curtains opening at Upper Gently's annual pantomime and Twirly stood dazed with wonder.

He was on the top of the world and it was lit by bright sunshine. Far down to the right the sea was bluer than it had been at Taranto. To the left, green valleys and purple hills stretched to disappear in hazy horizons, like the Argen alps of Provence.

Ahead, a yellow path snaked through purple heather and golden gorse, like a sapper's tape through a minefield.

The air was sweet as a new shirt.

Budge halted and waved a hand in the direction of the sea where a stationary container-ship sat like an island made of Lego.

'That path we walked yesterday past the holiday camp, three hundred years ago that was all sea, right up to Dunster castle, which had its own harbour. Luttrell Arms was once a pub called The Ship Inn.'

He turned and squinted along the coast to the east.

'Smudge of houses is the fishing village of Blue Anchor. Got its name from hauled-in anchors plastered with blue mud.'

He pointed inland at the great heather-covered dome filling the horizon.

'Dunkery Beacon. Highest point on Exmoor.'

Twirly was suddenly impelled to don his new black hat.

From a whitewashed, half-hidden, trig pillar on a wall at nearly a thousand feet, Budge led down onto a lush grass track dropping steeply through old trees and new plantations.

At the bottom of a sloping field, where sure-footed cows morosely munched, cosily snuggled the village of Wootton Courtenay, with cottages, gardens and a church with a golden cockerel weather-vane.

Outside the Bright and Beautiful Tea Room Budge looked at his watch.

'Eleven o'clock. Doing well. Suggest we grab a coffee.'

The Major instantly allowed his satchel to slide off his shoulder and sank with a groan on to a low wall, massaging his knees.

The tearoom was delightful. Cool. Clean. Pine-furniture. Painted plates high on cream walls. And smelling of freshly baked bread.

A man wearing a blue apron burst through a curtain at the back with a look of genuine pleasure.

Budge dumped his backpack onto a chair by a blue-check table.

'Three glasses of chilled milk, two coffees, one tea,' he said.

The man beamed as if Budge had told him he had just won the Lottery and swished back through the curtain.

He instantly popped back his head.

'Can I interest you in our speciality, gentlemen? Dunkery Bacon.'

Silence.

'We're famous for it. Toasted soft bap with, slice of bacon, melted cheese and drizzled with Lea & Perrins.'

As they reassembled themselves into their packs Budge said, 'Loved your Dunkery Bacon.'

The Major added, 'And the name. Bright and Beautiful.'

The man smiled.

'Comes from the hymn, of course.'

Twirly knew that.

Sunday School, and Mrs Tarry.

He hummed, 'All things bright and beautiful.'

The man beamed.

'An Irish lady, Mrs Alexander, spent a holiday at Frackford Bridge just down the road. Wrote the hymn. She said 'the purple headed mountain' referred to heather-covered Dunkery Beacon; river running by was the River Avil across the road.'

Out of the village Budge stopped in the middle of the path to explain to the Major where they were.

' . . . and at the end of this field is the hamlet of Ford.'

Twirly pushed past them to cross a field full of buttercups and daises as pretty as a summer dress and sat on a stile to wait.

Around his wellingtons grew a mass of the tiny yellow herb bennet. He picked a few sprigs and stuffed them into the band of his hat.

'For luck, Twirly?' asked Budge.

'Always lucky for me. Old Annie Wentworth used to pay me for it – penny a bag.'

Budge stooped and picked some, and put it to his nose.

'Smells of cloves. She make wine?'

Twirly chuckled and shook his head.

'She used to do the laying-out in the village. Anybody died, you sent for her. Knew a lot of clever things, did Annie. Used to put the dried roots into the shifts they used for shrouds.'

Twirly watched Budge shudder and flick the flowers from his fingers; the Major arrived, and they were off again.

Beyond Ford, the path emerged from a spinney of sycamore and beech and began climbing the purple slopes of Dunkery.

At first a wide grass track cut a clear swathe through head-high bracken, neighbourly supporting crimson foxgloves and purple thistles. Now it became a narrow, increasingly steep path through sparse moorland, with pink stones and muddy puddles.

The sun was still glaring down at them, but as they gained height welcome breezes shook and teased the crouching shrubs of gorse.

Twirly's 'morning-after' headache was fading, but in its place he was aware of feeling as uneasy as a dog in a field of bullocks.

Suddenly a pheasant shot up from beneath his feet, squawking and whirling.

'STAB!'

If he had been more himself he would have whacked it with his hazel stick.

He watched it wheel away, still chortling, until it suddenly dropped behind high gorse.

He sniffed, with his eyes darting like a kite in the wind.

It's all this shrub, and stony hillside. The Herman Goering Jäger Regiment are probably hidden on the reverse slope.

He looked up at the summit ahead. The cairn on the top was strangely fuzzy-headed, like a full pin-cushion.

Budge and the Major stood having an O-group discussion:

'Can't understand it, Major. Been up here before – always traffic on the road running around the hill; and with this good weather there should be walkers everywhere. Now only us. Everybody else seems to be gathered on the summit.'

Twirly looked up at the summit again and understood the fuzzy pin-cushion. The black dots were heads.

He watched the Major anxiously fiddle with his satchel, while peering around the hillside.

'Look at that,' cried Budge. 'A small flash of light where the road comes over the horizon.'

The Major swung round.

Budge took out his binoculars.

'Angular shapes up on the road. Would they be horseboxes, Major? Hunting perhaps?'

He panned his binoculars down the road and mumbled, 'Just ahead of us – this side of the road – a group of people crouching in the bracken. With equipment of some kind. Hell is going on?'

The Major looked alarmed.

'Good Lord. An ambush?'

Budge, still at his binoculars, said, 'Some sort of tripod . . .'

Twirly sniffed.

'Mortars?'

Budge studied the road far down to the right.

'Hello! Yellow jackets. And a police-car.'

He lowered the glasses, puzzled.

'They've blocked the road.'

Movement ahead amongst the crouching group by the road caught Twirly's eye. A youth scrambled to his feet, held up a board, and quickly dropped into the bracken again.

The Major pointed and said, 'There's movement up there. Look! Amongst the horse-boxes.'

Twirly could see something moving down the road towards them. Yellow and black. A low-loader lorry?

Suddenly Budge cried, 'Its a coach! A horse-drawn coach.'

And he laughed and shouted, 'Ha! Knew there was something going on. They're *filming*. Those tripods are cameras. Closed the road to film the coach coming down the hill.'

Twirly could see the coach clearly now. Bright and shimmering, yellow, black and red. People on top. Four chestnut horses. Coming at a trot.

Seen it all before. The pictures.

Dick Turpin with Leslie Banks. *Scarlet Pimpernel* with Leslie Howard. *Wicked Lady* with Margaret Lockwood.

He fancied he could hear jangling spurs.

The Major growled.

'All right, Sir?'

The Major shook his head, turned away from the road and the coach, and scowled at the distant heather-covered hillside.

'Something not quite right, Corporal.'

Twirly heard him mumble something about snipers . . . or a lurking SP gun . . .

'Suggest you send one of your men forward, Corporal.'

Then it came!

That vacuum of intense silence that precedes a massive explosion of sound.

The Major shrieked:
'DOWN!'

The two old soldiers flung themselves flat and slammed their faces into the heather.

Chapter Twenty-two

The midday sun shone bright and warm on the forecourt of The Five Bells in Upper Gently, but Doll was tetchy. All morning she had waited for a telephone call from Budge.

As she had waited all last evening.

It's not as if he has to search for a telephone box which works. He has one of these walkie-talkie telephones; he can call from anywhere, anytime.

She could hear Shane rattling and banging in the back yard collecting the empties for the Wednesday brewery dray.

Funny boy.

Turned up this morning wearing a Foster's Lager T-shirt.

We don't sell Foster's Lager.

'SHANE! Where's the LUNCHES board?

Shane appeared, staggering wide-legged behind a stack of loaded crates and nodded towards the only car in the front-of-pub car park: a black Mondeo with a Cheltenham Museum sticker in the rear window.

'It's out there, Mrs Burnlystock. In front of the car.'

Doll scratched her elbow and jangled her bracelets.

She knows the car, and the strange man with thick glasses sitting inside eating his own sandwiches and reading the Guardian.

Here every Wednesday.

After his sandwiches he comes into the pub for a half-pint-with-a-handle and drinks it in the empty Club Room, and sometimes does some drawing that he covers up if you go in.

'It's going to rain, Mrs Burnlystock,' called Shane cheerfully as he disappeared to search for more empties.

Stupid boy. It's July fifteenth – St Swithin's day. Can't rain today.

She looked up to the horizon above Bancombe Bottom Wood in the general direction in which she supposed Twirly must be walking.

Her heart nose-dived.

The bright blue sky ended in a wall of menacing cloud, black as a funeral.

Twirly clutched at the heather.

VROOM! VROOM!

The ground thumped from the double blast and he flinched from the noise that hurt his head. He looked up to see two low-flying aircraft swinging away along the valley.

They banked steeply and disappeared behind a distant landscape, trailing behind them a creeping barrage of ricocheting echoes.

The stunning silence which followed was pierced by screams.

Twirly lifted his head. Up to the left the coach was continuing down the road.

But not at a trot.

Nor even a spirited gallop.

This was a lurching, headlong, out-of-control disaster.

Bolting terrified horses.

Flailing forelegs.

A driver, too scared to shout, stood on the buckboard heaving backwards on a fistful of reins.

Twirly could hear the screeching iron-rimmed wheels, twisting and striking sparks from granite road-chippings.

Suddenly it was close enough for Twirly to see the wild eyes and flared nostrils of the crazed horses.

He heard the Major gasp beside him.

And more screaming and shouting.

Two cameramen jumped up from their hide and leapt away through the bracken, whilst one stood crouched in frozen fear like a rabbit in front of a stoat.

Now the bolting horses swerved off the road on to a grass track where stout wooden posts allowed *them* to pass through – *but not the coach.* It slammed to a smashing halt with an explosion of splintering timber.

The leather pole-straps tore like strips of paper and the shafts splintered like matches snapped between fingers.

The driver, still grasping the reins, was snatched forward and tossed into waist-high bracken.

The back of the coach reared into the air and a large and probably empty trunk was hurled from the roof to bounce noisily on to the road.

A big brown bundle soared through the air and thumped into bright yellow gorse.

Twirly jumped to his feet and watched the coach slowly keel over like a floundering ship. The bodywork twisted and a door swung open. Three fancy-dressed people tumbled out on to the verge to the sound of smashing glass, with more screams and shouts.

Then silence.

Stunned *still* silence, all fearing what was to come.

The Major snorted, and Twirly watched the ex-officer scramble to his feet aware that his country needed him.

'ANYONE HURT HERE?' he called.

It was the signal for the film industry to return to life.

Coughing

Groaning.

Cursing.

Chuckling.

Retrieving hats and knocking them back into shape.

Touching displaced hair arrangements.

Adjusting deep necklines to make them respectable.

Flexing knees and elbows to see if they were still capable of performing.

Embracing and sobbing.

Someone – Twirly thought it might have been the blackboard boy – wittily called, 'CUT!' and there were loud guffaws of relief.

A young man from the rear of the coach in a long blue coat began leaping through the heather after the horses.

'Leave them, Chris,' called the coachman, now on his feet removing bracken from his hair and wiping blood from a grazed forehead. 'They'll stop when they've had enough.'

A man came running down the road towards them. He wore high yellow boots and a fake tan.

'Everyone all right, darlings?'

'We're all right, Steve,' the coachman called, but he nodded grimly towards the smashed coach and added, 'The *Porlock Flyer* is in a bad way. Six months work there.'

Even as they studied the damage, the offside large rear wheel imploded with a loud crack, and the iron rim with dangling spokes rolled on to the road. The coach groaned a crunching death gurgle and lurched over at an even more alarming angle.

'Right, children!' called the tanned man, clapping his hands for attention. 'Vehicles are on the way down. Everyone back to the hotel to regroup.'

Twirly heard someone in the shuffling, mumbling group ask, 'Where's Harvey?'

Everyone turned to examine each other.

Steve raised his voice again.

'Harvey?'

Silence.

'WHERE IS HARVEY?' demanded Steve.

Someone said, 'He was riding on the rear-dicky.'

Twirly looked at the Major.

Both had seen it.

The flying brown bundle . . .

They dashed across the road and recklessly high-stepped across the bracken and into the gorse.

Twirly got there first.

The brown bundle was lying awkwardly, half buried by the thorny bush of green and yellow, and Twirly ripped the vicious branches aside.

Heavy stage make-up could not disguise the greasy greyness of the skin, nor hide the red bubbling from the mouth like a cluster of deadly-nightshade berries.

204

Nor dim the eyes staring in astonished disbelief – a look Twirly had seen so many times before.

The Major crashed down to kneel by the body and listen for signs of breathing. He looked at Twirly and shook his head.

Twirly watched in surprise as the Major gently inserted his hand under the white lace ruff, already tinted by the berries.

'Sir?'

The Major continued groping.

'His body tag, Corporal.'

'But, Sir,' whispered Twirly. 'He's a 'civvy'.'

The Major started and stared anew at the grey lifeless mask.

'Civilian?' He nodded. 'Course he is – poor sod.' And he struggled to his feet.

The film people stood in horrified silence, each on their marks doing a piece to camera.

The tanned man called, 'Julie. Get an ambulance here immediately.'

The Major held up his hand.

'Better make that the police. This man is dead.'

Instant gasps. And wailings. A fair-haired lady in a cloak of green and gold stepped forward and pointed and screamed, 'Who *is* this man? He is not one of us.' And with both fists raised she advanced towards the Major.

Twirly recognised her immediately.

Anna Fielding.

The tanned man rushed forward and enveloped her in his arms as she slumped into a sobbing heap.

The tanned man looked at the Major with pleading eyes.

'You sure?'

Twirly, still kneeling, put his hand on the forehead of the man who had been Harvey and carefully lowered the greasy eyelids.

Many times – too many times – he had knelt in mud, and damp undergrowth, and on iron-hard sand as hot as a kitchen hearth, and done this for boys too young to die. Not just out of respect for the unfairly departed, but more for the benefit of the unfortunates detailed to bury them in hurried shallow graves.

Hard enough to shovel earth onto a face you have lived and laughed with. Even harder if the eyes you once knew were wide open, questioning your every move.

A pale-faced Budge came stomping over the bracken in slow motion and called, 'Hell's going on, Twirly?'

He gave a quick nervous glance at the brown bundle in the gorse and turned away.

The Major retrieved his jungle hat, slapped it twice against his knee, and carefully placed it in position.

'Corporal. Get the men together.'

He turned to Budge.

'Mr Ballflower, get us away from here, if you please. This is not our show.'

Twirly stood and looked over at the Bambi-eyed girl whom the director had called Julie, and who had now taken over comforting the sobbing star. She became aware of his gaze and looked up, but made no attempt to focus properly. Twirly knew she wasn't seeing a real person. Only Anna Fielding, and Steve and Chris and Harvey were real. Twirly was merely an extra in a film she was already trying to forget.

He turned away and fell-in at the rear of Budge's advancing column of three.

They marched through the urgently descending crowd of pinheads and ignored the questions.

What? How? Who?

The Major turned to shrug and give Twirly a knowing look.

For fifty-odd years the two old soldiers have brushed aside idiotic questions from people who wouldn't want to know, or wouldn't want to understand, the answers.

Budge paused on the summit of Dunkery Beacon. The now-deserted great cairn was surrounded by a collection of stubby pillars, stone-walled circles, and tribal offerings of discarded Coke tins and foil wrappers.

In the sky a tarpaulin of dark cloud was being dragged slowly over from the west, obliterating the bright blue promise of the morning. Distant Porlock Bay lay as grey as stolen roofing lead. Twenty miles beyond crouched the Welsh mountains the colour of Twirly's hat.

Breezes which had merely teased, now violently shook the bracken, like beaters on a shoot.

Get those walkers off the hill!

Half-an-hour later the purple slopes were behind them, and they moved rapidly down through soft green fields with gates marked by yellow arrows. Cows stood surveying them, like embarrassed bystanders watching mourners pass through a cemetery.

By a narrow village green surrounded by pretty pink and cream cottages Budge stopped and said, 'Exford. Lunch.'

They overtook a man wearing a crumpled tweed hat, walking slowly with a stick, each step a triumph. In one hand he carried a small plastic bag with bright red contents.

Twirly stopped and nodded at the bag:

'Strawberries?'

The man's face changed slowly from the exertion of the old into a smile which gradually involved the whole of his seen-it-all face. Small blood-shot eyes shone like hooded rear-lamps on a tractor.

He looked Twirly up and down as if he was mentally measuring him for a suit, then shuffled nearer, and turned to ensure that Exford wasn't listening, and wheezed, ''Tis venison.'

His smile lasted until he was certain that Twirly understood, then he glanced at Twirly's rucksack.

'Walking far?'

'Land's End.'

He slowly measured Twirly for another suit, and turned to study the southwesterly horizon as if expecting to see something appear if he looked hard enough.

He turned back to Twirly and steadied himself. He lifted his stick off the ground, and gently tapped Twirly on the leg.

'You'm better get moving, lad.'

In the flower-decked Crown Inn a smiling young waiter – 'I am coming from Roosendaal near Rotterdam.' – recommended the Exmoor game soup.

Excellent.

They supped in silence until the Major quietly said, 'Must have broken his neck. Wouldn't have known a thing.'

As they prepared to leave the Dutchman asked, 'Do you wish that I fill your water-bottles?'

'Dank oo vel. Heek hartelðk dank,' nodded Twirly, survivor of the snow-buried Ardennes and heated frost-bitten fighting around Venlo on the River Maas.

Twirly took up position in the rear as Budge led them between a school and the garage of Jones and Sons, and past Exmoor Park Maintenance Depot.

In North Court Farm, people on white chairs on their private riverbank waved to them. In a tidy orchard the trees were loaded with Discovery apples. A path rose painfully steeply between high grassy banks.

Near the top Twirly watched Budge pause for breath and heard him say, 'Room Hill – a thousand feet.'

The path levelled where a combe on their left dropped down to a deep-cut river.

'The Exe,' he said.

Twirly looked down the steep sides covered in tufty grass, dislodged mud, loose rocks, shrubs, and snaking brambles.

Budge took off his pack and squatted down on a rusty water-trough.

'How'd you like to scramble down that lot, Twirly?'

Twirly sniffed. And shuddered.

Been there. Done that. February 1943. Tunis.

The First Parachute Battalion was ordered to force the Austrian Mountain Division from the summit of Djebel Mansour – highest hill in the area.

Over on the left was Point 646 which the French Foreign Legion was supposed to have taken, but hadn't. Along the ridge on the right was El Alliliga which the Guards were supposed to have taken, but hadn't.

In a bloody battle, the Austrians were driven from the summit and the para-battalion, which lost half its strength, dug-in. Twirly was amongst the medics who made a precarious sliding descent with loaded stretchers followed by staggering walking-wounded.

Then RAMC Sergeant Eddie Prudden led a handful of volunteers back up for another sweep-and-carry.

Halfway up they were met by the battalion coming down – ordered to retire.

The medics continued to the top and brought down everyone they thought might survive the carry.

Back in the shelter of a deep wadi, Twirly was slumped exhausted with the other bearers, when Prudden scurried along at the crouch and hissed, 'Whippet, a man in a bad way from S Company is fretting about a lost wedding ring. The MO wants someone to go back up and get it.'

Twirly groaned in disbelief.

'Sarge? Back up there? To find a wedding ring?'

Prudden was fiddling with the entrails of a field blood transfusion set and hardly looked up.

'Get going, Whippet. You're not searching for a sodding ring. You're looking for an arm.'

Twirly squatted down by Budge on the water-trough and fumbled in a pocket to produce comforts for the troops: three more squashed sandwiches courtesy of the *Waverley* and the British Legion; three crumpled sachets of brown sauce; three Discovery apples.

The Major added three squirts of brandy to their three mugs of water.

As they dropped down a geometrically interesting path through fields of oblivious cows, over-friendly horses, and tall silver-grey skeletons of thistles, Twirly detected the first drops of rain.

By the time they crossed a stone bridge to climb up to the Royal Oak in the village of Withypool, the drops had got their act together to form an impressively heavy shower.

Twirly watched the Major order his knees to charge uphill, and they gallantly obeyed.

That evening Jake's Bar was crowded but strangely silent.

The ceiling was criss-crossed with beams as black as ebony, and the cream walls busily adorned with hunting prints, stuffed fox heads, mounted deers' feet, and a startling wooden-shafted iron-tipped assegai brought back by a local survivor of the Zulu war.

Tucked behind a pillar Twirly discovered a signed photograph of General Eisenhower who, in May '44, found time to arrive on horseback and sink a quick beer before setting forth to lead the invasion of Normandy.

But Budge appeared to be more interested in the melancholy drinkers.

He hissed, 'Know who these people are?'

He breathed across his beer, 'They're the Dunkery Beacon film crew . . .'

Above the a low hubbub Twirly heard someone say, ' . . . those three walkers . . .'

The Major stepped over to the grey-haired lady in a lavender cardigan whom they had met earlier when she had been tucked into a tiny reception kiosk like a railway ticket office between the stairs and the restaurant.

He spoke quietly.

She turned to study the film people for a moment, then briskly collected three menus and strode over to Twirly and Budge.

'No one in the restaurant tonight. Follow me.'

Twirly peered around the *La Cupule* Restaurant: dimly lit, and quiet as a chapel of rest.

No hunting prints here.

Pink wall-lights illuminated gold-framed pictures of places Twirly had known: Salerno, Algiers, the tilted tower of Pisa, and the temples of Paestum and Hephaisteion, but all without the litter of battle rubble and smashed tanks.

Heavy curtains were pink and blue. Chairs were gold with blue velvet seats. The blue carpet was soft as undertaker's velvet. Tablecloths were white as bed-sheets hung in surrender from nervous mortar-damaged farms along the banks of the Rhine.

The lady led them to a table in the corner and lit a blue candle standing amongst vertical blue napkins and gleaming glasses and enough knives and forks for a Darts Club dinner.

While they studied menus a young man swerved in with a frosted bottle of white wine that he held before the Major.

The Major read:

'Pouilly Fuisse, Vincent Vielles Vignes.'

He rubbed his chin and murmured, 'Think we should check the price first.'

'Oh no, sir,' said the slim young man, nodding his head in the direction of the bar:

'…it's paid for.'

Chapter Twenty-three

Thursday 16th July *Day eleven*

On this glorious morning Budge set a brisk pace along by the river Barle heading for Dulverton.

He stayed in Dulverton in 1965 when his father attended a YMCA conference in the town hall, and early one morning they walked by the river as it slid along at an average speed of almost fourteen miles an hour, so his father said.

This morning he was delighted to discover that the river was exactly as he remembered it: fast flowing, crystal clear, and joyous.

Although now only nine o'clock, the ready-for-anything sun was high in the clear blue vault of sky, causing the river to sparkle like a moving conveyor-belt of diamonds. Glistening pendants of dew still clung to shaded clumps of water forget-me-not and bankside meadow rue.

At sharp bends the exuberant river leaned over to reveal small beaches draped with dangling tree-roots.

Where black gleaming boulders broke the surface like cruising dolphins, the river leapt beside them and chuckled, whipping up foaming white surf. In quieter stretches over beds of shimmering pebbles, the water murmured like well-behaved voices in grammar-school corridors.

The river-meadows were silent and still: nothing moved, except for a squadron of workaholic bees doing the early shift and rummaging in an erratic bush of gorse.

Crickets scraped with early-morning delirium, undeterred by Twirly whacking at thistles with a newly-cut stick of hazel.

Randy up-all-night rabbits still gambolled irresponsibly on a sunlit grassy ridge on the bank opposite.

'Wonderful walk,' called the Major, storming along behind.

Below South Hill farm, a ragged line of stepping-stones stretched across the river like a rosary. Rusty holes in the great granite blocks once held iron handrails.

'You phone Doll yesterday?' called the Major.

Budge scowled, and stopped, and took his machine from his pack.

'Phone her now. Catch you up.'

'It's *you*,' said Doll. 'Expected you to ring *yesterday*.'

'Difficult day yesterday, Doll . . .'

'Are they all right?'

'They are fine.'

'How's the Major?'

'Fine, but tired. Done a hundred miles now, Doll. Walking every day.'

'Don't you give them a day off?'

'Can't do it.'

'Not even *Sundays*?'

'The thing is . . .'

' . . . and you the son of a vicar?'

Budge thought he heard Doll jangling her bracelets.

'What about Twirly?'

'He's doing well. Passing me just now.'

Twirly pointed to a buzzard squatting on a post in the middle of the field.

'Is he eating?'

The buzzard tore viciously with its beak at the ragged victim clamped between its claws.

'With enthusiasm, Doll.'

Twirly, now several paces ahead, lunged at a five foot high thistle and felled it in a single stroke.

'Don't be too long Budge before you call me again.'

The water raced through a wood of ancient oak trees standing as silent as Quakers in a prayer meeting.

213

In some places the path rose fifteen feet above the river and immediately dived down to dip into sparkling pools surrounded by tree roots and slippery boulders.

The Major and Twirly were rocking along well ahead.

In a patch of bracken and high foxgloves, a slim young lady in a loosely flapping blouse and tight yellow trousers drew three handsome red Labradors to the side of the path to allow Budge to pass, and the smell of wet river banks and pungent bracken was instantly suffused by a heady perfume.

'Nice day,' said Budge.

Her reply was a long, cautious smile with dipped eyelashes.

Beautiful river – the Barle.

The Major waved from his seat on a walled circle in the middle of a field from which grew a clump of beech trees. Twirly was ahead standing by stone-built pillars supporting stout steel hawsers, and Budge remembered his father explaining they were installed to prevent debris being carried down-river by winter floods.

In the great flood of August 1952 the main damage came not from a fifteen-foot wall of angry water, but by the fearful flotsam of fencing posts, feeding troughs, and uprooted full-grown trees.

'Mid-morning break,' declared Budge when they reached the riverside paddock of Tarr Steps farm at eleven o'clock.

They sat at picnic tables to drink coffee, with the farm's famous warm doughnuts dribbling their chins with scalding jam.

A handful of families were busy preparing picnics, or calling back their dogs, or throwing, or catching, or playing inventive versions of cricket.

Along the seventeen great slabs of the much-photographed clapper bridge, a few brightly-clad children lay full length pretending to fish.

The Major nodded at the slabs.

'Prehistoric?'

Budge shrugged.

'Some say the name 'Tarr' comes from the Celtic *tochar*, meaning a causeway, suggesting it's Iron Age. More likely to be part of a medieval pack-horse route.'

A small green car appeared on the opposite bank at the head of the ford running alongside the bridge.

It hesitated.

'Too deep,' warned Budge.

But the intrepid car crept forward into the Barle, throwing up a huge bow wave, to the screaming delight of the children on the slabs.

Midstream, it stalled.

A window was wound down and an etiolate-faced passenger peered into the watery depths.

'Twit,' said Budge and, with eyebrows raised, watched Twirly scramble from the picnic table and leap down to the car park.

He reappeared, directing a mud-covered Land Rover down to the water's edge, where the driver dismounted and unwound a cable from the front bumper. Taking this, Twirly waded carefully into the water in his shining wellingtons.

With rolled-up sleeves, he groped about in the river at the front of the marooned car, then stood and waved.

The cable tightened, and the car slowly emerged from the depths, dripping like a surfacing submarine.

Tarr Steps rang to tiny cheers and polite clapping.

Storming along the Hawesbury road on the other side of the bridge, they passed a hotel where the only activity Budge could see was a man morosely creosoting a shed.

The road rose gently, and soon the Barle was glinting twenty feet below at the bottom of a tree-covered slope, and they stopped to lean on a wooden fence.

'Did the man in the car give you anything, Twirly?'

Twirly stood with his eyes closed, smiling like the *Buddha of Polonnaruva*.

'Twenty quid.'

'You give anything to the Land Rover man?'

'Split it.'

'Fifty-fifty?'

'Sort of. Gave him five. Kept fifteen.'

Now they were once again by the river, climbing up tree-covered banks and zooming back down to the water's edge, walking as fast as they had on the flat.

They passed the hill forts of Brewer's Castle and Mounsey Castle, and arrived at a particularly wide stretch of river where on the opposite bank stretched a deep line of rushes, backed by a green meadow.

Budge thought he heard distant laughing, but decided it was the river chortling over some particularly amusing stones.

'How far to lunch?' called the Major.

'The Lion in Dulverton is about an hour. All right?'

The Major nodded but frowned.

'Knees complaining – and the feet singing. It's the pace you know. We've been going like Pollock's forced march to relieve Jelalabad.'

Budge looked around.

The path at this point consisted of large smooth boulders lapped by the rippling river.

He slung off his pack, wrenched off his boots, peeled off steaming socks, and plunged his feet into the icy water.

'Five minutes paddling time.'

The Major did the same.

Budge watched Twirly arrive and stand with a disapproving glare. Finally he took off his rucksack, sat down on the rocks, and gingerly lowered his wellingtons into the water.

'Nice,' he said and distributed three small plums.

'Tree near Withypool Post Office,' he explained.

The water swirled happily around their legs and Budge watched Twirly skilfully skimming flat stones across to a patch of rushes with yellow iris flowers.

'Think there's a moorhen in there,' he said.

'HELLO!'

A woman's voice.

'Hello there!'

The voice again.

'Would you fellows kindly consider moving on? We were bathing when you arrived, and we dived into the rushes. *The water is FREEZING and we want to get out!'*

Still no sign of anyone, although Budge detected movement in the rushes.

Budge called, 'Can't see you. But why don't you just get out?'

The water chuckled and babbled.

And the woman's voice again.

'We are skinny dipping.'

Pause.

'We aren't wearing *costumes.'*

Budge noticed the Major slowly lift the brim of his jungle hat, while Twirly scratched around for another skimming-stone.

'We've got to put boots back on,' Budge called. 'Take ages. Just get out and run.'

He looked at the Major for confirmation.

'We won't look.'

But they did.

A plumpish girl with moorhen black hair leapt out on to the bank, swooped up a handful of garments, and disappeared behind a group of pollarded willows. She was followed by a shimmering, dripping shapely figure as white as the basilica of *Sacré-Coeur,* with streaming shockingly blonde hair.

'Let's go,' said Budge, lifting his dripping frozen feet from the water.

As he walked he remembered the gorgeous Inga-Lisa.

Twenty-five years ago he was in Sweden where he took the sleeper to Lapland beyond the Arctic Circle to walk from Abisko to Kvikkjokk on the two hundred and twenty mile Kung's Leden *path pioneered in the 1930s by Swedish Boy Scouts.*

Back in Stockholm he visited the Carl Milles sculptural garden, to see the Flying Angels *perched on pillars and other wondrous works.*

One evening in the Kallamästare *fish restaurant in the old town of* Gamla Stan *he became aware of her as he toyed with his* sursild. *She was tall, tanned and fiercely blonde, sheathed in a green slip of a dress and little else, and stood swaying like a daffodil.*

She smiled at him and wandered over – lonely as a cloud.

'You are English, I think,' she purred.

She let him take her everywhere.

Lunch at the Operakällaren *with its chandeliers, and breathtaking prices. They dined even more expensively in romantic cubicles in the seventeenth-century* Stallmästaregarden.

In the lofty Moorish courtyard restaurant within the Grand Hotel, *with its balconies on the fourth floor, and indoor lawns of real grass in front of the orchestra, he cruelly abused his credit cards.*

In a poorly lit bar she softly took both his hands.

'John, do you know about Biffidder Yin?'

His heart pounded. He didn't.

She had a word with the barman, and he produced a bottle of Beefeater Gin.

At Arlanda airport he asked for her address so he could write.

'No, John,' she sighed. 'Don't write. Torbjorn is so jealous. Yes?'

On the plane he sat overcome with angst, *and gazed sadly at the clouds, and moaned to himself the mantra she had taught him:*

Ett tva tre,

Fyra fem sex,

Sju atta - nio tio.

They stormed along the river path and paused at Marsh Bridge where a smiling lady sold them piled-high ice-cream cornets. They marched through Kennel Farm, where shortsighted chickens pecked at pebbles in the rough track.

Over a five-arched bridge they crossed into Dulverton near the old maternity hospital, now the headquarters of Exmoor National Park.

New to Budge was a bronze statue of Lorna Doone on a grass island near the car-park, commissioned by the president of the American Lorna Doone Society.

The bar of the Lion was busy.

The Major got the beers in and collected three menus from a dark-haired girl with a ponytail.

He reported, 'Special of the day is smoked trout salad.'

'I'll have that,' said Twirly.

The Major raised his eyebrows, but Twirly quickly downed the remains of his Bishop's Finger, slapped the empty glass on the bar, and snapped smartly to attention.

'Back in a minute, Sir.'

About-turn-to-the-right and out of the pub.

The Major called after him, 'We'll be at the far table under the Steam Fair poster.'

'Hell's he up to *now?*' growled Budge.

The Major shrugged and studied the menu.

Budge continued, 'Doll was very concerned about him.'

'Yes, she would be. Think I'll have the tuna-stuffed peppers.'

Budge chose the ham ploughman's, then read aloud the poster.

'Steam Fair, Thorverton, Sunday 19th July. Largest assembly of steam vehicles in the Southwest. Logging and steam-ploughing. Swap-shop and . . . '

Twirly reappeared carrying a large pale blue bag with the legend *Lance Nicholson*, which he briskly stuffed under his chair.

'Quick shop, Corporal?'

'Yessir.'

'Well?'

Twirly leaned over to check the bag was still there, and sniffed.

'Last night, Sir. On them velvet chairs. My old trousers didn't look right. Been and bought a new pair.'

The pony-tailed girl placed a handful of cutlery wrapped in red paper napkins on their table.

'Not jeans I hope, Corporal? Mess regulations . . .'

'No, Sir. Not jeans. The man said they were knitted cotton with an elasticated waist. Weigh only eleven ounces.'

The Major nodded in approval.

'Capital. Colour?'

'Chocolate.'

'Practical. Well done, Corporal. Very well done.'

The waitress carefully slid the trout salad in front of Twirly and paused to look at the Major for approval.

'Ah yes,' said the Major. 'I took the liberty, Corporal of also ordering you a plate of chips.'

Even as he spoke the chips arrived.

Twirly looked stunned, and studied them, then peered at the Major.

Other-ranks don't smile at officers – might be mistaken for insubordination.

'Sir,' he said quietly.

The Major noticed for the first time that Twirly had eyes similar to the Geordie batman who was with him throughout Korea, and who usually managed to present him with a mess-tin of something edible in the evenings, while the remainder of the Mess were obliged to dine on Compo.

Budge said, 'Anyway, Major. Who *was* this Jean? Was she the queen of trousers?'

The ploughman's and stuffed-peppers arrived.

'There was no Jean, Mr Ballflower. Comes from *Gene*, the old word for a sailor from Genoa.'

Medieval English sailors often saw Genoese in Mediterranean ports, with their trousers ending just below the knee. Very practical. Began wearing them. Referred to them as 'Gene's breeches'. *Eventually shortened to* 'jeans'.

'What about denims?' asked Budge, pressing a fork into a pickled onion.

'Ah,' said the Major . . .

In the sixteenth-century a heavy twilled cotton was woven in Nimes in the south of France. Called serge de Nimes.

Then in the Californian gold rush of the 1840s a Bavarian immigrant undertook the horrendous 13,000 miles sea journey around the Horn of South America with a large stock of merchandise to sell to hopeful miners.

This included several bales of this material, now known simply as denim, *which he intended to sell as tent material.*

Sold most of his stock to the 'forty-niners', but couldn't shift the denim. No one wanted tents that sagged when wet and wouldn't dry.

But one day he was asked for a pair of heavy-duty trousers which could stand up to the rigours of mining and an unrelenting diet of beans and rancid bacon.

The Bavarian was not in the habit of refusing the odd dollar and he quickly got a tailor to make up a pair from his non-selling stock. An obliging mining engineer reinforced the stitching with copper rivets.

The miner was delighted.

So was the Bavarian.

Soon he was employing hundreds of workers and he – Mr Levi Strauss – became a millionaire.

Outside the Lion, Budge said, 'Let's do this fast. Three miles to go.'

They checked into the Anchor Inn at Exebridge.

Budge threw his backpack on to the single bed, and his portable telephone rang.

It was Doll.

'Budge, m'duck. Arthur Wilkins says English Heritage people have been back poking around Fish House all day. Measuring everything. Even the outside toilet.'

A long pause.

'Something's up, Budge. Do you think you should warn Twirly?'

Chapter Twenty-four

Friday 17th July *Day twelve*

Twirly sat at a picnic table in the rear of the Anchor Inn with his Morris man's hat full of black and red blackberries.

An early morning blue sky was streaked with white clouds like swollen vapour trails from a squadron of Lancasters.

Stretching from the corner of his table to a scorched brick barbecue hung a long strand of glistening thread, spun by a spider with great aspirations.

A good sign: spiders don't waste skills on complicated constructions when bad weather is on the way.

Twirly looked around. This was a place popular with loose bowelled rabbits. Last night a local told him about rabbits and food supplies during the war.

Every night except Sundays, the GWR ran a 'rabbit-special' along the old Barnstaple to Taunton line, and then up to Smithfield's Market in London. Fifteen thousand rabbits at a time. From Dulverton station alone they used to pick up two thousand a night.

'Morning, Corporal.'

The Major stared at the blackberries.

Twirly nodded towards the pub.

'She wants them for a pie. You have the porridge, Sir?'

'Mushroom omelette, Corporal. Capital.'

'Budge about?'

'Only just down for breakfast. Not particularly communicative. Probably worried about his schedule. Or perhaps he's weary too. A 48-hour pass would not go amiss.'

A cheeky robin made a heavy landing on the table and Twirly rolled a blackberry towards it. A quick sideways blink of disgust, and it was gone.

Budge snorted at the heavy traffic outside the hotel.

At a hexagonal toll-house like a Crawford's biscuit tin they scurried across a confusion of road junctions, dodging late-for-work drivers who drove directly at them and hooted in annoyance when they missed.

Half-an-hour later, by a trig point seven hundred and eighty feet up in a field of shoulder-high maize, Budge stopped and looked back.

Below stretched a crumpled map of dark woods, with green meadows, and fields of yellow rape, and blue flax, dotted with half-hidden hazy villages. Ten miles away lay the grey horizon of Dunkery Beacon – still in mourning.

'Right,' he said. 'That was Somerset. Now for Devon . . .'

When he rang this morning, his foreman insisted on reminding him that everybody was booked to begin work on Monday, third of August. Two weeks away and a hundred and thirty miles still to do.

Hell's bells.

Not sure the old warriors can keep up this pace.

He stretched his legs, one after the other.

Not sure I can.

'Let's go,' he sighed.

In the village of Bampton a large plaster swan with outstretched wings perched on the porch of a white building smothered in flowers – the fifteenth century Swan hotel.

In a bar, with the only-just-opened smell of polish and disinfectant, Budge ordered three pints of Wivelscombe Tawny Bitter.

The lady served the beers and smiled.

'Lunches start at twelve.'

A man in a dark suit peered around the high back of a Tudor settle.

'Morning,' he called waving an invitation to join him.

'Assume you are walking the Exe Valley Way.'

Budge sipped his beer and sat down by the dark suit.

The Major nodded towards the mass of flowers filling a deeply recessed fireplace.

'Wonderful display.'

The man pushed away some papers in front of him.

'Flowers are important in this village. Once won an award in the Village-in-Bloom competition. You heading for Dulverton or Tiverton?'

'Tiverton.'

'Ah.' The man drank from his glass of red wine. 'I apologise for the miserable route.'

The pub lady brought three menus.

The man continued, 'It was originally intended to make use of the railway that closed in 1963. Could have been one of the finest long-distance walks in England, from the city of Exeter along the Exe valley to Exmoor, and onto the coast at Barnstaple and Bideford. Marvellous.'

'The Lake District attracts six million walkers a year. Just think what that could have done to *our* local economy – Tiverton and Bampton as prosperous as Keswick and Kendal

He sipped his wine again.

'But in fact, none of the route from here to Tiverton *is* along the old railway. It's all narrow high-hedged lanes with no pavements. Eight miles shared with cars and tractors. Every morning a milk-board tanker goes through like an enema to keep the lanes open.

'What happened?' Budge asked.

'Lethargy. Lack of vision. Perhaps a touch of corruption?

He picked up a pen and slid it into an inside pocket, and held up a finger:

'However. There *is* another route. Two miles longer, but most of it on footpaths. A high-level route with wonderful views across the valley. 'You got a map?'

On the village outskirts they crossed a stone bridge over the River Batherm and took an ancient footpath threatened by an upstart housing estate.

After a mile of gentle climbing they were high on Bampton Down ridge. The dark suit was right. Magnificent views in all directions.

At the end of an almost buried grass lane the path passed in front of two cream cottages with slated roofs and paddocks with horses.

Three Corners Farm.

'What we got here then?' said Budge.

A white Devon County Council minibus stood alongside a blue build-it-yourself horsebox. Behind them, in a bed of nettles, partly concealed under a green tarpaulin, crouched a rusting steam engine.

Budge knows about steam.

An old Burrell 8-hp double crank compound.

He saw Twirly gasp, and stand like Paul on the road to Damascus, then leap forward to dive under the cover. He clambered up onto the footplate and peered at the array of rusting controls – chuckling and making noises like a vet consoling a sick dog.

'Used to drive one of these . . .'

Budge watched him wrestle with a jammed brake-wheel, and rattle an immovable reversing lever, and smack a rust-red firebox door with the remains of a shovel.

'Me and Billy Hargreaves. Towing a Marshall threshing-drum and straw-elevator. All over the county.'

Budge *also* had a Damascus moment and remembered the Steam Fair poster in the pub and Doll's admonishment about Sunday walking.

He could feel his knees grinning . . .

His eyes narrowed, and he smiled for the first time that morning.

He spoke carefully with mellifluous innocence:

'You interested in steam at all, Major Legge Wellesley?'

From the pristine gardens of Shute Farm a splendidly maintained terraced path dropped steeply through recently mown bracken.

In the hamlet of Cove, opposite a cottage with a bell-tower, a bridleway ran down a harvested hay-field. On the hillside ahead rose a green expanse of fir-forest. Down across a stream, a wicket-gate opened into the plantation.

The accountant-looking man in the pub had said vaguely, 'Go up through the wood.'
> *But here the path divided three ways. Not a waymark in sight. Hell!*

While Budge pondered, Twirly pressed a foil-wrapped biscuit into his hands.
> 'Girl doing the rooms,' he explained.
> Budge chose the middle path, and pushed into the gloom of the tightly packed trees.
> The gloom got deeper, with yet another choice of ways.
> *Blast!*
> He had a map, and a compass, but again he took a chance.
> Initially he followed deep horseshoe marks but these soon disappeared and the track became a confusion of fallen branches and unexplained lumps of spongy turf.
> Gloomier and danker.
> Bright green patches became pools of black stagnant water. Brambles snagged their shirts. Hidden rocks tripped them. Lengths of rusty wire from fallen posts snatched at their feet. Tree trunks swathed in green moss edged in even closer and they were obliged to cower beneath the branches.
> Twirly called, 'We lost, Budge?'
> 'Of course we are not lost. We're in Yonderdown Wood.'
> Twirly sniffed and stood pointing.
> 'Only it's that clump of red-fly toadstools. Noticed them because they're earlier than we see them in Withington Woods. We passed them several minutes ago.'
> Budge glared at the group of red, white-speckled, flat-topped fly agaric toadstools surrounded by a cluster of small red knobs, and vaguely recalled seeing them earlier.

He leaned against a bank of orange soil sprouting root tentacles of a long dead tree and shuddered. It was like the interior of the Crichton family mausoleum that he had opened up last year to install a cremation urn.

There he had groped in the chaos of greasy spiders' webs, and gasped at the foulness of the damp air, and tripped on scattered timbers of collapsed coffins, and crunched queasily over unthinkable . . .

'You all right, Mr Ballflower?'

Budge glared into the gloom.

The Major continued, 'Only I'm a little concerned about the lichen on the tree trunks. It's changed sides. We've shifted our line of advance, Mr Ballflower.'

Budge wearily brushed a hand across his forehead.

The Major said quietly, 'Do you suppose I might have a look at your map a moment? And may I borrow your compass?'

Ten minutes later they stood blinking in bright sunlight on a dazzling white concrete farm road.

The Major said, 'Gogwell Lane, I believe.'

He produced a small bottle of Lucozade and his brandy, and they sank on to the grass verge.

Refreshed and walking again, Budge made up his mind.

Steam fair and rest-day on Sunday. Sod the walking.

The walk from Firebeacon Farm was glorious, and views to Middlehill two miles across the sun-filled valley were astounding.

They passed quickly along delightful trails of soft red earth and sheep-nibbled grass, until in Knightshayes Home Farm they were checked by a rope stretched across the path.

A flurry in a barn, and a young woman in a nicely contoured green pullover with trousers tucked into wellingtons and wearing enormous pearl earrings rushed to lift the barrier to allow them to pass.

She smiled at Budge with a sort of explanation.

'Expecting the cows.'

The village of Bolham consisted of a handful of cottages, a school, a shop selling ice-cream, a high sadly surplus railway bridge – and the three-star Dower House Hotel.

The Major was delighted with his room.

It is an English tradition that single rooms must be miniscule, overlook the hotel's dustbins, and be adjacent to whining service lifts.

This was a proper room.

A tall sash-window overlooked well-ordered gardens where a grey squirrel scampered in low urgent bounds across a smooth expanse of lawn, dodging yellow umbrellas scattered like primroses.

A full-length mirror adjacent to a power point made the room appear larger. Pictures on the walls looked pleased to be there.

Tucked away in a pale wardrobe were a trouser press, a folding ironing-board, a Morphy Richards iron and a Kenwood hairdryer.

The Major purred with pleasure. A complete *dhobi wallah* kit.

He removed his Corrymoor mohair knee-length socks. Off with his Lord Winston shirt. Off with his breeches. Off with the admirable Alex Tilley's Endurable briefs.

From a bottle of Hindon water on a silver tray he filled a heavy-based tumbler, and enlivened it with a generous tincture of brandy.

Finally, he sank slowly and blissfully into a great bath of perfumed whispering froth like a moustachioed Ophelia.

After dinner – roast breast of duck with lime and orange marmalade for the Major; tenderloin of Wiltshire pork with sage and onion stuffing for Budge; and steak and kidney pie for Twirly – the Major insisted they deserved a nightcap.

The waiter suggested he deliver the drinks to the television room.

'It's quieter.'

Twirly held up his hand.

'That noise. The knocking and laughing. Is that skittles?'
The waiter was impressed.
'Indeed it is, Sir,' and sped off calling, 'Coming table four . . .'
But he skidded to a halt: and pirouetted to return and whisper, 'Does Sir skittle?'

It was a sad tale. One of the Dower's best players was inconvenienced – his wife's mother again – and it was important that the hotel thrashed The Four in Hand from Tiverton.

'Do a bit,' admitted Twirly.
The waiter almost wept.
'If Sir could possibly consider . . .'
Twirly took his leave and weaved along behind the waiter.

The television room was a maroon and gold haven with subdued pink wall-lights and a television inanely talking to itself. A crop-headed, sharp-nosed comedy actor playing the part of an archaeologist was spitting with excitement about a broken tea-cup he had found in a medieval midden.
Budge snorted and switched him off, and the quasi archaeologist shrank to a bright dot and disappeared.
The room was crowded with oversize chairs and sofas like a furniture-shop window.
Budge sank down into a great pile of soft gold velour.
'Impressed by the way you rescued us from the wood, Major. Thank you.'
The Major shrugged and lowered himself onto a grey velvet sofa as large as a crouched elephant.
'Far East Training School at Kohta Tinggi, southern Jahore. Taught jungle navigation.'
Budge swirled his brandy balloon.
'Expect Yonderdown Wood *is* like a jungle.'
The Major chuckled.
'My dear Budge, a Malay *Sakai* aboriginal would consider Yonderdown Wood to be open ground. He would build an *atap* on

229

stilts, plant fruit trees, grow purple hibiscus flowers, cultivate paddy fields and raise a platoon of snotty-nosed, doe-eyed offspring.'

He inhaled the brandy.

'The Malayan jungle is dense, Budge. Really dense. Like moving about in a full broom-cupboard in a hot boiler-room.'

From the distant skittlers came a muffled cheer.

Budge said, 'Doll is worried about English Heritage measuring up Twirly's Fish House.'

'English Heritage? Why on earth would they do that?'

'Probably because they own it. Twirly has it for a peppercorn rent. Expect they plan to do it up and open it to the public. Only one other like it, and that's near Glastonbury.'

'And Twirly?'

A slight sound caused them both to turn to look at the door.

The brass knob was turning.

Twirly?

But it was a white jacket and check trousers which appeared around the door.

'I trust the meal was to your liking, gentlemen.'

The Major put his glass on a low table and jumped to his feet.

'Ah, Chef. Meant to come and find you. My roast duck was the finest I have ever tasted,' and he stepped forward with his arm outstretched.

Too late he saw the right-sleeve was empty and pinned.

'I'm sorry,' he stammered. 'I didn't . . .'

The ruddy-faced chef chuckled, raised his left arm and grasped the Major's hand.

'Don't worry about the arm, Sir. Jerry took that from me years ago.'

The Major shrugged his regret, then studied the smiling face in astonishment.

'But if you don't mind me saying so, Chef, you look too young. . .'

The man threw back his head and laughed.

'Not *that* Jerry. The other bloody Jerry. Some of his leprechauns decided they could best serve Ireland by blowing up my cook-house - Wellington Barracks in Dorset.

The Major shook his head.

'Very unlucky . . .'

'No, Sir. *Not* unlucky. In fact, just the opposite. They *killed* two of my cooks, *and* a poor squaddie doing jankers, *and* the lady who cycled into camp every morning with the papers.'

Saturday 18th July   *Day thirteen*

Budge was awakened by the sound of rain tapping on the sill of the open window. Tyres swished on the road beyond the trees.

At nine o'clock, crouching in rustling wet-gear, they scampered across the gleaming A396 road and briskly passed Bolham Primary School – *'Alice' is to be performed by the pupils on Wednesday.*

A dripping newspaper-board outside the ice-cream shop announced: *LIME REGIS DISASTOR.*

Budge turned to check he was being followed by his cocooned companions.

'Hell you got on your head, Twirly?'

The hood on Twirly's orange waterproof had fallen back to reveal his head encased in clear plastic decorated with pretty pink flowers.

Twirly growled into his jacket, 'It was in a little box in the bathroom.'

Budge snorted.

'It's to wear in a shower.'

Twirly looked up into the cascading raindrops.

'Well?'

They passed the gates to the National Trust Knightshayes Court, and splashed along Curly Lane.

By ten o'clock they were in the old lace-making town of Tiverton. Opposite a Garden of Remembrance they turned off the road into an area where empty children's swings stood observing a weeping two minute silence.

The sky was a troubled inferno of swaying, heaving curtains of rain.

231

An optimistic blue and white sign said *Tiverton Castle*, but Budge thought the red Devon sandstone building with Georgian windows looked more like Social Security offices than a stronghold of the realm despite its impressive gateway and castellation works.

At the lych-gate to St Peter's he said, 'There's some carvings here I need to see.'

John Greenway was a sixteenth century Tiverton cloth merchant who managed to gain membership of the exclusive London Merchant Venturers – wily merchants who built armed vessels to export goods across seas made dangerous by piracy.

In 1517, now wealthy, he donated a chantry chapel to St Peter's and commissioned masons to carve images of some of his ships on the outside parapets.

In 1983 the carvings were restored at a cost of £150,000 using stone from the original quarries in the Devonshire fishing village of Beer.

Budge noted that whilst he stood squinting up at the carvings with eyes pummelled by raindrops, the Major and Twirly sensibly stood silently pious inside the church porch, dripping a rhythmic chant on to the encaustic-tiled floor.

When he had seen enough he shook himself like a dog leaping from a lake and joined them by a shelf between two brass vases of Michaelmas daises where a visitors' book lay open.

He took a pen and signed:
John Ballflower, Upper Gently – 18 July, 1998.
He ran his eyes up the page.
And his dripping eyebrows lifted.
A few lines above his entry he read:
Annabelle Clayton, Royal Tunbridge Wells.
Sophia Forrest, Toronto.
He checked the date – 15 July, 1998.

The girl with eyes like emeralds was here three days ago.

Chapter Twenty-five

A town astride the River Exe once had two fords, and was called Two-ford Town. *This became* Twyford-ton. *And eventually* Tiverton.

While Budge visited the Information Centre in Phoenix Lane, the Major and Twirly went to the rose-garden opposite dedicated to those who died in the Burma campaign.

In the Four-and-Twenty Blackbirds Tea Shoppe they fortified themselves with rum-laced coffee.

When they left the town the rain was still hammering on their hoods, and they splashed along a puddled concrete road, with damp water-meadows stretching over on their right.

A fortress of high chain-link fencing loomed out of the rain blocking their progress. A dripping sign warned: South West Water Waste Treatment – KEEP OUT.

There was no waymark, but Twirly spotted a narrow passage squeezed between the concentration-camp fence and a high briar-filled hedge.

Budge fumed, 'Amazing, Major. They pamper motorists with signs as big as garden sheds. Scatter verges with arrows the size of field gates in case drivers fail to notice there's a bend. Paint white lines to help feeble-minded drivers locate the middle of the road – but find it impossible to send a man out with a tin of yellow paint for a morning to daub a few footpath arrows.'

The Major, buried deep inside his noisy hood, grunted.

'Quite right, Mr Ballflower, *ghastly* weather.'

Twirly led the way over Mid-Devon District Council's amusing version of a stile, and disappeared between the overhanging hedge and the fence, scurrying along at a crouch, like a runner in a First World War trench.

For more than an hour they squelched across soggy meadows, waded through boot-filling streams, and scrambled over slimy green fences where no stiles could be found.

Stretches of muddy forest tracks took them through a car-wash of low branches and spiteful, gangling brambles.

'This is rubbish,' fumed Budge.

On the other side of the Exe they could clearly see the railway embankment where they *might* have been strolling but for the incompetence of councillors and the machinations of bastard landowners.

At twelve-thirty they arrived at Bickleigh's five-arched 1630s bridge, which the guidebook claimed was the inspiration for Simon and Garfunkel's 'Bridge over Troubled Water', and they stormed over despite it being raked by 9mm raindrops.

At twelve-thirty-one they put in an attack on *Fisherman's Cot*, and burst into the bar.

The silence, after the constant tattoo of raindrops, was deafening. The dryness of the air stung their eyes and made them blink.

They threw back their hoods and stood surveying each other, and Budge quickly checked for booby-traps and the customary 'NO BOOTS' signs.

There were none.

'Take off those wet clothes, lads,' cried a cheerful young lady in a crisp blouse looking dry enough to self-ignite.

She reminded Budge of the Salvation Army songster he met in Stoke-on-Trent.

'Pegs by the door,' she called.

'Three rum and blackcurrants,' he sang, to the tune of 'Rescue the Perishing'.

By the time they had peeled of their wet-suits and loosened their steaming shirts, the drinks were lined up on the bar.

He watched Twirly, flushed and glistening, remove his shower cap and extract wet money from a rain-filled pocket to order three chaser-pints of Cotleigh Brewery's Tawny Bitter.

At a table far from rain-scudding windows they fondled and studied menus enclosed in padded maroon folders, dry and comforting as hot-water bottles.

They had chicken and chips.

Wonderful.

While they were weighing the merits of sponge pudding against treacle tart with custard, the Sally lady called, 'It's stopped raining.'

Windows at the far side of the bar were still obscured by sliding water, but drops were no longer bouncing from picnic tables in the flower garden which stretched down to the Exe.

Budge waited for the Major and Twirly to exclaim, 'Oh good!'

But they didn't.

Now! This is the time.

'Men,' said Budge. 'We've been walking for two weeks. I think we should take a day off. Good for all of us.'

He turned to the Major.

'Tomorrow will be Sunday, and we'll be in the village of Thorverton. You could attend morning-service.'

He then turned to Twirly.

'We might go to the steam-fair. Look around. Grab some lunch. And there'll be all kinds of events in the afternoon.'

He awaited a response.

None.

Twirly sat staring out at the glistening garden.

The Major unfolded a large white handkerchief which he had somehow preserved from damp.

Eventually he turned to Budge.

His eyes were moist. His voice was soft.

'Mr Ballflower, on behalf of the men . . .' and he snuffled the handkerchief below his nose and mopped his bedraggled moustache.

He suddenly pushed back his chair, eased himself to his feet and jutted up his chin.

'Delightful as is the prospect, Mr Ballflower, one is obliged to ask, how would this affect our schedule?'

Budge strode over to the pegs and returned with their combined wet-gear and beamed at the Major.

'I think the words are – "if necessary we'll temporize to meet the exigencies of the service."'

And to Twirly, he said, 'And when opportunities occur – we'll cheat.'

Their pace along the valley road was fast.

The Major said, 'That sign, Mr Ballflower, EXETERIO. Some connection with Roman incursions into the valley?'

'It says, *Exeter ten miles*, Major.'

For a mile beyond Bickleigh Castle the going was flat until they reached the white buildings of Traymill Farm. Here the tarmac lane narrowed and a strip of grass sprinkled with buttercups ran along the centre and began to climb.

After nearly a mile they gained five hundred feet according to the map, and they passed a damp farmyard stuffed with dripping wrecks of agricultural machinery, looking like the toy-box of a spoilt child. Somewhere a damp dog made a half-hearted protest.

At a bend further up the hill, opposite the neat flower-box fronted Little Stone cottage, Budge peered into a large green metal barn. It was full of aircraft engines and propellers.

A sign rising from more flower-boxes declared *Arrow Aviation Services Ltd.*

Soon the sun had driven off the clouds and the valley below was shaking itself dry.

At the top of a steep combe in almost vertical fields, cows that might have been trained by Chipperfields grazed precariously above Pitt Farm.

'We'll stop here for a moment,' said Budge. 'We've finished climbing. Now downhill all the way to Thorverton.'

They sat on a high grass bank and Twirly produced a bag of crumbled pastry and jam.

'Tarts from Dower House skittles team.'

They each scooped out a handful.

The views were spectacular.

Budge was reminded of balcony seats in an Imax cinema as they sat overlooking the half-mile-wide green valley floor. The newly arrived sun glinted on the Exe meandering below around an ox-bow island near Chitterley.

Suspended above the valley in the rear of retreating clouds arched a rainbow looking so solid you could train roses up it. A radio-tower on Christ Cross two miles away reminded Budge of the seventy foot statue of the Redeemer in gleaming white marble standing with arms outstretched high above the town of Maratea on the Italian coast, carved in 1965 by Bruno Innocenti and inspired by the statue above South America's Rio de Janeiro.

He watched Twirly lead the way down into Thorverton at a cracking jolting pace, his flat black hat bobbing like that of an Italian priest late for confession.

At four-thirty they entered a village of cottages so brilliantly white they dazzled the eyes. Flowers bloomed everywhere: in tubs, pots, baskets, and concrete troughs lining two small bridges across a stream bordering Jubilee Green.

The seventeenth century Thorverton Arms had been a coach staging-house on the Cullompton to Crediton route, and Budge's guidebook said it was originally called The Dolphin.

'Tea and cakes for three wise men,' called Budge in a loud voice.

A smiling man appeared.

'Wise men?'

'Wiser than we were two weeks ago, that's for sure,' said Budge.

After dinner at a table beneath a golden-framed Pears soap poster of a blue velvet boy blowing bubbles, Twirly took his wellingtons into the rear car park and found a tap where he scrubbed them Household Cavalry clean.

Back in the bar, his eyes were caught by the intense gaze of a rotund, weather-beaten man.

There's somebody who knows how to dodge gamekeepers, and can probably still set a snare.

He nodded.

The man nodded back.

Sunday 19th July *Day fourteen*

After mid morning coffee Budge sat in his room overlooking the courtyard with the Ordnance Survey 1:25,000 map spread before him.
He needed to devise a suitable walking route into Exeter.

The Exe Valley Way runs reasonably enough from Thorverton along by the river to the villages of Brampford Speke and Cowley, but then dismally follows the unattractive A396 into Exeter for over a mile.

Must be something better.
He eventually located a route which included a stretch between Brampford Speke and Stoke Cannon actually running for half-a-mile along the shamefully lost hundred miles of railway, then up over the 300-feet Huxham Brake, passing the lofty Roman signal station on Stoke Hill, and joining the Exeter Green Circle Walk to drop easily down into the city via Duryard Valley Park, the University, Hoopern Valley, Bury Meadow Park, and Queen Street to the Cathedral.
Perfect.
Well pleased, he packed away the map and guide books and went down to the bar to meet the Major and Twirly for coffee as arranged.

'Manage to find your church, Major?'
'Church of St Thomas of Canterbury. Has a memorial to a young lieutenant of the Devons attached to the 11th East African Division – King's African Rifles. Buried in Imphal.'
'Tell them of us and say, for your tomorrow we gave our today.'
Budge looked round the bar.
'Twirly?'
'Be with us in a moment. Some old boy, a fellow poacher I suspect, took him for a long walk in the woods to show him a secret bunker.'
'Air raid shelter?'
'Good heavens, no. Called an Operational Base. This chap

was an explosives expert with a secret guerrilla unit of local men when Jerry was expected in 1940.'

'Of course,' sighed Budge.

It was one of the best-kept secrets of World War II.

When England was daily expecting invasion from across the Channel, volunteers with intimate knowledge of the area and able to live off the land assembled under tight security in six-man groups.

A thirty-three-year old Guards Officer, Peter Fleming, brother of the 007 Ian Fleming, devised training programmes to show them how to fight an underground war. During the day they worked. At nights and weekends they trained.

If the invasion happened they would leave their homes and take to underground shelters built in great secrecy in woods and embankments. These were stocked with food, ammunition and explosives. Here they would stay, unsupported, carrying out guerrilla attacks on the occupying troops for as long as they were able ...

They received no pay. And until a long time after the war, no official recognition.

With muddy wellingtons Twirly hastened into the bar where Budge and the Major stood waiting.

'Right!' he said.

'You find your dug-out, Twirly?'

'Great,' said Twirly. 'But in a sorry state. Ought to be restored and opened to the public. A part of our history. Should be taken over by English Heritage and ...'

He stopped.

The Major and Budge were exchanging guilty glances, and looking as uneasy as if they were caught in an orchard with pockets full of apples.

He glared at them.

'What's wrong with English Heritage?'

The Major waved his hand.

'Nothing. Worthy institution, Corporal. Suggest we get to the fair.'

Twirly looked his officer up and down and was impressed.

Although he was wearing the clothes that Twirly had seen every day for a fortnight, he still managed to look as if he was dressed in his Sunday-best.

Perhaps it was the sprig of bright yellow laburnum stuck in his jungle hat like a fusilier's cockade.

Twirly pushed out of the bar. He knew the way. Edward had told him.

'Turn right from the pub, a mile down the road, just over the river, on Latchmore Green.'

Passing a yard on the edge of the village he heard Budge behind him call, 'Site of the old railway station.'

A grey stone building stood on a slight rise.

A pre-Beeching wagon-height gauge still hung like a gallows.

Soon Twirly's nose twitched.

Coal smoke!

He turned and grinned.

The Major strode along as if the battalion was marching behind him accepting the freedom of some city and he gave a jaunty wave.

It was at the river-bridge that Twirly first heard the music, a confusion of jangling and shrill trebles, with heavy thumping earth-moving bass.

Fairground organs! Glorious.

He quickened his step, knowing they would keep up.

At the gate he paid.

It was breathtaking.

Like a hundred Upper Gently feast-days. A field of colour; and the noise of rumbling machines and hissing steam; and the smells of hot coal and oil, all beneath a canopy of swirling smoke suspended from a bright blue sky.

Curving away from them ran a line of shimmering-wheeled giants contentedly rocking and rumbling, with gleaming paintwork and dazzling brass.

Twirly turned to urge them on, struggling to suppress a stupid grin.

Budge looked like someone who had just scored double-top.

The Major had his chin up, with cane at the slope, marching along the line of engines and nodding as if he was inspecting a magnificently turned-out guard of honour.

Each engine swayed with its own thudding rhythm of slapping drive-belts, and swishing pistons, and whirring fore-mounted dynamos and sliding rods moving as smoothly and sweetly as the hands of a district-nurse.

Every firebox threw off face-scorching heat and Twirly grinned as familiar showers of sparks spewed onto mini-volcanoes of glowing ash scorching the turf.

Billy Hargreaves would have loved it.

Beyond the line of engines they pushed through the dawdling crowd, past the swings and magical whirling roundabouts, ignoring touting stallholders proffering fistfuls of hoops.

Twirly was stopped by a cookhouse smell of a roasting pig revolving on a spit, and he poked a finger to a corner of his mouth to stop the dribbling.

He grinned and spoke with his mouth full of bun and slices of hot pork as tender as pancakes, with crunchy sticks of greasy crackling, and generous dollops of apple sauce.

'This day off – great idea, Budge,' he spluttered.

And he could see that Budge agreed.

The Major insisted on stopping at an air-rifle range.

He won a fluffy pink rabbit that he gave to a wide-eyed little girl who backed into her mother's skirt.

At a darts booth Twirly scored enough playing card pips to win a blue vase which he dropped into a rubbish bin.

Now the fairground-organs.

The line of exotic fantasies lit by a million coloured bulbs produced a pandemonium of sounds, all in competition with each other. Magically clashing cymbals. Jerky kettle-drums. And bright turban-wearing, eye-staring figures slowly revolving and tapping triangles.

At one point Twirly thought he recognised the tune, *Ma, he's making eyes at me*, but he wasn't sure.   It was buried in the contrapuntal confusion.

They walked to the rear of an organ labelled *Winnie's Waltzer* to watch the concertina-cards folding through their mechanisms and Twirly nodded at the owners seated on folding chairs surrounded by thermos flasks and Tupperware boxes, smiling like proud parents at a baby show.

By a display of small stationary steam engines all clacking and chuffing away, Twirly turned to look for the Major.

'Sir,' he called, and pointed at a small green shoebox-sized device.

'Stuart Turner R3MC steam generator.   Designed for Airborne.'

In the Parachute Field Ambulance the softly spoken Corporal Young used to jump with one of these clutched to his chest, and once down, no matter what chaos was going on around him, never failed to provide lighting for the quietly swearing surgical teams operating in farmhouse cellars and barns.

In the main arena, the band of the Royal Marines from Lympstone were playing.   They marched off to *The Ride of the Valkyries* – the march of the Parachute Regiment.

Twirly glanced at the Major, who smiled, and touched his jungle cap with his cane.

Wildly echoing, almost undecipherable tannoy speakers declared it was time for the Obstacle Race.

The crowd cheered as four gleaming engine gladiators snorted into the ring with steam-whistles blasting.   A muddy jeep-and-trailer rushed around the mud-scored field dumping bales of straw in four lines. At the head of each line a sack of coal was dropped.

Twirly recognised the engine in the left-hand lane as an old Burrell but, unlike the dusty oil and chaff-covered engine owned by Billy Hargreaves, this was a shining vision of red and burnished gold.

A blast from the steam-whistle of an imperious Fowler-showman's thirteen-ton engine, by the judges' platform, sent the four panting engines surging forward.

Each engine had only a driver – no stoker – and Twirly knew the toil involved as they whirled small steering wheels and juggled with regulators to slalom and slide between the bales.

When they reached the coal-sacks, all engines were more or less level.

The crowd cheered and urged, drowning the noise of the distant fair-organs.

The drivers frantically forced their engines into a tight turf-churning turn, jumped from their machines to pick up a coal sack and, after a weaving stagger, heaved them on to rear coal-bunkers.

And off again.

Twirly noticed that the Burrell driver lost ground here.

People sportingly cheered in encouragement, but the race was now with the other three as they thundered down the field towards the finish.

The crowd roared.

Twirly gasped.

For in the arena just beyond the boundary rope . . .

. . . stood Aunt Maggie.

'STAB.'

Chapter Twenty-six

Young Twirly Whippet, his brother and his three sisters required more attention than his mother could spare, so at the age of ten Twirly was sent to live with Aunt Maggie, a mile from Upper Gently at Cassey Compton.

Sunday School taught him what he shouldn't do.

Upper Gently village school taught him what he could do.

Torkin Saturday morning cinema club taught him what other people did.

His maternal grandfather taught him about rabbits, pheasants, trout, salmon – and gamekeepers.

His paternal grandfather, a regular soldier who was sent to Peking in 1900 to fight the Boxers, taught him how to survive the army.

In 1942, at the age of seventeen, he lied about his age – and the army taught him when to duck.

Aunt Maggie taught him everything else.

She never shouted.

She never pointed.

To Twirly she didn't even appear to walk, but just hovered in her long skirts - although he knew she had feet because every evening he polished her buttoned boots.

Today the spirit of Aunt Maggie is part of his early-warning system.

Thus it was that Twirly saw what no one else had noticed: the driver of the Burrell was slumped between the coal-bunker and the firebox door.

He pushed through the spectators; ducked under the rope; and with whirling legs sped towards the runaway engine which was now heading directly for alarmed spectators.

He was vaguely aware of shrieks and scattering people and toppled chairs and abandoned bags.

He leapt up onto the footplate.

With one foot on the unconscious driver, he grabbed the reversing lever with both hands and heaved it backwards, and snatched the regulator to slam it closed; then leaping to the steering-wheel, he spun it with the fury of a wild eyed dervish.

The runaway slithered to a halt with a furious snort of expelled steam. Coughs of frustration belched from the chimney; the spud-chains clanked; and the red and gold wheels pushed through the boundary rope and spitefully crunched two folding chairs into the turf.

The driver's face was a mask of grey and he lay with eyes closed and a boot pressed against the red-hot firebox door.

Suddenly the engine was surrounded by people shouting and a breathless, thick-set man scrambled up on to the footplate, thrust Twirly aside and yelled down at the driver,

'DICK!'

'We all need a drink I think,' said Budge when Twirly rejoined them, flushed and silent.

'Absolutely,' said the Major and, with chin-jutting determination and Twirly close at his heels, he cleared a way through the idly wandering crowd.

'That was well done, Twirly Whippet,' called Budge from behind.

The Major agreed.

'Astonishingly percipient, Corporal. Commendable initiative.'

Budge thought he heard him add something about 'brigade shall hear of this . . .' but it was drowned by the still-thumping jollity of the steam-organs.

Twirly strode with his head hidden beneath his black Morris hat, neither seeing nor hearing.

The beer-tent was deserted except for a few groups of men with red eyes outlined by smoke-mascara engaged in earnest discussion. Budge suspected they were talking horse-power, and pounds-per-square-inch, and the price of Best Welsh Coal. All vitally more important than fun-races and marching military bands and the antics of rogue engines.

Budge said, 'Beer or tea?'

Twirly took a deep breath and considered.

'Tea – with plenty of sugar.'

'Quite right.   Sweet tea, I think,' said the Major.   'Then perhaps back to the hotel.'

When they met in the bar before dinner Budge noticed the Major was wearing a smart blue and red cravat he hadn't seen before, and he appeared to have shaken off the weariness of the last few days, and, if possible, looked an inch taller. He nodded imperiously around the bar and beamed continually at Twirly like a proud owner at Ascot.

Twirly ignored this attention and kept his nose studiously near the top of his pint glass.

The barman slid a dish of peanuts in front of them and the Major collected a few between his fingertips.

'Mr Ballflower, our programme for tomorrow?'

Budge scooped up a handful of nuts and unloaded them into his mouth.

When he stopped chewing, he said, 'Walk into Exeter – about seven miles. Quick look at the cathedral with the longest stretch of Gothic vaulting in the world. Perhaps a quick lunch in the *Thai Orchid* on the cathedral close, originally built to house the cathedral's stonemasons. Then an easy three miles to the village of Old Wheatley and a bed-and-breakfast near Pocombe Bridge.'

'And after that?'

'Next day, lunch at Dunsford, level walk along the river, and spend the night in a pub on Dartmoor. And that marks a . . .'

A kerfuffle by the door doused the pub's general rumble of conversation.

The bar-staff looked apprehensive.

'THERE HE IS!'

Budge stared in alarm. A stocky, flush-faced man stood pointing directly at him, then pushed forward, crashing against tables, and colliding with chairs.

Who the hell?

246

He had an uneasy feeling that all this morning's map research was about to be tossed out of the pub window.

Twirly recognised the man instantly.

He was the owner of the steam engine.

The man lurched at him with both arms outstretched.

'You just disappeared. Looking all over for you. Then somebody said you was a walker and staying here.' A huge smile spread over the man's face like rings on a pond.

Twirly sniffed; and the man pumped his hand as vigorously as if he was using the Burrell's water-lifting pump by a canal bridge.

'How is he . . . Dick?'

'In the Royal Devon in Exeter. Heart attack. That stupidly heavy sack of Best Welsh . . .'

The man took a handful of their peanuts and turned to the Major.

'Don't dare to think what would have happened if your friend hadn't been quick off the mark.'

He turned back to Twirly, beamed very close into his face, and said through pulped peanuts, 'Don't even know your name.'

'Whippet – but they call me Twirly.'

The man suspended chewing.

'Twirly?'

'Twirly.'

Budge slid the empty peanut dish to the barman, who instantly refurbished it.

'Right. Had to find you to thank you, but there's something else.' He reached for the dish and took another handful.

'Tomorrow have to get the Burrell to Rewe Garage where I've got a low-loader parked. Then I load her up and get back to Fowley near Okehampton where I farm.'

He explained, 'Not sensible to bring the low-loader into the ground tomorrow morning. Everybody desperate to get away, and only one exit. Chaos. Everybody rushing about like woodlice under a kicked brick.'

He turned back to Twirly.

'Getting *Empress Gladys* into steam and driving the two miles to the garage is a two-man job. And now Dick has gone . . .'

He put his large hand on to Twirly's arm.

'You're obviously a steam man. Any chance you can give a hand?'

Twirly looked at Budge for an answer.

Budge needed to have things explained.

'Are you driving your engine to a garage two miles away and you want Twirly's help?'

The man nodded.

'Then you want him to help load it onto your low-loader?'

The man nodded again.

'What time you expect to finish the loading?'

The man calculated aloud,

 'Leave the ground about half-seven . . .'two-miles . . .

'should be at the garage by half-eight . . .

'loaded by nine.'

Budge, too, made calculations.

Finally he said to Twirly, 'If you want to do it, that's no problem. The Major and me will walk the Exe Valley Way and see you at the garage at nine.'

The man appeared to be speechless with pleasure, and scooped the dish empty of nuts.

But Budge was not finished.

'You say you're going to Okehampton?'

The man nodded.

'You pass Drewsteignton?'

'More or less.'

Budge turned to the Major.

'How important is it for you that we visit Exeter, Major?'

The Major raised his eyebrows.

'Hadn't thought about Exeter. Mary and I went there once. Three days at the *Royal Clarence*. Our twenty-fifth. Splendid. But not really bothered.'

Budge retrieved the one peanut that had escaped the steam-man's mechanical-grabber and spoke carefully.

248

'You got room for three on your low-loader?'

'Cab holds five.'

Budge looked across into the dining-room where the boy in blue was still blowing bubbles by the side of an enormous gilt mirror.

A young girl appeared behind the bar with an armful of menus.

'You dining, gentlemen?'

Budge thought she was the most beautiful creature he had ever seen – and the glorious smell of Sunday roast and Yorkshire pudding flooded into the bar.

He slowly chewed the single nut and turned to the Major.

'If Twirly helps our friend, and we ride with him, we can be on Dartmoor tomorrow-midday.

That saves us two days hard walking.'

He took the menus, smiled at the young lady and said, 'And can you please bring us four brandies? Four *large* brandies!'

Monday 20th July   *Day fifteen*

It was just after six on a glorious morning when Twirly arrived at the show-ground.

The churned-up turf was glistening with dew, and lightly peppered with morning-after debris.

He sniffed with pleasure and the air was sharp with the smell of soot and smoke and still-warm oil. Around him the steam-fair was rousing itself with grunts, and coughs, and unhurried dismantling noises.

The *Empress Gladys* stood in the engine-park unattended, but Twirly saw that the damper was open and providing draught for a kindling of torn cardboard and oily rags just inside the firehole, from which smoke idly curled.

'Morning,' called Robert, the steam-man, carrying an armful of scavenged timber. 'You had breakfast?'

Twirly shook his head.

'Good.' Robert threw the timber down, and from the foot-plate retrieved a large blue thermos-flask and a package wrapped in a tea-towel.

'From Mrs Dunmore where I stay. Tea and fried-egg sandwiches.'

Robert carefully introduced four shovels of Best Welsh on to the now blazing kindling and soon a heavy breathing of drawing air meant that Gladys was awake. Shortly her boiler, still warm from last night, began singing like frying bacon.

A rag was wiped across the glass of the Bourdon's Patent Pressure Gauge:

'Twenty pounds. We'll move off when she touches one-forty,' and he handed Twirly the battered shovel.

It was almost fifty years since Twirly last stoked an engine. He climbed up onto the foot-plate, rolled up his shirt sleeves and slowly teased Best Welsh onto the growing pyre.

Robert grinned.

'That's right. Keep it bright. Don't let it go black.'

He added, 'She'll take more'n a hundredweight getting to Rewe.'

The frying sound increased, and the fire crackled, and escapes of truculent steam hissed from a dozen apertures and a nipple dripped scalding water.

Soon, beneath his feet, Twirly felt Gladys begin to gently rock.

The chimney snorted clear smoke that drifted aimlessly into the clear Thorverton morning and he was aware of Robert moving around with oilcan in one hand, oily rag in the other, touching and patting and caressing and sweet-talking *Gladys.*

The foreplay suddenly ceased.

The time had come.

Robert swished a flapping shirtsleeve across his forehead, and with both hands began to push firmly at the thirty-six-inch flywheel.

Gladys responded magnificently.

The flywheel began to cautiously turn, until, gaining confidence, it quickly settled into a musical trundle which set the whole engine rocking with innocent ecstasy, and the coiled water hose beneath her belly swung gently like a pendulum, and Twirly swayed with it, and became misty-eyed.

'Good girl,' whispered Robert. And to Twirly he said, 'She's ready to go.'

Twirly checked the fire and peered at the water gauge. He looked at his watch: it was seven-thirty.

Budge and the Major briskly followed the Exe Valley Way along the water-meadows to Nether Exe and turned left along Green Lane to cross the A396. They arrived at the garage near Paddleford Bridge as Robert and Twirly finished adjusting the securing chains which kept *Gladys* in her place on the great green and black Scammel.

They took their seats in the cab behind the gloriously grimy Twirly and the grittily sweaty Robert.

Through Stoke Cannon.

Past St David's station.

Over the River Exe roundabout.

Through confusing industrial estates.

Onto the A30.

Past Pathfinder Village.

And, just after ten, off the A30 on to the Cheriton Bishop road; and five minutes later into a lay-by near Highfields bridge, where beneath a silent and still blue sky stretched the expectant plains and pastures of Dartmoor.

Goodbyes.

Thanks.

And gleaming *Gladys* – EMPRESS *Gladys* – made her stately exit over the bridge.

Budge stretched his limbs and flexed his knees.

'England's last great wild place, Major.'

He waved an arm towards the west where a distant hint of mist obscured the horizon.

'Ten miles over there – the highest point in England south of the Pennines. High Willhayes – two thousand feet.'

He turned to Twirly.

'Hell is that?'

Twirly's black Morris hat hung from his rucksack, and in its place he was wearing a striped black-and-white high-domed cap printed 'Seattle International Steam Fair – 1997.'

'Robert,' sniffed Twirly in explanation.

'He give you anything else?'

Twirly fingered the cap's large peak, and looked inscrutably toward the distant hills.

The Major shuffled impatiently.

'When you are ready, Mr Ballflower.'

A signpost indicated: Veet Mill and Drewsteignton. The upright was marked with the letters M and W.

The Two Moors Way. A 100-mile long-distance footpath running south from the coast at Lynmouth and crossing Exmoor and Dartmoor.

Budge led down a tarmac lane between wooden fences and a field of sweet-smelling recently mown hay from which the sun was coaxing a gentle haze of departing dew.

At the grey buildings of Winscombe Farm the tarmac ended abruptly, and the route became a lumpy grass track beneath a quiet tunnel of high hedges, with a whispering stream dancing alongside.

The long silence was shattered by a call from the Major.

'What do you suppose this is, Mr Ballflower?'

He was standing by a grassy bank pointing.

Half-hidden by a holly bush, in a rough granite niche, was a large dark polished stone, like a pumpkin studded with dimples.

Budge went back and studied it, and fingered it.

'No idea, Major. Except its marble - probably Ashburton.'

He looked around for clues but there were none, and he recalled once discovering an impressive Barbara Hepworth dominating the silence of a cathedral cloister in the Midlands.

They continued downhill swishing their boots through dead leaves piled between high banks.

A cockerel crowed.

It came from beyond the hedge and beyond the stream that had now become a brick-walled leat.

Further down the green tunnel the hedge thinned to reveal a group of grey thatched barns. Veet Mill.

On an area of mown grass stood a group of large boulders like garden-sheds at a County show.

'You go ahead, Major. Where the track meets the road, turn right and go steeply up the hill into Drewsteighton. On the square there's a church, a post office, and a pub. See you there.'

He crossed the leat by a little footbridge and moved slowly amongst the boulders. Some had been cleft in half by enormous forces and he ran his stonemason's hands over the polished surfaces that gleamed like burnished gunmetal.

'Can I help you?' said a voice.

Chapter Twenty-seven

The road from Veet Mill climbed steeply between high banks of Queen Anne's Lace cow-parsley.

The Major looked round at Twirly who was lagging.

'All right, Corporal?'

Twirly snatched off his new loco-driver's cap to squeegee his gleaming pate.

'Corporal, you limping?'

Twirly stopped and considered.

'Think I am, Sir.'

'Blister?'

Twirly firmly shook his head.

'Don't get blisters, Sir.' But he glared down at his left wellington.

'In One-Para you were put on a charge if you got a blister – self inflicted wound.'

He hobbled up to the Major.

'Butter. Always rub my feet with butter.'

'Butter?'

Twirly nodded. 'Swipe a couple of blocks from breakfast every morning.'

Ugh!

'You rub anything on *your* feet, Sir?'

'Vaseline Intensive Care,' snapped the Major.

Twirly sniffed.

'It's the same, Sir – but yours *smells* nicer.' And he sat down on the grass bank, drew off a boot, plunged in his arm, and withdrew a small black dice of Best Welsh.

He held it up for the Major's inspection, then made as if to toss it away, but instead he reached to drop it into the deep grenade-pocket of his Commando rucksack.

The Major stared.

'Think you'll need that, Corporal?'

Twirly sniffed and thrust his black-socked foot back into his boot.

Standing amongst the boulders Budge stared at a young man with a high forehead and dark beard. His overalls were covered with white dust, and he held a stubby mallet and chisel.

Budge said, 'You a stonemason?'

The man stepped forward with a hand outstretched.

'Sculptor.'

Touché. A world of difference between an artist and an artisan.

The young man continued, 'Peter Randall-Page.' And he waved his arm around the site. 'This is my banker-shop.'

'John Christopher Ballflower. Ballflower Stone Restorations. That marble piece back there on the path. That yours?'

The man smiled.

'Put it there eight years ago. Called it *A Secret Place.*'

He took Budge to a barn behind the mill house and put down his apple-wood mallet and boaster chisel, and slapped a four foot high boulder of Dartmoor granite.

'Start work on this next week. Commissioned by Devon County Council. Memorial to Joe Turner, founder of the Two Moors Way.'

He walked all the way around the stone, stroking it fondly.

'I'll slice it in two. Install one half on the northern boundary of Dartmoor. Other on the south of Exmoor. You like a coffee?'

Budge smiled his thanks but waved a dismissive hand as he recrossed the footbridge.

The sculptor called after him, 'If you walk past here when the Turner stones are in place, be certain to pass your stonemason's hands over my pattern of drilled holes.' He smiled. 'You'll feel the three hundred million-year old granite talking to you.'

Up in the village of Drewsteignton, Budge found the Major and Twirly sitting on a low wall on the empty always-afternoon square.

Outside the shop a newspaper hoarding declared: *Prescott forecasts Golden Age of bus.*

By the doorway of the thatched, yellow *Drewe Arms,* a brass plate acknowledged: 'Auntie Mabel Mudge's seventieth anniversary as landlady'.

The Major leapt to his feet.

'The corporal and I were wondering, Mr Ballflower, how many miles to lunch.'

Budge looked up at the Mediterranean sky, inadvertently directly into the dazzling sun. His eyes instantly watered and clamped shut, leaving an image of the golden Disk of Phaistós gleaming in the indigo darkness.

'Do you know, Major, that in the mountains of Crete, walking distances are always spoken of in hours, never miles.'

Twenty-five years ago he spent four-months studying Aegean and Greek architecture on Crete. It was here that he met the incredibly attractive Kaite Athanassakis, an architectural student working as a guide in the Palace of Knossos.

He persuaded her to join him on the long climb to the snow-covered, eight-thousand-feet summit of Mount Ida.

After the nine-hour expedition they revictualled and recovered at the Doxa *bar in the mountain village of* Anoyeia *with* raki *and* mandarini *and* paximdoa *bread and* souvlkia *kebabs.*

She glowered at him with her Minoan almond-eyes and quietly sang him Greek love songs. He bought her a shawl, hand-woven in the village.

They both promised to write. They never did . . .

Budge looked at his watch.

'Before we left Thorverton I made a telephone call – someone I know – and lunch will be at half-past-twelve.'

They dropped easily down a field path to cross a stream into the blue-green Rectory Wood, ignoring a path to the left signposted Fingle Bridge.

A sun-dappled track rose knee-creakingly steep up through the trees and opened on to a field scattered with golden buttercups. At the top of the climb Budge stopped by a stile surrounded by friendly foxgloves.

This north-eastern section of Dartmoor is intensely cultivated and the landscape resembles a patchwork coverlet of browns, yellows, and every shade of green, thrown haphazardly over a crumpled un-made bed.

Breathtaking.

Beyond the stile an immaculately manicured National Trust path wandered through high bracken over Piddledown Common.

'Hunters' Path,' said Budge.

On their left, four hundred feet below at the bottom of a thickly wooded gorge, ran the unseen River Teign.

He watched the Major blissfully swishing past yellow gorse that the sun had coaxed into smelling of coconut to seduce a flutter of brown fritillary butterflies.

'You been here before, Major?'

The Major turned and looked blank.

'Castle Drogo,' said Budge. 'Last castle to be built in England. Designed by one of England's greatest architects – Sir Edwin Landseer Lutyens. Commissioned by Julius Drewe.'

The young Julius Drewe returned to England after several years as a tea buyer in the Far East, and established the Home and Colonial Stores, a chain of over a hundred grocery shops.

Their success made him a millionaire.

He managed to convince himself that he was the descendant of Drogo de Teigne, a Norman Baron who came to England with the Conqueror and who had given his name to the parish of Drewsteignton. He decided it was his duty to build a suitable family seat here on Dartmoor and work began in 1910.

In the National Trust's modern admission complex the Major nodded towards the Swedish-looking cafeteria.

'Is this lunch?'

Budge shook his head and chuckled.

'A couple of years ago I attended a three-day symposium here on the problems of working with granite. Met Pamela. She is fixing a private lunch for us in the old Servant's Hall.'

A dawdle of National Trust pilgrims drifted through the glorious gardens towards the massive fortress of towers and battlements, perched like a granite extension to a tree-covered rocky spur.

Budge said, 'This entrance, Major, is not as grand as Lutyens wanted. He originally envisaged a victoriously triumphant gateway. Even erected a mock-up of canvas-and-timber to sell the idea to Drewe. But Julius was beginning to look at the escalating costs, and wasn't convinced, especially when the canvas blew away in an autumn gale.'

In the reception hall a beaming National Trust lady in a pink twin-set with a swaying pearl necklace kindly suggested they leave their packs by the fireplace, between two fire-screens which Budge said were cut from sixteenth-century paintings by seventeenth-century vandals.

'Castle took twenty-years to build, Major, and still not finished,' and he pointed out two rough-cut stubs of granite protruding from the fireplace arch still awaiting the attentions of a stonemason.

'Granite – incredibly difficult to work. But Lutyens made brilliant use of it.

'On the castle's first floor there's a display of his work.

'Gate of India in Delhi.

'Cenotaph in London.

'And on *Royal Clarence* notepaper, where you once stayed, Major, his first sketches for Drogo which he did while waiting for a London train.'

In a green-and-gold stippled drawing-room Budge stopped beneath a portrait of a gorgeously dressed look-a-like Lord Fauntleroy.

'Adrian Drewe, eldest son.

'In a glass case down the passage is that actual suit he's wearing and the toy bugle he's clutching. In the Great War he served in 262 Siege Battery, Royal Artillery, and was mentioned in despatches. Eighty-one years ago this month, aged twenty-six, he was killed near Ypres, when a shell wiped out everyone in his battery headquarters.'

A small memorial room created by Mrs Drewe contains her son's school and college mementoes, and a full-length hand-coloured photograph. A bronze figure of Victory *dedicated to his son was commissioned by the devastated Julius, for whom life was never quite the same.*

At the head of a staircase beneath a high vaulted roof, Budge tapped Twirly on the shoulder and pointed to a large oil painting.

'Mr Drewe in a favourite Burberry cloak ready to do a bit of fishing. See the large fish at his feet, Twirly? A thirty-nine pound salmon. Drewe had it stuffed and it's in a glass case where we're having lunch.'

Budge looked at his watch.

'Pam will be waiting for us. Let's go.'

She provided a magnificent game pie, followed by Mrs Drewe's favourite: strawberries and cream.

From the castle a wide bowling-green-smooth path ran along high above the gorge. The views were stunning.

The Major said, 'Always a delight to walk a National Trust path.'

Budge held a kiss-gate open.

'Official figures show visitors to the countryside, mostly there to walk, spent 8.4 *billion* pounds last year.

'Our footpaths are a national treasure. All ninety thousand miles should be removed from the indifferent care of local authorities and handed to the Trust for safekeeping. No other country in the world has a network to match it, and, typically, it's only the English who don't know.'

Down by the river, a sunlit field-path was dotted with sprawling picnickers who had no desire to walk to Land's End. Where the river was wide the crystal clear water slid along in great slabs at deck-chair

259

speed. In the narrows it broke into scurrying ripples of multi-coloured bubblepack.

By three-thirty they sat in *The Three Crowns* in Chagford.

Twirly insisted on buying three pints of Eldridge Pope *Royal Oak,* and Budge noted that he extracted a ten-pound note from a brown envelope bearing oily thumbmarks.

'How are the knees, Major?'

The Major fumbled under the table and rubbed them reassuringly. 'They loved that spot of twenty-four-hour leave.'

'But how about *you?*' persevered Budge.

'Me? I'm bruffed.'

'Bruffed?'

'Quite bruffed.'

An irritating chirruping disturbed the peace of the pub.

Budge remembered his mobile telephone and scowled.

Only Doll and the banker-shop know his number. And the banker-shop has been forbidden to call unless it's an emergency.

It was Chris, his foreman.

'Budge. Sorry to have to call you. It's Lambley Park.'

In the 14th-century a French monastic order established a monastery beside the Fosse Way, four miles to the east of Upper Gently.

It never prospered, and when in 1536 Henry suppressed religious houses that could not show an income of £200 per annum, it was one of the first to have lead ripped from its roof.

In exchange for £53, the site was granted to Sir James Lambley who rearranged the stone and timbers into a fine Tudor house with magnificent outbuildings – leaving succeeding generations to struggle with its maintenance.

Situated on the banks of the River Coln, it had always suffered from damp; but a greater problem is the unpleasant odour that unfailingly appears during hot weather.

It was perhaps because of this that the Lambleys usually made a point of dying young; and the expensively introduced herd of Pére David deer disappeared in a single season; and water fowl stayed away from the lake built by Lancelot Capability Brown, or dived into it and drowned.

It was also perhaps because of this the 1940s prisoner of war camp on the estate was a failure. It was not only the Italian POWs who attempted to escape. British guards continually went AWOL.

In 1948 the house was cautiously opened to the public to provide much needed funds, and initially proved a popular destination for coach parties from the Midlands.

Unfortunately, the recurring smell meant that too often visitors tended to scurry to the toilets, then leave, ignoring the dusty treasures of the house and the more-or-less freshly cut sandwiches on sale in the orangery.

The Duke's eldest son, the Marquess, then had the brilliant notion of filling the stables with crates of perfumed dried flowers from China, and bussing in ladies from Compton Abdale and Upper Gently to make up nosegays and sachets of pot-pouri. These sold well, and on days when the offending odour appeared, the stable doors were thrown open, suffusing the estate with heady Asian aromas and the problem appeared to be solved – or at least hidden.

A substantial lottery grant meant that the house fabric could be restored, and Ballflower Stone Restorations was commissioned to carve twelve thousand pounds worth of mullions, dripstones, balustrades and delicate Gothic tracery. Installation was to commence the first week in July.

A month ago a Health and Safety man arrived from Brussels demanding that he be allowed to investigate complaints of 'noxious emanations'.

Armed with a Gallenkamp olfactometer and a crowbar, he probed around the paved and cobbled courtyard.

A sudden loud CRACK startled the watching staff, and a large slab slid aside and the inspector disappeared into a black cavity.

He had located the source of the smell – the monastery's forgotten five hundred-year old cess pit.

A European Notice of Closure was issued next day. Budge's restorations were put on hold.

Budge stomped outside The Three Crowns seeking a better reception for his telephone and he leant against the wall of St Michael's churchyard opposite.

'Yes, Chris, what's the problem?'

'It's the engineers who are clearing the cesspit. Apparently the monastery was built along Carthusian lines, with individual cells for the twenty-three monks.'

'So?'

'Each had its own *necessarium* connected to a main conduit, Budge. The engineers say they are not dealing with a single cesspit, but a winding six-hundred feet long sewer.

'They say it'll take until the end of September to clear the whole system and the Notice of Closure will stay in place until then.'

Budge swore.

'There's worse, Budge.'

'The Duke says the extra work will absorb most of the lottery money, and if they can't open to take advantage of what's left of the summer, he won't be able to pay Ballflower Restorations to begin work until some time next year.'

Budge hunched his shoulders so that St Michael, patron saint of Brussels, wouldn't hear, and he swore again.

Chris said, 'I'm trying to arrange a meeting with his lordship, but he insists he'll only deal with you.'

'You have to come back, Budge – preferably tomorrow.'

Chapter Twenty-eight

In The Three Crowns, Chagford, a despondent Budge led the Major and Twirly into an alcove secreted behind a bubbling fish tank.

The Major briefly perused the dinner menu and replaced it on the table.

'Returning to Gently, Mr Ballflower – is it unavoidable?'

'Unavoidable. Probably away for three days.'

He saw the Major adopt his noble chin-up pose:

'Mr Ballflower. You are obviously obliged to do what you consider to be your duty. If you will be so kind as to indicate our line of march, Corporal Whippet and I will continue the campaign.'

He turned to Twirly.

'Isn't that correct, Corporal?'

Twirly sniffed and picked up the menu.

Budge was stunned.

They thinking of continuing without me? Unbelievable.

A jovial and substantial man in an unravelling pullover burst into their sanctum.

'Evening, gents,' he said, and he slapped on to the table a small dish containing a dusty posy of plastic flowers.

'What can I get you?'

With large red hands outstretched like mangrove roots, he raised his eyebrows.

'You fancy fish?'

Budge looked at the fish tank of swirling baby sharks and pulsating Chinese lanterns, and slug-like creatures slouching over slimy gravel on the bottom.

'No. Not the fish.'

'Liver – with mash?'

Budge reflected.

'Do me fine'

He watched Twirly snap shut the menu, and both he and the Major acquiesced.

'Three livers,' confirmed the man, 'with mash.'

With a podgy finger he marginally adjusted the position of the plastic flowers and swirled his substantial bulk away.

Twirly eased himself to his feet and stretched his legs.

'I'll get three more in.'

Budge took the top off his replacement pint.

'You going to be all right on your own, Major?'

The Major looked askance.

'I'll *not* be on my own. I have Corporal Whippet.'

Twirly bent down to retrieve and examine an ancient potato chip from the floor.

Budge continued, 'Reception says a First Western bus leaves here at seven-thirty for Exeter station. Should be in Cheltenham by midday. Tonight, before you go to bed, Major, I'll go through the map with you, and list the accommodation I've booked.'

He studied their hideout. Copper and brass plates hung from dark timber uprights. Faded hunting prints haphazardly punctuated the cream walls.

'Did you visit the church opposite?'

The Major nodded.

'D'you see the ghost of poor Mary Whiddon – murdered on her wedding day?'

'It was her day off, but I saw the processional cross. Aluminium. From a Zeppelin shot down in 1916 . . .'

Budge was not listening. He was worrying about the finances of Ballflower Restorations, and Lambley – and his two walking companions.

But most of all he was worrying about the liver with mash.

Tuesday 21st July   *Day sixteen*

It was a fresh morning and a quarter-past seven.

Budge stood opposite the pub, by an octagonal market-house with dormer windows and slated tower, where the man promised the bus would stop.

He tapped an unhappy foot against a pile of crates stuffed with vegetables which must have arrived at goodness knows what hour. His stomach rumbled. The Three Crowns declined to start serving breakfast until seven-thirty.

Must organise a meeting with the Duke as soon as I get to Gently. If we can't start installing as planned, we could be in big trouble.

An Ansell's brewery lorry larger than the market-house trundled around the square.

Have to see Doll. Although she won't be pleased about me deserting the two ancient itinerants.

A wild-eyed *kamikaze* pigeon crash-landed on to the top crate and began pecking at a protruding lettuce.

I'm hungry as hell. Will I have time to get something at Exeter?

'Nice morning,' said a lady pensioner, obviously a fellow passenger. Her handbag looked large enough to hold a full English breakfast.

He nodded; and wondered if the crates contained fruit.

'Morning, Budge.'

Twirly!

A warm serviette-wrapped parcel was pressed into Budge's hand.

'Hell's this?'

'Two bacon sandwiches, a hard-boiled egg, and some toast.'

Budge protested, 'They don't start serving until . . .'

Twirly placed a finger at the side of his nose and sniffed.

'See you in three days.'

And he was gone.

At nine twenty-nine the Major stood by the reception desk on which was a glass dish of Fox's Glacier Mints.

At precisely nine-thirty Twirly appeared properly accoutred in full FSMO.

As they left the pub the Major waved to the girl peering into her luminous screen and noted that the glass dish had been scooped empty.

Clear of Chagford; down Manor Road; up on to Padley Common.

Just after ten o'clock, the Major, breathing heavily, paused amongst boulders on the thirteen hundred-feet summit of Meldon Hill.

He watched Whippet fumble in his pocket and hand him a Glacier Mint.

A slight breeze jostled collapsed brown bracken, and rustled a carpet of last year's golden beech-leaves.

Despite a hint of morning mist the views stretched forever.

Below them to the west lay a tight net of dark green hedges enclosing pale fields, and white and granite-grey farms. On the slope rising out of the South Teign valley stretched a prominent pepper-and-salt field of daises and buttercups, topped by a barn with a shining silver roof.

The Major unfolded Budge's Dartmoor 25:000, and he and Twirly held it between them like choirboys in an economical church.

To the southwest the great dark mass of Fernworthy Forest hid the map's reservoir from view. South-south-west rose the mottled moorland of Chagford Common.

'When we're up on that horizon we should be able to look down on England's fourth highest pub. Budge suggests we have lunch there.'

He waved towards a great dun-coloured ridge on the left.

'Hamel Down – about two-thousand feet. Behind that lies Widecombe-in-the-Moor where Budge has booked us with Mrs Gregory at Honeybag Cottage.'

Twirly took the map and folded it.

'Maps – wonderful things, Major.'

A choice of rough tracks twisted down from the summit.

Twirly continued, 'Before we dropped over the Rhine they gave us escape maps printed on silk. A bloke in 'A' Company sewed his inside his trousers. He was took prisoner when we kicked our way into Greven.'

The Major stopped to listen.

'He and two others managed to escape. Outside a kraut village they tried to check the map to see where they were.

'A Jerry *polizist* on a bicycle appeared and tried to arrest them for indecent exposure.'

The Major chuckled.

He also has a map story.

When HE dropped with 154 Gurkha Parachute Battalion to take Rangoon - part of operation Dracula - some sticks dropped wide. A week later a patrol from the Border Regiment with the 17th Indian Division were astounded to discover a Gurkha who had made it back through Jap-infested jungle to British lines.

He insisted he couldn't have done it without the map that an RASC driver had sold him for three cigarettes.

The interrogating officer was intrigued; not many maps of the Burmese jungle existed. He asked to see it.

It was a map of the London Underground torn from a Letts pocket diary.

On either side of a narrow lane between high hedges and boulders the size of Tibetan *chortens* were two signposts. To the right: Two Moors Way to Gidleigh. To the left: the Mariners' Way to Hurston – a route said to have been used by ship-seeking sailors journeying between Bideford and Dartmouth.

They continued ahead to the wide open moor, shimmering beneath a blazing sun.

The terrain was a mixture of velvet-soft grass and ankle-wrenching clumps of sedge grass. At first, deep tracks ran parallel to an intake wall.

Down on the right a few sheep nibbled unconcerned amongst groups of wild Dartmoor ponies, chestnut, white, and grey, which once worked extensively in tin mines but were now left to their own devices.

'Sir?' said Twirly, pointing to a yellow panel on a low boulder on the edge of the depression of Metherall Brook.

They detoured to investigate.

It wasn't yellow.

It was polished brass.

Dedicated to the memory of Joyce Lorna Scott. Loving wife, mother and friend.

The Major extracted a tube of Jaffa cakes from his satchel, purchased from Chagford's Spar shop.

'Time for a break don't you think, Corporal?'

Twirly instantly unslung his rucksack and they dropped down on to the grass to lie back and study the big blue sky.

'You have brothers and sisters, Corporal?'

'A brother and three sisters.'

'Ah. A houseful. Must have been quite a problem for your mother.'

Twirly sniffed in agreement.

'Especially when people called. She sometimes sent me down the lane to borrow a cup of sugar – it was the cup we needed.'

The original tracks disappeared, and the going got rougher.

Twirly groaned as he stumbled against clumps of moor-grass. Tough heather stems snatched at him like trip-wires. Hidden boulders the size of footballs threw him sideways and concealed cavities had him staggering like a Saturday-night drunk.

Stab!

'Over there!' cried the Major.

He stood waving Budge's written instructions.

'Mr Ballflower is insistent that we divert over to the right to see the ancient stone rows below Hurston Ridge.'

Twirly watched the Major flounder eagerly towards a double row of knee-high granite spikes running up a green, sheep-grazed slope.

'About 2,000 BC. Nobody knows what they're for,' he puffed. 'Astronomical? Processional way?'

Twirly didn't follow, but stood and watched, and called, 'Perhaps they played skittles.'

Up on the saddle of the ridge they stood looking down on to a new wide-screen landscape. In the distance lay a vast fir-plantation.

268

From left to right ran a three-mile stretch of road, a grey strip stamped onto lush green verges, with minibuses, cars and lorries all moving silently along at an identical speed, reminding Twirly of straw bales on a conveyor belt.

By the side of the road a white building shimmered in the sun.

The Major waved his cane in triumph.

'Warren House, Corporal – and lunch,' and he set off like a terrier that has spotted a rabbit.

Twirly sped after him, kicking his way through purple and white heather and scattering shrapnel of sun-dried cow dung.

The Major slammed to a halt at the corner of a chain-link compound stacked with propane gas cylinders and public house essentials. He turned to Twirly. His face flushed and creased with pleasure.

He tapped his cane lightly on Twirly's shoulder.

'Brigadier Ballflower will be proud of us, Corporal.'

He preened his moustache.

'Kindly fall out the men for lunch.'

The Major squinted as he entered the crowded bar. After the bright sunshine it was dark and vaguely smoky, and he remembered Budge's note that the pub's fire hadn't been allowed to go out for a hundred and fifty years.

He eased off his satchel, commandeered an empty table in a far corner, sank down on to a bench, swung his brown brogues up on to a chair opposite and leaned back against ancient dark panelling, watching contentedly as his Corporal weaved through the massed raised elbows towards the bar.

'The Day's Special is Chagford sausages with beans and chips,' said Twirly, as he placed two gloriously overflowing pints on to the table.

'Perfect,' purred the Major.

By one-thirty they were marching along wide grassy tracks through waist-high bracken, and the Major called back, 'Mr Ballflower suggested that we spend a few moments looking at the ruins called

Grimspound – a Bronze-age settlement. Conan Doyle came here one night and was inspired to write *Hound of the Baskervilles.'*

He was disappointed with Twirly's dull reaction to the collapsed encircling boundary wall and the remains of stone huts.

It reminded him of King George III seeing the sea for the first time. After watching the rolling incoming waves for several minutes the permanently confused monarch asked, 'Is that all it does, Charlotte?'

High up on spectacular Hameldown Tor at almost two thousand feet the Major thought it sensible to regroup and check the nominal roll. He slid down on to soft grass with his back to a stubby trig-pillar.

He took from his satchel a bottle of Bulmer's Number 7 cider purchased from the pub, and was impressed by the alacrity with which Twirly produced his bottle-opener and mug.

'Unfortunate tendency these days, Corporal, for the vulgar and impercipient to drink directly from bottles like hand-reared suckling-calves.

'No finesse.

'No colour appreciation.

'No nose-tingling bouquet.

'No excited taste buds.'

He sighed.

'Might as well take it intravenously.'

Twirly burped in agreement.

High above, the sun blazed in a blue sky stretched over the whole of Dartmoor. The trig-pillar was as warm to his back as a storage heater. There was a stillness beyond silence.

The Major emptied his mug and waved his arm in a wide arc.

'You know, Corporal, great pity Mr Ballflower is not here for this. Must be the finest walk in all England. We are on top of the world, you and I.'

He peered around the pillar at Twirly, but his chin was on his chest and his eyes were closed. Nevertheless, he continued, 'Magnificent. And what's more, Corporal, from here its downhill all the way into Widecombe … '

He raised his eyebrows in a brave attempt to lift eyelids which had become ridiculously heavy .

'All the way. . .

'Widecombe. . .'

'SIR!'

The Major shook his head and blinked himself awake.

'Sir! It's three o'clock.'

The Major glared at Twirly, wondering if they had been formally introduced.

Then, 'Quite right, Corporal. Duty calls.'

He groped around for his weapon, and desperately tried to remember the operational plan.

In Widecombe Mrs Gregory greeted them like favourite uncles.

'The teapot is warmed and the kettle is on the boil. Mr Ballflower was quite certain that you would arrive in time for tea.'

She flowingly indicated a silver cakestand.

'Fairy cakes I made this morning.'

The Major carefully lowered his satchel on to plumped-up floral cushions in a bay-window and watched Twirly polish his wellingtons against the backs of his legs as if he was in the presence of the Pope.

'I don't do evening meals,' said Mrs Gregory, 'But the Old Inn is just up the road. They do wonderful food.'

Twirly detected a hint of pride . . .

Although the armada of day-coaches had long left Widecombe, the cosy labyrinth of the seventeenth century Old Inn was still cheerfully bustling, and a dense phalanx of thirsty customers formed a formidable barrier in front of gleaming beer pumps.

The Major and Twirly formed a two-man patrol and insidiously pressed themselves into this cold war of fixed smiles and subtly manoeuvred elbows.

The Major quickly identified a weak point and eased himself into the gap, covering his action by saying, 'Do you know, Corporal, that if you go into a bar in Japan and say "knickers" they serve you with a brandy?'

Twirly inserted an invidious elbow between two bodies and skilfully positioned it on the bar top.

'You been to Japan, Sir?'

The Major manoeuvred his right hip to the front and squeezed alongside Twirly.

'Korean War. Got some leave at Kure on the Japanese island of Honshu. Weird people. All grinning and bowing. Don't care for them. Of course, it doesn't help if the little blighters once used to whack you over the head with a rifle-butt.'

Twirly grunted in agreement and, with impeccable timing, fluttered a five-pound note above his head and called, 'When you are ready, Kevin, mate.'

They were served instantly.

With hunched shoulders protecting their pints, they backed away from the action and retreated to the safety of an empty table beneath a group of Uncle Tom Cobley pictures.

'How'd you know his name was Kevin, Corporal?'

Twirly sniffed.

'Mrs Gregory told me. He's her grandson,' and he tilted his glass to the Major.

'*Meh-heh-beh*,' grinned world traveller Twirly.

'*Selamat minum*,' replied the Major.

The Major studied the menu and decided upon baked carp with soft-roe stuffing.

'Gammon and chips,' said Twirly.

'You familiar with the Gammon bomb, Corporal?'

'Yellow plasticine explosive stuffed into cloth bags?'

'The very same,' said the Major, and he watched Twirly swirling his pint glass and gazing into its depths in search of his past.

'When I was wounded in Italy the 1st Para Brigade went back to England and left me behind. Posted to Fourth Para – the Wessex – with black lanyards and webbing. Captain Jock Gammon was in command of their Vickers team. It was *him* who invented the bomb. Nice bloke. Put me on a charge once.'

The Major looked around the crowded bar and noticed a plump, perspiring man sitting at a single table with his legs wide apart like a trombone player. One fat hand held a half empty pint glass – the other grasped a yellow walking-stick.

He was glaring at their table.

He raised the stick accusingly, and the Major braced himself, waiting for him to speak.

Chapter Twenty-nine

Doll Burnlystock stared aghast.

'Budge Ballflower! What *YOU* doing here?'

A carton of Babycham slipped from her hands and thudded onto the bar-top as she leaned over to peer through the open door.

'Twirly with you?'

Budge held up his hands in supplication.

'Just me, Doll.'

Her glare almost propelled him back through the door.

'You've left *them?'*

Budge gave a smile that he hoped was reassuring.

'Just a couple of days, Doll. Got a problem with Lambley.'

'Where are they?'

'Dartmoor.'

'DARTMOOR? Isn't that where the bogs are?'

'They're not in any bogs, Doll. I had to come back for an urgent meeting at Lambley Hall.'

He looked at the Guinness Toucan clock behind her. It was ten-past six.

'At this moment, Twirly and the Major should be in the village of Widecombe-in-the-Moor, in the tender care of Mrs Helen Gregory.'

'Mrs Who?' She whirled around to the shelves behind her and began to aggressively stack the Babycham.

This activity quickly calmed her.

'How is Twirly?'

'He's fine.'

'And the Major?'

'Spry as ever, and still fighting his lonely widower's war.'

Doll turned back to face her pumps and Budge – and reached for a glass, and smiled a conciliatory smile.

'Usual, m'duck?'

Budge's lunchtime meeting with the Marquis of Lambley and the contractor from Crawley was not a success.

The Marquis was in a foul mood.

The contractor's representative wore a yellow jacket and pink shirt, and every time 'effluent' was mentioned he dabbed his mouth with a fragile handkerchief.

A second meeting was arranged for four o'clock with a civil engineering firm from Pontefract, miraculously discovered by Budge's foreman, Chris.

The Pontefract man, in his sixties and with hands of cracked linoleum and wearing a battered white safety-helmet and polished black boots with industrial toecaps, spent the afternoon with his lad and a measuring-rod striding about the walls of the old priory, making notes with a small blue pencil on a folded envelope.

In Widecombe's Old Inn the man with the yellow stick bellowed, 'You're walkers!'

The Major smiled, politely nervous.

'Can always tell. Them who arrive by car burst in talking loud and *demand* a drink. Them as walk, come in quiet, knowing they've *earned* one.'

His face creased with a massive wink and he looked down to study his almost empty glass tankard.

'Anyhow,' he smilingly confided, 'I seed you coming down from Hamel. You're staying at Helen Gregory's place.'

With a gulp, he disposed of the remains of his beer.

'Expect you've come to see the 'cathedral of the moor'.'

The Major recalled Budge's notes.

St Pancras church is known as the cathedral of the moor. A tall tower rises 120 feet above the ancient settlement of Wide Combe and is probably the most impressive in Devon.

The Major said brightly, 'We've also come to see the village of Uncle Tom Cobley.'

The man spoke slowly, beginning with a murmur and swelling to an ear-filling blast, like the sound of Notre Dame's thirteen-ton Emmanuel bell.

'T-o-m C-O-B-LEY?'

And a smile grew, and slowly lit his ruddy face, and he rocked with laughter, and prominently waved his empty tankard

'Tom Cobley,' he chuckled, ''tis all twaddle. Best joke on Dartmoor. If I weren't so dry . . .'

The Major noticed the tankard was held upside down.

'Mr Whippet. Kindly refresh this gentleman's glass, if you please.'

Twirly leapt to his feet, snatched up the tankard and speedily departed to find friend Kevin.

The man beamed. The joke was getting better.

'Do you know, every year thousands of visitors come to this town. *Thousands.* And they're NOT here to see the prettiest village on Dartmoor. NOR to see our great church.'

He gave a quick glance in the direction of the bar to check on the re-supply situation.

'They come in their big coaches for . . .'

And he counted expansively on his podgy fingers.

'Toilets;

'Tea;

'And Tom Cobley.'

Another burst of raucous laughter..

Twirly arrived at a quick trot and pushed the pint into the waiting hand, and the man urgently nodded his thanks, and rapidly lubricated his throat.

'But 'tis all flim-flam and fiddle-faddle,' he confided in a loud whisper, furtively checking for unwelcome lurking listeners.

'Tom Cobley never were *nothing* to do with this village. Not never. Was a Spreyton man. T'other side of the A30. His marked grave is beside Spreyton church door. His name is in the Church Register. And they have an Old Tom Cobley pub.'

He paused bright-eyed to check that his joke was being understood; and edged his chair nearer by almost an inch.

'Y'see, old Tom borrowed a horse from the carrier – bloke called Pearce – so he and six mates could visit our Fair.

'Never got here! Lost up in Gallaven Mire.'

He laughed aloud again, and banged his stick, and plunged his happy face deep into his tankard.

'Bob!' called a red-shirted man in a hurry who poked his head around the door. 'Two coaches coming from Coventry tomorrow afternoon. That all right?'

The tankard was lowered, and the red-shirt was subjected to a quick recognition check, which it passed.

'Ah. That'll do.' He nodded briskly.

The red-shirt said, 'Right. I'll drop in the top hat and smock. Shilstone Rock Stables say they'll have Snowball up here by two o'clock.'

He disappeared as if he was snatched away by an elastic cord.

The tankard rose back into place and the man's twinkling eyes darted back and forth between the Major and Twirly like a table-tennis ball.

A wide Cheshire-cat grin enveloped his face and he flashed a wink as subtle as a dropping garage door, and he gurgled into his tankard.

'Tom Cobley? Tis better'n farming sheep.'

Wednesday 22nd July *Day seventeen*

'Black treacle or honey with your porridge?' asked Mrs Gregory.

'No porridge for me, thank you,' said the Major. 'Just toast.'

Mrs Gregory rubbed a hand down her cream and green apron.

'You need more than toast for walking,' she said. 'Your friend says you're walking to Princetown, and he had porridge *and* fried potatoes *and* two eggs.'

'Actually not feeling too good, Mrs Gregory. Didn't sleep well.'

Mrs Gregory looked horrified.

'Bed not comfortable?'

The Major held up his hands.

277

'Bed was perfect. But Mr Ballflower left me a large sheaf of notes and directions. Lot to think about. Responsibility. Not allowed to lose men on Dartmoor.'

'You can't get lost between here and Princetown – not unless a mist comes down.'

A mist?

The Major shuddered.

Budge had reminded him that Dartmoor mists were notorious for distorting distances, and disorienting even experienced navigators.

With Princetown eleven miles away there will be no time to rectify errors.

Beneath a grey granite sky a grassy track led steeply up through golden gorse and startled sheep.

The Major stopped to stand hunched and breathing heavily.

'Sheep, Corporal. Either grazing frantically as if they've just discovered something illegal. Or lazily chewing as if they can't stand the stuff. Or just standing trying to remember if it's Wednesday or Thursday. *Never* sensibly lying down taking a kip.'

'Sheep always have trouble sleeping, Sir. Some people say they try to drop off by counting imaginary walkers climbing over a stile.'

The Major walked with his map open, checking every feature they passed.

Essential to know their precise position in case the dreaded mist comes down.

By ten-thirty they had crossed Dunstone Down and were outside Ponsworthy Post Office, kept by Carol Dry. Next door a shop boasted it sold everything from brandy to boot-laces.

Twirly mumbled something and disappeared inside, and the Major, grateful for the pause, sank on to a low wall by a surprisingly narrow bridge over the River Webburn.

The road out of Ponsworthy was painted with white elongated letters warning, TAKE MOOR CARE. Soft grass verges were studded with grey boulders, thickets of gorse, clumps of new green bracken, and sheep joyfully playing 'last-across-is-a-cissy.'

The Major noted that Budge had written 'SEE' by Ouldsbroom Cross between the untidy pinnacles of Sharp Tor and Yar Tor.

The cross was a sorry affair: a shapeless six-foot upright of rough granite.

It was originally one of several crosses marking routes across the moor to Widecombe church, and was uprooted in 1825 and dragged on an ox-drawn sledge to Leusdon Farm two miles away. There its arms were knocked off and it became a gatepost. Only returned to where it belonged in the 1950s.

The Major was aware he was unnecessarily breathless and, although the going was easy, he was sweating as if they were slashing at the jungle in Malaya's Cameron Highlands.

'NAAFI time, I think, Corporal.'

Slumped on a bed of soft grass sprinkled with sheep-droppings, the Major watched his Corporal produce a plastic pack.

'Mrs Gregory said you didn't have breakfast. The girl in the shop said you'd like these.'

The Major wasn't sure, but he chewed through a crumbly and sticky jam tart and licked his fingers.

'Very good, Corporal.'

In the distance ahead, perhaps half-a-dozen miles, a slender mast poked into the leaden sky. He consulted the map.

'The TV tower ahead, Corporal, marks Princetown. Today's objective. And Dartmoor prison.'

The prison was built in 1806 to rehouse French prisoners from the Napoleonic Wars who were previously held in appalling conditions in rotting hulks on the River Tamar.

Originally intended for 5,000 men, the prison was soon crammed with a population of 10,000 and conditions became worse than on the hulks. The death rate was four a week. Escape attempts were rarely successful due to the moor's bogs, and mists, and vile weather.

The Major watched Twirly gaze at the tower above the prison.

'In One-Para – R Company – we had a Sergeant Cooke who was an old soldier. When we were in North Africa in November '42 he was captured at *Oued Zarga* and taken to a prisoner of war camp in southern Italy.

'After a couple of months he escaped by thieving a set of overalls, a bicycle, toolbox, and a ladder. Rode out of the camp pretending to be a visiting electrician.

'He cycled for days, bluffing and hiding and living off the land, and when he got to Rome he rode into the neutral Vatican, still posing as an electrician, found an Irish priest and told him he was a Roman Catholic prisoner-of-war.

'The priest arranged for him to be shipped back to England in exchange for a sick Italian prisoner.'

The Major said, 'That story true, Corporal?'

Twirly shrugged.

'Don't know, Sir. All sergeants lie a lot.'

A sheep with rheumy eyes gingerly edged forward and sniffed Twirly's wellingtons, and retreated in dignified disgust.

'You ever do confined-to-barracks, Corporal?'

'All the time, Sir.'

The Major nodded.

'You got another of those tarts?'

They left the road where squealing children were paddling in the East Dart river beneath an ancient clapper-bridge, and followed a rising lane lined on both sides by lichen-covered boulders as big as London taxis.

At a bridge by a bend, where a footpath sign pointed across a flat meadow, Budge had marked on the map: SEE the house.

This is the only remaining example of the strange Dartmoor custom of a house-in-a-day.

On Midsummer's Day in 1835, while the local gentry were living it up at Holne Ram Roasting, a young couple Tom and Sally Saterley, using materials secretly collected and hidden beforehand, erected a single-storey house. And because the house was built in one day between sunrise and sunset, with smoke coming from the chimney, the house and land became theirs by ancient squatters' right.

Through the hamlet of Huccaby, and into Hexworthy.

By a row of horse-stables sheltering beneath dark fir trees being fingered by a fidgety breeze; and below a sullen sky, the white Fountain Inn gleamed like a Nepalese guest-house.

A sign by the door in fluorescent orange announced: *Walkers welcomed, dried, fed and watered.*

The slightly feverish Major took his large white handkerchief and dragged it across his sweating brow.

'*Namaste,*' he breathed.

He followed Twirly to an empty table between the open door and a plant-filled window.

'You'll cool off here, Sir,' he said. 'I'll get them in.'

The Major sighed and did as his Corporal directed.

Still five miles to do this afternoon.

'You all right, Sir?' said Twirly, standing like Father Christmas with two pints of Newton Abbot bitter.

'Fine, Corporal.'

The beer was good and cooling and he watched Twirly restlessly step over to the window and peer out past the barricade of green plants.

'Sit down and relax, Corporal. There's no sign of mist, and Dartmoor doesn't do snipers.'

'Like to see what's going on, Sir.'

The Major noted that his eyes continued to twitch and dart like a snake charmer's mongoose, even when he was pretending to read the menu.

'Ham salad for me,' said the Major.

'Think I'll have the home-made faggots.'

The Major checked the menu again.

'You have to decide – peas or beans, Corporal.'

Twirly sniffed and turned again to peer out of the window.

The Major heard a car door slam.

'Corporal, decision time! The young lady with her notepad is coming over. Peas or beans?'

A man's voice said, 'I should have the beans.'

Twirly shot to his feet.

A familiar figure filled the open doorway.

The Major struggled up and held out his hand

'Mr Budge Ballflower, I presume?'

Budge grinned.

'Probably,' he said.

Budge was surprised to see how sun-tanned – or wind-tanned – they both looked. Although creases around the eyes appeared to have increased, especially the Major's.

'Not expecting you until the day after tomorrow.'

'My foreman worked wonders. Found a northern company to take over the contract and complete on time. Caught the first train I could.'

'How is Doll?' asked Twirly

'Brisk as ever, but worried stiff about you two. She's sent you a present, Twirly – in my backpack.'

'You see Ratcher?'

'No, but Alf Smith says your cat has put on weight and he thinks it's pregnant.'

'Ratcher is a tom.'

'Alf Smith has always had problems.' He waved his hand above the half-empty glasses. 'Same again?'

The Major held up his hand.

'Not me, Budge. But would appreciate a gin.'

'Gin?'

'Medicinal – works like quinine.'

'Hell you want quinine for?'

The Major shrugged.

'Perhaps a *chota-peg* – a double if you would be so kind Budge'

The young lady with the note-pad appeared again.

Her young eyes shone; her cheeks as rosy as Victoria plums; swishing luxurious chestnut hair – she might have just returned from a canter around Laughter Tor.

'Gentlemen?' she said.

'Great lunch. Now let's go!' said Budge, looking around for his backpack, and resuming command. 'Two hours to Princetown; and our pub; and dinner; and kip.'

Hell. Missed these two old remnants.

At the bottom of an ancient walled track a new wooden footbridge crossed the River Swincombe alongside ancient half-submerged stepping-stones.

'Lot of activity around here once,' called Budge. 'Miners scratching for tin,' and they moved at speed between dead roofless hovels built of monstrous blocks of moss-covered granite.

Over on their right a white mist lay sullen in the valley.

Budge waved his map.

'West Dart Valley.'

At Cholke Head where multiple streams came together in a swampy depression, Budge took long precarious leaps from tuft to tuft. He looked back.

The Major in his brown brogues was skipping like a young Topsy negotiating the unstable ice-flows of the Ohio.

Twirly in his wellingtons was happily slopping through the bog like a naughty boy in a puddle.

The map indicated that beside the rough and twisting grass track lay a *kistvaen* burial chamber with the name Crock-of-Gold. Local legend says ancient excavators struck lucky here. But Budge found nothing but a crushed Coke can amongst the scattering of granite boulders and broken slabs.

Twirly distributed Glacier Mints as compensation.

The rough moorland walk suddenly became a wide man-made stony track. Budge checked with his Dartmoor Guide.

During the First World War, conscientious objectors from the prison were given the task of building a road across the moor from Princetown to Hexworthy. But the war ended and the work was abandoned.

Budge closed his guide book and said, 'Road built by 'conchies'. Should have been shot.'

He saw the Major quickly look back at Twirly, who stood stunned for a moment, and then stormed forward and pushed past.

His expression was oddly fierce.

He pointed ahead with a stake he had picked up at Swincombe.

'This way?' he demanded.

Budge stared. He had not seen Twirly this angry since the lurker in the Mendips ten days ago.

Twirly continued striding.

Budge hesitated, and called after him, 'Straight on into Princetown. Turn left. Plume of Feathers by the roundabout.'

He turned to the Major.

'Hell's all that about?'

Chapter Thirty

Twirly stomped into his room at the Plume of Feathers, flung his rucksack onto the end of the bed, and swore.

Off came his wellingtons and sticky socks and onto the bed with his feet up on his rucksack – the approved 'rest' position of British infantry during a forced march.

Stupid going off like that.

Not Budge's fault. He knows about Romans, Crusaders and the Retreat from Mons. But he knows nothing about OUR war. Except the coloured bits they made into films.

He watched two flies circling the frilly orange lampshade. The outer one – the wing-man – was finding it difficult to keep up.

Down in the bar, Budge collected a rum-and-black and a packet of crisps and found a slate table with metal legs hiding behind the fireplace.

Don't care for Princetown. Been here before. An organised walk to see Merrivale standing stones.

The town is a dismal waiting-room for pale-faced prison visitors.

The Major slid into the hideout clutching a glass of gin with a slice of lemon.

Budge now saw that his suntan was undershot with grey, and the usually keen eyes looked as if they needed a new battery.

'You all right, Major?'

The Major offered a wan smile and slid a chair across the stone floor with a noise like a displeased cat scratching a window pane.

'Has Whippet…?' he began.   But at that moment Twirly arrived.

Budge instantly stood.

'This one is mine, Twirly. Owe you an apology. Senseless remark back there. The Major has told me about your unit.'

Twirly sniffed.

'It's for me to apologise, Budge. Conduct contrary to good order and military discipline. I'll have a pint of best.'

Back at the table Budge thoughtfully crunched a mouthful of crisps.

'Would you like to know we've covered a hundred and fifty miles – one way or another.'

He watched the Major peer into his glass like a fortune-teller at a fair.

'So how many now?'

'About another hundred.'

'In how many days?'

Budge poked into his crisp bag.

'Well,' he said, 'today is Wednesday, 22nd of July . . .'

Twirly lowered his glass and turned to the Major.

Twenty-second of July? That was when the bomb went off in Jerusalem.'

With a long finger Budge skilfully retrieved crisp particles from the corners of the foil bag.

Twirly continued, 'We were stationed in the Syrian Orphanage with the Argyll and Sutherland Highlanders. The building shook. Jerusalem shook.

'Big panic. Sergeant Armstrong bellowed like a bull. We grabbed shell-dressings, piled into jeeps and rushed to the smoke and dust.

'One wing of the King David, right opposite the YMCA, had gone. Concrete floors hanging down like washing. Pile of rubble as high as a couple of haystacks. Somebody shouted, "Two hundred people under there!"

'In three days we only brought out six alive. Hundred dead, mostly civilians.'

Budge crushed his empty crisp packet into a tight ball and stuffed it into an ashtray.

'Suicide bomber?'

Twirly sniffed.

'Not *him*. Polish bloke called Menachem Begin. Said it was a victory against the British. Made him Prime Minister.'

'It was weird for the Paras,' continued Twirly. 'In May, when we were chasing across Germany, we had been releasing these people from filthy hovels, and them who had the strength were hugging and kissing us. Now, five months later, they were dropping live grenades in our pockets!'

Budge's crisp packet creakily unfurled and leapt out of the ash tray.

Thursday 23rd July *Day eighteen*

It was a grey morning and the Information Centre in the old Duchy Hotel was asleep – and knew nothing.

Budge waved a hand.

'Conan Doyle is supposed to have written *Hound of Baskervilles* in there. Took the name 'Baskerville' from his hackney-carriage driver.'

But only he heard . . .

They trooped past the site of what was once England's highest railway station at 1,373-feet; past the Fire Station; and past coloured houses attempting to conceal the dismal grey slabs of the prison. The church peeped over the trees like a nosey schoolmaster peering over a school wall.

They stamped along the granite chippings of the old railway track on an embankment high above hummocky grass. On either side were rush-lined puddles, and bright green patches which they say can swallow a horse-and-cart.

The Big Brother radio tower up on the right noted their escape – but did nothing.

Budge wondered if the beautifully carved twelve-feet long granite corbels were still on King's Tor, hidden under bracken like the ruins of a fallen Mayan temple.

Originally intended for the widening of London Bridge, they were abandoned in 1968 when an American with two million pounds to spare bought the bridge as a souvenir, and took it back in numbered bits to Arizona.

Where the old railway curled below Ingra Tor, they crossed the road at Criptor Cross to leave the Moor behind. On Ward Bridge they looked down on the placid River Walkham, and Twirly distributed 'hard-tack' biscuits, thieved from the house-trusty's trolley in the Plume of Feathers when the 'screws' were not looking.

Budge maintained a brisk pace up a narrow lane with high hedges and verges of curly brown bracken.

Through Sampford Spinney and on to Plaster Down.

Over on the right, about six miles distant, Budge recognised the silhouette of the church of St Michael-of-the-Rock perched a thousand feet above sea-level.

Charles Kingsley, in Westward Ho!, *tells of a wealthy merchant caught in a storm at sea who promised the row-the-boat-ashore saint that if he was saved he'd build a church on the first land he saw. Off Plymouth he caught sight of this extinct volcano, and lived to keep his promise.*

On soft verges they followed the road into the ancient market town of Tavistock astride the fast flowing River Tavey.

By one o'clock they entered a busy square where severe windows glared down from municipal offices in a grand castellated building sprouting pinnacles and tall chimneys.

The Pannier Market, housed beneath a high-pitched roof with huge stone arches, was bustling like a souk in the medina of Marrakesh; Budge winced, remembering a fiercely expensive carpet and a free cup of mint tea.

He led them into crowds moving slowly through the heavy aroma of almonds, honey, fruitcake, cheese, varnish, paraffin and smouldering joss-sticks. High above the stall of Odds and Suds –

288

Devonshire soap makers - an amused Queen Victoria looked graciously down from an ornate gilt frame.

'Food time,' said Budge.

Bob's Cafe looked hopeful.

Three-decker Breakfast Sandwich – 2 bacon, 2 sausages, black pudding and a fried slice.

But Bob was too busy to feed three walkers.

At Duke's Coffee House, under a slated lean-to supported on green pillars, lucky eaters were cruelly dawdling over their lasagne-and-chips, while a hungry queue stood drooling like dogs hoping for fallen crumbs.

'Not here,' decided Budge.   'Let's go and see Saint Eustachious.'

The parish church across Bedford Square, built of green Hurdwick stone quarried two miles north, is dedicated to the Roman officer who converted to Christianity, and was martyred for his sin.

On the edge of the churchyard, near the ninety-foot church tower, Budge located the ecclesiastically respectable Café Liaison.

He found an empty table.

'Twirly,' he said. 'I'm going to look in the church. Order for me. Anything that can be served and eaten *quickly*. Still have six miles to do.'

The church's barrel-ceilings are supported on three rows of wonderfully slender quatre-foil pillars, and Budge ran his fingers over two-inch vertical chisel marks made by hard-hitting fourteenth century masons converting *horse's head lumps* of glistening granite into perfect curves and folds.

He decided the pulpit was probably Beer stone, or maybe even Caen. It was often quicker and easier to ship stone from France than transport it along Devon roads.

In the north aisle he found a floor-slab under which lie the leg-bones of Ordulf, first-century Earl of Devon, founder of Tavistock's dissolved Benedictine abbey, and Budge wondered where the rest of him lay.

The faithful Twirly stood waiting with food.

Devonshire Double-over: chunks of lamb, potatoes and carrots sealed in a fold of flaky pastry, doused in cider-gravy and served with hand-cut chips.

The moment they left Tavistock the walking became awful.

Muddy overgrown footpaths.

An absence of waymarks.

Stiles either cat's-cradles of scrap timber, or obstacles of trampled brambles and barbed wire.

Hard foot-slapping roads between claustrophobic hedges.

Really awful.

Budge fumed.

How can councils not know that their local economy benefits more from visitors who come to walk than they do from a dwindling farming industry? And why is that farmers are allowed to forget that walkers are historically more a part of the countryside than they are? Hunters and gatherers roamed here long before the farmers arrived.

Budge had hopes of a respite in the Hare and Hounds at the optimistically named crossroads of Chipshop; but it was closed to wayfaring walkers at three-fifteen in the afternoon.

Climbing up from the deep cleft at Catsbridge, he sat on a bank of nipplewort and watched the Major and Twirly plod unsmiling towards him.

Should have found a better route than this.

Finally, just before four o'clock, they arrived at the bottom of a steep hill where the River Tamar marks the border between Devon and Cornwall, and the Royal Inn opposite Horse Bridge was mercifully open.

They slumped into this one-time nunnery.

With head bowed, Budge begged forgiveness and asked to be blessed with three beers.

'Buddlemead Farm?' said the landlord fingering a carefully manicured ginger moustache. 'Out of here turn right and along by the river for a hundred yards.'

He looked quizzically at Budge.

'You staying there?'

Budge nodded.

'Mavis and Arthur. Lovely couple.'

He brightened. 'You know they don't do meals? We start serving at seven. I'll book a table. My name is Paul.'

As they left, Paul called after them, 'Hope you've got torches.'

Budge didn't understand.

The ginger moustache lifted in a smile.

'They don't have the electric,' he shouted.

'We didn't hear your car,' said Mavis, drying her hands on a black towel.

She wore a long necklace of wooden beads that rattled like dried broad beans in a potting-shed drawer.

Then she saw their packs.

'Don't get many *walkers* here.'

She turned her head to call, 'We don't get many walkers here, do we, Arthur?'

She waited for a grunted agreement, then said, 'Most people round here have cars or bikes.'

But she made them a pot of tea and offered them cakes as if they were normal people.

Budge splashed himself with cold water from a tin basin and decided it was time to head for Saint Paul and food.

He committed to memory the position of a blue enamel candlestick by the side of the bed, and shook the box of matches to ensure it was full.

Outside his room, on a chair beneath a picture of the Destruction of Sodom and Gomorrah entitled 'Lot 7', stood a storm-lantern already alight and filling the creaking passage with the throat-rasping reek of paraffin.

291

Twirly was standing inside the front door.

'The Major's not joining us for dinner. Mrs Wentworth has filled two hot-water bottles for him and is making some oxtail soup with parsley dumplings.'

'Is he all right?'

'No.'

'Will he walk tomorrow?'

Twirly sniffed.

'If he can *stand* – yes.'

In the Royal Inn Paul comforted them with pork and pease pudding, followed by rhubarb pie and custard.

Friday 24th July *Day nineteen*

Budge sat yawning on his sagging bed.

He peered out at the drizzle and watched drips from the thatch running along the bottom edge of the open window.

'Fifteen miles,' he groaned.

The parlour where breakfast was served was as cold as his banker-shop on a Monday morning.

'Where you walking today?' smiled Mavis, wearing two cardigans and holding a teapot snuggling in a knitted tea-cosy.

'Want to get to the Jamaica Inn on Bodmin.'

She stared and put the teapot on a cork tablemat to insulate it from the cold table.

Twirly entered carrying his rucksack.

'Been to see the Major.' His words condensed in the cold air.

'And?' asked Budge.

'He's coming down. Just wants tea and fruit juice.'

Mavis Wentworth stooped to look out of the weeping window.

'Will you have full English breakfast? I've got some nice lamb kidneys.'

Budge nodded.

'Mr Wentworth would look in and say good-morning but he's outside with the vet who's come to castrate the pony.'

Budge raised his hand with a weak smile.

'Think I'll skip the kidneys.'

Budge was horrified when he saw the Major.

He stood in the doorway like an alabaster statue. His cheeks were sucked in as if he'd bitten on a sour gooseberry.

Twirly leapt up with a mouth full of kidneys and fried bread and guided him to a chair.

The Major gave Budge a thin smile of reassurance.

'Be all right once we get going.'

Budge nodded.

'Need to leave soon as we can.'

At eight-thirty they stood encased in crackling wet-gear.

Through the open door, they scowled at the dismal morning.

Mrs Wentworth appeared, followed by her husband.

'Arthur says he has to go into Stoke Climsland for a bag of Heygate pellets. He don't mind going early. Seems stupid to walk . . .'

The battered Land Rover took them over the long stone bridge that marks the border between Devon and Cornwall: the scene of a bloody battle on another July day when the Earl of Essex led an army of Parliamentary troops into the county in 1664.

A dripping sign read: KERNOW.

Twirly sat amongst the swirling chaff and sniffed knowingly.

'That's foreign for 'Clear Off!'

The half-hearted drizzle of Devon became serious rain in Cornwall.

At the church of Stoke Climsland they scrambled stiffly from the vehicle.

Budge pushed his hand through the open passenger's window, past a black-and-white collie on the front seat with a grin as evil as any he had carved on a Guiting-stone gargoyle.

'Thanks. Great help.'

Mr Wentworth shook his hand with no change in his look of incomprehension, pushed into gear, and drove off.

The remains of an abused footpath post leant unwanted against a white cottage. A narrow passage ran steeply down to an overflowing muddy stream.

'This way,' sighed Budge.

Beyond the stream they trudged past immaculate farm buildings where a central bell-tower bore the Prince of Wales' feathers. A row of tractors in assorted colours stood gleaming and dry in a shelter as smart as a car showroom on Berkeley Square.

Budge turned in his clammy hood to remark to his fellow peasants on the splendour of this place, but they were busy discussing who should carry the Major's satchel, with the Major repulsing Twirly's advances with trembling dignity.

Budge cursed as they slipped and skidded on paths of mud, with footwear increasing in size and weight with every step. He groaned as they pounded hard tarmac lanes, shedding a disgusting trail of mud-clods. He swore as he searched for non-existent waymarks, and clambered over wet and slippery pretend stiles.

He decided he hated Cornwall.

From Baddaford Farm the lane dropped down to a clutch of houses, overlooked by a tall church tower.

He checked his soggy map.

The village of Linkhorne – with a pub!

A concrete pillbox – one of the five thousand built in a hurry to meet Hitler's expected invasion – had been sensibly converted into an open-sided bus-shelter. Inside, above a wooden bench, hung an unfamiliar black and white flag.

A few yards further on, lashed by the rain, stood Church House pub.

Three rum-and-blacks with a dash of hot water, if you please, landlord.

The pub was closed.

Opposite, sheltering in the church porch, stood a beaming vicar.

Communication was difficult because of enthusiastic bellringing in the tower above.

'A competition organised by the Guild of Bellringers,' explained the vicar. 'St Mellor's has a peal of six-bells.'

Budge forced himself to return the smile, and nodded at Church House across the road.

'The pub. What time does it usually open?'

The Vicar shook his head.

'Doesn't. Been closed for four weeks.'

Budge blundered back onto the lane.

'You still got those Glacier Mints, Twirly?'

While Twirly fumbled in a pocket, Budge pushed back his hood, exposing his head to the rain.

He looked around . . .

The population of Linkhorne had taken cover from the pounding precipitation and retreated from the deafening bell-ringing, and looked as deserted as a dripping plague-village.

He looked harder. 'Twirly!' he demanded.

'Where the hell's the Major?'

Chapter Thirty-one

The Major was alone, grey and grim-faced, as he advanced through the pounding rain, alternately sweating and shivering inside his plastic mobile sauna, jolting from one complaining knee to the other.

He hesitated and peered into the downpour.

Budge had disappeared, but a few yards ahead the glistening red shroud of his corporal still bobbed along like a marker beacon and the Major followed.

Moments later ghosts of hunched houses and a grey church loomed out of the gloom, and the Major saw the Corporal stop to stand in the centre of the empty road.

Now he could see Ballflower in front of the church talking to a vicar framed in the porch like a fair-weather-man on a Swiss weather-cottage.

He groaned.

Now there will be a long discussion about barrel vaults, and bosses, and curiously carved corbels.

He looked around him.

On his left a massive wayside shrine contained a representation of the flag of Saint Pirran who brought Christianity to the pagans of Cornwall. Beneath the flag ran a wooden bench looking considerably more comfortable than last night's bed.

Without undue effort, he called to Whippet, 'Taking shelter for a moment, Corporal.'

Ignoring the Sandhurst edict that a message is not properly sent until it is acknowledged, he slipped into the bunker.

'Hell *is* he, Twirly?'

Twirly shrugged his shoulders and looked wildly around.

Budge was incensed.

'Find him! He's *your* officer!'

296

He watched Twirly set off back up the road looking to right and left, until he vanished into the obscurity of the Stygian rain.

Budge clamped his eyes shut and swore.

'Yes, Doll. Both disappeared in a deluge. Never saw them again.'

With a groan he set off after Twirly – and immediately the two appeared, almost holding hands like the Babes-in-the-Wood.

He sighed.

'This way!' he called.

Half-an-hour later they squelched into the dry warmth of The Manor House pub at Rilla Mill, threw off their wet-gear, and crouched around three rum-and-blackcurrants topped up with hot water.

'Not thinking of carrying on in this?' called landlord John.

Budge shrugged.

John came over to the table to say confidentially, 'Best thing you can do is go home.'

Budge thanked him for his advice and ordered chilli-con-carne for himself and Twirly. The Major sat with half-closed eyes and declined to even discuss food.

Halfway through the chilli a newcomer stamped through the door and shook his wet overalls.

'Think it's stopping, but the mist is coming in.'

Budge went to check.

Cornwall was fast being enveloped in a dense fog arising from the sodden ground.

Budge took Twirly aside.

'We could get a taxi for the Major.'

Twirly considered. Finally, he said, 'Would be difficult. Best just to take it easy, Budge. There's a lot left in him yet.'

Budge heaved up his pack.

'Time to go. Sure you can carry on, Major?'

The Major replied with a zombie nod and Twirly helped him to stagger to his feet.

From the village a footpath ran along by the River Lynher, and came to a lane where high black hedges parted the dense walls of opaque white and they trudged along this trench like fleeing Israelites crossing the Red Sea.

Shadowy villages occasionally invaded this nothingness.

Starabridge

North Darley

Henwood

At Sharptor, on the edge of Bodmin moor, an unhappy imprisoned dog barked.

Beyond Wardbrook Farm a lost soul with thin wet hair plastered to his scalp was condemned to sawing up old fence-posts.

Budge approached with his map and explained they hoped to walk down to Withey Brook and continue west along by Snallcombe Plantation, but there appears to be two tracks dropping down from this point.

'Does it make any difference which we take?'

The man continued sawing.

Eventually he stopped and sluiced surface water from his face.

Without looking at Budge, he resumed sawing.

'Not to me, it don't.'

Withey Brook was a chocolate-coloured stream full of undulating pondweed. Although they floundered up and down the bank there appeared to be no suitable crossing, and Budge decided that, as they were already at saturation point, they should just blunder across.

He swore as his boots filled and chilled, and he paddled to the opposite greasy grassy bank.

The Major plunged into the stream in his brown brogues, stepping like a flat-footed Jacana bird, and Twirly, in his wellingtons, plunged in to steady him.

Budge leaned down from the bank and reached for the Major's hands, but the Major stumbled, and knocked Twirly from his balance. Twirly fell to splash on his back amongst the pondweed with his wellingtons in the air, completely submerged and spluttering like a cat dropped into a canal.

Budge watched him scramble up on to the bank and rip off an his wellingtons to empty them of Withey Brook; then he crept up to him to whisper:

'Twirly. When I took the Major's hands . . . they were red hot.'

Twirly looked him in the eye.

'He's got malaria.'

Budge gaped.

Malaria?' he hissed, and turned to stare at the Major.

He turned back to Twirly.

'You get malaria in hot deserts and steaming jungles. Not on bloody Bodmin.'

'It's recurring malaria. He gets it.'

Great!

'Yes, Doll. Unfortunate. One of them fell in a brook and drowned; the other died of malaria.'

Budge's map showed that in about two miles they should arrive at the young River Fowey with a road leading them easily to the village of Bolventor and the famous Jamaica Inn.

But the Bodmin white-out denied recognition of any geographical features and, with map in one hand and compass in the other, he led them in an erratic route, clambering over wet walls, stumbling on churned-up turf, passing boulders which turned into scowling sheep which crossly scrambled up and bleated off into the white unknown.

After an hour of blundering they came to yet another wet wall barrier, but Twirly cried, 'Budge! To the left. There's a gate.'

Sure enough, a gate stood just beyond a strip of asphalt, and to Budge's relief it opened with a push.

He winced when he noticed that the Major now looked more ghastly than he did at the pub and that Twirly was now carrying his satchel and continually nudging him upright.

'Are we lost?' asked Twirly.

Budge snarled, 'We are *not* lost, Twirly. It's sodding *Jamaica Inn* which is lost.'

He stamped off angrily, and too late realised he was in a hollow of bright green sphagnum moss dotted with white heads of bog cotton.

Hell!

His boots instantly disappeared, and he sank above his knees into a sucking mire.

Chapter Thirty-two

Doll looked at her clock and rattled the bazaar of bracelets on her wrists.

Budge had promised to telephone as soon as he rejoined them. But not a word.

Two days had gone by, and now it was four-thirty in the afternoon.

She had tried several times to ring his portable telephone but the wretched thing wasn't working.

It was essential she speak to him for several reasons.

Shortly after he left, the dreaded Cynthia turned up again, insisting she *MUST* get in touch with the Major.

This time she was accompanied by a portly tweed-suited man who murmured, 'Absolutely,' every time she spoke.

Must be her lawyer – although she called him 'Humphrey'.

And later in the afternoon the brewery's obnoxious Beer Services manager arrived to say Cheltenham museum had made a generous offer for the Roman stone. Budge's stone. The brewery had accepted the offer 'in principle', but the decision was hers.

The museum had also agreed to cover the cost of removing the stone and making-good afterwards, and at the same time the brewery would carry out the improvements she had been demanding for the last six years.

Budge knows very well that the stone is his if he gets Twirly safely to Land's End before he rushes back to start the Lambley contract, but it's only right he knows the position.

Then last night Mickie Balding came in with a shocking story about Twirly's Fish House. Of course Mickie makes up a story a day, but there's no smoke without fire.

So where IS Budge?

'Probably with his feet up in a bar,' she snorted.

Budge stood struggling like a cow stuck in a muddy gateway. Twirly watched in horror, but only for a moment.

He ripped off the rucksack and satchel and tossed them to the feet of the Major who stood swaying like a dead carline thistle.

'BUDGE!' Twirly cried in a parade-ground voice. 'Stop struggling. Take off your pack and chuck it back to me.'

He stepped gingerly forward into the wobbling, sucking green until his wellingtons were all but submerged. He watched Budge fumble with his straps and twist round to hurl his pack, his face contorted with alarm.

With his fence-post stick, Twirly hooked the backpack and hauled it towards him. He shouted, 'Now, Budge – SIT DOWN!'

Budge stood paralysed.

'SIT!' commanded Twirly.

Budge hesitated, then plopped backwards.

'Now lay back to spread the weight.'

Budge lowered his shoulders on to the ooze.

'Now put your hands above your head and reach for my wrists.'

Twirly sank down and slithered forward on his belly with his arms outstretched until he could grasp Budge's trembling cuffs.

'Now,' he said quietly, 'pull out your right leg.'

Budge snorted and swore and pumped his leg up and down until it came clear of the greedy quagmire.

'Now the other leg!'

More snorting, more swearing, until the other leg was dragged clear with the morass falling away like melting snow from a steaming roof.

'Now, when I say 'push', you dig in your heels and push like hell. I'll pull.'

Budge pushed.

Twirly pulled.

And Budge moved a few inches.

Twirly edged back on his elbows, and lifted his boots and slammed his toes into the bog like Clint Eastwood in the ice of *The Eiger Sanction*.

'PUSH!'

'PUSH!'
'PUSH!'

But this time when Twirly slammed down his toes, he found firm ground. Wet but firm.

'Almost there, Budge!' he called.

Another couple of heaves and Budge was lying amongst tufts of marsh arrowgrass, gasping like a trout in a landing-net.

Twirly turned to the Major who stood shakily holding out his half-bottle of brandy – uncorked. His face was afire and glistening with sweat.

'Could I exchange a swig of this for a sup from your water bottle, Corporal? I seem to have foolishly exhausted mine . . .' and his parched lips croaked to a halt.

Budge sat up, still heaving.

'Bodmin should be banned,' he gasped. 'After you with the brandy.'

'What now, Budge?' asked Twirly, assembling himself into his rucksack and the Major's satchel.

Budge sighed.

'Need to go around this lot, Twirly. Then head north-west. Hope to pick up the Bolventor slip-road or the A30.'

He scrambled to his feet and clawed up his backpack.

Twirly followed him to the left, and the terrain changed. Not bog. Nor roughly tufted moor. But shallow surface-water like the water-meadows of the meandering Booky Tweet.

Presently Twirly stopped, and held up his hand like an Indian brave in *The Last of The Mohicans*.

'Listen!' he demanded.

Budge stopped.

Twirly turned and silently splashed along into the mist.

There was the noise again.

Moorhens!

He prowled a few more paces, then rushed back to where Budge and the Major stood as patient as refugees.

'It's a lake,' he cried. 'Not a puddle. Not a pond. But a bloody great lake! Your map show a lake, Budge?'

Budge stood as if he had been hit by a flying duck, then he furiously groped for his map, his eyes shining.

For a few seconds he twisted and turned his map, then advanced on Twirly with his fist raised.

He thumped him on the chest.

'Dozmary Pool! You've discovered Dozmary Pool.'

The mystic pool where the dying King Arthur instructed his faithful Sir Belvedere to hurl his Excalibur sword, and where a gleaming white arm arose from the water, grasped the weapon, and sank with it below the surface.

Budge stepped forward so that he and Twirly were only a nose apart, and he said quietly, 'But what is more important, Albert Valentino Whippet, I now know *exactly* where we are.'

He laughed, and brushed lumps of moss from his chin, and turned to the Major.

'Hang on for a bit longer, Sir. Within the hour the Corporal and I will have you tucked up in bed surrounded by vestal virgins fanning you with cool frigidaire breezes and serving you with iced exotic fruits such you have never seen before.'

The map was gloriously correct.

A grass-edged road ran up the west side of the pool and Budge knew that it ran directly up to the front door of the Jamaica Inn.

He watched Twirly lift the Major's arm and curl it along the top of his rucksack, and the two of them strode off up the road like a courting couple. Budge rushed after them, took the Major's cane, and they marched along together, the three of them, with eyes down, ignoring the damp cocoon of white haze enfolding them, seeing only the road. Just the hypnotic road.

All we need now, he thought, is Dorothy and Toto in front.

Twenty minutes later the mist ahead momentarily glowed yellow, followed almost immediately by another brief golden suffusion, but this time with the unmistakeable sound of a car.

'We're there,' Budge said.

The Major stiffened and struggled free of their embrace.

'My cane, Mr Ballflower, if you please.'

He straightened his saturated jungle hat and Budge watched as he drew himself upright.

Chin up.

Cane at the slope.

A rasping clearing of the throat.

'Right. Lead the way, Corporal. Bags of swank now. Show these HQ wallahs what we're made of.'

The fog shrouding the slate-clad Jamaica Inn swirled across the cobbled courtyard, drifted around a handful of cars and two sleeping snub-nosed tour coaches, and did its best to smother the outdoor lighting.

In the brightly lit reception office a matronly lady greeted them with raised eyebrows.

'Surely you haven't walked in this?'

Twirly sniffed.

Budge nodded.

'We started this morning in Devon.'

She turned to her glowing crystal screen, but caught sight of the perspiring flushed Major.

'You all right, Sir?'

'Malaria,' said Twirly.

She slowly handed the Major a key dangling from a piece of slate.

'Shall I call a doctor?'

Budge saw the Major smile for the first time that day as he held up his hand.

'Thank you. But almost certainly I know more about it than him, my dear – benign tertiary Malaria. Know what I have to do, and I have my chloroquine tablets. Thank you. Most kind.'

He turned to Budge.

305

'Mr Ballflower, I will be much obliged if you will advise the mess President that I wish to be excused appearing for dinner this evening.'

He turned, swinging his satchel and his key, and began to mount the red and blue carpeted stairs, but paused.

'Corporal Whippet – fine performance today. I'll be speaking to Brigade. Meanwhile, kindly ensure the men are properly fed and watered.'

Again he set off, this time a little shakily, only to pause once more.

'And advise them we are to be pulled out of the line in the morning.'

He turned to continue climbing – and collapsed on the stairs like a puppet with its strings slashed.

Budge, now scraped and scrubbed, stretched on his bed watching the mist folding and curling around a weeping lamp outside his window.

It is finished - we can't go on.

The adventure is over.

He was surprised at his reaction.   Relief and regret – plus a strange feeling of deep emptiness.

Must call Doll and tell her. Not now perhaps. In the morning, after breakfast.

Meanwhile – dinner.

He searched the Smugglers' Bar with its dark timber counter and granite footrest, but there was no sign of Twirly, although the barman said he had been in the kitchen earlier persuading chef to make a bowl of hot beef broth, which he'd taken up to the Major's room with a jug of iced water.

Neither was Twirly in the large Du Maurier dining room, now almost empty; so he ordered a bottle of house red and the roast saddle of venison with juniper and thyme.

Saturday 25th July *Day twenty*

Budge leapt to the window of his sunlit room and gasped with astonishment.

During the night the Jamaica Inn had miraculously emerged from a damp, sinister chrysalis and bloomed into a slate-coloured butterfly surrounded by sparkling green and rolling hills.

Above, the heavens were clear and dazzlingly blue, with an eager sun warming the window-sill to his touch. The air was sharp and clean and smelled of peppermint.

It's going to be a wonderful day.

Then he remembered . . .

He drooped and sighed.

Must go and see the patient.

He groped for his shirt.

Bang! BANG! The door was kicked.

'Wakey-wakey!'

Twirly's voice.

'Wakey-wakey!

Rise and shine,

The morning's fine,

There's a mangle to turn,

And money to earn,

For father's been took for a soldier.'

'Budge. We leave in an hour.'

Hell!

He slumped against the MFI wardrobe.

Now what?

Has he booked an ambulance?

Or worse?

Budge rushed to the door.

Twirly stood beaming and pristine as a new tube of toothpaste, hair combed, wearing his clean Hawaiian shirt, and wellingtons shining like twin ebony umbrella stands.

He pressed a steaming mug of tea into Budge's bewildered hand.

'Had dinner last night in the special room reserved for coach-drivers – there's a discount. A party from Burnley is going to Newquay. The driver's agreed to take us.'

Budge gaped.

Twirly's face fell.

'You *did* say we had to get to Newquay?'

Budge clapped a hand onto Twirly's shoulder.

'Four-square!' cried the stonemason, beaming like Sunny Jim leaping from a carton of *Force*.

The route he had envisaged involved two days walking to the coast.

With transport, they could be in Newquay in two hours.

Wow!

'But the Major?'

'Look out of your window.

'He's down there stomping about like an impatient bridegroom. Two poached eggs and a kipper for breakfast. Been to see the du Maurier exhibition. Now he's raring to go.'

'His malaria?'

Twirly chuckled.

'Reached its climax when you were up to your arse in bog. Always goes quicker than it comes. Still got a slight temperature, and a bit wobbly, but he's taking the pills. Shall I nip down and order you a full English?'

Budge stood numb.

Who are these guys?

Chapter Thirty-three

At eight-thirty the blue-and-white Morpeth Tours coach was full of bubbling expectancy.

'Your people are good timekeepers,' said Budge.

Sandy, the driver, grinned.

'Fourth day of the tour. Early call at seven. Breakfast at half-past. Pack. On to the coach. Every morning for a week. Pensioners. Indestructible.'

Sandy turned to Twirly and confided, 'They prefer to sit near the front – they think they get there sooner. There's plenty of seats at the rear. I'll drop you at Hotel Victoria, if that's all right.'

He lowered his voice.

'If I was you I'd come forward as soon as we pull into the hotel forecourt. The instant I cut the engine they struggle up from their seats and block the gangway checking that overhead bags haven't gone missing during the journey. Then they all join in a quick game of Where's My Handbag?'

He looked at his watch.

'Right! Let's get moving.'

By the time the coach reached Brockabarrow Common, Twirly and the Major were swaying together with eyes closed like day-old puppies. Had they been conscious at Indian Queens, Budge would have told them the story.

In 1616 an English tobacco trader arrived in Falmouth from Virginia with his attractive almond-eyed wife, a North American princess with the name of Matoaca. Their London-bound stage stopped overnight at The Old Inn on Kelliers Common.

The landlord was overwhelmed, and decided to rename his pub in honour of the royal visitor. However, he considered INDIAN

PRINCESS not grand enough and chose to call it THE INDIAN QUEEN.

The story has a sad ending.

Despite all of London feting her, she became horribly homesick and asked to be taken back to Virginia.

On the homeward-bound ship she instantly fell ill and was put ashore at the Thames port of Gravesend where it was customary for river-pilots to be dropped.

There she died.

Budge learned the story in 1991 when he was replacing mullions in the Gravesend church of St George. He watched people from Virginia unveil a bronze statue of the Indian princess dressed in buckskins with a single-feather head-dress.

The plinth of Caen stone bears her old Indian nickname meaning 'little-mischief' – POCAHONTAS.

Just before ten o'clock they reached Newquay. The coach swung into the forecourt of the creeper-covered Victoria, and Budge saw two waistcoated porters burst from the hotel's conservatory entrance skilfully propelling brass-hooped trolleys.

He leapt to his feet.

'This way!'

Pushing his backpack before him, he bulldozed through the avenue of elbows already forming along the gangway.

'Great!' he said to the driver, and pressed a folded something into his hand.

Close behind him Twirly fumbled in his rucksack and produced a small white parcel and accompanied his sniff of appreciation with a wink.

Bank Street was already busy with intrepid holiday-makers.

Amusement arcades were preparing for a day of hilarity, and Kiss-Me-Quick shops stood eager to dispense seaside tat at only slightly more than daylight robbery. Budge threaded them past family convoys burdened with all the bright paraphernalia of a jolly day on the beach and they kicked their way through areas participating in Newquay's highly successful 1998 Litter Festival.

'What d'you give to the driver, Twirly?' called Budge.

'Pot of greengage-and-walnut chutney.'

Budge turned to stare.

'Mrs Wentworth gave it me yesterday. Homemade. To cheer us up if we got lost on the moor.'

On Central Square the born-again Major held up his cane like a Japanese tour leader.

'Mr Ballflower. Corporal Whippet and I need to do some shopping – of a personal nature.'

Hell's Bells.

Budge scowled at his watch.

'See you down on the harbour in half-an-hour.'

Budge sat on a green bench in front of the white patio of the red-roofed Harbour Hotel.

The tide was out and the small stone harbour was bottomed with glistening yellow sand. Around a grass-topped island in the centre lolled a handful of yachts connected to land by a tangle of lines like an ancient telephone switchboard.

Stretching for almost a mile to the north ran a golden beach punctuated by rocky headlands. A fragile footbridge restrained a tiny island from floating away.

To the left a shimmering, endless diorama of sea stretched three thousand miles to Newfoundland.

It was bluer than the Mediterranean between Amalfi and Capri. Bluer than the midday sky above the Glaoui city of Ouarzazate. Bluer than the bottomless lake of Torneträsk beyond Sweden's Arctic Circle.

Budge checked his watch again, and wondered what the two ancient warriors might be up to.

'You wearing clean socks, Corporal?'

Twirly pondered.

'Think I washed them the day we were at the steam fair.'

The Major sighed.

That was a week and several bogs ago.

'The problem is, Corporal . . .'

But Twirly slung off his rucksack and, beaming like Jack Horner, produced a pink paper bag.

'New socks, Sir. Doll sent them with Budge.'

'In that case, Corporal, follow me.'

Budge's portable telephone rang.

Doll.

One: She is being pestered by the Cynthia woman who insists it's essential she gets in touch with the Major.

Two: Cheltenham museum has made an offer for the Roman stone – his stone.

Three: There's a rumour in the village that English Heritage are going to open Twirly's Fish House to the public.

'Apart from that . . . how are they?'

'They are fine, Doll. The Major had . . .'

'How is Twirly?'

'He is fine, Doll . . .'

'Tell him I rang.'

Budge thumbed through his Guide to Newquay.

The 'new' of Newquay is not particularly new. It dates from 1439 when the Bishop of Exeter gave the inhabitants of Towan Blistra permission to build a new quay.

He was suddenly impelled to look up towards the promenade.

Hell! I'm catching the instincts of an old soldier.

Sure enough, there they were, passing in front of the Beach-Goods shack, marching along like two guardsmen.

They both looked surprisingly tall and upright and were kicking their feet out like Bluebell Girls.

And that's when he saw the Major's boots.

New brown boots with red laces.

Twirly, too.

His wellingtons gone. His trousers tucked into red socks; and he also was wearing new brown boots.

They stamped to the steps where Budge sat and slammed to a halt.

'Sah!' snapped Twirly.

And Budge noticed that Twirly's redundant wellingtons were hung from his rucksack 'at the reverse', exactly as the Duke's boots hung from the saddle of the stallion Copenhagen in the London funeral procession of 1852.

'I approve of the boots, Major.'

The Major beamed.

'Ready for the big push.'

Budge folded the morning's copy of *The Times* purchased from Newquay News and Spar.

'You will be pleased to know, Major, that your savings are safe. Yesterday, 25th July, Gordon Brown vehemently denied that the country is heading towards recession. "There will be no crash-landing he promises."' Budge sighed and dropped *The Times* in the adjacent waste-bin.

At the top of concrete steps on to King Edward Crescent, Budge was delighted to discover a wooden post bearing a black acorn logo and a yellow arrow.

Wonderful.

From here the South West Way is marked all the way to Land's End.

This long-distance route, apart from being England's longest at 630 miles, is also the best marked and maintained, and the least threatened by farmers and landowners, largely due to the diligence of the voluntary South West Way Association.

It is estimated that the path generates three million pounds a year for the local economy.

The grey, inelegant Atlantic Hotel squatted on the summit of a bank of thistles. Below it sat the Headlands Hotel, a delightful Victorian whimsy in yellow and red brick. Surprisingly, *both* hotels built by the unloved Silvanus Trevail.

Budge saw the Major tip his cane to his hat as they passed the war memorial.

A white huer's hut, where a lookout once watched for the arrival of pilchards, shone in the sun like a wedding-cake.

They crunched along the soft sands of Fistral Beach where roaring white waves skilfully juggled a flotsam of brightly clad figures crouching on surfboards.

Budge sighed.

Surfing. Florida 1975. Whatever happened to the nubile Angela who still owes him six dollars?

A flight of steps dropped down the steep flank of Pentire East to the Fern Pit Café on the banks of the River Gannel. A notice read*:*

Open to the public daily rain or shine
Footbridge free
Ferry 60p as and when you wish to cross

The slate-clad café displayed an 'OPEN' sign large enough to be seen from the opposite side of the river, and a blackboard offered: *Snacks – Freshly cooked lobster'*

They took a table on the terrace.

'Lobster?' asked Budge.

'Tea,' sniffed Twirly.

She looked gorgeous.

Probably seventeen, thought Budge.

She swerved between the green clothed tables, slim as a tightly rolled rug. Her hair black and glossy, her eyes dew-washed sloes.

Budge noticed that even the Major jerked himself upright and snatched off his floppy jungle-hat.

'Do you have cake?' asked Budge.

She lowered a small notepad and spoke carefully, as if she was taking a pronunciation test.

'We have Garden of Eden Cake.'

Her sloe eyes studied all three.

'It is full of forbidden fruit.'

Budge smoothed the green tablecloth.

314

The Major gave a little cough.

Twirly said, *'Ne. Parakalo. Malista – tria. Efharisto poli.'*

The dark eyebrows lifted, dazzling white teeth smiled and, with a slight bow, she glided away between the tables.

Budge watched her go, then turned to Twirly.

'She's Greek,' Twirly said.

'You been to Greece?'

Twirly squinted across the river to the far beach where a mass of coloured windbreaks resembled a resupply-drop of colour-coded parachutes.

'When Jerry was pulling out of Greece, they dropped us on an airfield to the West of Athens – to hurry him up a bit.

'My battalion, 4th Wessex, went in first to take the airfield, but the wind speed was thirty-five miles an hour. Too high. We were dragged along the deck like leaves on a concrete drive. Fifty of the battalion had broken arms or legs. Three killed; one was a medic.'

The Major grimaced.

Twirly continued. 'Greeks were great at first – cheered and made a fuss. Then the royalists and communists began scrapping with each other. Then the communists turned on *us* with the Stens and mortars we had dropped to them a year before.

'Tricky street-fighting. We had four hundred casualties. They were right bastards. Our Medical Officer, Captain Irwin, climbed from an ambulance at the Acropolis Museum, fifty yards from the Parthenon . . . CRACK! Shot in the head by a sniper.

'But the worst was when trade unions in England claimed we were murdering innocent workers and the TUC sent out a delegation – in the middle of the war – to check.

'We were assembled in a theatre where the General Secretary, a bloke called Tewson, told us we could talk freely as our officers had promised there would be no recriminations.'

'And?' asked Budge.

'The blokes lit fags, or got in some badly needed kip, then we were ordered back on to the streets to be shot at again. The union men went back to England to do whatever it is union people do in wartime.'

Twirly squinted.

'I think they organised a dock strike.'

The tide was out and from the Gannel footbridge they strode across the firm wet corrugated sand of the wide Crantock beach.

Black-backed gulls defiantly ignored the three pairs of boots, reluctantly fluttering aside at the last moment and screaming with indignation. Their brown, fat youngsters merely froze, and threw back their heads with plaintive, high-pitched whines.

Up on the headland of Pentire West stretched pastures manicured to National Trust standards. One field was a gilded carpet of bright yellow corn-marigold. In another, newly mown hay lay sunbathing in long curving lines, filling the air with the scent of summer.

Around Kelsey Head the walking was magnificent with cliff-edge paths skirting deep inlets and secret coves. Far below, frothy white waves ceaselessly assaulted dripping black rocks, while heavy-bodied Fulmars hovered on cliff face thermals with disdainful ease, often suddenly appearing above the cliff edge like old-time cinema organists.

Twirly pointed to a distant shape, a long Noah's Ark sitting hazily on the horizon.

'Container ship,' said Budge.

Twirly squinted.

'Ten miles away?'

'Down on the beach the horizon is about three miles. Climb up twenty feet and you can see for six miles. From up here, you can probably see for fifteen miles.'

Twirly walked off muttering, 'When you're clinging to a floating piece of green plywood the size of a sheep-hurdle, you can only see as far as the next wave.'

Hell is he talking about?

Budge guessed the hazy, purple headland ahead might be St Agnes. But here, just below them, stretched the glorious half-mile long Holywell beach.

Down on rolling dunes of hot Sahara sand, National Trust boardwalks led them easily through plantations of dusty marram grass and patches

316

of spiny blue-green sea-holly and purple sea-bindweed and into the centre of crowded seaside holiday-land.

They threaded past sandcastles, and sunbathers, and rugs, and sand-covered sandwiches, and small children who stared at these overdressed aliens who were probably escaping from an episode of *Dr Who*.

Behind the beach was a toytown of holiday chalets and they bought three bottles of beer and take-away pasties from noisily busy Treguth Inn. Up in the silence of deserted Penhale Point they threw off their packs by a bench in memory of Michael John.

While Budge unwrapped the still steaming pasties, Twirly laid out the yellow silk identification triangle he had carried on the drop over the Rhine, and covered it with assorted offerings:

Handful of brown sauce sachets.
Handful of tomato sauce sachets.
Three Jaffa oranges from the Jamaica Inn fruit bowl.
Gold foil mints from a flirting housemaid.
A package wrapped in a Waitrose bag…
'What's in the bag?' asked Budge.
'Greengage and walnut chutney from Mrs Wentworth.'
Budge raised his eyebrows.
'Thought you gave that to the coach driver.'
'She gave us three – one each. And she didn't say *if* you get lost. She said *when*.'

The Major collected his haversack rations and sank on to a mattress of soft grass and purple thrift in the shade of a great Sitting Bull of rock.

Just off the headland floated the twin islands of Gull Rocks, with a white yacht lay becalmed on an unbelievably blue sea.

He sighed and smiled.
You would have loved this.

Lunch over, the Major stood, and did a quick check:
Cane. Satchel. Hat. Tablets.
'Think I'll get going, Mr Ballflower. My doctor says, movement is your friend, Major Legge-Wellesley.'

Budge blinked awake.

'Right, Major. Just follow the waymarks. Keep the sea on your right. We'll be just behind you.'

Twirly hurriedly put away a postcard he was laboriously writing and scrambled to his feet.

The Major was grateful for the cooling *punkah wallah* breeze which danced over the edge of the cliff.

The track was wide and level. Low clumps of Inca-gold gorse enriched a royal-purple carpet of ling heather. Inland of the path, low piles of pink and brown shale were spread in front of a sinister Ministry of Defence chainlink barrier surrounding Penhale Camp, with ugly gulag buildings and aerial masts and perimeter lighting.

An unfriendly sign warned of 'Non-iodizing Radiation and High Voltages'.

A suspicious gull, hovering just ahead of him, was obviously in the pay of the Ministry, and probably a cleverly-disguised drone camera.

He strode past long-dead mine shafts, crowned with barbed-wire and surrounded by yellow tormentil and clumps of Persil-white clover.

Now ahead and far below, the Major could see the golden sands of Perran beach, as empty as a forgotten wartime runway, and the path suddenly turned inland and became vertiginous, with a grass-covered cliff dropping steeply down on the right.

Now a junction.

One track continued ahead, but one turned sharply right, heading down the cliff. This was obviously the one most walked, and this was the one he took.

But it quickly became alarmingly narrow, and threaded along a deep, boot-wide cleft between large rocks, and he was only able to progress by slowly sliding one foot in front of the other, crouching, and steadying himself on the boulders on either side.

Sweat in his eyes made it difficult to see where he was placing his boots.

He crept forward and stopped . . . *'Arrgh!'*

Immediately beyond his boot the cliff ended with a sheer drop to the beach, fifteen feet below.

Blast! He had fallen for the trap he often warned about at jungle school. A SPUR path may look more walked than the main trail SIMPLY BECAUSE IT COMES TO A DEAD-END – and the double-wear from retraced steps gives the appearance of heavy use.

With no room to turn his feet around, he must shuffle backwards and call to the others admitting his mistake.

'Budge!'

But then . . .

'You all right up there?'

A woman's voice, coming from the beach below.

He swished an arm across his dripping forehead and leaned forward to peer over the edge.

There was indeed a woman, staring up at him.

'You all right?'

The Major pressed his hands harder into the boulders and blinked his eyes clear.

But she was still there.

He groaned, and shook his head in disbelief.

The woman appeared to be completely naked.

Chapter Thirty-four

'Is there a problem, Major?'

The Major stood transfixed, both hands pushing against the boulders lining the narrow track.

Budge pushed forward to investigate.

Hell the old fool come this far? Obviously NOT the path. This trench is more like a Roman ankle-trap.

He placed a hand on to the Major's sweaty shoulder and pressed him gently aside so he could look down on to the empty beach.

Except the beach *wasn't* empty.

On the sand immediately below the rocky overhang stood a woman.

A voluptuous blonde woman.

A quite naked woman.

Unmistakably a natural blonde.

STEADY, Budge.

The apparition lifted an arm and pointed and with a reassuring smile called, 'There are plenty of footholds.'

She nodded sideways at two children standing in a circle of sandcastles, with plastic spades and not a stitch of clothing.

'They've been up and down there all day.'

The bewildered Major turned to look at Budge.

The woman continued, 'You'll be all right. I can talk you down if you like,' she said, and she clambered on to a three-foot high rock platform at the foot of the cliff and reached up.

'Hand me down your stick.'

The Major perilously transferred his cane, and Budge steadied him whilst he shakily turned about like a nervous old lady preparing to get off a bus.

The woman called, 'Your *right* boot. Move it down. More to the right. Bit lower. THAT'S IT! Now the left boot . . .'

320

Two minutes later the perspiring Major was standing on the platform, reclaiming his cane and flushed with triumph.

'It's a doddle, Mr Ballflower,' he called. 'Remember, don't use your knees – feet and hands only.'

Old fool. I know how to scramble.

As he followed the siren's instructions, Budge wondered how the shorter-legged Twirly would cope. But he checked himself. The seventy-three-year old could still climb trees like a squirrel and had a two-week old scar to prove it.

Safely down on the beach, Budge watched the Major shake the woman's hand as he mumbled words of thanks, all the time keeping his eyes firmly out to sea. Twirly, on the other hand, seemed unaware that she was unclothed, and enthusiastically related how they were all from Upper Gently, and were walking to Land's End, and would she kindly accept this pot of homemade Devonshire greengage-and-walnut-chutney?

He also pressed a handful of Glacier Mints on to the two children and asked their ages.

They were six and seven.

Budge stood awkwardly and watched the two old soldiers depart with brave waves of farewell, kicking up clouds of sand as they ploughed along the beach, eager for the next operational hazard, and looking for Rommel.

'Thank you,' said Budge softly. 'Don't know what we would have done . . .'

He shook her hand, staring into her chuckling soft grey eyes, resolutely refusing to look anywhere else.

She smiled and tossed her blonde hair.

'It was nothing. It made a welcome change from watching interminable building of sand castles.'

They turned to watch the departing warriors and she laughed.

'They move fast. Don't you ever lose them?'

Budge shook his head.

'Unfortunately, no.'

They laughed again, and Budge realised he was still holding her hand.

He remembered the soft hot hand of the blonde who asked if she could sit by him on the cog-railway trundling up the 7,000-feet Mount Pilatus, overlooking the Lake of Lucerne . . .

Finally, he sped after his charges.

Foam-edged sheets of water slid back and forth beneath his boots, while further out waves rushed threateningly towards him, but suddenly capitulated just feet away in angry thundering cascades and retreated back towards the horizon hissing with frustration.

Up in a gloriously blue arena of sky, herring gulls wheeled about in a lazy air display which deserved to be accompanied by Vaughan Williams.

He looked around for skylarks. There were none. There ought to be – right now there ought to be.

In the soft sand, by an outcrop of rock, Twirly and the Major sat awaiting orders to continue the attack.

The Major had inserted a white handkerchief beneath his jungle hat so that it hung down over the back of his neck like a Foreign Legion kepi.

Twirly crouched under his black Morris hat like an Algerian orderly.

Budge slammed to a halt.

'*Attendez, mon braves,*' he growled in his best Beau Geste voice. '*Le fort de Perranporth est pres d'ici.*' And he waved his hand towards the end of the beach where dark hordes were gathered.

He loved Twirly's smile of recognition.

Twirly's education had been in the private sector: sixpence a session on Saturday mornings in Torking's Roxy Cinema.

Suddenly Budge crumpled into a laugh.

'Wow! What did the young lady do for your fever, Major?'

The Major raised his eyebrows.

'She was very kind.'

Budge looked closely. Beneath those fluffy-white eyebrows the Major's eyes twinkled and danced like wicked fireflies.

He chuckled. 'Come on, pass us your brandy, you old lecher.'

They broke camp, and fell-in, and advanced at a plunging pace through minor sandstorms surrounding their boots. The constant pounding of the sea sounded like distant gunfire.

Over on the left a stream of rust-coloured water poured from a rock in the dunes to form a large pool and a wide shallow stream meandered down to the sea.

From an ice-cream snack bar, a zig-zag stairway alive with people climbed up grey and red cliffs. A large board announced: *Welcome to Perran Sands.* A smaller sign read: *Your lifeguards are Mike and Fifi.*

Out at sea, far ahead, Budge could see the Bawden Rocks like moored ships awaiting instructions from a harbour master.

Now they rounded the grey-green outcrop of Cotty's Point, and the whole of bustling Perranporth lay revealed, with boulders, holiday-makers, houses, hotels, and sun-flashing cars.

The sea was alive with an enormous shoal of screeching, waving, splashing people, watched enviously by timid, trouser-rolled paddlers who bobbed up and down on the water's edge with waves tickling their ankles.

Determined young men streamed back and forth across the beach, some bronzed and gleaming, some pale as supermarket chickens, all purposefully clutching colourful surf-boards.

Families sat having holiday fun within the confines of gently billowing canvas screens which staked out their territorial claims. Seaside smells of salty seaweed and wet rubber combined with a homely whiff of barbecue burnt-offerings and Budge recalled his mother's gritty sandwiches and thermos-flasks of odd-tasting lukewarm tea at Bournemouth.

High above in the dazzling sky, weaved whirling stunt kites, controlled by unseen string-pilots.

At the far end of the beach the shimmering white arches of the Seiners Arms Hotel resembled a film star's villa on the beach of Positano.

Budge twitched his sweat-soaked shirt away from his backpack straps like a Wimbledon player who wishes he was doing better:

'This way,' he cried, and they splashed like wild horses across the confluence of shallow streams sliding across the beach.

'Dinner is from seven,' said the smiling man in the Seiners Arms as he presented them with room keys as if they were medals for bravery.

The dark-haired girl called Jo in the Information Office next to the hotel in Porth Street, asked, 'You walking the coast path?'

Budge nodded, and she recommended the annual guide published by the South West Way Association.

'You Australian?'

'Perth.'

'Good on ya,' said Budge.

'Welcome to Perranporth billabong,' winked Jo.

Bathed, cooled, and perfumed, Budge strolled amongst the coloured umbrellas on the hotel's beach-side patio, contentedly swirling the clinking ice in a gin, lime and lemonade.

And there was Twirly.

He was still in his walking gear, but with pink bare feet, standing by a white plastic table covered with an assortment of brushes and yellow cloths, looking like a street trader in Naples.

Budge nodded at the two pairs of new brown boots, with red laces removed.

'The Major's as well?'

'Told him I'd treat them to their first proper polish – up to stick-man standard.'

'He coming down to dinner?'

Twirly shook his head.

'But he's fine. Taking an early night, but given the kitchen an order for iced melon, steamed lemon sole with spinach, Cornish junket – and a glass of chilled Chablis.'

'Right,' said Budge.

He watched Twirly dip two fingers into an open tin of Marron Rouge Kiwi, and with a swirling action, smear it across the toes of all four boots.

Budge said, 'I never thanked you . . .'

Twirly stopped swirling and studied his chocolate-coloured finger-tips.

' . . . for extracting me from the bog.'

Budge continued, 'Very impressive. Done it before?'

Twirly lifted a boot and treated the toe to a squirt of spit.

'Once dragged a bloke out of a minefield . . .'

With a yellow-cloth he slowly worked the spit-and-polish paste into the toe-cap.

'Half-way up Italy. Far side of the River Garigliano. Bloke's foot had been blown off by a Schuh mine.'

'Shoe mine? They had a mine for blowing off shoes?'

Twirly put down the boot, and picked up another, and chuckled.

'Jerry had these small mines – half a pound of explosive packed in a wooden box – couldn't be detected by our Polish mine detectors.'

Twirly stopped his boot ablutions and looked out across the beach to the restless blue sea.

'Jerry made us keep our heads down.'

Budge sipped his drink.

'Sounds dicey.'

Twirly reached for a pint glass Budge had not previously noticed and sniffed:

'Budge. That's what medics did.'

A screeching seagull with its under-carriage down, boldly alighted on the edge of the table. Twirly swooshed it away.

'Ah yes,' said Budge. 'These conscientious objectors in your unit? They parachute with the others?'

Twirly took a long drink and stared at Budge as if he was speaking Swahili.

Budge persisted.

'They were volunteers?'

Twirly passed the back of his polish-smeared hand across his mouth.

'All paras were volunteers.'

He picked up another boot.

'Some of these 'conchies' were great at volunteering. Blokes in my unit had shiny scars on their arms from when they volunteered to be guinea-pigs for antidotes against mustard gas, which everybody thought Jerry would use. When he began bombing London, five hundred of them volunteered to act as navvies for the Sapper unexploded-bomb squads. When the blitz stopped, they volunteered to drop with paras as medics.

'My unit in 6th Airborne was 224 Parachute Field Ambulance – a hundred strong. Thirty of them were conchies.'

Budge looked across the beach.

It was now almost deserted except for a few dawdling couples not wanting the day to end.

The wind-breaking-screens had been rolled and taken away. A few scavenging seagulls wandered around picking and pecking.

He emptied his glass.

'Vaughan Williams volunteered to be a medic in the First War. Drove an ambulance on the Western Front. See you at dinner in half-an-hour, Twirly.'

Sunday 26th July *Day twenty-one*

Budge found the Major and Twirly in the breakfast room at a table beneath a suspended crabpot, overlooking Perranporth sands.

The Major beamed.

'Morning, Mr Ballflower!   We can recommend the Fisherman's Fry-up.'

'Feeling better?'

The Major nodded enthusiastically, gulped urgently, and said, 'Still taking the tablets, of course. Twirly says it's Sunday. I asked for an early breakfast so I could go to Communion. He can't come – still has work to do on the boots. You care to join me? St Michael's, just down the road?'

Budge shook his head.

'Need to study the guidebook I just bought. Anyway, I don't do Communion, Major. In fact, I don't do church at all. An unbeliever, I'm afraid.'

Budge could see the Major was shocked.

'And you a vicar's son?'

Budge grinned.

'Perhaps *because* I'm a vicar's son.'

'Good heavens,' said the Major, and he cruelly stabbed a golden grilled sprat spread-eagled on a 'soldier' of fried-bread. But he brightened instantly and produced a paperback from beneath his chair.

'Thank you for the *Medieval Masons*. Fascinating.'

Budge nodded. 'Pleasure.'

The Major looked puzzled.

'Book belong to one of your brothers?'

Hell's he talking about?

The Major waved his empty fork.

'The name inside is Dr J.C. Ballflower.'

Budge nodded. 'That's me.'

'Doctor?'

'Did a PhD on English Monasteries.'

He watched the Major thrust his fork to skilfully skewer a scallop wrapped in bacon.

'Ah!' he said.

It was ten o'clock when they left the hotel, heading past the Youth Hostel and towards the cliffs overlooking Shag Rock. By ten-thirty they were on sun-soaked Cligga Head looking back along the golden two-mile strip of Perran beach.

'Once the city of Langarrow,' said Budge. 'Now buried under those dunes. Stamped out by storms and sand for being sinful. You get to Communion all right, Major?'

The spectacular cliff path wandered amongst fenced-off shafts and red-brick ruins.

Piles of coloured shale poised in danger of tumbling over crumbling cliffs.

'This place once crawled with toiling men. Copper and tin mining.'

He read from his guidebook:

Slowly turning wheels, slapping belts, sliding rods, slimy slurry streams of yellow, red, and grey, and tall spewing chimneys of stone with brick toppings . . .

He watched the Major and Twirly suddenly crouch, and a great yellow and white glider hissed over their heads. It dropped down towards the sea, then soared up and away like a released cage-bird.

He saw the Major raise his eyebrows at Twirly.

'From Trevallas airfield,' said Budge.

Spitfire squadrons were based here in 1942 protecting convoys from attack by German fighters. Canadian Hurricanes, with bombs slung beneath their wings, regularly flew from these cliffs to attack enemy destroyers off the Breton coast.

The path passed dangerously close to the cliff-edge, and they stopped to look down at furious waves pounding noisily into the dramatic cleft of Hanover Cove.

'Magnificent,' breathed the Major.

'The cove is named after a Falmouth Packet brig which smashed onto those rocks,' said Budge. 'December 1763. Thirty-crew – only three saved.'

'Some say the cargo of 60,000 gold coins is still down there.'

Budge watched Twirly peering down into the thrashing foam, making quick calculations.

'Coffee in half-an-hour, in Trevaunce,' he said.

In the Driftwood Spars Hotel the perspiring Major insisted the coffees be augmented by three pints of Hick's Special Draught, to replace lost liquids.

On the gloriously flat and wide cliff top path on Agnes Head the views were breathtaking, and Budge opened his map.

'About a mile offshore – those are the Bawden Rocks. Twenty miles to the north is Trevose Head near Padstow. Down in the haze to the south is St Ives Head, perhaps fifteen miles.'

All quite wonderful.

They stood in silent Sunday-morning worship.

Behind an inland wall stood a long line of sad-eyed cows, and Twirly gave them a friendly, 'Hi-up!' The captive cows moaned with envy, and chewed reflectively, hoping there would soon be a letter from home.

Ahead Budge could see the ruined buildings of Coates mine. In Cornish, *Wheal Coates.* On a lower path a stone tower with brick arched windows and a chimney of yellow stone and red brick stood prominently like a clenched hand with a raised finger.

The pumping house of the 636-feet (106 fathoms) Towanwroath shaft was built in 1873 to lift water from this never very prosperous copper and tin mine. The mine closed seventeen years later and the ruined buildings have been splendidly restored by the National Trust.

Budge could clearly see the great slot in which a massive metal arm – the bob – slid up and down, day and night, pumping water from the lower levels in the same way that the village pump worked.

Down on the beach at Chapel Porth cove, in the National Trust open-fronted stone-shelter, they had pasties, followed by Hedgehog Surprise, a creation of ice-cream smothered in clotted cream and rolled in honey-roasted hazelnuts.

'Watch your steps, men,' called Budge.

The path rising from the cove was narrow as a sheep track. A grass bank dropped down almost vertically onto the smooth wet sand, where three lifeguards sat by a red tractor.

On Mulgram Hill the path became wide and flat and wandered amongst screes of all colours scattered around ruined engine houses, fenced shafts, and a small thick walled stone tower, probably built as an explosives store.

'Great Wheal Charlotte,' said Budge. He wandered over to examine the remains of an old bob wall looking like a triumphal arch which would not have been out of place on the Forum site in Rome.

Suddenly the industrial moonscape was left behind, and a perfumed path ran between a field of yellow corn dotted with bright red poppies and a dazzling display of blazing gorse and rich heathers.

The ceiling of Porthtowan's Commodore Inn was draped with fishing nets, lobster pots and coloured floats. Framed photographs on the cream walls were of sailing ships, wrecks on beaches, lifeboat crews, and assorted naval ships.

A red and blue poster announced the St Ives Annual Festival with Trelawney's Thread-the-Needle street dance; Redruth Silver Band and Camborne Prize Band to be in attendance.

Budge ordered three pints of St Austell Bosun's Bitter.

'Going far?' asked the grey-bearded landlord with rings in both ears and built like an ex-navy stoker.

Budge was about to reply when Twirly suddenly slammed his hand on to the bartop. With a quick glance at the Major, he pointed accusingly at a photograph behind a polished artillery shell.

'That picture?' he said.

He strode over to examine it more closely, then turned.

'What's *this* doing here?'

Chapter Thirty-five

'Know what it is?' called the ex-stoker landlord of the Commodore.

Twirly did.

It was a framed photograph of a Horsa troop carrying glider.

He nodded and returned to the bar.

The landlord explained to Budge and the Major:

'Caption says: Horsa glider on Portreath airfield, June 1943, before taking off for Africa.'

'Africa? Hell for?' snorted Budge.

The Major sighed and turned to the landlord:

'Think we are going to need three brandies.'

'Shall I make them doubles?'

The Major nodded, carefully aligned his moustache, rested his elbow on the polished bar, and began:

'It was like this, Budge. . .

'When the Allies decided to attack the 'soft under-belly' of Europe, a seaborne landing on Sicily was planned, backed up by British airborne troops already fighting in North Africa.

'Paratroops were to be dropped from C-47 Dakotas. Glider troops would be carried by American Waco gliders, already lying in crates awaiting assembly on Oran airfield in Algeria.

'But the 48-foot long Waco, built by Western Aircraft Corporation of Ohio, presented a problem: it could carry fifteen men, or a jeep, or a field gun.

'But not a jeep WITH a field-gun, Budge – and without a towing vehicle a field-gun is of limited use.   However, the 67-foot long Horsa glider, designed by Airspeed Aviation and built by English furniture manufacturers, could carry twenty-five men, or a jeep WITH a trailer or field-gun

'So Horsas were essential.

'The brave decision was made to fly these out from England to Africa, in time for the operation.'

It was a remarkable undertaking.

Four-engined Halifax tug-aircraft took off from Holmsley airfield in the New Forest and flew to Hurn near Bournemouth to pick up the gliders. These were then towed to Portreath airfield From here the tugs and gliders took off again for Rabat in Morocco – a flight of 1,300-miles, 300-miles further than the glider's recommended maximum range.

The Major took a sip of his brandy and glanced at the landlord to confirm the veracity of his words:

'To avoid enemy radar the flights skirted the western coasts of France and Spain, flying at wave-top height.

'The lumbering Horsas were exhausting to fly for even short flights, and the usual two-man crew was increased to three, working in thirty-minute shifts on the ten-hour flight.

'Forty-one gliders took off from Portreath.

'All but four arrived.'

Budge looked from the Major to the landlord, to Twirly:

'And then?'

The Major continued:.

'On July 13th 1943 – that's fifty-five years ago last Monday when we were in Shipham – a thousand glider men took off from Sousse, on the east coast of Tunisia. The fleet of gliders included the Horsas which had been towed to Africa from the cliffs just above us.'

Twirly moved from the bar, walked over to the open door, and stood in the sunshine.

'They flew for over three hundred miles to the island of Sicily to make a night attack on a bridge near Syracuse, to protect a sea-landing to be made by Montgomery's 5th Division at first light next morning.

'Unfortunately there was a massive cock-up.

'Invasion-fleet gunners had not been warned about the airborne operation.

332

'They blasted the tugs and gliders out of the sky, and three-hundred and fifty glider men were drowned.'

The Major swirled his brandy . . .

'Of the one hundred and thirty gliders leaving Tunisia, only fifty-two reached the island.

'Only twelve found the designated landing-zones.

'Only two reached the bridge.

'One of these crashed into the canal bank and exploded.

'In the other were twenty men of the 2nd South Staffs, commanded by a young Lieut.Withers. They rushed the bridge and captured it. 'Chunky' Curnock, the platoon medic who had been a miner in civilian life, treated the wounded and removed the explosive charges from the bridge.'

The Major lifted his eyes to check that Budge was comprehending; and took a ruminative drink.

Twirly remained gazing at the beach, and the sky, and the never ending sea.

The Major swirled his brandy:

'The First Parachute Brigade took off three days later in a hundred Dakotas to take *another* bridge, thirty miles further north. The *Ponte Primosole* over the river Simeto.

'This was Twirly's brigade.

'Twirly at that time was a lance-corporal-acting-unpaid, and as the brigade's official Hygiene Section he had acquired his own jeep and water-trailer. He, with a driver, and three medics was detailed to go in by one of the handful of gliders transporting vehicles.'

The Major called, 'That correct, Twirly?'

But Twirly was fifty five years and nine hundred and fifty miles away, and the Major continued.

'It was hoped that by this time the trigger-happy naval gunners would have got things sorted out.

'They hadn't.

'Of nearly two thousand parachutists, only three hundred reached the bridge. Of the nineteen gliders, only four reached the island.'

Through the pub door came the distant roar of the sea and the plaintive cries of seagulls.

333

Budge called, 'And *your* glider, Twirly?'

Twirly turned and looked across his brandy glass into the bar with its pictures of the sea and ships, its nets, its floats, its red and white lifebelt.

He looked down at his shiny new boots – and walked back to the bar and spoke softly:

'In our glider were two pilots, one of them from Macclesfield. Up front, by the cockpit-door, was an RE sapper, 'Bill' Bailey, and an RASC driver called Jock. The jeep and water-trailer were lashed in by thirty-one yellow chains. In the back was me and two RAMC lads.'

He peered into his brandy to check he was remembering correctly.

'They shot down our tug, and we ditched in the dark.'

The sun streamed through a large window with dust dancing in the beam. A couple of customers strolled over to the bar with their beers.

Budge said, 'And then?'

'Glider broke up. Jeep and trailer went down like parapet-stones dislodged from a bridge. The tail where we were strapped was shattered. We shouted and splashed and grabbed, and then three of us were clinging to this chunk of pale-green, ribbed plywood.'

Outside the pub an adolescent two-stroke squealed past like an angry chainsaw.

Twirly sighed and pulled himself upright.

'Hung on all night. Freezing. Hands stuck to the plywood-ribs. Mouth dry with salt. By the time it began to get light, the two medics had slipped away. And I knew . . .'

Twirly shook his head.

They wouldn't understand.

Not about Aunt Maggie.

Not about her being there in the water. Hanging on to this bit of tail-plane. And glaring at me, as she always did when she disapproved of what I was about to do . . .

Couldn't see properly: eyes stinging: lashes caked together.

But she was punching a finger at me. Kept jabbing.

334

Then I realised she wasn't pointing at ME, but over my shoulder.

Managed to twist.

Can see it now.

THERE WAS THIS BLOODY GREAT SHIP.

And then a wave away was a boat with sailors and men in green berets, and a dozen arms reaching out . . .

Budge said , 'And then, Twirly?'

Twirly finished his brandy and carefully replaced the glass on the bar.

'Three Commando were going-in to take a bridge seven miles to the south of ours. Somebody spotted me and my piece of glider. They put out a boat, prised my hands from the plywood, and dragged me out of the water . . .

'On board the LST they stripped me; warmed me; gave me hot Bovril; found me dry clothes, and they gave me that rucksack lying over by the door.'

Budge slid from the bar stool, silently shook hands with the landlord, and lifted on his backpack. By the open door he bent to pick up the Commando rucksack, and held up the shoulder-straps for Twirly.

He meant to say something, but his vocal-cords were as taut as ropes on a brick-hoist. Instead, he blinked his eyes clear and headed for the beach, croaking quietly over his shoulder:

'C'mon, let's go'.

He set a brisk pace across the beach, and over a new footbridge crossing a wide, shallow leat. A handful of mobile homes surrounded an old mine building, now transformed into a striking three-storey house with arched windows and a timber gallery.

The stone engine-house was built in 1862 as part of a scheme to revive the Wheal Lushington in the hill behind. But it never actually got working. The engine shipped from Ireland lay rusting for many years until it was finally broken up for scrap.

The corner chimney lost the normal upper section of brick.
when it was removed to provide foundations for the bungalow next
door.

On the thin path wandering steeply up from the beach, the Major
paused to massage a knee.
    'You all right, Major?'
    'How far now?'
    'Four miles. Be there by five o'clock.'
    The Major made a sobbing noise.

While Budge stopped to check his map, Twirly and the Major
stomped ahead along crumbling cliff-edges, kicking through screes of
pink and red shale, high-stepping over concrete platforms and
ignoring health-and-safety warnings of dangerous cliffs and old mine
workings – and passed conical cages where Kerrier District Council
kindly invited bats to make use of deep shafts below.
    He watched them stop where a deep combe lay across their
path, and heard them utter mutinous groans as they descended the
steep flight of more than fifty steps, moving awkwardly sideways,
with arms raised like surf-board riders.
    As they crossed a stream he called down, 'Map says this is
"Sally's Bottom".'
    He heard Twirly growl something rude about Sally and her
bottom.

The Major, breathing heavily, stopped at the corner of a high chainlink
fence, with the excuse of issuing emergency rations of Kit-Kat bought
from the pub.
    Budge nodded at the jumble of low buildings, and
complicated cat's cradle of aerials behind the fence.
    'That's the old Portreath airfield, where Twirly's gliders took
off. Was once nine hundred acres of good farm land and three
hamlets. In 1939, farmers and villagers were told the land was
required to build an airstrip. They were promised this would all be
returned to them at the end of the war.
    'But politicians have always lied.'

'When it was no longer wanted as an airfield, the Ministry of Defence blundered in and took it over, increased the height of the fence, gave it the sinister name of Nancekuke, and proceeded to do unmentionable things, without our permission, in the sacred name of freedom.

'In off-moments, locals still mumble darkly about the whereabouts of twenty tonnes of lethal nerve gas.'

'Welcome to the Portreath Arms Hotel,' said a smiling man outside the yellow pub with windows outlined in black.

It was five o'clock and Portreath was deserted. A few yachts and motor-cruisers rocked gently at their moorings in three docks of the long narrow harbour.

The blue glistening sea was empty, except for a great chocolate-coloured off-shore rock like an upturned coal scuttle. Although the sun had lost its heat and was preparing to leave for other climes, the walls of the pub still hummed with warmth.

They sat on a flower-surrounded bench beneath a hanging sign of a lifeboat with red sails and Budge flicked through his South West Way book.

Portreath was once a main port for the shipment of copper to Swansea, and in the 1840s seven hundred loads of ore a year sailed from here.

During periods of bad weather enormous piles of ore accrued waiting for conditions which allowed colliers and cawl boats to navigate the tricky harbour entrance.

The same ships returned loaded with Welsh coal to feed the pump-houses that kept the mines from flooding.

The smiling man re-appeared with a handful of menus.

'Eating later, gentlemen?'

Budge realised he was desperately hungry. The lunchtime Cornish Hedgehog was but a sweet memory.

'Suppose we ought to have fish . . . being on the sea,' said Budge.

The man nodded.

'Our fish is always good. Today we have some particularly fine pilchards. Stiff, shiny, and bright-eyed – don't get them any fresher.'

Budge looked at Twirly and the Major. They were slumped on the bench looking stiff and shiny, but with no bright eyes, and not particularly fresh.

'If you all agree on the pilchards you could have Star Gazy Pie.'

The Major stirred and an eye flickered momentarily.

Twirly gave a subliminal sniff.

'It's a traditional Cornish dish. Not on the menu. But I can probably get Sharon to do it for you.'

Budge said, 'Sounds great,' and he nodded towards the recumbents.

'They'll absolutely love it.'

Sharon herself brought in the Star Gazy: a large round pie-dish with pilchard heads protruding from the edge of golden pastry like wide-eyed gargoyles. Bursting up through the centre was a finial of tails garnished with parsley.

A space on the table was quickly cleared.

'Pilchards stuffed with onions and herbs; chopped hard-boiled eggs, bacon, milk, cider vinegar and a pinch of saffron. Pastry lid brushed with Cornish cream,' recited Sharon.

'Looks amazing,' said Budge.

It was.

Monday 27th July *Day twenty-two*

It was another gorgeous morning.

The Major slapped his sides and sighed with pleasure. He'd had a good night; breakfasted on cold ham and tomato, taken his tablets; now he was ready for action.

High up on the gorse and heather of Western Hill the views were again breathtaking.

Five miles to the south-west a lighthouse gleamed white against the dark blue of a hazy horizon.

By the path, a display of tall, brilliant saffron-orange montbretia waved a sedate greeting to the still-climbing sun.

At the bottom of the hill a squadron of whirling seagulls was conducting a screeching low-level attack on the town.

He saw Budge gazing up into the sky where a single early morning skylark was pouring out its soul in a trilling matins.

Poor Budge. Not just seeing a soaring skylark. He was remembering emerald-green eyes . . ..

Budge suddenly turned and said, 'Major, do you think we might see . . .

But the Major held up his hand and interrupted:

'No, Budge. They said they were only here for another week. That was ten days ago. She'll be back in Toronto by now.'

Budge nodded.

'Y'right, Major.'

The skylark dropped twenty feet, but instantly soared back up to continue its high-level *Te Deum*.

The Major looked back across the harbour.

The tide was out, revealing an attractive beach. The handful of boats which yesterday afternoon had bobbed in the three narrow docks, now sat marooned on wet sand.

On the far side of the harbour, perched high on a rocky headland, stood the white watchtower they had passed yesterday. It was by this tower that Laurence Binyon is said to have written the words, 'They shall grow not old . . .' Now it was caught by the morning-sun and was glowing like the white-washed *chorten* of Pulchowki sitting high above the valley of Kathmandu.

Twirly, who had stopped to cut himself a new stick, joined them and unwrapped a foil package to distribute three slices of fried bread.

'Concentrated energy,' he said.

Budge scrunched the salty bread, and imagined the harbour as it once must have been: a tangle of masts and rigging, and chutes, and derricks rising above overflowing bunkers of ore and coal.

According to the guidebook the harbour once contained a lime-kiln, a fish-palace, huge warehouse, a blacksmith's, and a stable for pack-ponies. A tramroad built for the movement of ore was the first above-ground railway to be built in Cornwall.

But progress impatiently scraped aside this history to make way for lucrative car parks and holiday homes.

He recalled the time he looked down from the 260-foot bell-tower of Piazza Bartolo Longo onto the excavated first century city of Pompeii, where the honeycomb of walls has survived thanks to a preservation order provided by Vesuvius.

On Reskajeage Downs a road gradually nudged in on the left, threatening to push the path over the cliff-edge. Budge cautiously leaned over to look down at the maritime battlefield where a foaming sea angrily attacked a chaos of dripping boulders and a litter of rocky-islands.

Budge checked the map – Deadman's Cove.

In a patch of white mayweed-daises with oversize yellow centres stood a green and gold National Trust sign.

Car Parking – One Pound.

Customers were snoozing safely in their shimmering cars, unaware of the drama taking place three hundred feet below.

The Major lurched on to a National Trust bench surrounded by purple ling.

'Quite beautiful, Budge,' he sighed. 'How long to lunch?'

Budge sat beside him.

'Be there in an hour. Level walking.'

Across the road stood Hell's Mouth Cafe offering All-day breakfasts, Cornish cream teas and ice-cream.

Cars rushed along the A3301 desperate to discover leisure in Hayle or Redruth. Budge and the Major watched Twirly carefully prop his stick against the bench, then skilfully dodge across.

Budge grunted.

'Funny lad,' he said.

340

The Major gazed at his new boots, still shining like conkers newly prised from padded shells.

Budge continued, 'Did you see the card he wrote to Doll?'

The Major leaned forward and with a white handkerchief gave his boots a superfluous flick.

Budge said, 'Here we are on this spectacular coast which can knock spots off *any* in Europe with shops full of marvellous postcards of beaches, boats and harbours – and he chooses a picture of a *flower*.'

The Major folded his handkerchief and returned it to his shirt pocket.

'Flower?'

'Yes – a rose.'

Twirly skipped across the road clutching three dripping ice-cream-cornets, grinning like a young scrumper.

The Major turned and frowned and stared at Budge.

Extraordinary. He must be the only person in Upper Gently who doesn't know.

Chapter Thirty-six

On Navax Point the Major stood in the insect-buzzing bright sunshine, smiling and swaying and flexing his abused knees.

A brilliant white trig-pillar stood in the centre of a pointillist carpet of heather and flowers, like the Dagaba in Ceylon's Peradeniya Botanical Gardens.

The blue sea could have been the Indian Ocean.

The air was as heady as the early-morning bouquet of cedar-wood and scented oils in the bustling Laksala arts and crafts centre in Colombo.

'*Sadhu Sadhu*' – Blest, Blest – he murmured, like an entranced pilgrim climbing up Adam's Peak.

He poked a burnished new boot into the coloured carpet.

Mary would have known the names of all the flowers: the masses of yellow wort, aromatic pink patches of yarrow, clumps of blue self-heal, which she said was a cure for throat infections, and clusters of pale purple small-scabious, a certain prevention against pimples and freckles.

He followed close behind Budge and striding around Godrevy Point he stopped and gasped.

It was a breathtakingly theatrical moment - as if the Covent Garden curtain was pulled aside in a private viewing of the most spectacular set of the season.

On the right, perched on a hamburger-shaped rock half-a-mile out on the sunlit blue sea, stood a lighthouse close enough for those in the boxes to touch.

In the wings on the left a huge sprawl of cars shimmered in the heat.

In the orchestra-stalls at their feet, fingers of green and black rock groped across sand towards the sea. Children played in pools, dug in the sand, and oiled bodies lay supine in a Bedouin encampment of striped canvas.

Centre-stage curved a magnificent, flat, three-miles-long golden Circus Maximus beach, ending in a distant headland covered in a twinkling mosaic which Budge insisted was the fishing village of St Ives.

'But first – lunch,' cried Budge, and he led them through dunes, hairy with marram grass, to a pyramid slated roof with a timber gallery, where the owner-designer, Ray Sapak, created a crab salad in front of them, served with a bottle of chilled Chardonnay.

As they crossed the Red River on to the beach Budge called, 'You been to St Ives before, Major?'

The Major shook his head.

Budge said, 'You'll absolutely love it.'

He said it with such conviction that the Major looked up into the blue heaven expecting to see skylarks.

Budge chuckled as he watched the Major and Twirly speeding along the flat beach at the British Army regulation marching speed of two thirty-inch paces a second, splashing through the shallows of the incoming tide as it slid indolently backwards and forwards across the firm sand.

Still in the rear, Budge checked his watch. They had been advancing along the beach at this pace for just over two miles – almost three quarters of an hour.

He tilted his head. A noise puzzled him.

Not a screeching seagull.

Not a pilchard-seeking *huer.*

Not the pounding Atlantic; nor the hissing retreating waves.

He strained to hear.

It was THEM.

They were singing.

And he realised he was stamping along in step with them and, to his surprise, he began to sing a contented *Onward Christian Soldiers,* and remembered Sunday School Rogation Walks.

Budge glanced at his guidebook: *Leave the beach at the lifeguard hut near the foot of Black Cliff.*

And over on the left he could see the hut.

'LEFT WHEEL!' he called, amazed he knew the words.

He was even more amazed when the two instantly turned away from the sea. They stomped dustily across the soft sand towards cliffs where mobile homes stood along the top, lined up like the bows of a flotilla of landing-craft.

They scrambled up the steep foot-sliding dunes and persevered through a maze of caravans, chalets, shacks, and a redundant concrete pill-box.

Marker posts guided them to the estuary where two rivers flow, and here the glorious seaside picture was switched off.

Budge groaned.

It should have been a colourful scene of a wide stretch of blue glistening water, backed by a bright green golf course and the tower of Lelant church.

Intead it was a scene of dirty desolation, where a sad road of black mud ran alongside a grey river, wandering through a landscape of rusty cars, rotting ribs of boat skeletons, ginger railway-lines, and filth and rubbish.

They stopped and stared in disbelief.

The tang of iodine sea air that had propelled them along the beach was replaced by a stench of wet wood and old oil.

'Hayle harbour,' groaned Budge.

He recalled that the guidebook said this was once Norwayman's Wharf, always crowded with ships bringing fresh-smelling timber from the pine-forests of Scandinavia.

The Major called, 'Hey! Look at this.'

He was peering down at a dishevelled motor-cruiser which was squatting on the black mud and leaning against the crumbling harbour wall like a drunk in a pub yard.

He pointed with a flick of his cane.

'Something odd about that boat, Mr Ballflower.'

Budge peered.

The Major said, 'Saw this bobbing about in Portreath harbour last night when I was walking off the Star Gazy Pie.'

'So?'

'Tide was out when we left this morning. It's only just creeping back in *now*.'

Budge stared.

What's he talking about?

'It means it must have travelled here during the night, Major.'

Budge said, 'Guide book says there's a pub ten minutes from here, beneath the railway viaduct.'

But the Major protested, 'Odd to be sneaking along the coast at night, don't y'think?

'Another thing,' he continued. 'Look at it. Tatty as hell. Yet the midships canopy is newly painted. Bright red with a white stripe. Some sort of identification?'

Budge said, 'Perhaps . . .'

The Major was insistent.

'Look at the aft cabin windows, Budge. Newly barred. And look at the size of the padlock on the cabin door. What the hell they got in there?'

'Perhaps expensive diving equipment.'

'Tosh!' snorted the Major. 'Diving people can afford something better than this wreck.' And he strode to the stern and again wielded his cane.

'And it's registered in Dublin.'

Budge shrugged.

'Major. Dublin is only two hundred miles from here. Why shouldn't it be here?'

The Major glowered.

'Anyway, it's called, *WE OURSELVES.'*

Budge stared at Twirly, who was studiously coiling a short length of insulated wire he had just ripped from the rusty shell of a gutted Ford van.

'Come on!' he called. 'We need that drink. All getting dehydrated.'

As he strode off along the rutted and puddled track he pointed to the church tower beyond the estuary.

'Major. There is something you should *REALLY* worry about.

'When this coastpath was planned, a ferry could take you from here across to Lelant. But Hayle let it go out of business. Now we have to walk along a busy road.'

He stopped to face his followers and his face suddenly creased in a grin.

'BUT – at Lelant we can catch a magic little shuttle train which managed to hide from the quack-doctor Beeching. It'll have us in St Ives in time for tea.'

The air inside the Royal Standard was heavy with stale tobacco-smoke and spilt beer, although it was empty, apart from three men at a corner table who had their heads together as if they were planning to raid a betting shop.

Budge headed for a table near a breezily open window and called, 'Make those halves, Twirly. Need to get out of here.'

To the Major he said, 'Your boat from Dublin - don't you like the Irish?'

The Major snorted.

'Mr Ballflower, the Irish are charming. Beautiful country. Mary and I used to holiday every year in the south-west. Roaring Water Bay. Skibbereen. Always stayed at a wonderful pub in Schull.'

Budge looked around to see what was keeping Twirly at the bar.

The Major continued, 'Mary loved to shop in London, and one December we took with us the little daughter of Mrs Platt, who still helps me with the cleaning. Her friend came along, too.

'After lunch in a steak-house in the Brompton Road we crossed the road to Harrods. The two girls went by a traffic island a few yards further along to our left. As I pushed against the glass door, there was this enormous WUMPH!

'Because I *felt* it rather than heard it, I knew it was a bomb.
'Shouting.
'Crashing glass.
'Chaos.
'The two girls came running – crying, sobbing. Mercifully unhurt.

346

Twirly arrived with three half-pints.

The Major said, 'Haven't been to Ireland since. No time for a people who allow their wild ones to blow up children visiting Father Christmas.'

Twirly distributed the drinks.

'Barman is very friendly. Full of information.'

He lowered his voice.

'First: the three men are Irish – and he's never seen them before.'

He brightened and beamed.

'Second. We don't need to walk along the road to Lelant. In six minutes there's a train from the station just around the corner. It stops just down the line at St Erth. Catch the little train there, which waits. Due in St Ives at three-seventeen.

'I told the barman to keep the change.'

Budge sat erect, attempting to control his idiotic smile as the St Ives shuttle train swayed and rattled along by the beach. It hammered through gorse-filled cuttings and clattered beneath footbridges draped with waving walkers and threw blasts of sea-air through open windows, and double-hammered over joints and shouted at plate-layers' huts; and slowed only slightly when wheel-flanges squealed on acute bends.

He watched Twirly perched on the edge of his seat like a youngster on a school outing.

The Major sat upright as a Maharaja on a richly caparisoned elephant.

The brilliantly blue sea nonchalantly rolled its waves and did its best to ignore the proud little train's dashing blue-and-gold coaches – descendants of Great Western's grandly named Ocean Coast Line, built by the legendary Brunel.

As the train slowed to a halt at Porthminster Beach the driver turned to smile triumphantly through his glass partition.

Budge waved and stepped from the train – and looked around, and sighed.

What a pity.

It was not a proper seaside station.

Not as it should be, with white-fretted canopies, slender gold and black pillars, and porters in waistcoats leaning on luggage barrows with iron wheels and large wicker baskets labelled RUSH.

St Ives's original station was outrageously flattened in 1971 to make way for a car-park and the Ocean Coast Line is now obliged to sneak to a halt in a set-aside former goods-yard.

'Enjoy your walk,' called the driver, pocketing the last of Twirly's Glacier Mints.

Budge glared around him.

The large car park was crowded, jammed with every car in the south-west.

And people everywhere.

People with sunshine smiles. People in laughing groups. People dawdling. Purposeful we-might-be-late people, swerving and weaving.

PEOPLE.

But not dressed *correctly* in seaside holiday clothes.

The ladies were wearing long dresses and Ascot hats – or skirts short enough to frighten horses and set dogs barking.

The men wore crisp white shirts and floral ties, or had top-hats and morning-coats.

Children, who should have been on the beach, were wearing Sunday-best.

Somewhere a band was playing 'She'll be coming round the mountain'.

Hell's going on?

Twirly said, 'Is today Monday, 27th July?'

Budge considered.

'Yes.'

Twirly pointed to a poster pinned on the garden-shed ticket office: *St Ives Annual Festival, Trelawny's Thread-the-Needle street dance. Monday 27 July.*

Budge waved his street map above his head, and they pressed through the throng and passed below the rocky outcrop which nineteenth century survivors of Sevastopol had dubbed *The Malakov.*

They passed a smart hotel built over Pednolver tin-mine displaying menus, photographs of seductive bedrooms – and FULL signs.

They pushed along the narrow Warren with cottages in Mediterranean colours, tiny gardens and overflowing flower boxes.

They jostled along Lambeth Walk, a narrow causeway a few inches above a sparkling frivolous festival sea.

Past West Pier, and the new lifeboat house, and the toilets, and a plaque announcing that General Booth once preached Salvation here.

Past a grim and grey Woolworths that hadn't been told of the Festival. Past Fat Willie's where it's *always* Festival. Then in front of the black and white Sloop Inn which claims to date from the thirteenth century, or fifteenth century, or seventeenth century, depending upon the state of the tide, where they abruptly ran aground on a solid bank of people.

Budge turned to a Cornish pixie wearing a chequered bowler hat.

'What's happening, Constable?'

The rosy cheeks smiled.

'Festival opening, sir,' and she nodded her hat over at the harbour wall where a group of important people wearing gold chains stood on a decorated platform beneath a tall white flagpole.

Budge said, 'But we have to get to the Grey Mullet.'

'In Bunker's Hill, just round to your left, sir,' said the bowler hat. 'But you'll have to wait I'm afraid. The Mayor will finish his speech shortly, then they'll raise the traditional festival flag, everyone will clap, and St Ives will begin to flow again.'

She gave a puckish smile and Budge was disappointed to see she didn't have pointed ears.

Suddenly the important people began clapping.

The Mayor folded his script and slipped it into an inside pocket and the crowd surged forward as if a penalty was to be taken.

A large man in a red and gold coat stepped forward with a folded flag. A youthful Admiral of the Fleet assisted by two sea-cadets reverently took the flag, and fumbled with it – and disaster struck.

A toggle in the corner of the flag pulled away from the ancient fabric. The general hub-bub was instantly converted into a single tsunami gasp. The 1998 Festival appeared to be doomed.

Budge groaned.

'Mrs Herbert promised to have tea ready for us. We'll be here for hours.'

Twirly looked at the Major.

The Major's raised eyebrows signalled to Twirly.

Twirly snapped to attention and mumbled, 'Sir!'

He pushed towards the platform with a powerful elbow-stroke and snatched the fragile fabric from the despairing officials.

One of the sea-cadets began to cry.

Twirly shrugged off his rucksack, dug his hand deep into the grenade pocket, and retrieved a dice of Welsh coal, poked it into the frayed corner and twisted the fabric into a little parcel around it. With a piece of insulated wire he happened to have handy, he made two loops into a clove-hitch, and pressed it over the coal parcel.

The wire was threaded into the eye-lashing in the flag-halyard held by the distraught sea-cadet and fixed by a round-turn-and-two-half-hitches and the repaired flag was thrust into the hands of the Admiral.

Twirly stepped from the platform and the crowd parted like the Red Sea before Moses.

The flag was raised.

The St Ives Festival was launched.

The Major beamed.

'Well done, Corporal.'

Budge said, 'When did you learn to do that?'

Twirly sniffed.

'Just then.'

Mrs Herbert tucked the blue and white tea-cosy over the St Ives souvenir teapot.

'You joining the street-dance?'

Three teacups were held poised in silence . . .

'You should. Everybody does, but they're always short of men. The girls will grab *you* with eager arms. Handsome men like you.'

Twirly sniffed.

'Do you suppose I could have another of those nice cakes, Mrs Herbert?'

A line of gentlemen partnered a line of ladies threading through the labyrinth of St Ives' flag bedecked alleys, with two bands blasting out the same repetitive tune, and everyone singing the Trelawny song:

Lift up, lift up your gates on high,
And let Trelawny's men come by.
And we'll march up,
And we'll march down,
Until we come to London town.

At intervals the cry went up: 'UPALONG!' and the men instantly moved to the right to face a new lady partner and the whole nonsense began again.

As Budge leapt, and whirled, he was reminded that walking-boots are not ideal for dancing and the noise was hurting his head and the fixed grin was becoming painful.

Hell am I doing here?

His newest partner, a bright-eyed girl with moist hands, told him that she normally worked in the Information Office and she was delighted he had joined the dance.

They danced up steps and along the high pavement of Fernlea Terrace and past the Regent Hotel which the guidebook said was originally built as a mine engine-house, and before D-Day became the HQ of an American general. Down Tregenna Hill, and Street-an-Pol; past the Guildhall. They squeezed along crowded Fore Street, the *Chandri Chowk* of St Ives, and soberly jogged along Teetotal Street.

All the time clapping bystanders crowded the narrow streets singing over and over again the same words:

Lift up, lift up your gates on high . . .

351

Budge was gasping.

Not many people have walked two hundred miles to be here. Not many people have to walk twelve miles tomorrow.

He must escape.

To desert his current partner would be ungallant. He would wait until the next UPALONG manoeuvre.

Along the Wharf the crowds were denser and Budge saw that Twirly's flag was still flying.

'UPALONG!' cried a hundred voices.

Now.

He turned to push himself into the throng of bystanders, but his hand was suddenly grasped by fingers as soft as dog-rose petals – but with a grip as firm as a slave-master's shackle.

He turned, and was blinded by a blur of green.

The deep mystical green of the waters around the Faraglioni rocks off Capri.

He blinked his sweat-dripping eyelashes.

Two eyes gleamed like emeralds held in the brown hands of an *amudes*-clad boy in Sri Lanka's Ratnapura.

Softly spoken words slid easily beneath the tumult.

'Good evening, Mr Budgineer.'

Chapter Thirty-seven

Budge pulled the green-eyed girl from the melee of dancers, pushed through the spectators and pressed her against the promenade rails.

He stared into her eyes.

Hell's bells. She's beautiful.

'Sophia! The Major said you were back in Canada.'

She tossed her sunlit hair.

'And Aunt Annabelle had decided you would not reach here for another five days.'

They both laughed together, and a maple-leaf pendant swung backwards and forwards across a valley of golden tan.

He moved his hands to her bare arms. The loose floral dress was *exactly* right for the street celebration.

Right for him, too.

'Can hardly believe it . . .'

Stupid thing to say.

She again burst into laughter, and her eyes danced like twinkling starboard-lights.

Green is an amazing colour. Always difficult to get right in a stained glass window. But when it works, it's heavenly.

'Your aunt. She here?'

She waved an arm toward the dancers.

'In there – somewhere. And the Major?'

Budge chuckled.

'Last saw him being propelled along by a perspiring lady of impressive proportions.'

'And Valentino?'

'Twirly? He didn't care to dance. Said he was going to see a man about a fish.'

Now they could hear both bands playing, not quite synchronized, and distorted by echoes and changes in volume as they jostled through the St Ives honeycomb.

They turned to look across the harbour where rich, gently rocking yachts haughtily ignored the beat of the thumping bands and ragged singing.

And then we'll shout,
And then we'll sing,
And teach this dance to the English king.

'You're wearing the same perfume.'

She turned to him and smiled.

'We ought to find the others.'

But Budge placed his hand in the small of her back to keep her against the rails.

'Find any interesting churches?'

'Oh yes. Several. A beautiful church in a Devon village called Ottery St Mary. All towers and gables. Gorgeous colours. Tombs smothered in family shields. Some of your work there?'

Budge shook his head.

'Been there to look, not to work.'

'Sherborne Abbey, too. Incredible fan-vaulting.'

'Once replaced some Purbeck capitals there,' said Budge, and he flicked some of the sunlight from her hair. 'I suppose you're right. We should go and find them.'

Annabelle was rescued from the dance near Trewyn Gardens.

The Major was discovered sitting on stone steps at Salubrious Place. He leapt to his feet and snatched off his jungle-hat.

'Good Lord!'

'Not dancing, Major?' laughed Annabelle.

'*Been* dancing, Ma'am. Now just doing a little R-and-R and a spot of shopping.'

The Major was surprised how pleased he was to see the sprightly Annabelle. He had also forgotten how attractive she was.

Silver-grey hair. Bright oyster-blue eyes. Slim and erect as an army nurse. Wearing a straw hat with a blue ribbon – probably bought for the dance. Cream dress with pleated skirt, similar to the one Mary always wore at church fêtes in their Residency gardens.

He loved her bubbling smile, suggesting involvement in a secret joke.

They found Twirly on duty outside the Union pub in Fore Street.

He was standing with a pint in his hand, running a repeat of an old war with a man as rotund as a middle-ground buoy wearing an unravelling blue pullover.

'He saw the *Abdiel* go down in Taranto harbour,' he said by way of introduction. 'Lost my second jeep and trailer there.'

The Major looked at his watch.

'You ladies staying in St Ives?'

'Tregenna Castle, up on the hill,' said the niece.

'May I make a suggestion?'

Whilst prancing arm-in-arm with a slender lady topped with a hat as large as a kan tok *basket, he had noticed the blue,red and white flag of Malaysia flying from the* Jalan Toh Lee *restaurant in Chapel Street.*

'Sounds wonderful,' said the aunt.

The olive man in a shiny suit who met them at the door was apologetic.

'It's the Festival, sir. Unless you have a reservation . . .'

'I understand. *Saya faham,'* smiled the Major.

The aunt beamed.

The Major continued, *'Kami mahu meja untuk lima orang.'*

The olive man considered, then clapped his hands together.

'Silakan masuk. Follow me.'

He ushered them upstairs to a small room heavy with spices, where flickering candles threw shadows of hanging paper dragons onto walls festooned with Kanchipuram silks.

Perfect.

Exotic crimson and gold *Kain Songket* silk brocade cushions from Terengganu were scattered over gold-sprayed Macau rattan chairs arranged around a circular table of Lanna teak. The Major guessed that the assortment of gleaming brass and enamel finger-bowls came mainly from Varanasi. Underfoot was a soft *shyrdak* carpet with bold, swirling designs. Almost certainly from Kyrgyzstan.

The Major nodded with pleasure.

'I see you are a world shopper.'

The olive man displayed several gold teeth.

'Trago Mills,' he said.

The Major consulted briefly with the olive man, then turned to the others.

'Our host has agreed to serve us a special Malaysian menu.'

He looked around for approval.

Annabelle said, *'Ji hā. Shābāsh.'*

The Major blinked.

Yes. Excellent.

He raised his white eyebrows.

'The Far East?'

Annabelle smiled.

'Fourteenth Army.'

'Good Lord.'

Through a beaded curtain emerged a slim girl shrink-wrapped into a purple *cheong-sam*. She slid to the central table bearing a shallow basket of pre-meal *samosas*.

The Major leapt to guide the ladies on to chairs.

Annabelle bathed him in her laughing eyes.

'My parents were in India during the war. When I became eighteen I joined the Women's Auxilliary Service in Burma. April '45. We set up *Chinthe* mobile canteens for troops on Ramree Island. They were assembling for the invasion of Rangoon.'

The Major sat between her and Sophia, shaking his head in disbelief.

'Extraordinary. Rangoon!'

Sophia leaned forward.

'You were there too, Major?'

The Major glanced swiftly at Sophia, and then back to the aunt.

'A few of us were put into Malaya to annoy the Japs, we were there for there for eleven long months. I got into a terrible state. Black-water fever. Tick-typhus. Chronic malaria. Running ulcers. Leech bites. Home sickness.

'Eventually evacuated back to Trincomalee by submarine.'

He waved a crumbling *samosa.*

'As soon as I could stand, they bundled me onto a Mark VI Liberator and I was flown to Jessore, then down to Kalaikunda airfield. Posted as jungle-warfare expert to 153 Gurkha para battalion waiting to do a drop on Elephant Point. Part of the Rangoon job.'

The Major watched Annabelle's eyes widen.

He laughed and waved a finger.

'Knew your lot. Used to send my batman down to get some of your apricot jam.'

Annabelle threw up her arms and laughed.

'Saya suka! The little tins of apricot jam. Everybody loved them.' She shook her head. 'We could *never* get enough from Bulk Issue.'

Her faced danced with pleasure in the light of the candles.

Budge stared around the table.

Who ARE these guys?

The beaded curtain rattled open and in swirled the shrink-wrapped girl bearing a large silver *thali.*

The Major beamed at the precisely placed skewers of chicken and beef *satay,* with chunks of cucumber, and *ketupat* palm-leaf parcels.

With a flamboyant gesture to the aunt, he invited her to begin.

As she dunked a *satay* into her dish of spicy sauce, she squinted happily at the Major.

'We think your walk is absolutely wonderful.'

'Wonderful,' repeated the niece, although the Major noticed this appeared to be aimed exclusively at the stonemason sitting opposite.

357

The aunt continued, 'When do you expect to get to Land's End?'

A large rattan-fan in the ceiling began to revolve slowly.

'Three days walking, so...' and he quickly calculated ...'We'll be there on Thursday. Thursday afternoon. That evening – a celebration dinner at the Land's End hotel.'

The Major was aware of significant eye-communication which flashed between aunt and niece.

The fan thudded as it slowly increased speed, tossing a welcome breeze around the room. The Major turned to smile his approval at the olive man standing by the curtain.

Twirly leaned forward to reach for another *satay* and sniffed.

'All being well,' he said.

The fan leapt to helicopter speed and a small vase of purple orchids toppled on to the *thali*.

The Major looked round in alarm at the olive man, who plunged his arm behind the curtain and the fan instantly slowed.

'*Terima kasih,*' called the Major.

'*Sama-sama,*' smiled the olive suit.

The meal continued with *mee rebus* noodles, spicy *prawn sambal*, cakes of *tahu bakar* in peanut sauce, *gushtaba* meat-balls floundering in spicy yoghurt, *otak otak* fish paste wrapped in banana leaves and *nasi lemak* coconut rice with anchovies and peanuts.

Dessert was *gula melaka* sago pudding with palm-sugar syrup.

'Are we having coffee, Major?' asked Budge.

Annabelle looked at her watch and nodded to Sophia.

'Ought to be getting back to the hotel, dear. Early morning tomorrow.'

She turned to the Major.

'Hope to get to the Tate, then back to Tunbridge Wells, then Heathrow – and Sophia takes a flight back to Toronto.'

Tomorrow?

Budge looked desperately across at the Major.

The slowing fan paddled to a halt.

'Tomorrow?' he said in the sudden silence.

Both the aunt and Sophia nodded.

The olive man stepped forward clasping his chubby, ring-adorned hands and bowed slightly.

'Everything satisfactory?'

Budge winced.

Satisfactory? Tomorrow? Get out, you idiot.

He glared at Twirly, who was secretly shovelling gold foil chocolates into a trouser pocket.

A taxi was called to take the ladies back to *Tregenna Castle*.

Addresses were exchanged.

The Major said, 'I really must renew my acquaintance with Tunbridge Wells.'

The aunt smiled.

'That would be nice.'

Budge studied a visiting card.

Sophia Forrest, Forrest Flowers, Toronto.

She said, 'I'll write.'

Budge nodded.

She won't. They never do.

The taxi departed, and they walked in silence via the Memorial Gardens and deserted Fore Street, back to the Grey Mullet.

'Great meal,' sniffed Twirly.

Tuesday 28th July *Day twenty-three*

Another beautiful morning; with high-flying gulls complaining about the scandalous shortage of fish.

The sea air was sharply fresh.

Ancient harbour smells of seaweed, diesel, and damp rope were submerged beneath the prosperous aroma of a hundred bacon breakfasts.

Budge discovered the Major on parade on the steeply sloping cobbles outside the Grey Mullet. Massive granite blocks were hidden behind a confusion of flowers, with an obese cat dozing on stone steps, refusing to move.

'How are you this morning, Major?'

The Major gave a thin smile and saluted with his cane.

Twirly stepped over the cat, flourishing a slim volume.

Budge scowled.

'Hell you got there, Twirly?'

Twirly sniffed.

'Second-hand. Got it yesterday when you were dancing.'

Budge took the book.

'South West Peninsula Coastal Path – St Ives to Plymouth'

Budge flicked it open and read: *First published 1977.*

He handed it back.

'It's twenty years out of date.'

'So are me and the Major,' sniffed Twirly.

Up narrow Rose Lane; along The Digey where shops were yawning and stretching; a quick look down a hip-squeezing passage into white-washed Hick's Court; down on to Porthmeor Beach Road, and to the bone-white Tate Gallery of St Ives, the drum shape recalling that this was once the site of the town's gasometer.

Budge looked anxiously up at the entrance terrace.

Twirly shook his head.

'You won't see them, Budge. Don't open till ten.'

The glistening sands stretched soft, tide-washed, and braced for the morning invasion. A row of yellow surfboards lay lined up as precisely as the keys of an old piano.

A lady in a white smock marched across the sand carrying a pile of cartons to a beach café still in its bedclothes.

A man in jeans with a pirate's beard struggled without enthusiasm to erect a sandwich-board announcing: *Boat trips to Seal Island – one hour.*

Out at sea a wallowing fishing boat was harassed by a noisy paparazzi of scavenging seagulls.

Overlooking an immaculate short-back-and-sides bowling green, sat three elderly people on varnished brown benches waiting for something to start – or finish.

A leaning Coast Path sign by the public toilets pointed to a path leading from the pavement.

'This way?' called Twirly, with a chestnut paling he had just wrenched from the remains of a fence.

The South West Coast Path Association warns that this section of the 630-mile route is 'rough, rocky and severe'.

'Guess so,' said Budge, and he watched his charges march off, as innocent as Kitchener volunteers.

Beyond Clodgy Point the path narrowed to a track wending through dark green grass dotted with pink thrift, passing impressively close to the edge of a deep cove with near vertical walls.

Budge stopped on Hor Point. This small headland with its superb views across the bay was purchased by the National Trust when the Council threatened to make it a household refuse tip.

Hellesveor Cliff.

Pen Enys Point.

Always through lush grass scattered with buttercups, and low hedges of gorse.

Trip-wires of dwarf mallow playfully snatched at boots.

Waist-high hedges of white and crimson honeysuckle blessed them with heady perfume.

Uneven paving stones rocked across soggy patches where bubbling streams fought like lemmings to get to the sea.

Bright, starry, yellow wall-pepper snuggled against low granite walls, both survivors from the Iron Age kingdom of Dumnonia and older than Christianity.

Budge called, 'We'll rest at the trig-pillar on Carn Naun Point.'

He chuckled as Twirly stopped to consult his new guidebook.

It was eleven o'clock when they sank on to hard boulders meanly upholstered with multi-coloured lichens to share a can of Newcastle Brown.

Then off again, moving at speed.

Budge watched Twirly pause by a gorse bush to snatch a tangle of red thread-like dodder and give his still gleaming boots a quick flick.

Ten minutes later, at River Cove, they met a group of walkers waiting to see seals on Carrack Rocks.

'Going to Zennor?'

Budge nodded.

Twirly quickly nodded, too.

They earnestly recommended a fast inland alternative to the coastal path.

Budge studied his map and turned to his co-pilot.

'All right?' But Twirly was already stomping along this inland path by a noisy stream. At Trevail Mill the path dived into a tunnel of purple fuchsias.

At Boscubben Farm they crossed an ancient Cornish cattle-grid stile of large granite kerbstones laid over a shallow pit and joined an old miners' path parallel to the coast through walker-friendly flat meadows dotted with holiday-making cows.

They passed Tregerthen Farm once owned by Virginia Woolf, and Higher Tregerthen where D.H.Lawrence and his wife Frieda lived during the First World War.

Frieda was discovered to be a cousin of Manfred von Richthofen, the notorious Red Baron fighter-pilot, and the locals accused her of signalling to off-shore Germans. They were given three days to leave.

At Tremeda Farm a notice pleaded:

> *Do not let the black dog follow you.*
> *Tell him to go home.*
> *If he continues please take him to the Old Chapel hostel in Zennor.*
> *Thank you.*

In Zennor, Budge led them to the eastern entrance of the churchyard. The roof of the old lych-gate had long gone, but stone benches still remained either side of a central slab where bearers once rested the coffin while someone ran to fetch the vicar.

Tables in the shady small courtyard by the entrance to the historic Tinners' Arms were crowded with booted, tanned-faced, hungry lunchers, as were the tables and benches inside.

Twirly investigated down a couple of steps and found a small empty room.

They chose locally-smoked mackerel.

'You seen the mermaid in the church?' asked the landlord as he pulled another three pints of St Austell Hicks Tinners Ale. He handed over the change and growled confidentially, 'I'm packing this lot up. Keeping a pub is a mug's game.'

A grizzled local, half-hidden by hanging coats, leaned forward to Budge. His weathered face bore a permanently etched grin. He winked and breathed quietly across the top of his pint.

'David's all right. Been saying that for twenty-five years.'

By the granite steps up into the churchyard Budge found the Major plucking burrs from his long socks.

'You going to be OK this afternoon, Major? It's four miles to our next beer-and-bed.'

The Major grimaced.

'Same ups and downs?'

'The same.'

'Can't wait, Mr Ballflower.'

'There's a local museum in a mill-house at the bottom of the hill,' said Budge.

The Major probably didn't hear.

In the church of St Senera, Twirly found the fourteenth century mermaid carved on the end of a pew.

'She's no Esther Williams,' he sniffed.

The Major signed a Veterans' visitors' book on a shelf beneath a Burma Star stained-glass window.

Budge's portable telephone rang.

Doll.

'Your man Fred Glenning is in here. Says you have forbidden him to call you, but your scaffolders arrived this morning at Lambley. He wants to know if you're still aiming to be back on Friday.'

'Tell him, "Yes".'

'That's three days time, Budge.'

'Right.'

Silence, then, 'Is Twirly near you?'

'I can see him.'

'That story about English Heritage and Fish House is true. They're going to do it up, make information panels, and open it all to the public. Fred says they want you to quote for some new stonework.'

Twirly waved his guidebook towards the sea and called, 'This way, Budge?'

Budge nodded.

Doll said,

'Are YOU going to tell him, m'duck?'

Chapter Thirty-eight

From the top of the amphitheatre of Carnelloe Cliff an audience of nodding gorse and heather sloped down to a glistening stage of idling waves.

A matronly yellow and grey passenger ship made a dignified entrance-left, leaving a foaming train of bridal white.

'Scilly Isles ferry,' said Budge.

In Porthglaze Cove he gazed down at the expanse of sapphire blue creeping in to stroke the base of craggy cliffs; and noted the colour change of shallow waves sliding like smiles across white sand to become pools of brilliant Sophia green . . .

On National Trust Boswednack Cliff he checked his map.

'Major,' he said. 'The red and grey whale of rock out there . . . Gurnards Head. Interesting because it was an Iron-Age hill-fort, and you can see the two defensive ditches astride it like hoops on a barrel. However, what is even more interesting . . .'

He looked up, folded his map, smiled at the Major like a teacher saying that's the end of school for today.

'Ten minutes walk inland gets us to our beds for the night.'

In the hamlet of Treen they sat at picnic tables by a red postbox let into the wall of the yellow Gurnard's Head Hotel. They slowly and silently downed cool draught Bass and contentedly watched speeding holiday traffic taking risks at a sharp bend.

Eventually Budge spoke.

'Two more days, and fifteen miles,' he said.

Dinner was perfect.

For Budge, the duck.

The Major: plaice with Greenland prawns.

Twirly: chicken and chips.

For dessert: Speciality of the House. 'Thunder and Lightning' – ice-cream, black treacle and a ladies-finger biscuit, all generously doused in gin.

'If you don't mind, Budge,' yawned the Major.
    'Me too,' said Twirly.
    Budge nodded and raised his brandy glass in a 'goodnight' salute.

It was a pleasant evening.
    He strolled back down the lane towards a weary sea doing a good job on the night shift, past a sheep-dip trough sunken into the verge, past the white house with blue downpipes and shutters, past Treen Farm B&B where a black and white dog had growled at Twirly, and Twirly had growled back, with Twirly winning.
    Beyond the dozing handful of houses the path was of soft, sweet, whispering grass, where motionless bracken stood watch over small white flowers which had already closed for the night.
    He crossed up and down over deep defensive trenches dug with antler picks, and ox-shoulder-blade-shovels. In ten minutes he was on the rocky headland, and he scrambled up to a no-longer-needed coastguard hut wedged high in a cleft, perched like an abandoned Navajo cliff dwelling.
    To the east a long chunky line of cliffs, tipped with gold, disappeared into tomorrow. To the west, three miles back along the coast, he could just make out the Carracks looking like two sleeping whales blissfully ignoring fidgeting seals which guidebooks insist are there.
    Further to the west, an enormous fiery sun was being forced down into the horizon, mildly protesting by setting fire to windows in the hamlets of Porthmeor and Bosigran.
    High above in a sky drained of blue, a buzzing insect aircraft also headed west – probably taking the green-eyed girl back to her flower shop.
    By the time we get to Land's End she will have forgotten England – too busy selling bunches of begonias and bright red maple leaves.

He stood, creaked a little, and slowly wandered back to the hotel.

Wednesday 29th July *Day twenty-four*

'Hell's bells!' snorted Budge as he stepped into the gale that was giving Cornwall a wild shaking.

Behind him the Major emerged warily from Gurnard's Head Hotel trussed up to his nose in his gaberdine jacket. Twirly followed, encased in his orange waterproof, aggressively clutching to his chest the bayonet chestnut paling he had taken up to his room the previous night.

Budge protectively squinted his eyes and scowled up at the sky, no longer a high barrel-vault of lapis lazuli, but a low ceiling of turbulent boiling pitch.

He cautiously peered around the corner into the face-slapping, eye-blinding, south-westerly. Beyond the headland, yesterday's distinct sea horizon had become an angry haze where the troubled sky merged with a furious sea as dark as Carthusian marble. Angry white lines rushed towards the cliffs like charging Scots Greys. The wind boomed and howled like an artillery barrage, and a larch-lap-panel by the picnic-table rattled like rifle-fire. Overhead a power-cable attached to a bracket near a bedroom window tugged and screamed to be set free. Budge peered at his silent volunteers.

Crouched, expressionless – awaiting the whistle to move.

'Need to watch your step, lads. Suggest we keep close together.'

He bit his lip; blinked; put his head down; thought of England, and pushed himself into the blast.

'This way,' he cried.

He heard the Major shout, 'Warn the men, Corporal: we're taking no prisoners!'

Halfway down the peninsular he turned on to a path running left to follow the line of the cliffs and the brunt of the wind now switched from its frontal assault, but continued a right-flank enfilade with gusts leaping up over cliff edges with powerful sideways thumps, and the sudden flurries kicked mid-stride boots off balance, making walking a hazardous stagger.

The path passed close to the deep, rocky cleft of Zawn Duel where, far below, the sea pummelled the drowning rocks in a milk shake of white fury, and the wind howled like a train whistle in a cutting.

A small signboard, green with age, probably once warned – DANGER. Now Budge thought it was just big enough to trip the unwary into the boiling zawn.

He turned to yell, 'Careful!' into the blast.

Sometimes the path passed leeward of rocks or low granite walls and the wind declared a brief truce.

Sometimes wide grass tracks became thin and stony grooves, and greasy clapper bridges led to squelching bogs with unstable islands of tussock sedge and wobbling paving stones.

Sometimes red earth paths teetered precariously along crumbling cliff edges where tossing strands of thin gorse strained to cling by fingertips. Idiotically twisting paths contorted like narrow sheep trails through purple heather quaking with terror.

But always the rude roaring bullying wind.

Eventually, in the silent lee of a lichen-covered wall, Budge stopped and fumbled with cuffs to find his watch.

Half-past ten.

He turned to the Major who slowly held up a reassuring 'OK' thumb as if he'd been asked for a situation report. Twirly remained undercover, crouched deep inside his hood.

Budge looked around.

A few feet up from the path, massive boulders were piled to form a cavity the size of a small hen-coop.

'This way,' he cried, and they squeezed tightly side-by-side into the refuge to sit on a patch of grass.

The wind still howled, but here they were safe from the buffeting; hoods no longer slapping and crackling, their limbs were their own, and, for the moment, the gale was someone else's problem.

'Bloody hell,' breathed Twirly, and they all guffawed at this remarkable burst of wit.

Budge sat expectantly.

This is where Twirly produces his morning treat.

This morning – nothing.

Budge slapped his knee and laughed louder than the wind.

Like a sitting hen turning its eggs, he shuffled and clucked and juggled his elbows, and eventually gave birth to a folded green pullover and held it aloft like a cup at Wembley.

'In here, gentlemen – wrapped in three yards of kitchen foil – WARM SAUSAGE SARNIES.'

Budge joyfully watched Twirly's eyes glowing in wonder.

'From the kitchen?'

Budge nodded.

'Nigel did them?'

Budge nodded again.

Twirly grinned in unbridled admiration.

The Major, looking as wise as an owl, gave a slow nod of approval.

A sudden marauding seagull, sensing food, scudded up from nowhere, but was instantly blasted away by an angry burst of south-westerly.

In expectant suspense, the green pullover was slowly unwrapped . . .

Budge wiped the last crumbs from his lips.

Far below, the sea still tirelessly raced to attack the cliff, encouraged by the bellowing wind.

Newly fortified, he watched with scorn the thrashing gorse and the trembling boot-tripping heather.

People tucked safely inland at Gently know nothing of such hazards and invasions. At Lambley, the land-lubber scaffolders will be working secure and unaware. Doll will protest if it even dares to drizzle.

'Jolly good, Mr Ballflower,' breathed the Major flicking food particles from his jacket. 'Men have got medals for less.'

Budge folded his pullover away.

'Sorry there were no sachets of brown sauce, Twirly.'

369

No response.

He turned his head.

Twirly's hood was pressed against the wind-polished boulder as if it were a pillow stuffed with Chinese eider duck down.

The Major shrugged.

'You must understand, Budge, that ex-army men who spent long periods in action, learned the knack of instantly falling asleep anywhere, anytime, in any conditions . . . and they still do it today . . . some even falling asleep . . . in the middle of . . .'

'Major?'

Down in Portheras Cove, where enormous boulder stepping-stones took them across a bright, bubbling stream, they were again protected for a few moments from the fury of the wind. Budge waited for them at the top of the road running up Pendeen Cliff, and they sheltered together behind a six-foot-high white wall surrounding the lighthouse.

Budge said hopefully, 'It's open to visitors.'

The Major looked out at the tossing sea, and sighed.

'Do they do food?' Twirly grunted.

Budge groaned, 'This way,' and he led them back into the fray, leaving the road to take the blustering footpath down to the stream emptying into Enys Zawn.

Up above the Avarack rock-pile Budge halted until they stood in a buffeted group.

'All OK?'

The Major pointed inland to a grey straggle of houses less than a mile across the valley.

'Pendeen,' announced Budge.

The slope between the houses and crumbling cliffs was covered with a desert of red and pink spoil, surrounded by a desolation of collapsed walls, ruined buildings, and tall chimneys.

'Corpse of the dead Geevor mine,' said Budge.

The land of the Cornovii has always been associated with tin.

In 330 BC, Pytheas of Massila is said to have sailed to Britain to discover the source of metals brought back by intrepid Phoenician traders.

Truro County Museum has a 150lb ingot of Cornish tin, bearing Roman markings.

In 1716 a mine was registered on this site called Wheal-an-Giver (mine of goats), and by the end of the nineteenth century more than three hundred men worked a hundred miles of stopes beneath these cliffs, many under the sea.

Eventually prices plummeted and the mine closed, although water-pumps were kept going in the hope of a reopening. But in 1991 this life-support system was switched off. The levels filled with water and Geevor became history.

But,' said Budge, 'all is not lost. Geevor now has a mining museum, a shop, a short length of underground adit open to the public – and The Big Bob Café.'

'We can be there in fifteen minutes if we move with alacrity.'

Budge took a quick glance out to sea. Huge waves still surged forward to explode at the foot of orange and black cliffs, but the tops were no longer being viciously whipped. The Scots Greys had finished their charge. The wind was becoming bored.

They hurried down to Trewellard Bottoms and entered the lost city of Geevor.

Propped against a wall of square red stones, a sign hand-painted in a hurry promised: CAFE - SUN TO FRI 10 TO 5.

The feebling wind looked around to find a new game, and suddenly decided to become kind, and gently nudged them up a twisting trail marked by rough white arrows daubed on wall corners, tilted posts and convenient heaps of debris.

They stumbled past entrances to murky tunnels with sagging timbers, great settling tanks of green slime, ancient shorings, a frozen waterfall of phosphorous green and gold bleached out of red rock, and tall Y-shaped concrete posts with protruding rusting bolts reminding Budge of Organ Pipe cacti in California's Sonoran Desert.

The Big Bob Café was bright as a new pin.

Packs off. Feet up. Pints procured.

'Will they ever mine tin here again, Budge?'

Budge shook his head.

'Tin still here, but the mining always involved colossal risks. We don't take risks any more. Health and Safety has made the country sterile. We all sit waiting for Godot.'

The lunch speciality was Miner's Lunch Pasty: a fold of pastry with mutton and vegetables in one half, and stewed apple with cinnamon and raisins in the other. Served with two small jugs. One of hot gravy. The other of warm custard.

'We loved the Miner's Pasties,' said Budge.
     The lady smiled.
     'Did you know that down at Levant they are hoping to get the whim engine in steam?'
     'Today?'
     'Now. Oldest surviving beam engine in Cornwall.'

They scurried along stonewalled Maggie's Lane, and five minutes later they skipped down steps to an underground chamber beneath a building perched on the edge of Levant Zawn.
     Hot oil. Hissing steam. And the sound of enormous power.

The 27-inch cylinder engine was built by Harvey's of Hayle in the 1840s to haul skips up from 278 fathoms. When the mine closed it was saved from destruction by the remarkable Trevithick Society, and since 1966 has been owned by the National Trust.

A man in overalls, wiping his hands on an oily rag, introduced himself as Milton, one of the 'greaser-gang' volunteers.
     He took them up into a chamber where a massive cast-iron 'bob' rocked slowly and majestically like an enormous see-saw.
     Milton affectionately stroked the beam with his oily rag.
     'You going to see how we've restored the entrance to the man-engine shaft?'

Conditions in Levant were always dangerous:
     High temperatures.
     Constant risk of flooding.

372

Long walks to lode-faces.

Descents and ascents of flimsy vertical ladders in a darkness lit only by candles attached to helmets by lumps of clay.

And then in 1837 a Matthew-Loam man-engine was installed to reduce accidents on the ladders. This involved a rod made up of sections of nine-inch square pitch-pine suspended from a rocking 'bob' over an 1,800-foot shaft.

Five times a minute this rod rose and fell twelve feet.

Attached to the rod at every twelve feet were tiny platforms.

A miner descended by leaping – in the dark – from these platforms on to similar platforms in the side of the shaft, then at the right moment leaping back on to a lower-platform on the oscillating rod. This risky procedure was repeated until the required depth was reached. The reverse process would carry the miner 'up to grass' at the end of his shift.

On the afternoon of 20th October, 1919 the rod broke away from the 'bob', and crumpled down into the blackness in a bloody and splintered heap.

Thirty-one miners died.

Above the Crown mines where two restored engine-houses cling to the cliff-side, Budge took off his jacket.

The wind had gone inland. The heavy cloud was breaking up, with the sun making furtive appearances.

He checked his watch and called to the Major and Twirly, who were plodding through the maze of ruined arsenic flues and buddles and crumbling chimneys.

'Just over an hour to go, men.'

He sighed and rolled his shoulders.

And one more day.

'I thought of doing roast stuffed chicken,' said Mrs Cargeeg of Nanweddon B&B when she brought in a second pot of tea.

Three hours later a recovered Major dabbed the corners of his mouth with a starched napkin.

'Chicken was perfect, Mrs Cargeeg. As was the ginger pudding.'

She smiled.

'You walking again tomorrow?'

'To Land's End.'

Mrs Cargeeg grimaced.

'Weather forecast not good again, I'm afraid. Jim says now the wind's dropped, there'll be a mist. Could be thick. Have to watch your step on some of them cliff paths. Would you like coffee?'

The Major nodded at two photographs signed 'Jerome', in silver frames, squeezed on to a family-filled sideboard.

'Sons?'

'No. Brothers. Harold was in the Engineers – killed in North Africa.   Stanley was a gunner in 137 Field Artillery.   Died in a Japanese prisoner-of-war camp.'

'Just two coffees would be fine, Mrs Cargeeg. Mr Whippet has gone into your garden to clean boots.'

'Major,' said Budge. 'Your friend Quintin said *you* were captured by the Japanese.'

The Major ran a finger around the top of his cup and leaned back to look out of the plant-blocked window at Twirly polishing as furiously as a shoe-wallah in Cairo.

His equipment was arranged on an old mangle by a rust-red anchor sprouting from a bed of beach-pebbles. In the distance a whale-backed heather-covered pennisula was topped by a single chimney like a candle on a first-birthday cake.

'That's right.'

'And you escaped?'

The Major nodded, and rose stiffly.

'Care for a spot of brandy, Mr Ballflower? Bought a new bottle in St Ives.'

'Rather hear about you and the Japanese.'

The Major watched Twirly spit on a toe-cap.

'In that case I think we *both* need a brandy.'

Chapter Thirty-nine

'Jungle in the Far East, Budge, was an awful place for soldiering.'

'Danger always present.

'Constant need to identify every sound.

'Never ending *extreme* discomfort.

'Heat.

'Sapped energy.

'Terrible thirst – a ration of one water-bottle a day filled with muddy water tasting of chlorine.'

'Some poor lads couldn't take it. Walked off into the rough and went 'missing'. Had a man who actually willed himself to die.

'Some developed a craze for alcohol. Not unknown to drink a tin of Brasso filtered through a shell-dressing.'

Budge shuddered.

The Major poured two measures of brandy into Mrs Cargeeg's water-tumblers.

'Where do you want me to begin?'

'How'd the Japs get you?'

The Major grimaced, sipped his brandy, and forced himself back more than fifty years.

'It was after the first parachute supply-drop.

'Two Liberators flew from Jessore with three tons of explosives and ammunition to a drop-zone we prepared on the Sungei Sui between Bidor and Tapah.

'All went well, but absolutely essential we got the stuff dispersed quickly amongst Chinese guerrilla units.

'We split ourselves into teams. Myself and two others, with six *Sakai* porters, set off to contact a camp, strangely enough, near an old tin mine near Larek, thirty miles away, fifteen miles north of Cameron Highlands.

'On the third day, I was doing 'tipper', carrying a desperately heavy rucksack, route finding, and occasionally *parang* slashing.

'In the centre of the column with the porters was Sergeant Stanley armed with a Sten, a sub-machine-gun mass-produced in engineering-shops across England. Got its name from the initial letters of the inventors' surnames, Shepperd and Turpin, and EN from Enfield small arms factory. Excellent weapon, except it was liable to jam.'

The Major took more brandy.

'Bringing up the rear and armed with a sixteen-round Winchester 30 carbine, was Vanrenan, a Dutchman who had been manager of a rubber plantation when the Japs arrived.

'Some of us had been in the jungle for a year, and our bones stuck out like sticks in a bag, and our sickly yellow skins were mottled with the purple spots of leech-bites.

'We were making good progress, then at Kinding Estate – disaster . . .

'I turned a bend, and a hundred yards away were half-a-dozen Japs looking as surprised as me – but with aimed weapons.

'"*Killy-kollack. Te o agero!*" they shouted.

'No point in starting a war. Nothing we could do. The Japs rushed us. The porters dropped their loads and ran. Didn't blame them. Japs were only interested in *us* and our supplies.

'They surrounded the three of us, and poked us, thumped us, and kicked us, and hurried us along for about twenty minutes until we came to a clearing with two lean-to shelters.

'Stanley was instantly clubbed to the ground – and it looked as if Vanrenan and I were to receive the same when . . .

'*Tomare! Mou ii!'*

'The shout came from one of the shelters.

'A young, clean-shaven officer appeared and instantly began shouting questions in English. "Where the rest of your party? You land with the Australians at Johore? You parachute?"

'He then noticed the pip-and-crown of a lieutenant-colonel on the epaulettes of my black-with-sweat shirt. He leapt to attention and saluted.

'"I educated in England. You are English gentleman. You no lie me."

'I told him we were soldiers who had been obliged to retreat into the jungle when the Japanese invaded in 1941.'

The Major nodded at Budge.

'Incredibly there *had* been 'stay-behind' volunteers, and several had somehow survived in the jungle and made contact with the guerrillas. Did an extraordinary job annoying the Japanese.

'The officer began to search my pack.

'Unfortunately he found a map dated 1944 . . .

'He glared.

'"You lie me!"

'He nodded to one of the guards, who smartly stepped forward and downed me with a heavy thump on the head with his rifle-butt.

'I blacked out, a prisoner of the Imperial Army.'

The Major stood with his brandy and stepped over to the window to watch Twirly still toiling at the boots.

'That island out there – with a single chimney?'

Budge checked through the window.

'Not an *island,* Major. Cape Cornwall.'

The Cape was once thought to be England's most westerly point, but sophisticated measurement proved Land's End to be the winner by a thousand yards. The single chimney was designed to provide a great up-draught to aid ventilation in a mine six hundred feet below, but it worked too well and was abandoned. In 1987 the Cape was presented to the National Trust by H J Heinz, famous for its 57 varieties.

The Major sipped more brandy and lowered himself onto a chair.

He heard Budge say. 'But you escaped . . .'

The Major grimaced.

'When I came to, the jungle was getting dark, and I was lying face down in one of the shelters with my wrists tied behind me and my ransacked pack by my side. A guard stood outside with rifle and bayonet. And surprisingly, for a jungle patrol, beyond him burned a camp-fire.

'I lay with my head throbbing, attempting to identify a confusion of noises.

'Apart from the normal jungle night-sounds of tree-frogs and cicadas and grasshoppers and angry mosquitoes, and the deep booming of black siamang apes – and the coughs and snorts of the Jap soldiers – there were others.

Shufflings.

Draggings.

Growled commands.

Suddenly the officer appeared silhouetted at the front of the awning and gazed down at me for several minutes before speaking.

'"English Colonel. You must not think bad of Japanese soldier. You must not think bad of Japanese emperor: he does not want these things to happen to English soldier."

'I asked him about Vanrenan and Stanley.

'He briefly looked into the blackness beyond the bonfire, then said, "War between Japan and England a very bad thing.".'

'I knew then that I would not see Vanrenan and Stanley again.

'I also knew I had to get away immediately.

'The chances of surviving tomorrow did not exist and my mind raced with the speed of desperation.

'I raised myself up as well as I was able and said, '"As an intelligent officer of the Imperial Japanese Army you cannot believe that I would be foolish enough to attempt to escape alone into the jungle. May I therefore ask that you at least permit me to sleep this night by unfastening my wrists?"

'He considered, and studied me – too long I thought. But suddenly he dug his hands into a pocket of his breeches and pulled out a small penknife. By the light of the flames I saw clearly its cheap coloured enamel and shiny blade.

'Leaning over and without a word, he cut the bindings, then straightened. As he turned to leave, I was astounded to see by the light of the fire that his eyes were welled with tears. The bastard was weeping.

'He suddenly stopped, as if he was about to say something, but he grunted and disappeared.'

In the stillness of the Nanweddon dining-room the Major attempted to focus on the sideboard photographs of the two boys wearing army greatcoats and jauntily-tilted forage caps.

Budge stood.

'Time for bed, Major. Twirly will bring your boots up.'

The Major ignored him.

No permission has been given to withdraw. Been here many times. Especially on hot nights. Leaping out of bed, with a shout. Scaring Mary. Scaring myself...

The sentry re-appeared at the mouth of the shelter, his bayonet gleaming in the firelight.

'Now.

'Must do it now.

'With the minimum of movement I opened my pack and dragged out my green woollen blanket – best bit of kit the army ever gave us – which I had sewn up two sides to make a sleeping bag.

'Writhing like a kitten playing on its back with a ball, I ripped off my boots, and stuffed them into the bottom corners.

'Fluffed-up every other bit of kit I had, and arranged it down the sack as best I could.

'Whenever the guard peered into the shelter, I froze. My head was pounding and I could taste thick blood in my mouth.

Soon, the camp's grunting and rattling pans developed into the sounds of mild ribaldry. The patrol was obviously supplied with 'hooch', the potent sugar-flavoured rice spirit which the Chinese called White Stag Whisky.

'Feigning restless sleep, I threw out my arms and groped for odd items of clothing and equipment which were strewn within arm's reach, and shoved them down into the bag. With my legs drawn up tight under my chin, I hoped my bag looked full enough to contain a member of His Majesty's Forces.

'Just above my head the shelter canvas was pegged into the ground. During my arm- stretching movements I loosened two of the pegs.

'I estimated that shortly the guard must be relieved, and hopefully the new man would have partaken of the 'hooch' and be less sensitive to my movements.

'That's when it must happen.

'Although I was trembling with anticipation and fear, I must have dozed, and was awakened by soldiers mumbling and snorting as they entered the shelter and threw themselves down, not bothering to remove clothes or boots.

'Outside the guard *had* changed, and the new man had bouts of a wheezy cough.

'I knew I had to wait until the men were asleep. Fortunately they were restless, noisy sleepers, which would make any actions of mine less noticeable.

'I was now ready to go.

'When the guard began his next coughing session, that would be my signal. I would take nothing with me, and go barefoot.

'As I lay I tried to visualise where the track entered the camp. I would make for that. From the shelter I could see that the clearing allowed glimpses of sky – and there was a silver moon.

'Eventually the guard began coughing . . .

'With a desperate push of my legs, and rapid fumbling with the edge of the canvas, I pushed myself out into the night, leapt up, and began running. The guard was still head-down with his coughing and, by great fortune, I found the track.

As I ran with my arms outstretched to fend off vegetation, I began counting. When I got to twenty I stopped running. Standard jungle training.

Stop. Push yourself off the track; stand still; listen.

'Presently, above the noises of the night and the thumping of my heart, there was a dull thud.

'Again, standard jungle practice: one of the guards had heard a noise and tossed a stone or clump of earth.

'If the noise was made by a human, the source would freeze. If it was an animal, it would move resentfully away, with no attempt at silence.

'Accordingly, I began to lurch away, slowly, and clumsily – and trying not to scream.

'On the count of ten I began running again.

'Wildly.

'Painfully.

'As fast as I could force myself.

'Suddenly my feet were thrashing in empty air.

'I landed heavily on hands and knees, engulfed in water. Gasping and choking, I splashed along a stream. Stumbling and falling.

'Eventually an opening appeared in the banks on either side. A crossing place!

'I clambered up to the right to join another track, much wider now, and began running again. Exhaustion was ordering me to slow down. Order ignored. Faster. My body screaming with pain from constant buffeting, bare feet stamping on sharpened knives. Suddenly, I tripped and thudded to the ground. Get up. Get up now! Gasping with pain, I prised myself up, and off again. On and on. My legs were beginning to flail wildly. I fell again and landed with my face buried into undergrowth. I lifted my head.

'There came a groan louder than I had heard before.

'And I realised it came from me.

'Not from my throat, but from the bottom of my bowel: for just beyond my outstretched arms were boots, and gaitered legs, and the dark butts of rifles.

'The world flashed a blinding red, and I plunged into the blackness of eternity.

'I was aware of drifting back through a humming tunnel of coloured lights, and felt my face being gently bathed.

'Through my puffed and bloody eyes, I could see an olive girl with almond-shaped eyes bending over.

'I groaned with relief.

'The girl gave a little cry, and turned, and called, '"*Cepat! Sila datang!*"

'Someone came running, and knelt with a face next to mine.

'I knew the face.'

' "Ling Fam" I whispered.

' "Colonel *tongste*"

381

'Ling Fam, who I had met at Ipoh HQ.

' "You very bad. You sleep. *Tidur.* We make you good."

'My olive-skinned nurse slid back into view and carefully prised open my punished mouth with a bamboo spoon, from which flowed something soft and sweet. Could have been palm syrup.

'I closed my eyes and realised I was probably sobbing.

'They tended me for six weeks and made me good, then walked with me for sixty miles to Pangkor where the submarine *Tantalus* was waiting to take me back to Ceylon.'

Budge spoke quietly into the silence of the room.

'Did you find out what happened to the other two?'

The Major took Mrs Cargeeg's water-jug and slowly topped up his brandy.

'Immediately the war ended, Force 136 parachuted thirty teams to make initial contact with prisoner-of-war camps. I managed to drop in the Kedah region with a four-man team: two medical officers from 44 Airborne, a signaller, and an armed escort.

'Before I finally left the penninsula I went back to the Larek camp area, where a headman offered to show me the graves dug by villagers after the Japs moved on. Proper graves marked by Christian crosses of bamboo.

'The headman asked if I needed to identify the bodies.

' *"No. That is for other."*

'The headman nodded.

' "Very wise, *Tuan.*"

'The way he said it made me ask just how they met their deaths.'

The Major paused and sipped his diluted brandy.

'You see, Budge, it wouldn't have been sensible for the Japs to shoot them. Would have given their position away. They knew there were Chinese in the area.'

The Major shook his head.

'Such brave men.'

He looked at Budge. Probably the same age as the rubber planter when he died.

He stuck up his chin, and forbade his lips to tremble.

'Apparently it took *several* clumsy blows of a *chankol.*'

'*Chankol?*'

'A long-handled Malayan spade, Budge.'

Twirly burst into the dining room with his bag of cleaning kit and four gleaming brown boots.

'Footwear ready for your inspection, Sah!'

The Major took his boots and said quietly, 'Perfect. Thank you, Mr Whippet.'

Twirly studied him.

'You all right, Sir?'

'Just a little weary. Think I'll go and shake centipedes out of my *charpoy* and inspect my person for leeches.'

Budge put a hand on the Major's shoulder.

'Sleep well, Major. Last day tomorrow. Dinner at Land's End . . . all being well.'

The Major held up a cautionary finger.

'Corporal. Can you hear that distant thumping?'

Twirly put his head on one side.

A faint regular throbbing.

'A helicopter, Sir.'

The noise got louder and nearer and more threatening.

Very low.

With no diminution.

Must be landing.

Finally, the noise rapidly slowed and stopped, leaving behind a great vacuum of silence.

Twirly watched the Major frown and clutch his boots about him. He headed for the stairs, and stopped, and turned. His eyes were stern as steel.

'Corporal. I suggest the men put out trip-wires tonight. Stand-to at first light. Everyone alert for snipers.'

Chapter Forty

Thursday 30th July   *Day twenty-five*

Budge was nudged awake by the low moan of Pendeen's foghorn.

Twenty seconds later it nudged him again.

He squinted, sat up and peered out of the small bedroom window.

The garden of Nanweddon Farm was being probed by fronds of curling white mist.

Beyond that – nothing.

No sky.

No horizon.

No sea.

Cornwall had disappeared overnight.

He should have guessed the last day would be like this.

No dramatic cliffs or mind-bending seascapes.

No towering rock-castles defending England.

No cheering crowds or massed bands.

Only an undercover arrival, censored by fog.

But the smell of frying bacon was *real* and not to be ignored.

'Good morning, Ballflower', said the Major, a napkin tucked beneath his chin. He nodded towards the window.

'Gunners have done a good job putting down smoke.'

A beaming Mrs Cargeeg charged into the room with a plate of steaming cholesterol.

The Major, with the authority of mess-president, explained, 'Took the liberty of advising our host that you qualify for the pre-operation allowance of *two* eggs. I have despatched Corporal Whippet outside to search for a reel of Sapper's guiding tape.'

The pork-and-herb sausages were the best Budge had ever tasted. 'A bit murky out there, Major.'

The Major bullied butter onto a thick slice of toast.

'Jim Cargeeg has looked in. Says the mist will lift in a couple of hours. Recommends we delay leaving. Pity to walk Europe's most spectacular coast with our heads in a bucket.'

Twirly entered with glistening eyebrows and hair.

'Think it's lifting.'

Budge looked at the sideboard photographs of the two brothers grinning with eager innocence.

'I think we should get going. Six miles, and it'll all be finished.'

Twirly winced.

All be finished.

He remembered his mother.

'Never forget, Twirly. Milking is never finished *until the cooler has been cleaned and pails put away.'*

He would watch her eyes moisten, and he knew she was thinking of grandad who was shot by a sniper on the River Sambre in November 1918.

Down in the village they were already waving flags to celebrate the Armistice and the end of the Great War when Stan Whitlock delivered the telegram..

The Major said, 'Right. We move off at o-nine-thirty-hours, Corporal. Get the men fell-in.'

'Do be careful,' said Mrs Cargeeg. 'Jim he do say Hermon Hill is terrible tricky in mist.'

She dug deep into the front pocket of her floral apron and pressed on each one of them a Mars bar.

She said, 'You never know . . .'

On the road just below Nanweddon the dishevelled but imposing Porthledden House loomed like a shadowy *Marie Celeste*. Peeling wooden gates hung loosely fastened by blue binder-cord.

Budge snorted. The ex-chairman of De Beers Company wouldn't like that.

At the age of twelve, local lad Francis Oates started work at Botallack Mine, and at the end of his shift, four times a week, he walked the seven miles to Penzance for evening classes in mineralogy.

Later, he found work in the diamond mines of South Africa, and became chairman of the De Beers Company. Back in England, he purchased Cape Cornwall and built this once fine mansion. After his death the house became a hotel and fell into disrepair.

By a grass-topped wall a green and gold sign announced that the lost-in-the-mist Cape Cornwall Golf Club was pleased to invite non-members to its Spa, Restaurant, and Accommodation.

Further down the road Budge was surprised to find the shadowy car-park full of figures and vague shapes. At the far side, a mine ruin appeared to be topped by a gantry.

A few more paces and the figures became young soldiers with green berets drinking from brown enamel mugs. The vague shapes became military vehicles. The mine ruin became a helicopter.

'Morning,' cried a cheerful officer, looking younger than Budge's nephew studying Economic History at Royal Holloway.

Budge nodded.

'All a bit sinister – this.'

The young man chuckled.

'The *mist* is sinister, Sir. Not us. We're on an exercise. Some of the men are already down in Cot Cove with inflatables. Due to make a beach insertion on Whitesand Bay, two miles along the coast. But can't do it in this visibility.'

'And the helicopter?'

'These chaps are due to join them with a fast-rope low-level landing from twenty feet above the beach.'

Budge searched the haze for Twirly and the Major, and found them amongst a group by a field-kitchen stove.

Twirly was busily handing out much-travelled Sharp's toffees.

The path climbed steeply from the car-park between high stone walls, and at the top, by a stone-slab stile, a narrow lane led off to St Just. Ahead a black cinder path ran through high bracken, and a silver and black National Trust sign warned of hidden mine shafts and instructed: KEEP TO FOOTPATHS.

Budge wondered if they should make a detour to the left in search of the Bronze Age burial mound of Carn Gloose, but the still swirling mist looked hostile, and Budge was not sure what there was to see even on a clear day. He also felt that this was not his companions' day for archaeology.

On either side of the descending path were circular walls enclosing old shafts, with red-edged triangular signs and dramatic silhouettes of falling persons. Additional signs reminded: HIDDEN SHAFTS. KEEP TO FOOTPATH.

Down near the beach in the wide bracken-filled Cot Valley, shadowy young soldiers stood amongst the enshrouded foundations of nineteenth century ore-crushing stamps, and dressing-floors. On the road lurked three large black inflatables. A Sergeant of Marines wearing a camouflaged smock and bright yellow life-jacket nodded a curt greeting.

A small stone bridge crossed the fast slowing Cot stream which once powered a dozen water-wheels in the valley.

The bridge is the voluntary handiwork of the remarkable Willie Oates of St Just who died in October 1987. Mr Oates built steps up the steep valley side, secured paths at the top, and provided stone benches for the weary.

A rocky outcrop on Herman Hill marked the top of the climb. A grass path running inland was signposted: *St Just Youth Hostel.* Ahead, a level path ran between the base of a towering cliff, and a mist-filled void dropping down sheer to the sea.

Budge stopped to peer into a gloomy narrow cave in the cliff.
'Adit,' he said.

Seeping water was always a problem in Cornwall's mines, and sloping adit passages like this assisted drainage, as well as sometimes providing access for miners.

Further along the path were two more adits; one had collapsed and through the now thinning haze Budge could see the bracken-filled trench soaring up the cliff-face.

At a circular wall with a triangular sign warning OPEN SHAFT, the path turned sharp left up a few stone steps, and instantly turned right again, leading up to hazy Gribba Point.

'Take ten minutes,' said Budge, and he slung off his pack and dumped it onto one of Willie Oates' benches.

Twirly fumbled in a pocket, and distributed crumbly biscuits he had acquired in St Ives, and they wordlessly stretched full-length on the path.

The cliff was as quiet as Gently Wood when gamekeepers are about, the mist smothering even the sound of the sea breaking on rocks below.

High above, ragged hints of gauze-covered blue sky began to appear briefly, as shy as young coneys.

He turned his head, and the smell of damp grass reminded him of Fish House, and he idly supposed he could hear Ratcher purring.

He sat up.

He COULD hear Ratcher purring.

A slow and irregular growl.

But it wasn't Ratcher.

'There's a boat down there,' he said.

But the mist swallowed the noise again.

Budge, horizontal further along the path, called, 'Doubt it, Twirly. Not so close in. Not in this mist.'

Twirly sniffed, and smiled. He knew better.

It'll be smugglers. Saw the film. Frenchman's Creek. *Jean Simmons. Stewart Granger. Boats sliding in and out of mist . . .*

Suddenly Budge sat up.

'There *is* a boat.'

The sound rolling up the cliff was now unmistakable. A throaty engine bubbling and ticking over, far below.

The Major sat up.

'You're right, Corporal.'

Then he pointed and cried 'THERE!'

Folds of mist had parted, and for a few seconds a motor cruiser could be seen on the grey sea, stationary and close inshore to the cliffs.

Twirly watched the Major scramble urgently to his feet.

'Damn!' he exploded. 'Look at that! See that red mark on the cabin roof. It's the boat we saw in Hayle. It's the *We Ourselves* from Dublin.'

Twirly watched Budge slowly stand.

'So what, Major? It's a boat from Dublin. It's allowed to do a bit of fishing, even when it's foggy.'

The Major demanded:

'Budge. Do you know what *We Ourselves* is in Gaelic?'

Budge bent over to calmly brush shreds of bracken from his trousers.

The Major fired the words like a burst from a Schmeisser.

'It's SINN FEIN, Mr Ballflower.'

Twirly leapt up, and he and the Major peered down into the disintegrating gauze.

Budge sighed loudly.

'It's ten-thirty. Could be at Land's End by one o'clock if we get moving . . .'

Twirly silenced him with a wave of his hand.

'*Listen.*'

But the only sound was the faint stuttering of the boat, and a hint of breaking waves, and a couple of mewing seagulls which had been grounded by the mist.

Budge began to move off.

'LUNCH,' he called over his shoulder.

The Major angrily struck a gorse bush with his cane and called, 'Mr Ballflower. The Corporal and I suspect something odd is going on.'

389

Budge whipped round and snorted, 'Major! We're *not* going down to find out. We're going to Land's End. That's the 'operational plan' – remember?'

The Major stood his ground.

Twirly cried:

'We don't have to go down. If you look you'll see heads bobbing about in the bracken.

'They're coming up, Sir.'

Twirly, closely followed by the Major, pushed up from the path through gorse and brambles, to a shoulder-high boulder where they crouched like artillery FOU observers.

Now they could hear the sound of thrashing undergrowth. The heads got nearer.

Budge clambered up beside them and growled, 'Still think we should get out of here.'

Suddenly, only yards away, the head and shoulders of a man appeared amongst the thin swirls of mist, kicking his way out of the bracken on to the path. Others followed. Soon there were six of them.

Twirly held up his hand for silence and watched them head for the circular stone wall with the OPEN SHAFT sign.

A man in a long brown coat grasped the triangular warning sign and lifted it completely off the post. Another clambered over the wall and bobbed about. He appeared to lift a wooden hatch, then vanish.

A wooden device like a small gallows with a dangling rope was slid on to the empty signpost in place of the warning sign.

Two men urgently hauled on the rope, and eventually a long green wooden box appeared.

Budge swore.

'Hell's bells. It's guns.'

After about ten-minutes five similar boxes had been brought to the surface and the first man reappeared and closed the hatch. The slip-on derrick was removed and dropped inside the wall and, with a box apiece balanced on their shoulders, the men plunged back into the bracken and began working their way down the cliff.

Budge licked his dry lips and croaked, 'You got any of that brandy, Major?'

'We must tell the police,' said Twirly.

Budge pulled his brick-sized telephone from his pack.

He jabbed at it several times, then shook his head.

'No stupid signal. Have to go to St Just. It's about a mile. Hide yourselves until I get back,' and he kicked through the bracken down on to the path.

The Major called, 'We will employ delaying tactics until . . .'

Budge swung round and pointed a threatening finger.

'Do nothing, old man. No stupid heroics,' and they watched him set off along the grass path with urgent strides.

'Right, Sir,' said Twirly. 'Let you and me take a *shufti* at that shaft.'

Propped inside the shaft-wall was the displaced triangular warning sign with the wooden derrick and tangle of rope. The wooden hatch was secured by a metal bar fastened by a large galvanised padlock.

'We need delaying tactics, Corporal.'

Twirly nodded.

'You got your Mars bar, Sir?'

Three minutes later it was all done and sorted.

Twirly had rolled over the wall, produced his tin of storm-proof matches, ripped wrappers off two Mars bars, and pressed melted brown gunge deep into the padlock and encased it in molten toffee.

He gave a deep job-well-done sniff.

Will set like concrete. Let Paddy try and get a key into that lot.

They scarpered up through the gorse towards the cliff top.

Above them in the departing mist loomed a row of shapes like huts on an allotment.

'Up there, Sir.'

They flung themselves over the remains of a dry-stone wall and pressed themselves into straw stubble.

Twirly looked back at the hut shapes – great drums of rolled black plastic. His mind was racing…

'They're coming back,' interrupted the Major.

The column of heads pushed up through the bracken. Below them the red-topped cruiser lay at anchor, no longer screened by drifting mist.

Twirly watched the leading man arrive back at the shaft, climb over the wall, and crouch to momentarily disappear.

He shot back upright.

The remaining men rushed to peer over the wall, then turned to scan the cliff side, and began to spread warily along the path in both directions.

Now all movement was halted and the man in the long brown coat appeared to be giving orders.

'I've got this idea . . . ' whispered Twirly.

The Major hissed, 'Holding an O-Group. Pointing at the cliffs – and back at the boat. All look pretty heated.'

A pistol shot shattered the silence.

'Good Lord,' exclaimed the Major.

A second shot.

'They've shot away our handiwork, Corporal.'

Twirly watched the men pushing and pointing, all looking unhappy, but guessed they were probably now able to open the hatch.

Sure enough the boxes began appearing again, although these were deeper and squarer.

Eventually, five of the men, led by the long brown coat, set off down the cliff bearing the boxes.

The sixth man stood by the hole nervously scanning the cliff side – with the pistol in his hand.

The Major hissed, 'Had to leave him on stag, Corporal. They can't lock the cover.'

'I've got this idea,' insisted Twirly. 'Those black bales . . .'

Working with the speed and strength of desperation, they heaved and pushed until five of the bales were perched along the cliff edge.

Twirly gave the order: 'NOW, Major!'

They hurled themselves at the first bale, and away it went, leaping and bouncing high into the air, hurtling unstoppable down towards the sea.

The others followed in quick succession.

After the third bale Twirly thought he heard a cry of alarm – or pain – from deep down the cliff.

On the launch of the last bale they both sank on to the stubble, soaked in sweat, and gasping like marathon runners.

The Major recovered immediately.

'Where's the sentry, Corporal?'

They slithered along the line of the wall.

Twirly slowly raised his head.

'He's still by the shaft.   Twitchy as hell, Sir. Knows we are up here. But can't leave his post.'

The Major peered and declared with excitement, 'Look at that! You can see right into the stone-enclosure from up here. The cover's open, looking a bit battered.'

Suddenly the Major demanded, 'Any good at throwing, Corporal?'

Twirly considered.

'Could always knock a pigeon out of a tree. Drop a potato into a bucket from three hundred yards.'

The Major impatiently shook his head.

'Grenades?'

Twirly nodded.

'When I was with the battalion.'

The Major hurriedly pulled out his brandy bottle, took a quick swig, and thrust it at Twirly, who did the same.

'Stones, Corporal. A handful of stones from the wall.'

It took only a moment for the Major to stuff a clean handkerchief into the bottle with a tail hanging out, and turn it upside down, and for Twirly to set it alight with his storm-proof matches, then grab up the stones and toss them far to the left where they fell into the gorse.

The sentry leaped in alarm, and took a few paces towards the stones away from the shaft.

393

In that instant Twirly stood, snatched the flaming Molotov cocktail, and, tense as a sapling of willow, hurled it arching towards the shaft.

It trailed a line of flame, which for a second looked as if it had detached itself from the bottle, but it was still furiously alight when it disappeared centrally into the hole.

Twirly and the Major dropped to their knees and stared in wonder at each other, and the Major thumped Twirly so hard that he rolled over into the stubble.

'Bull's eye, Corporal!' he hissed.

They waited and watched.

Nothing.

Just the sentry jumpy as a wagtail.

'Did you hear the bottle land?'

Twirly shook his head.

The Major whispered, 'Take a bit for the timbers to catch fire. Hopefully there are explosives down there . . . mortar bombs . . . rockets . . .'

'MAJOR! The men are coming back up from the boat.'

The Major scrambled up.

'C'mon, Corporal. Let's get the hell out of here.'

Twirly ran at a crouch behind the wall and slithered down on to the path.

He heard the Major close behind him.

They came to an adit entrance.

'Quick, Major. In here.'

'No! Not this one,' cried the Major. 'Will search this first one. Better the next.'

They pushed into the narrow entrance and pressed into the black interior, stumbling over fallen rocks and thumping against rough sides.

Twirly scrambled up onto a rough ledge, and heard the Major burrowing noisily into the blackness.

'Quiet, Sir! Stay still, whatever happens.'

From outside came the sound of muffled gun-fire.

The first cave.

This was no pistol – but something substantially more lethal.

Another sharp burst of about five rounds.

Now the light at the entrance was blocked.

Somebody there.

Twirly pressed himself into the jagged wall until it hurt.

BRURRP!

The air was ripped by a head-splitting blast, with the scream and slap of ricocheting rounds peppering the rocks by his head.

Light returned to the entrance, and Twirly blinked his eyes free of dust, and licked dry grit from his mouth.

He was certain the gunman had moved on, but he continued to crouch, still making himself part of the rock-face.

Finally he hissed, 'You all right, Major?'

A couple of dislodged stones tumbled down, but that was all.

'Major?'

Stab!

He scrambled down from his perch, and pushed into the depths of the cave, stumbling and hurting, until he fell against a soft shape.

He found a limp arm, and ran his hand along a shoulder, and felt a face.

He knew at once, and shuddered.

Too many times, as a sweating parachute-medic groping desperately in the dark, he had found this warm stickiness between his fingers.

Chapter Forty-one

Budge was loping along at an urgent pace towards St Just when he heard the distant gunshot.

Hell!

Then another.

His mouth, already dry, became chalk.

No longer a job for a St Just policeman on a bike.

He looked desperately around. Immediately below in the bottom of the valley stood a white house with red-brick outbuildings.

They will have a telephone which works.

But a distant noise down on his left made him turn towards Cot Cove, now clearing of mist.

THAT'S IT!

To hell with open mine-shaft warnings.

With a roar, he plunged off the path and leapt into the shoulder-high undergrowth cloaking the sides of the valley. He rushed wildly towards the cove, flailing his arms like a mine-exploding Sherman.

Bushes of gorse ripped his clothes.

Bamboo lashed his legs.

Brambles tore at his face.

Down.

Still down.

Bellowing like a madman . . .

The sun was shining in Upper Gently as Doll Burnlystock, licensee of The Five Bells, frog-marched her LUNCHES sign on to the grass and buttercups opposite the church of St Amand.

The honey-coloured Guiting stone of the seventeenth century church glowed with warmth like a freshly baked loaf, and Doll had always taken comfort from the fact that the French bishop Amand is recognised as the protector of wine-makers, brewers and innkeepers.

The sound of crunching gravel announced the arrival of the black Bentley bringing Jack Heygate for his obligatory pre-lunch pint.

'Morning, Doll.'

For almost two hundred years the Heygate family have owned the local flour mill. The original was recorded in the Domesday survey and was water-driven: today it consumes more electricity than the rest of the village, and its great hopper lorries make daily journeys to the docks of Southampton and Falmouth.

'Heard anything?'

Doll adjusted her lilac blouse, smoothed her black skirt and rattled her jewellery.

'Budge telephoned last night. Should be at Land's End about now.'

Her swinging pub-sign detected a slight breeze and creaked.

'All being well,' she said.

In the dark depths of the adit, Twirly patted the Major's face, desperately searching for the source of blood.

He found it on his forehead.

Twirly braced himself.

And now . . .

The Saturday-morning cinema club seriously failed Twirly.

He was aware that a bullet from a villain's gun tended to produce a neat hole, sometimes adorned with a trickle of red which might have been lipstick.

However, Hollywood had failed to mention that an invading bullet can accumulate shreds of clothing, fragments of flesh, muscle and bone to produce a fearsome bundle which punches out a large crater as it exits.

In the dark, Twirly gently explored the Major's dust-filled hair for an exit-wound.

Mercifully – nothing.

Back at the forehead he fingered again the soggy mess.

He remembered a bloody-faced man of 2-Para being hustled into the Regimental Aid Post during street fighting in Barletta.

A spent bullet had struck without enough force to penetrate the skull, but it churned a furrow along his brow before falling away.

The Medical Officer had murmured, 'Tangential, Corporal,' and Twirly had slapped on a shell-dressing, and the man cheerfully rejoined his platoon. Pale, heroically bloodied – and not yet feeling the pain.

Twirly put his head close to the Major's face, listening in vain for breathing.

He grabbed his wrist and with three fingers fumbled to find the radial artery as laid down in the Royal Army Medical Corps Training Pamphlet No.3, November 1944, paragraph 341 – and found it.

Weak and slow, but probably normal for the Major.

'Major,' he whispered.

Then, 'MAJOR!'

No response.

Twirly gently shook his arm.

'Major. It's the men, Sir. They're waiting. Lined up and ready for inspection. They need you on parade, Sir.'

The Major moved his head and groaned.

'That you, Whippet?'

'It's me, Sir.'

The Major shifted, as if to get more comfortable.

'Whippet. We still in that bloody cave?'

'Sir!'

'Can't see a damn thing. Have I gone blind?'

'It's the blood, Sir. Your forehead is bleeding.'

'The Irish. Have they gone?'

'Not sure, Sir. Don't think they intend leaving until they've found us.'

'Bastards.'

Twirly produced a grubby handkerchief and rolled it into a pad.

'Press that hard onto your forehead, Sir, while I take a *dekho*.'

He crawled backwards across the rubble.

Soon he was able to stand and move stealthily toward the adit entrance.

He hesitated, arrested by an odd noise out there, like someone whacking a water barrel. But it disappeared.

The mist had cleared, and he cautiously peered out as if he were checking for gamekeepers; then he staggered as the noise reappeared, exploding above him with sudden deafening loudness, and he was almost thrown back into the adit by a powerful blasting wind.

The air was filled with whirling leaves and shreds of bracken and a pumelling of small stones, and just feet above him the sky was filled by a great black shape.

Down a single rope slid a fast series of bodies.

He turned back into the cave and with an hysterical shriek yelled above the head-blasting thump of the rotors, 'IT'S THE COMMANDOS, MAJOR! IT'S THE BLOODY COMMANDOS.'

He leapt out onto the path as if it was VE day and saw a couple of marines run off to the walled mine-shaft. Another, hunched over an automatic weapon, rushed directly towards him.

He heard the double-clack of a round being put up the spout, and the soldier yelled, 'DOWN. GET DOWN!'

Twirly threw himself down as the soldier continued to hurtle towards him and he called as calmly as he could, 'Care for another toffee?'

The green-bereted soldier slammed to a halt, with his face a few inches away.

From the corner of his eye Twirly could see people leaping about in the bracken.

'You OK?'

Twirly gasped, 'Fine.' He nodded back to the cave. 'But my mate is walking-wounded in there.'

The soldier leapt over Twirly into the mouth of the cave:
'THE MARINES ARE HERE' he shouted.

The Major staggered dramatically from the adit with his bloodied face, supporting himself rather grandly against the rock entrance like Sir Donald Wolfit taking a twenty-seventh curtain call.

The soldier stepped forward to steady him.

The Major held up a fending hand.

'Thank you, young man,' he said. Then motioning back towards the cave, he said, 'Can't find my hat. My jungle hat. It's in there somewhere – right at the back.'

A few moments later the soldier reappeared, slapping the hat against his leg and raising a small cloud of orange dust.

He studied it for a moment.

'This badge. It's a Marine Commando badge.'

The Major carefully and sensitively positioned the hat above his gory, glistening forehead.

'It was given me by a Marine when we linked up on Elephant Island, at the mouth of the Rangoon River – fifty-three years ago.'

Twirly watched the helicopter bank and roar away, taking its echoing rotor noise out to sea.

A perspiring corporal as broad as he was tall and nursing a weapon as large as a Bren, stomped along the path towards them.

'You all right, Sir?' and without waiting for a reply nodded down the cliff.

'Boat section boys will be with us in a moment. Soon round up these villains.'

Twirly could see green berets bobbing up the cliff and, far below on the brilliantly blue sea, wallowed the red-marked boat – with a black inflatable alongside.

The Marine-corporal stared at the Major's bloody forehead.

'You've been wounded.'

Twirly watched the Major begin to shrug, but the Marine-corporal snapped, 'There's a medic coming up the cliff. He'll sort you.'

The Major asserted himself.

'Thank you, Corporal, but I've already been seen by my own excellent medic.'

Twirly sniffed . . .

Classified Nursing Orderly Class II after a two week course at Boyce Barracks – with three days confined to barracks for doing something rude with a Thomas splint.

The Major said, 'However, I would appreciate a drop from your water-bottle, I appear to have emptied mine. Bad form, of course.'

Now the perspiring boat-section arrived, bursting onto the path with much shouting and pointing and dispersing and covering flanks.

Twirly looked in amazement at a bundle dumped on the path, 'That backpack! Where did that come from?'

The corporal shrugged.

'Belongs to your mate. It was him who got us to come here. Insisted on coming in one of the boats.'

Twirly and the Major rushed to the column of arriving Marines – and almost in the rear was Budge.

His expensive Ex-officio shirt torn and bloody.

His Fjällräven trousers torn and bloody.

His face torn and bloody.

But his grin was as big as a winner of gold.

He staggered on to the path, with a great noisy sob.

He held out his arms and rushed towards them.

'Good to see you, blokes,' and he embraced them both in his stone-lifting arms.

Twirly heard him mumble, *'alive,' 'heard those shots,' 'hell's bells'.*

Budge stiffened, and pushed himself clear, and snapped to attention like an ambitious guard-commander.

'Reporting for duty, Major.'

Then, alarmed, 'You've been wounded, Sir.'

The Major swished the words away.

'Spent round. Hell happened to you?'

'Took a short cut, Sir.'

Two soldiers came thudding along the path from St Just. One of them was the young captain in the car-park.

'What's the situation, Corporal?' he cried.

The corporal saluted.

'All in hand, Sir. Rounded up four men. Lance-corporal Letkins is down on the boat holding a fifth. And there's a body down on the rocks at the bottom.'

'Body?'

'Sir. Think he must have missed his footing. It's very steep. Looks as if an elephant jumped on him.'

The officer scowled.

'Adams will love that.

'Black balaclavas; black berets; pistol salute at the graveside; familiar-faced pall-bearers smiling at the cameras; beer and buns for the press. He'll bloody love it.'

Twirly felt a movement beneath his feet.

The path shuddered.

It was like the time he was taking a kip in the gardens of the 103 Nocera Military Hospital, between Salerno and Pompeii.

The path shook again and there was a rumbling.

Then that dreaded moment when all sound is siphoned into a vacuum, followed by:

WUMPH!

The earth exploded and everyone crashed down on to the deck with faces slammed into grass.

Twirly noted with approval that perspiring and bloodied Budge was amongst the first down.

The explosion rumbled into a mighty roar deep in the earth beneath them – and the bracken and gorse around them shook as if tossed in a gale.

Out of the walled shaft shot a column of red earth and blinding fire, climbing faster than a gusher.

A following cloud of angrily swirling black smoke rolled and lurched upwards like a burst barrage-balloon.

Branches of gorse were tossed into the air and fluttered about like autumn leaves.

Suddenly the sky became a lethal cascade of descending shrapnel. Rocks. Shards of timber. Twists of torn metal. And the air snapped and crackled like a Jubilee fireworks display.

Twirly, still slammed into the ground and with hands covering his head, felt a tugging at his boot.

He turned.

It was the Major.

His thumb was raised in front of a bloody grin, with eyes glistening like a desert pye-dog.

The shaft continued to roar and burp with explosions. Except it was no longer a shaft. The wall had gone. The stone steps had gone. The zig-zag path up to Gribba Point had gone. The shaft was crumbling into a fast-expanding crater, and Twirly watched two of the Marines paddle furiously away on elbows and knees.

The shower of debris slowed.

Heads were cautiously raised.

But Twirly's Molotov was not finished yet . . .

With a final angry roar the crater threw up a long dark object like a launched V-2.

Twirly squinted: a metal ladder.

It rose grandly above the head of the floating debris, and slowed, and gracefully curved in the direction of the sea, then turned earthwards, and hurtled down screaming like a Stuka.

You couldn't make it up.

Everyone knew what was going to happen, including the Marine and gun-runner, who leapt overboard from the red-topped boat.

With glorious precision, it smashed into the red canopy, and the boat rolled slowly over, showed its bottom – and sank.

On the road past Land's End airfield the Land Rover lurched and rumbled, and the Major dozily opened one eye, and saw that Twirly was asleep slumped against Budge, also asleep.

The Major heard the captain, sitting beside the green bereted driver, cough softly.

'You set out three weeks ago to walk to Land's End?'

The Major nodded, and Twirly and Budge stirred and opened their eyes.

The captain studied all three, then continued, 'Arriving by vehicle . . . that's not right, gentlemen.'

He motioned with his hand at the driver, who instantly pulled over on to the grass verge.

'You chaps. If you are up to it. I suggest we take you down into Sennen Cove. Have a quick reviver in The Old Success. Then we leave you to make a proper arrival walking over the cliff-tops. You staying at the hotel?'

Budge nodded.

'Right. We'll take your packs and tell them you're coming.'

He waited for a response, then smartly, 'Sennen Cove, Rawlings.'

From the circular windlass-house by Sennen Cove car park the path rose steeply up through bracken, wending past half-buried boulders like sleeping turtles.

The sky was crystal clear and Budge was reminded why this part of England is so popular with artists, who claim that the unique light intensity adds vibrance to colours and sharpens shadows.

The air was fresh with a gentle off-sea breeze.

He looked back at the Major coming up behind him, with his face now swabbed clean by the Royal Marine Corps and a khaki-bandage as neat as a cake-band beneath his jungle hat.

Twirly arrived last, having equipped himself with a staff, probably the remains of a broken sea-smashed deckchair, and he stood motionless at the top of Pedn-men-du.

Budge saw that the old reprobate's eyes were moist.

'Bloody marvellous, Budge,' he murmured. 'Been a lot of places. Never seen nothing like this.' And he turned to the Major who also stood moist-eyed and swaying with wonder.

'Isn't it bloody marvellous, Sir?'

Bloody marvellous that it's here. Bloody marvellous that WE are here. All bloody marvellous.

Budge inspected a wonderfully located coastguard's look-out, now deserted and unwanted.

Metal rings bolted on to nearby rocks probably once guyed a pole from which flags passed vital information.

Now coastguards and flags have been replaced by technology, and the coast is no longer watched by keen-eyed men from lookout to lookout, but monitored in a headquarters forty miles away, via a satellite that is up near the moon.

Enormous boulders precariously stacked on the two-hundred-foot high headland reminded Budge of building blocks in the rectory nursery.

Neat piles of coloured clothing and coiled ropes meant climbers were operating below.

This point was once the beginning of a mountain chain stretching south-west to Brittany, including the Isles of Scilly - the hundred-island archipelago said to have been the site of Arthur's engulfed Lyonnaise.

Budge began walking, but the Major called from behind, and Budge waited.

The Major looked as if he was about to speak, but he merely waved his arm at the rocks, and the coloured lichens, and the bracken, and the blue-as-heaven sea, and the blazing sun above. He passed sturdily on – chin up, still misty-eyed.

A cat's cradle of footpaths stretched half-a-mile distant to Trevescan Cliff where the Land's End Hotel crouched, gleaming white with tall white chimneys and a grey slate roof.

Budge led along cliff edge paths curling around Celtic bulwarks, and they looked down on battering foam, and secret coves, and tiny silver beaches lapped by languorous waves of creme-de-menthe.

Now they were near enough to see the confusion of coloured shapes landward of the hotel.

Seaward of the hotel curved a wrap-around conservatory overlooking a wide flat terrace which appeared to be the roof of a single-storey extension tucked into the cliffs, with glass walls reflecting the afternoon sun.

Budge waited for Twirly.

'Well, Twirly? There's your Land's End.'

But Twirly was not talking, and Budge supposed he was remembering a grey crowded troopship more than half-a-century ago, when a seventeen-year old lad sailed off to fight in five countries before seeing England again.

He recalled Twirly telling him his mother used to say, 'You went away believing in Father Christmas; and came back looking like him.'

As they neared the hotel Budge could see a wide staircase leading up to the terrace. It appeared to be lined by slim green bushes, dotted with seagulls.

The Major again called him from behind, and Budge turned to see him bending over, carefully straightening the creases down the front of his battered Norfolk breeches which had survived the 350-mile adventure. He righted himself, and fumbled with his hat.

'I suggest,' he called, 'That from hereon we advance abreast. That way we all arrive together.'

Quite right.

Now Budge recognised what the crafty Major had already seen.

The steps were lined not with bushes, but erect Commandos, the young officer standing central on the top step. Behind him waved the seagull plumes on the helmets of five Royal Marine bandsmen.

The Major was now marching tall, with his head thrown back, his white moustache bristling, his cane under his right arm, his left arm swinging like a metronome.

Twirly, unbidden, was marching like a guardsman, with thumbs flat on top of his clenched fists, arms swinging shoulder high.

Budge shrugged. It was churlish not to join them.

It was surprisingly easy.

An order was given. Not by the Major, but by the magnificent Twirly.

'Bags of swank, lads,' he called.

As they neared the steps the Major grunted, 'Well done, men.'

Then he softly warned, 'Remember. I am the senior officer present. Any saluting will be done by me – but keep in close.'

Budge was surprised to see so many people, and they appeared to be clapping, but it was difficult to see properly, and his lips were trembling.

Quite stupid.

Chapter Forty-two

The garishly painted prow figurehead looked down on the crowded Longships Bar.

The Major thought it was like half-time at Twickenham.

Chuckling, chattering elbow-to-elbow visitors all protecting their drinks: bright-eyed Marine Commandos made of west-country granite; comfortable bandsmen with gold epaulettes and buttons; a BBC Points West crew there to do a feature on Carn Greeb flints saying, 'Bristol says they can give us three minutes.'

He stood wedged between a flushed Budge and Twirly grinning like a *mahout* elephant-boy. His attempts to consume his lavishly topped-up scotch were frustrated by the need to continually acknowledge shoulder-thumping congratulations, and nodding appreciation for the number of drinks 'put-behind-the-bar'.

A grey-haired lady pushed through the throng holding aloft three room-keys dangling from scallop-shells.

She snuggled up to the 'celebrities' and smiled.

'We've been able to upgrade you to three adjoining Superior rooms in our new Boston Cairns complex.'

She consulted an *aide-mémoire*.

Over her shoulder the Major read:

Room 7 Whippet

Room 8 Legge-Wellesley

Room 9 Budgineer

Budgineer?

Wasn't that something to do with Painswick?

'We have also a table booked for you at this evening's Music-Dinner-and-Dance.'

Budge looked puzzled and began, 'How much....?'

The Major kicked him.

'Sounds wonderful. Thank you.' And he turned to growl briskly into Budge's ear,

'Gift horses and all that, Mr Ballflower.'

The lady continued, 'It's a black-tie event, and we realise that this may cause you a problem, but Housekeeping and Personnel have got together and agreed to sort something out for you from Waiter's Wardrobe. Perhaps if you will follow me . . .'

Emerging from the throng into the airy Reception oasis of palm-plants and upholstered bamboo furniture, she said, 'Only problem we have is providing black shoes.'

The Major smiled and turned to Budge and Twirly.

'Shoes?'

'We don't need shoes. We have *boots*. They got us here. We'll wear them tonight.'

Budge said, 'Quite right. *By their boots shall ye know them.* Matthew seven, thirteen – more or less.'

Twirly stood at the entrance to the dining-room, erect in black jacket and trousers, with his neck constricted by a stiff collar and bow-tie.

He gazed around in wonder. It was like the films.

Men in dinner-jackets.

Glamorous ladies with bare shoulders and sparkling dresses.

Swerving waiters.

White tablecloths, flowers, crockery, shining wine-glasses and dazzling cutlery; clinking forks, posh music, and the murmur of polite conversations.

The mixed scents of flowers, and grilled steaks, and perfumed bosoms: the larger the bosom, the stronger the perfume.

The Major appeared on parade looking magnificent.

Tall. Slim. Ruddy-faced. His snow-white hair immaculate and gleaming. A clean white bandage around his forehead.

Think I saw him once in a picture called Sons of the Empire.

Budge looked like a prosperous boxing promoter.

A hustling waiter said, 'This way, gentlemen,' and he led them bowing and swerving to a table near a small stage where a five-piece band was playing quietly, with a lady in a red dress plucking a large golden harp.

The Major said, 'Excellent turn-out, Twirly. Despite the jacket. Obviously made-to-measure – but perhaps not for you.'

The Major was fussed by the table setting and he held up a hand.

A laden passing waiter paused.

'Sir?'

The Major waved his hand round the table.

'The table is set for four. We are three.'

The man studied the table and nodded.

'I'll be back in a moment, Sir.'

The Major grunted, and studied the menu.

Fruit cocktail with Blueberries and Maraschino

Chicken Consommè Longships

Raspberry sorbet

Roast saddle of lamb –
  with a mushroom duxelles and fresh herbs
Stuffed Duck Leg, braised with Berni Potato, Red Cabbage,
  and Grand Marnier Duck Sauce
Seafood Ragout 'Newburg' in Light Lobster Madeira Sauce,

Hot Vanilla Pudding with Amaretto Sauce
Dark and White Chocolate Mousse with Mango Sauce
Cherry Crumble wih custard

Assorted West Country cheeses with Freshly Baked Breads

The Major recognised the light-hearted piece the sextet was playing when the fruit cocktails arrived. The *Butterfly Waltz* by Erkki Melartin. A favourite of Mary's, as was the fruit cocktail. He carefully rearranged the blueberries amongst the pears and peaches.

Budge said, 'Notice you never rush to begin eating, Major.'

The Major put down his spoon and fork.

'Only anyone who has been *seriously* hungry, Budge, can know the pleasure of having food set in front of you which will not

410

prove to be a hunger-generated mirage – but yours to eat *whenever* you are ready.'

'You also eat slowly . . .' said Budge.

The Major gathered up his implements again.

'Was it W H Davies who said,
What is this world so full of haste;
If we have no time to chew and taste?'

Budge said, 'Tried to ring Doll. Tell her we've arrived. No reply.'

The Major heaved over and extracted a small parcel from his jacket.

'While I remember, Twirly. Saw it in St Ives. Couldn't resist it. Mark of my esteem, don't you know.'

Twirly unwrapped it: a Parachute Regiment tie.

Budge and Twirly were seated facing the musicians. The Major was facing down the dining-room towards the entrance.

'Good Lord!' he said.

Budge and Twirly turned.

The Major thought her entrance was wonderful.

She was led by the arm-waving *maitre d'hotel* and accompanied by a consort of briskly advancing hotel staff.

Doll.

She glistened, and jingled, and waved royally to every table she passed.

Twirly leapt to his feet. The Major and Budge arose.

She made a perfect landing at their table, and threw out her arms, ruined her mascara, and proclaimed, 'M'ducks!', embracing each crushingly in turn.

A waiter held out the fourth chair for her occupancy but she was too excited to sit.

'Saw you on BBC Points West at lunchtime. I screamed, "It's them!" We all stood gob-smacked.

'Jack Heygate said, "Well I'm damned." Then, "How they getting back?"

'Couldn't think . . .

411

'Jack said, "I'll get Gary to collect them." '

'In a few minutes he was back. "Come on, Doll. Get your hat! Gary is outside with the Bentley."'

A waiter arrived with the consommé.

The Major watched Doll fondly studying Twirly across delicately balanced spoonfuls.

She said, 'You like this soup, Twirly?'

'Lovely.'

She bathed him in admiration.

'I'll make you some when we get home, m'duck.'

Twirly said,'Is Gary Baldey here?'

The Major saw Doll deciphering Twirly's interest.

'The darts team?'

Twirly nodded.

Doll beamed, 'The hotel is full, but they've booked him into a B&B. He's in the bar having something to eat.'

Twirly removed and folded his napkin, stood, and bowed.

'Excuse me, Doll, Major, Budge.'

Doll looked worried and consulted the Major.

'He's acting strange. Perhaps it's the dinner-jacket.'

She waved her arm at the surrounding splendour.

'Rose would have loved all this.'

Budge looked puzzled.

'Rose?'

The Major explained. 'Rose and Twirly were walking-out. Then he left for North Africa, and did Sicily, Greece and south of France.

'While they were advancing up Italy he was wounded by a mortar. The following week he learned that poor Rose had been killed in an air-raid on Sodbury rail tunnel.'

Doll sniffed.

The Major continued, 'Didn't want to come home. Signed-on for an extra three years.

'When he was fit he was posted to 6th Airborne.

'On Christmas Eve, 1944, the division was rushed over to the snow-bound Ardennes to halt Von Runstedt, then dropped over the

412

Rhine, chased up to the Baltic to halt Russian plans to invade Denmark; kitted out for a drop on southern Japan which mercifully didn't happen; finished up in Palestine.

Doll sighed:

'M'sister would have been so proud of him.'

Twirly was back in minutes.

'We thrashed the Sennington Arms.'

Doll smiled her approval and the Major watched her plunge a Marrakesh-souk arm under the table and grope for her Cloth of Gold handbag.

'Major! Got a letter for you. Cynthia insisted I deliver it as soon as possible.'

The Major gasped.

The hussy's caught up with me.

He took the letter, noted it smelt of chemical lavender, and proceeded to slide it into an inside pocket.

'No!' ordered Doll. 'Read it now. It's . . . it *might* be good news.'

Budge watched as the Major apprehensively fumbled with the envelope and unfolded the pale blue notepaper and read.

He threw back his head and laughed.

Never seen him laugh like this before.

Not during the walk. Not even before in The Bells.

Doll joined in the hilarity.

Twirly, who usually only grinned or sniffed, stretched his collared neck and laughed.

Budge was unable to resist and, using face muscles he had forgotten, joined them.

Loudly.

Outrageously.

A passing waiter asked, 'Is everything all right, Sir?'

They instantly simmered to a halt, and behaved.

The Major said, 'The Honourable Cynthia Withers is marrying that ghastly Humphrey Berkeley and he wants me to be best man.'

413

The laughing almost surfaced again. Mercifully, a burdened waiter arrived.

'You are the Stuffed Duck's Leg, I believe, Madam.'

Twirly suddenly put down his cutlery.

'Doll. What happened about English Heritage wanting the key to Fish House?'

Budge winced at Doll's murderous glare.

'Not had a chance, Doll,' he shrugged.

Doll sighed, and swung a toothpaste smile at Twirly.

'Wonderful news, m'duck. They are doing up your cottage. Returning the ground floor to how it was when the monks had it. Repairing the outbuilding and making it into an exhibition. Planting a monastery garden with herbs. Building you a new kitchen and bathroom. And you pay no rent, in return for opening it to the public "at all reasonable hours".'

Twirly helped himself to roast potatoes.

'Ratcher will like that.'

Budge knew the piece the musicians were playing. Frank Bridge's jolly *Cherry Ripe.*

Then a young violinist in a slim black dress with a white lace collar took centre stage and began playing.

Budge instantly recognised the first soft notes.

The Major, sitting with his back to the stage and facing the dining-room entrance, leapt in his chair and gasped.

Budge snapped up a hand.

'Sh! Vaughan Williams *The Lark Ascending.'*

He was back treading the soft grass of a sunlit Cotswolds escarpment.

Striding alongside wispy clouds along the airy Mendips.

High up on Dartmoor's green moonscape.

Strolling on cliffs above a magical blue sea.

Encouraged and serenaded by a solitary heaven-high trilling escort.

And always in the haze ahead - smiling green eyes.

414

The trundle of conversation and tinkling coffee-cups dwindled into silence and the lark music filled the room.

When the slim girl lowered her violin and smiled and bowed, the diners applauded for the first time that evening.

Budge said, 'She – the Canadian girl – would have loved that.'

The Major said, 'She did.'

The Major once said battle-experienced soldiers were often warned of the presence of snipers by tingling back-of-neck nape hairs.

Budge's nape hairs now stung like hornets, and he slapped his hand to the back of his neck, and swung around . . .

Two green eyes.

She's here.

He jumped up, and his chair fell backwards.

With long strides he made a bee-line to where she sat with her aunt. If there were tables or waiters in the way he was not aware of them.

She reached out a bare white arm towards him, as breathtakingly beautiful as he remembered.

'You said . . .'

'I changed my flight.'

Her soft smile of pleasure turned to horror.

'Your face! It's covered in scratches.'

Budge grinned.

'Been playing with the big boys.'

The violinists, harpist, cellist and pianist were smoothly replaced by an exuberant band designed for dancing, and on the first notes two couples of County Championship standard swept onto the floor with blinding confidence. Others, more cautious, awaited the anonymity of numbers.

The Major saw that Budge and the niece had vanished and Annabelle was sitting alone.

He stood and bowed.

'Excuse me, Doll,' and he strode to the table by the doorway.

An exciting day.

The sea-mist.
Appearance of the Dublin motor-cruiser.
Twirly's Molotov cocktail.
The exertion of tumbling the straw-bales.
Sustaining a head-wound in a cave blasted with gun-fire.
But strangely, THIS is the moment I'll remember . . .

The aunt squeezed her eyes, and chuckled wickedly.

'A pleasant surprise, Mr Legge-Wellesley.'

'I take it you are the magic-wand waver?'

She smiled like a fairy-godmother should.

'My brother, Sophia's father, owns a successful timber business in British Columbia. He is also a senior shareholder of this hotel group.'

The Major bowed slightly:

'We thank you.'

'Not me. Sophia. She is a girl who knows *exactly* what she wants.'

She made a signal across the room and a genie wine-waiter sped towards her table.

'Will you join me in a brandy?'

'I came over to ask if you cared to dance.'

'*Can* you dance in those boots?'

The Major raised his fluffy eyebrows and smoothed his moustache.

'Annabelle, I don't wish to boast . . .'

The aunt laughed.

'I think *all* men should boast a little. Modest men are so boring – and often have much to be modest about.'

She indicated the empty chair.

'First we'll have brandies, and talk. Then we'll dance.'

Sophia Forrest stood beneath the planetarium sky lit by a million stars with a large mottled moon casting a silver-sea highway towards the lost land of Lyonesse.

'It's beautiful,' she sighed.

'This way,' said Budge and he led her carefully past half-buried boulders towards the sea. Soon they could hear timid breakers stroking the rocks below, and the low growling call of restless guillemots.

'Here?' she asked.

'Nearer the sea.'

They stepped carefully on to soft silent grass and Budge found a couch of scented rock samphire enclosed by a crescent of granite which he said was probably in place before seas rushed in to make England an island.

'Here,' he said.

She should have followed aunt's advice and borrowed her shawl.

She shivered.

Budge quickly slipped off his jacket and draped it around her shoulders.

They sat close and she stroked his hands, as soft as cashmere.

'I would expect a stonemason's hands to be rough as pumice,' she said, and heard him chuckle.

'A stonemason needs to keep his hands soft and sensitive. Able to feel the way the stone wants to go. Fight the lay of the stone and you have a disaster. My old master-mason used to warn me, "You're not a convict smashing rocks on Dartmoor. The design is already in the stone. All you have to do is set it free. Think of it as undressing a beautiful woman."'

She snuggled up to him.

Perhaps I have been looking for a stonemason all my life.

A mile out to sea, a lighthouse waved its beam in a wide circuit, unhelpfully illuminating their grassy hideaway every fifteen seconds. Landwards, the beacon shone a warning red.

He laid her back by a king-sized boulder, and with her fingers she gently scratched at the velvet-soft lichen and listened to the rhythm of the softly, gently pounding, oh-so-unhurried sea.

The stars high above watched and shimmered in anticipation.

A sudden seagull rose shrieking in protest at some hidden affront, and swirled and squawked, then sank away beyond the cliff edge, and Land's End became silent again.

417

Now her hand found a clump of fragile thrift and she plucked a stalk and gently stroked it across Budge's back.

I ought to have known it would be here – at Land's End.

'You will just love Toronto,' she murmured.

Chapter Forty-three

EPILOGUE

Friday 31st July *Day twenty-six*

Twirly walked to the cliff edge with a man-sized mug in one hand and his black Morris-dancing hat in the other.

He looked at the scratched face of his Hermann Goering Jäger Regiment watch, and remembered the shattering day he took it from the wrist of the young blond *Fallschirmjäger* with furiously flashing eyes.

He peered across the sea in the direction of where he thought the distant scrub covered *wadis* of *Jebel Aboid* might lie.

'*Vielen Dank, Kamerad,*' he grunted.

It was ten-to-six and the chilled Cornish headland was awaiting the warmth of the sun.

To the east the sky was pale blue with a hint of pink. To the west it was naval blue. The silver-blue sea was still abed and lightly scored with criss-crossing lines made by early-bird fishing smacks.

He placed his mug on a granite pedestal and drew back his arm, and skimmed the hat far out to sea. Its arc was interrupted by a thermal rising from the cliff edge and it momentarily rose higher, but its flight was pre-determined and it sank, slowly and finally from sight.

'Done that.'

He thought perhaps he should thank someone.

But who?

His poor old worrying mother?

Mrs Tarry who taught him how to sharpen a pencil in the Infants?

PC Page – who never told his father, though he threatened he would?

Perhaps the unknown WAAFs who packed his parachutes?

Sgt Slater who taught him how to survive, but got himself killed in a glider which smashed into the trees of Diersfordter Wald?

Aunt Maggie, who even now is probably lurking in the waist-high bracken?

The always-beaming Doll?

Rose?

He heard a noise.

'Morning.'

The Major.

Also with a man-sized mug.

Twirly chuckled.

'The cook-house?'

The Major nodded and laughed.

'Martin. Nice chap. Has a brother who works at the Queen's in Cheltenham.'

He held up a napkin parcel.

'Did these for us.'

The bacon sandwiches were warm, and melted butter dribbled down Twirly's chin.

The pale sky in the east had softened from pink to orange.

A couple of fast-flying birds skimmed the sea on an urgent, secret mission. Dark distant headlands were beginning to show suggestions of green.

'Did Mrs Legge-Wellesley call you 'Major'?'

'Hated it. Said it showed lack of respect. Used to tell me, "*You're more than a soldier.*" It was always , "*Robert*".'

Twirly looked eastwards. The orange sky was turning bright gold. A thin gilded line crept slowly along the horizon.

The Major flicked crumbs off his jacket with the napkin.

'Do you know about planting brussel-sprouts?'

Twirly smiled.

'I usually come first in Gently's December Produce Show.'

The Major said, 'Mary had green fingers. Not me. But I fancy having my own sprouts for Christmas.'

Twirly nodded: 'Sprouts should be set out this month.'

'Perhaps you could come up to the Residency?'

'Right.'

Twirly looked east again where the sun was hesitating and keeping the world waiting like an old pro. Above, a weave of slender clouds had appeared and shone with a translucent glow like old gas mantles.

'Have you ever been up to the Residency?'

'Your wife once asked me to mend a gate.'

The Major shook his head.

'Don't recall . . .'

'It was only a gate.'

They both turned to watch the bright smudge on the horizon becoming increasingly intense. Suddenly the bright gold disc leapt up. Blinding. Searing the eyes. They turned to the west where the dark sky had become bright blue. Already they could feel the rising warmth.

'Wonderful walk,' the Major said.

Twirly sighed.

'Wonderful country, England. Do you think they will believe it back in Gently?'

The Major shrugged.

'Do you suppose *we* will?'

The world was stirring itself awake. No longer as quiet as a churchyard. Assorted noises came from the hotel. A cheeky motor-scooter screamed to a halt in the car park. Beside them, eager bees were touching-up a clump of golden gorse.

'Long walk, two-fifty miles,' said the Major.

Twirly nodded:

'But we survived.'

'Yes. Thank God.'

The sun was now rising rapidly into the waiting heaven.

'Amen,' said Twirly Albert Valentino Whippet.

421

Glossary

AWOL	Absent without leave
BLA	British Liberation Army
BMH	British Military Hospital
CCS	Casualty Collecting Station
COMPO	Military ration boxes issued in battle situations, usually designed for fourteen men, with seven variations of menu.
CO	Commanding Officer
DFC	Distinguished Flying Cross
DFS	Deutsche Forschungsanstalt für Segelflug (German Research Institute for Gliding.)
DZ	Dropping zone
EPIP	European Personnel, Indian Pattern
FSMO	Field Service Marching Order
FOU	Forward Observation Unit
GOC	General Officer Commanding
Housewife	Military issue personal sewing kit
LST	Landing craft (Landing ship, tank)
MDS	Main Dressing Station
MI	Medical Inspection Room
MO	Medical Officer
NAAFI	Navy, Army and Air Force Institutes. (Operated static and mobile canteens)
NCO	Non Commissioned Officer
O-Group	Orders Group
Ox and Bucks	The Oxfordshire and Buckinghamshire (2nd Battalion converted to Airlanding and became part of 6th Airborne Division)
PT	Physical Training
QAIMNS	Queen Alexandra's Imperial Nursing Service
QM	Quartermaster
RAMC	Royal Army Medical Corps
RAP	Regimental Aid Post
RTU	Returned to unit
RV	Rendezvous (Assembly point on dropping zone)
SEAC	South East Asia Command
SI	Sergeant Instructor
SN	Senior Nurse
SP	Self propelled (gun)
WAAF	Women's Auxiliary Air Force
WD	War Department